SOULFYRE

BOOK ONE OF THE GODSFYRE SERIES

SAMANTHA NELL

SOULFYRE

Book 1 of the Godsfyre series

Samantha Nell

Copyright © 2026 Samantha Nell. All rights reserved.

No part of this publication may be reproduced, distributed, or transmitted in any form or by any means, including photocopying, recording, or other electronic or mechanical methods, without the prior written permission of the publisher, except in the case of brief quotations embodied in critical reviews and certain other noncommercial uses permitted by copyright law.

This is a work of fiction. Names, characters, businesses, places, events and incidents are either the products of the author's imagination or used in a fictitious manner. Any resemblance to actual persons, living or dead, or actual events is purely coincidental.

Front cover image by An-Nhien Nguyen.

Editing by The Mystic Ink Pot.

Map art by Shepengul.

Chapter header art by Aila Designs.

Formatting by Aila Designs.

First printing edition 2026.

"It's time for you to look inward and begin asking yourself the big questions. **Who** are you? And what do *you* want?"

— *Iroh, Avatar the Last Airbender*

Table of Contents

Author's note	xi
The God Houses	xiii
Prologue	xvii
Chapter 1	19
Chapter 2	31
Chapter 3	45
Chapter 4	65
Chapter 5	69
Chapter 6	83
Chapter 7	87
Chapter 8	91
Chapter 9	101
Chapter 10	111
Chapter 11	113
Chapter 12	119
Chapter 13	129
Chapter 14	137
Chapter 15	143

Chapter 16 151

Chapter 17 159

Chapter 18 175

Chapter 19 185

Chapter 20 189

Chapter 21 199

Chapter 22 211

Chapter 23 221

Chapter 24 239

Chapter 25 243

Chapter 26 257

Chapter 27 269

Chapter 28 281

Chapter 29 291

Chapter 30 303

Chapter 31 313

Chapter 32 327

Chapter 33 337

Chapter 34 341

Chapter 35 349

Chapter 36 367

Chapter 37 371

Chapter 38 383

Chapter 39 389

Chapter 40 393

Chapter 41 399

Chapter 42 407

Epilogue 409

Acknowledgments 411

Author's note

This book contains explicit content that may be triggering to some people. The content warnings include sexually explicit scenes, explicit language, violence, gore, murder, drug use, physical abuse, and anxiety.

The God Houses

Current Day:

House Lucien
Elven descendants of *Bas*
Wielders of Death and Shadow

House Tozya
Fae descendants of *Eileamaid*
Wielders of Elements

Extinct:

House Moros
Human descendants of *Inntin*
Wielders of Minds

House Kazimyr
Fae descendants of *Gealach*
Wielders of Storm and Moon

House Deyanira
Elven descendants of *Ghrian*
Wielders of Stars and Light

Prologue

The Vulture

"Do you understand now?" the peculiar man asked. "Do you see what it will take to work by my side?"

The man slid a dagger across the desk, offering it to The Vulture. The dagger was clear, made of iridescent crystal. It was engraved with markings The Vulture didn't recognize, indicating it belonged to a language lost in time.

The Vulture gripped it in their hand, inspecting the blade that radiated overwhelming power, even now. Even when its power had faded and transferred to the barrier of Tevye.

"I will do what we bargained for," the Vulture replied, narrowing their eyes at the man. "Make sure he is there at midnight."

The man nodded, cruelty in his eyes. "Done."

The Vulture stood and stuffed the crystal blade in their bag with a determined look in their eyes. Their suspicions were confirmed. Whether they liked it or not, they knew what they had to do.

Who they had to kill first.

Chapter 1

Sun and Moon will always find each other in every life. Their souls are tied, where one goes, so does the other.

— *The book of Tevye*

Taryn

"Please," the Elven male begged. "I won't tell a soul!"

His frail body writhed under Taryn's grip, a weak attempt to fight off his attack. Taryn's hand tightened around the male's neck, then loosened as he took a step back. He unsheathed a knife from his belt.

"No," Taryn agreed. "You won't."

Before the male could respond, Taryn slid the dagger across his throat. Blood gushed out of the wound, leaving a pained gurgle in place of the words the male attempted to say. An empty silence followed in its wake.

Gods. This had to be Taryn's tenth kill of the week. His Guildmaster had sent him on a damned rampage. Of course, Eryx didn't divulge why he needed these people killed. His Guildmaster always gave vague answers, muttering that these people owed him a debt after stealing his drugs. Taryn didn't believe it. There was something else going on. Something... sinister.

What am I even doing with my life? The point had become unclear over the years. Taryn's body went numb as he willed the thought to pass. He snatched the bundle of salaroses on the counter and stuffed them into his cloak pocket. They were peculiar plants, onyx roses that had more use than vanity. They could get you high. They could be used in spells. They could be extracted for their poison. It was why Eryx needed them.

Taryn turned to leave. He stopped mid-step, looking back at the lifeless body, stifling any emotions that threatened to surface. No need for such *useless* feelings. He walked up to the body and closed the eyelids, sending the male to rest. It was the least he could do. It was *all* he could do.

Gravel crunched under Taryn's boots as he exited the flat onto the cobblestone street of Luciena. He veered right, pulling his cloak hood over his head. The dirty, brisk air bit his face, while a rat scurried from Taryn's footsteps, hiding away in the hole of a broken-down building nearby. Random shouting echoed into the alleyways of the slum, the usual civilian semantics bringing this area to life. The smell of urine and beer wafted up to his nose, blending into a familiar scent that belonged to none other than the city's poverty-stricken outer ring.

Taryn took in the slanted buildings surrounding him and frowned. Despite all the money the Luciens had in their coffers, they still refused to help repair this side of the city. Civilians took it upon themselves to make their own repairs, using shoddy handiwork to repair holes in the buildings with patched metal or scraps of wood. It had been this way for as long as Taryn had lived on this continent.

Looking overhead, he deduced it was around midnight due to the moon's position. Had he really been out that long?

He fastened his black handkerchief over the bridge of his nose and began his trek back to Lonskeep. Apart from his glowing silver eyes, Taryn blended into the darkness thanks to his black leather ensemble.

"Spare me," a voice croaked from below. Taryn glanced at a Human man sitting against the stone wall, a tin cup in his hand. Wrinkles lined his face, an unkempt gray beard reaching down to the ground. Taryn hesitated, looking around to make sure there weren't any city guards who would recognize him. He crouched before the old man, pulled out some change, and dropped them in the cup.

The man looked at him, the tin cup wobbling in his trembling hand. The scent of anguish and fear from the Human wafted up to Taryn's nose. He rested a hand on the man's arm and murmured a blessing in the Runean language. Taryn moved on. He couldn't stay in the city for long without risking capture.

Taryn thought of the homeless man as he walked toward the outer wall. He had seen himself in the man, recognizing that sunken look of hopelessness all too well. He bit back a feeling of shame as old memories resurfaced. Images of his childhood flashed in his mind – his grandmother's sunken cheeks in her last days, the sun blaring down on him as he begged on the streets after her passing.

Taryn grimaced, shutting the memories out. He wasn't that person anymore. That life no longer belonged to him.

His ears pricked beneath his hood at the sound of footsteps trailing him on the rooftops above. Taryn fought the instinct to grab the hilt of his broadswords. He wanted whoever followed him to think he would be taken by surprise when they revealed themselves. He turned down another alleyway, careful to distance himself from the main street.

Amateurs.

As anticipated, the footsteps above increased. Then, a flash of black as someone jumped from the roof into the alleyway with a heavy *thud*. An Elven male landed across from him, clad in dark clothing with a golden broach on his chest. The Elve drew his sword.

"The Vulture sends their regards," the male hissed.

Taryn's dark brows drew together at the comment. His eyes dropped to the male's right knee, noticing the slight hesitation in his stance, surmising that his left leg compensated for his right. *An injury left him permanently altered.* He pocketed this information like a letter, folding it and storing it away in his mind for the minutes to come.

The male lashed out his free arm, sending a streak of Shadow towards Taryn. Pure, black energy rushed towards him so fast, Taryn barely had the time to register the hissing sounds of the dead that followed the Shadow Magick.

Taryn's eyes went wide as he veered right, narrowly avoiding the Shadow. Taryn automatically retaliated with a blast of wind from his palm. His stomach lurched at the realization of who he was fighting.

Where the *hell* had this guy come from? Taryn was *sure* the Guild had taken out all the Shadow Wielders. He would have to work twice as hard to avoid getting hit while keeping this fight quiet.

The male fell backwards, Taryn's wind knocking him off his feet. Taryn lunged, swords out, ready to take the opportunity to strike while he was down.

The male rolled free as Taryn's blade jammed into the cobblestone, missing it by mere centimeters. The Elve sent another streak of darkness barreling towards Taryn, causing him to stumble backwards. The Shadow grazed the top of Taryn's hand as he pivoted out of the way, black energy fading into his skin like ink bleeding into paper.

Taryn felt the effects immediately, disembodied voices of the dead whispering in his ears as the Magick infiltrated his bloodstream. The cold, prickling Shadow began to flow strong in his veins, starting from his hand and expanding out to his arms and shoulders. It was a subtle pain, but the pain wasn't what Taryn was worried about. It was the fogginess creeping into his mind that caused him to slow.

"*Fuck.*" Taryn gritted between his teeth as he forced himself to move out of the way of yet another blast. His muscles tensed, sweat beading onto his brow as he forced himself to think back to everything he had studied on Shadow Wielders.

Shadow Magick was an Energy Magick gifted by the God of Death, a power only Elves could wield. Though the Magick didn't *kill* its victims, it spread like a virus, slowly paralyzing the body over a period of time. While the paralyzing effects were temporary, it was a lethal power to come into contact with. If you got hit, you might as well consider yourself as good as dead.

Unsure of exactly how long it would take to kick in, Taryn chose his next move carefully.

"We know *what* you are," the male said, coming to a slow stand as he unsheathed a crystal blade. "And we are going to rid the world of you."

Whatever Taryn had expected this male to say, it wasn't that. He had assumed this attack was for the Mrkynian Guild as a whole, not Taryn himself. Taryn's face hardened, his fists clenching.

The Elven male lurched forward, swinging the crystal blade. Taryn parried and moved back to create some distance, stumbling slightly from the numbness that started to creep into all four of his limbs. This wasn't an average sword fight. He couldn't afford to get hit again.

If he didn't act now, he was absolutely fucked.

The male began conjuring another blast of Shadow, forcing Taryn to unleash his God-given power to its utmost potential. He would deal with the consequences of blowing his cover later.

"If you know *what* I am," Taryn said as he released his blade. "Then you know what comes next."

He called on his most lethal power, willing it to the forefront of his mind. It awakened, greedily rising to the surface after almost a year of slumber. Overwhelming power bloomed, starting in his chest and traveling down his arms. Taryn felt the buzz of power humming beneath his palms, accumulating until he had enough energy within him to release outwards. He thrust out his palms and felt the jolt of electricity igniting every pore in his body. He aimed.

Lightning cracked through the air. A deadly flash struck the Elve. The male gripped his shoulder, groaning in agony as he fell, whipping another streak of Shadow at Taryn as he went down.

This male certainly had some grit.

Taryn growled in frustration as he advanced. Blue lightning lit up Taryn's face as he struck again. This time, he met his mark. Electricity skittered down the center of the male's chest, leaving behind the smell of burnt flesh in the air.

By now, Taryn's eyesight began to blur, the Shadow Magick taking its toll. Blackness intruded the edges of his vision as he knelt down and grabbed the male by the tunic. The male's head fell back, limp, but his eyes were open. Just barely.

"Who sent you?" Taryn demanded, his words slurred together as he fought against the Shadow poisoning. Every muscle in Taryn's body began to slow. He was running out of time. Taryn glanced at the golden broach attached to the male's chest – a gilded vulture.

It certainly wasn't the Lucien family that sent him. Their family emblem was a serpent, not a vulture. And if those who sent this attacker claimed they knew what Taryn *was*, they would surely have to be eradicated.

The male smiled at Taryn through his dying haze. "The dawn of the Salamoon marks a new age," the male croaked out. "*A stolen Death. A touch of Fyre…*"

The Elve's words faded as his eyes rolled into the back of his head, his body void of any life in Taryn's grasp.

Taryn dropped the male and stumbled backwards, slowly losing control of his motor skills. He couldn't think straight, unable to spare another second to ponder the male's words. Taryn fought for clarity, losing his balance and straining to see beyond the black film coating his eyes.

He staggered down the street as fast as his body would take him and headed for the sewer hole through which he'd entered the city. He prayed to the Gods he wouldn't pass out underground, removed the sewer lid and fell inside.

Taryn threw his room door open. He trudged to his washroom and gripped the sink, his vision blurring in spurts. There were two hands, four hands, then two again. When he unbuttoned his tunic, his hands felt like they were wading through mud. Black ink branched out like veins underneath his skin from hand to elbow.

It was a miracle he had stayed conscious this long. Taryn began to wonder if he would even pass out at all.

He thought he heard yelling, perhaps a name. Footsteps came closer.

Then, a voice. "You smell like shit," said a voice, possibly Raiden. "You *look* like shit too. What happened?" Raiden entered the room, a mix of blonde hair and brown eyes, expression taut.

Taryn looked at himself in the mirror. Dirt caked onto his bronzed complexion, a common trait for Runean Fae. His light brown curls clung to the sides of his face and neck from sweat, the hair covering the scar that went from his temple and down the side of his cheek. Taryn creased his angled, dark brows as he attempted to muster control over his mind, trying everything he could to block out the darkness.

Only his glowing steel gaze stared back.

Taryn raised his shaking hand, showing Raiden the blackness that lay beneath his veins. "I was attacked by a Shadow Wielder."

Raiden cursed, inspecting the black veins.

He relayed everything to his best friend, carefully excluding the contents of the Elven male's words. Taryn still hadn't had a moment to decipher them.

After Taryn was done, Raiden gave him a look of pity.

"What?"

"Eryx demanded to see you immediately. He wants to know why you took so long to return."

"For fuck's sake," Taryn muttered. Resentment flared as he changed into fresh clothing. His limbs felt like jelly, and the muscles in his legs strained to hold him upright. The Shadow Magick had taken its toll, leaving him weak and disoriented. Raiden helped him walk to Eryx's office, letting Taryn lean on him for support as he staggered from the Guild manor to the outbuilding where the Guildmaster resided.

Taryn entered the building alone, hand on the walls to prop himself upright as he crossed through the familiar stone hallways. His vision was blurred in and out of focus as he paused before the oak doors.

Calm. Collected. Controlled.

He recited the words internally as he pushed the door open.

Eryx sat behind his mahogany desk, frowning as he took in Taryn's current state. Lilac eyes narrowed as he noticed the dark patch of ink on Taryn's hand.

"Sit," Eryx said calmly.

Taryn stumbled to the velvet chair and sat before Eryx, taking in his cropped salt and pepper colored hair. Before Eryx could say any more, Taryn grabbed the bundle of salaroses from his pocket, now wilted, and threw them onto the desk.

"As requested."

Eryx grabbed the wine pitcher and began to pour, the silver ring on his finger glinting from the candlelight on his desk. "Wine?" Eryx asked. Taryn declined, grabbing a wine cup for himself. He lifted a hand sluggishly, desperately parched, and guided a stream of water through the air into his cup from a water basin nearby.

"And what of your hand?"

Taryn recited the incident for a second time, as best as he could, still trying to fight the murkiness in his mind. He again left out the Elven male's word—that he knew *who* and *what* he was. That was something not even Eryx could know, and Taryn prayed to the Gods Eryx wouldn't see past his lies. At the end of his recount, he confessed to wielding his lightning to get away.

Eryx closed his eyes and slammed his wine on the desk. "You did *what?*" He let out a bitter scoff. "We just convinced the monarchy our presence was annihilated, and you wield *lightning* in the *city*?"

Calm. Collected. Controlled.

Taryn breathed. "There weren't any other options. I was one more hit away from going down. What would you have me do?"

Eryx abruptly rose from his chair and walked to the arched windows behind him, his back to Taryn. "I would have done anything to protect the integrity of this Guild, that's what I would have done. I trusted you, and you compromised us."

The tattoo on Taryn's bicep began to burn.

"I just sent two spies to enter the city for a task that needed to be delicately handled," Eryx bit out. "Surely they will be singled out now, the Lucien's awareness of our presence now heightened, and executed for your irrational behavior."

Taryn's stomach sank. He had forgotten about the spies Eryx sent out. Taryn had helped prepare them to enter the city grounds for their next task. His head sank low in shame.

Eryx turned and strode back to his desk, throwing his ring at him. Taryn caught it, a questioning look on his face.

"Your irresponsibility has cost you," Eryx said. "I'm ordering you to finish what was started. *You* will go back out to the capitol tomorrow and retrieve the girl we are looking for—"

"Absolutely not. I told you, I am done with your petty assignments. Haven't I done enough alr—"

Eryx's deep laugh cut through Taryn's refusal. The burn in Taryn's tattooed arm flared. Taryn fought a wince, refusing to show Eryx the Oathmark affected him.

"You will do whatever I ask. You pledged your loyalty to the Guild, did you not? Are you not sworn by your Mark?"

The silence stretched between them as Taryn refused to reply. Eryx leaned back, a sly smile playing on his lips as he shook his head. "You think refusing this task cleanses you from all the blood on your hands?"

No, Taryn knew it didn't. But he could start to try.

"Get over yourself, boy. Where was the male that was sworn to my cause?"

Right, his *cause*. Eryx was fighting an uphill battle, attempting to reclaim the land as it was originally named: Mrkynia. He was the last living descendant of the old rulers, the most powerful criminal on the continent hellbent on taking his "rightful" place back on the throne after the Luciens usurped it. It was the original reason the Guild was created, but the organization had twisted over time into something unrecognizable.

Sometimes, Taryn didn't even think *Eryx* believed in his cause.

Taryn held Eryx's stare, choosing his words carefully. "I no longer have any interest in carrying out your petty assassinations."

"I'm not asking you to *assassinate* the female. I'm asking you to bring her to me, unharmed. Perhaps I'll consider moving you up in rank after your return. Wouldn't you like to run your own task force? It once was a dream of yours to see this Guild's mission come to fruition."

Taryn creased his brows at the proposal, looking down at the ring Eryx had thrown at him. It was a simple silver ring, no engravings or gemstones. Its purpose wasn't vanity. It was another method of control, just as Eryx's proposition was. The mere fact that Eryx gave it to him was a subtle threat in itself.

Now, Eryx would use flattery and propositions to get his way, and if that didn't work… Well, Taryn didn't want to experience Eryx's last resort to get him to conform.

"Fine." Taryn gave in. Eryx's smile grew, nodding at Taryn's submission.

Taryn felt it then. Something within him was brewing, changing. He was teetering on the edge of a tightrope, a silver lining between good and evil. Right and wrong. All he needed was one more push.

As he left his office that night, Taryn vowed to himself he would never allow anyone else to ever control him ever again.

No matter the cost.

Chapter 2

*Death is often thought to be the most lethal power in
the world, but that is a common misconception.
The strongest power of them all is the power of Mind.*

— *The Book of Tevye*

Airess

The corset, she thought, was an ironic metaphor for her life.

Strong fingers yanked the ivory laces at her back, constricting her, squeezing Airess so tightly, that she had no choice but to relinquish all breath as she stared at the ceiling.

"Hold still, my Lady," the seamstress ordered as Airess struggled for balance in the ridiculously high heels she had been told to wear. The lace on the shoes was so hardened, her feet had begun to blister. She sighed. It was the tenth dress she had tried on for the queen, and it was only morning.

"Tighter," the Queen Melanth of Luciena commanded from across the room. The queen had brought her ladies in wait for Airess' dress fitting this time, all of them sitting and laughing at the table adorned with delicate gold rimmed teacups and frosted sugar cakes. Her ladies voiced their agreement with the queen.

After all, how could they express anything *but* agreement? Melanth was the queen of one of the last remaining God Houses, ruling in the name of *Bas*, the Death God. To disagree with her was quite literally a death sentence.

The seamstress glanced at Airess through the mirror, a silent apology upon her features before yanking on the strings once more. Airess dug her nails into her palms and watched the females behind her make a spectacle of her dress fittings through the mirror. Melanth had Airess dressed and prepared as if she were a porcelain doll, a toy ready to be played with once Melanth was ready to make her move.

Shallow, Airess thought, *all of them.*

Airess clenched her teeth and seethed in silence. She imagined stepping off the podium and using her irrationally hard high heel as a weapon, bashing in Melanth's cold sneer and fleeing this prison of a castle. She wished she could scream at them. She wished she could *do something*.

But after a decade of being in Luciena, in this castle, Airess had mastered the ability to bite her tongue. To sit quietly. To not speak unless spoken to.

It was the only way she could survive this place.

"There. Perfect," Melanth said sharply, her chair scraping against the tiles as she came to an abrupt stand. Attendants scrambled to straighten the train of the queen's dress as she prowled towards Airess. The queen looked her up and down and assessed Airess for any damage, as one might do when inspecting property they might buy. Melanth's thin lips curved up in a smile as she regarded the seamstress, nodding in approval as she clasped her ring-adorned fingers together.

"You've outdone yourself, Esper, truly." Melanth's beady eyes finally met Airess, regarding her for the first time since she arrived in the room.

Perhaps in another life, Melanth would have been beautiful. Her porcelain skin, a common Elven trait, was flawless. Melanth's ebony hair shone in her tight updo as her head cocked to the side.

Yes, Melanth would have been beautiful, but there was no beauty that could be seen beyond her wicked soul.

"Only two more days until you marry my son," Melanth drawled as she stepped closer to Airess, brushing her cold fingers against her skin, pretending to make adjustments to Airess' bodice. Airess blinked, fighting The Sight that threatened to overcome her vision at the contact of Melanth's skin.

"Yes, my queen," Airess replied as she successfully blocked out The Sight. The power had a mind of its own, pushing itself to the surface of her eyes when a threat was sensed, as if yearning to expose the bright color of a poisonous energy. Airess often stifled the rare genetic ability, a defense mechanism that allowed her to physically *see* a person's energy and sense their feelings and truths. It was a power she used to her advantage often, and a well-kept secret from the royals.

Melanth stood behind Airess and met her gaze in the mirror, stroking Airess' long, flowing locks. "Such pretty white hair. It almost blends in with your wedding gown." Melanth stroked her hair, her fingers soft, yet the energy that buzzed around her screamed anything *but* soft. She felt, rather than saw, Melanth's cool jealousy.

Melanth snapped at one of her attendants. "The necklace."

She lifted Airess' hair as an attendant fastened a necklace onto her neck. Airess fought a frown as she brought her fingers to the gilded chained necklace, a sapphire encrusted snake at the center of her throat. The necklace represented everything about House Lucien, from the chains, to the coiled snake.

"Ah, the gold matches your eyes perfectly. Don't you agree, Lady Haeleth?"

The queen mentioned Airess' last name casually, but hearing it out loud brought up unwanted memories of her childhood she would rather forget. Memories of her father, Lord Haeleth, being slain before her very eyes.

"Yes, my queen," Airess repeated subserviently, always choosing her words carefully before she said them.

The queen stared at Airess in calculation, her gaze void of any warmth. Airess inwardly relished the queen's obvious jealousy of her beauty. At least, this, she had some control over.

Airess' hair reached down to her waist. Dark lashes framed her glowing golden eyes, freckles adorning her nose and cheeks. Airess' complexion was tanner compared to the fair-skinned Elves here in Luciena, indicating her halfling status. She was not a pure Elve. She was also half Human.

Her ears were pointed, but were not as long and lithe as pure Elven ears tended to be. The Elven people favored slender features, their elongated ears contrasting against the shorter length of Airess' half-Human ones.

"You will be my daughter soon. It's time you wear the family emblem."

The words struck a chord deep inside Airess that she actively pushed down into the depths of her mind. Airess' brows drew together in distaste at the words before forcing herself back into her usual docile mask.

But it was too late. Melanth saw her emotion, and smirked subtly at Airess' reaction.

This was the nature of their relationship. Melanth was both fond and resentful, always pulling a power play move to dig into Airess, to show her who was in control.

From the time Airess was ten years of age, she had been betrothed to Prince Arzhel Lucien. Melanth resented that Airess would eventually become queen, replacing her. Outranking her.

But she loved her for it, too.

Melanth, above all, craved power. She respected it. She sought it out everywhere she could. As if the queen *needed* more power, being one of the few Shadow Wielders left on the continent. Well, besides Arzhel, that is. Melanth's son harnessed a power of Death so strong, so lethal, it hadn't been seen in ages. The prince was rumored to have power akin to a God.

If Airess could scoff out loud at the thought, she would. If any of the citizens actually knew their queen and prince, they would surely compare them more to demons than Gods. She had learned as much during her decade long confinement in the capitol.

Melanth clicked her tongue. "So quiet today. Soon you will bear a prince or princess into the world. Are you not happy about that?" Melanth asked as she began to pace behind Airess slowly, drawing out her words.

"Of course I am." Airess inwardly grimaced, her words falling flat despite her attempt to sound genuine. She didn't want to become a mother, not with *that* asshole of a prince. Arzhel didn't want love, or a marriage, or even happiness. The prince and queen only wanted Airess for her *supposed* power, and to breed it within their familial line. That was the only reason she had been brought here as a child all those years ago.

Melanth's eyes narrowed and ordered her ladies in wait to leave. They filed out slowly, Airess thankful for the clacking of their heels overshadowing the pounding of her heart.

"Have you made any progress on your abilities?" Melanth asked, cutting to the chase. Airess expected this question, as it was asked of her every few months.

Reluctantly, Airess inhaled. She drew her breath deep inside, brewing it into power within her mind, sending the sensation down her arm, then to her hand. The surface of her skin buzzed, glowed. A golden orb faintly hovered over her palm, twinkling like a night star.

Airess watched Melanth's face soften as the glow illuminated the queen's face, hungry for power.

"I have been practicing, Your Majesty, and this is still as much as I can do," she drew out innocently. Airess, of course, was telling the truth, to some extent. She possessed a rare Magick that resembled the light of burning stars, something she had never seen before in anyone else but her mother.

"*The Gods gift us all differently,*" Airess recalled her mother saying in a distant memory, after asking as a child why her powers were so faint. Airess supposed she should be grateful to what little power she *did* have. Others were not so lucky, and had none at all.

Magick had died in Luciena. There weren't many Elves that had the ability to manipulate Shadow Magick anymore, and the ones that *did* have the rare gene running through their veins would be tracked down by the Lucien Dynasty and taken under their employ. Only the Lucien House members, or their guards, could legally possess such an ability. Any others who had the power and refused to join House Lucien were either executed by the monarchy or murdered by the Mrkynian Guild.

"I have a hard time—"

A wave of energy hit Airess' body, an aura so powerful, she felt it through the fitting room doors and down the hallway. Airess glanced to the twin doors that burst open beside her, the motion cutting Melanth off from whatever she was about to say.

Princess Morana Lucien walked through, her one-year-old babe in one arm and a glass of wine in her free hand. Airess' Sight pushed past her mental barriers and coated her eyes, revealing Morana's dark, heavy energy swirling around her like molasses. Airess blinked The Sight away, no longer wanting to see what her shell of a friend had become.

The princess was a younger version of her mother, aged eighteen with the same pale skin and dark hair cut short above her shoulders. Her eyes were colder and more calculated than Melanth's, her demeanor lacking any emotion.

Morana gave Airess a void stare, her eyes trailing down Airess' wedding gown before handing her child off to the nearest attendant. The queen finally dropped the subject and started conversing with the princess.

Yes, finally! She was thankful Morana had diverted the queen's attention. Airess narrowed her eyes, staring at the back of Melanth's head with a vengeance. "Bitch," Airess whispered.

Melanth turned around, face twisted into a scowl. "What did you say?"

"Oh, nothing. I just found a loose stitch." Airess motioned to the one white stitch that Esper hadn't caught. The queen huffed out a breath, eyeing the loose fabric like it was her enemy. "Esper, I expect that to be fixed."

Esper nodded intently, bending down to examine the skirts of Airess' dress. When Esper looked up, there was a mischievous smirk upon her lips.

The queen walked towards the princess. Airess watched them, how Princess Morana stiffened at the sight of her mother. She wished she could ask Morana what happened all those years ago, how they went from sneaking wine out onto the palace balcony to barely speaking months later. It was as if a flip had switched in Morana, her old best friend, and she was never quite the same.

Airess' mind went numb as she lost herself in her thoughts, thinking how the remnants of their girlhood died after Morana left.

Airess had finally made it back to her chambers for the day. She kicked off her heels and changed into her nightgown. She rubbed the blisters on her heels before sinking into bed and drawing the quilt up to her shoulders.

She was alone at last. Finally away from the queen, her chest released a breath that she had been holding all day. Airess was thankful to be in her bedroom that doubled as a prison and a haven. She felt this even knowing that two guards stood outside her bedroom doors, on strict orders to stop her if she tried to leave.

How warped was she to feel so at ease with her own confinement?

Airess didn't know. She didn't *want* to think about it anymore. She rolled on her side, rubbing the soft sheets between her fingertips as she gazed out the arched window beside her bed. Moonlight streamed through the window, brushing her face with a gentle warmth that offered quiet comfort. Airess hummed a gentle, lilting tune. It was a soothing ritual she could only do when she was by herself.

She looked out and wondered if anyone would take her from this place, save her from her impending marriage that she knew would ruin her. Her melody dipped, the note low in her throat. She knew no one ever would.

Why would anyone come for her? She was alone with no real friends, allies or even living family.

On the outside, she was believed to be a daughter of a late Lord, privileged to marry the prince.

On the inside, she was in a cage.

Airess closed her eyes, deep in thought. Tomorrow would be the engagement ball. The next day, the royal wedding.

The night of the royal wedding...

She changed melodies, humming a tune she had often heard her mother singing to her when she was a child. She envisioned her mother, happy and smiling as if she were still alive. The sorrow she had tried to bury earlier bloomed unexpectedly in her chest, a feeling she knew all too well. A feeling that always felt the same, no matter how much time had passed. Grief.

Airess had more rights as a child than she had at twenty years old, only allowed to stroll in the castle gardens if she wanted to get out. She wasn't permitted to go beyond that point, making her decade of confinement even more torturous.

She longed for the beaches from her childhood the most, the distant familiar feeling of the sand beneath her toes, the manor she was raised in—

Airess shook her head and shut off her train of thought. Dwelling on what cannot be changed wouldn't help her now. She could only focus on what she *could* control, and although it wasn't much, she did have one thing that no one could ever take away from her. A secret power, an ability her mother had drilled into her to keep to herself for as long as she could remember.

Dreamwalking.

Airess' hum faded off as she turned to lay on her back. She breathed in and out slowly, willing her raging thoughts away as she calmed her mind. She concentrated.

And left her reality.

Airess was falling through space.

Streaks of starlight rushed past her as she shifted into the astral, nothing but infinite starry blackness encasing her like a blanket as she traveled through the Dreamworld. The feeling was jarring, uncomfortable even, but she had grown accustomed to the sudden shift in planes. For she had been Dreamwalking aimlessly in her sleep for years now.

The starry space around her melted away like spilled paint, revealing the setting of her old childhood bedroom. Airess instantly knew she was in one of her past memories as she watched the younger version of herself nestle under the covers of her childhood bed. She must have only been six or seven in this memory, her mother still coming in to read her bedtime stories nightly.

Aesira, her mother, tucked her younger self in and smiled, "That will be all for tonight, my little one. It's time for bed."

"But wait, mama! I have a question."

"What is it, dear?" Aesira asked, narrowing her eyes in suspicion, knowing her daughter well enough to know she was stalling.

"Is Tevye real?"

Aesira sighed, lowering herself on the foot of the bed gently as she looked at her daughter. "Tevye isn't real, Airy. It's just a fairytale."

"Is time really frozen in Tevye? Do other beings and Magick really exist there?"

"Tevye is made up, Airess. It's only a bedtime story. Something to get little children like you to fall asleep!"

Her mother smiled a mischievous grin and began to tickle Airess. Childish giggles flooded the room, the last thing Airess heard as the dreamscape changed, just as quickly as it materialized. She was falling through space again until she landed somewhere solid.

Airess looked down at her astral body. She was barefoot here, her body resembling a ghost of translucent, golden light. She wore a simple maroon gown, the phantom material stopping just above her ankles, clothing she always appeared in while dreamwalking.

This was her dreamform.

She gathered her bearings and took in the foreign setting, a town she had never been to in the waking world, or the dreamworld, for that matter. It was daylight, and the oceanside town she stood before was bustling with life. Sunlight shimmered on the waves like scattered starlight.

She took in the architecture of her surroundings. It was vastly different from Luciena: square-shaped cream structures lined the shoreline, roofs made of orange clay tiling. Elven people walked— no, not *Elven people*— Airess squinted her eyes and walked closer to the bustling street.

"Fae," she said to herself in awe. "A whole town of Fae."

Pure Fae males and females crowded the streets. Airess could tell by their short, sharply pointed ears and elongated canines. They were wielding the elements all around her, some pouring water from the ocean nearby into buckets. Others moved rocks, guiding the earth with their hands, into wagons. Airess smiled at the rare sight. What a gift it was to dreamwalk, to see such a rarity of Magick.

After the war, it wasn't as common to meet any of the Fae on her continent. Luciena created their new world, eradicating elemental Magick from their country entirely and socially dividing the only two continents on the earth. The Fae who did exist in Luciena were Nobornes, powerless individuals who succumbed to working and living in the lower class.

The town and its people entranced her. Was this the great country Rune? She certainly had never dreamwalked here before. Not that she had any control of where she dreamwalked to in the first place. Unfortunately, there still wasn't a lot she knew about her dreamwalking abilities, and controlling where she ends up wasn't one of them. Airess had long since deduced this was the nature of the dreamworld.

She would go where it took her.

"Hey!" an older male yelled in Runean. The man hobbled by, walking right through her astral body. "Get back here!"

Airess turned to the group of kids running down the street, laughing as they held baskets of stolen goods in their arms.

"Follow me and run!" A Fae boy bellowed. He continued to speak, but he was yelling too fast for Airess to comprehend. Even though Airess had taken some lessons on the language in her schooling, she couldn't make out every word.

She felt her spirit being tugged onward, like a string pulling her forward from her chest. She knew the dreamworld was urging her to follow the group of juveniles. Airess obliged the sentient push to follow, knowing this to be the common nature of the dreamworld.

Airess chased them, like a ghost streaking through the night, running behind the group until they veered right onto another street, skidding to a stop once they gained enough distance from the old male. They were quite young, barely breaking their teenage years. Young females and males made up the group.

A boy with disheveled brown hair held up an engraved dagger, a sly grin on his face as he began to speak in Runean to the group, no doubt showing off his stolen goods.

"*So* this *is Rune,*" Airess said to herself, putting the pieces together as she looked around.

The boy with the dagger stopped mid-sentence, dropping his attention from the blade and looking in her direction. His gaze pierced through her, like he was seeing something he shouldn't. Airess stilled, her eyes going wide.

The sound of lightning cracked, a sound so close, yet so far away. The ground began to wobble at her feet. Airess' control slipped as the scenery around her blurred. She concentrated on stabilizing her body in the dreamworld, trying her best not to wake up.

Her efforts were in vain, the ground caving in at her feet as the dreamworld crumbled into nothing. She fell through that familiar starry void—

Airess sucked in a breath as her spirit sank back into her body, the sound of lightning ripping her from her dreams. The flash of electricity lit up her bedroom, the source coming from outside her window. She jumped out of bed and bolted to the window, looking out to the city's outer rings. Another strike cut through the night, originating from the furthest ring from the castle: The Poverty Ring.

Then, an eerie silence.

Airess pursed her lips in thought. An oddity, to be sure. The skies were clear tonight. This was no natural phenomenon. No, not natural indeed. The lightning had been wielded. Had the Mrkynian Guild breached the city once more?

If so, Airess supposed she should feel terrified. Fearful. Would the rebellion strike another hit on the capitol? Airess smiled softly at the idea, beginning to hum another comforting melody.

Yes, she thought, *come let this city burn.*

Chapter 3

'They will never accept us together, Evyen. Perhaps this is for the best.'
— *Written correspondence from Tinyrah Kazimyr to Evyen Deyanira (Pre-Division)*

Airess

Tonight would be the night. Airess had decided.

She had conjured up a half-baked plan, a last-minute effort to escape during the waltz tonight. Would her plan go sideways? Probably. It was more of a suicide mission than an escape plan, but she had to do something. She had to try.

The glass was cold beneath her fingertips as Airess pressed her body close to the bedroom window. Anxiety bubbled in her stomach, hundreds of guests beginning to file into the castle for her engagement ball below. If she wasn't a nervous wreck, she would take delight in how the differing ball gowns and suits looked like a kaleidoscope of colors. She usually found beauty in even the most mundane parts of life. It wasn't as if Airess had any other choice but to master the art of observation during her confinement.

She saw a flash of white in her peripheral, her head snapping to see a snow-white owl landing on a tree branch. Airess' face relaxed slightly at the sight of the familiar bird that showed up every once in a while. She watched it, its round head cocking to the side, milky gray eyes narrowing as if it were asking a question.

"At least we have each other," Airess whispered quietly, knowing even though the bird couldn't hear her, it helped calm her nerves in some odd, lonely way. It was strange—the bird, always seemed to appear, either outside her bedroom window or perched on a branch during her strolls in the gardens. Airess assumed it lived here from seeing it over the years, and liked to think the bird had grown fond of her.

Her chamber doors opened, a team of attendants entering, including the seamstress, Esper, to help her change into her ballgown. They bustled around the room, each one of them assigned to a different task. Airess sat in front of her vanity while hands tugged at her hair and face, applying fragrant face powder and roseate lipstain to her features.

She felt the cold sensation of the necklace queen Melanth had given her the day prior being fastened around her neck, the piece of jewelry feeling more like a branding than a gift. Airess sucked in as Esper pulled at the corset strings.

Finally, they were done. They dressed her in a long-sleeved royal blue gown, the sturdy corset sucking in her frame. The square neckline of the dress showcased her breasts. The skirt was conservative, not too large or too thin, the azure fabric spilling down to the floor. Her hair had been styled half-up-half-down, the front pieces of her hair curled in ringlets. She was the epitome of Luciena fashion.

Airess sighed, blowing a ringlet to the side and flattened her dress with sweaty palms.

The seamstress stood in front of her and smiled, her gaze lingering on the snake emblem at her neck. "A rather busy piece of jewelry," she muttered as she fished around in her bag.

Airess raised a brow in curiosity, intrigued by the seamstress's obvious dislike. Esper was a new addition to the royal staff, only arriving in Luciena a few weeks ago. Airess ought to warn the Human woman that such words could land her in a prison cell.

Esper brought out a thin necklace, dangling it in the air before Airess. "Consider this my wedding gift, dear. I would think less is best for such a beautiful dress, wouldn't you?"

Airess grabbed the necklace and inspected it. The golden chains were definitely old and dirtied with time. It was a locket, a small golden heart the size of a coin, considerably smaller in size than the statement piece she currently wore.

"Why thank you, Esper, but the queen gave me this necklace to wear—"

"*Meh*!" The old woman waved a hand. "Young ladies should be the ones to determine what jewelry they wear. Trust me, you'll want to wear *this* tonight instead." The seamstress's tone was uncharacteristically serious.

Airess didn't even get her reply out before Esper stepped behind her and unfastened the queen's necklace and replaced it with a locket. The new locket was fastened, the small heart resting above her breasts. Airess smiled softly as she touched it. "I love it. Thank you." It was probably the first gift she'd received by anyone in years.

Knock, knock, knock!

A fist banged on the door impatiently. Airess felt a burst of agitated energy hit her in waves from outside the door. Her heart began to race, her stomach sinking with dread. She stepped away from the mirror, rushing to the door. She stopped before it and hesitated, staring at the painted wood. She did *not* want to go out there. Airess could already feel the restless, heavy energy stirring on the other side.

"I believe that is the prince, my Lady," said an attendant, verbally urging her to open the door. Airess nodded, as if reassuring herself, and opened the door.

A pair of luminescent crimson eyes met hers, belonging to no other than the prince. Arzhel Lucien was tall and slender. His raven hair was slicked back, the dark color contrasting against his pale skin. Like his sister, Arzhel was a spitting image of the queen, sharing her sharp nose and cheekbones. The dark circles under his eyes were prominent today—never a good sign for Airess.

"Let's go," Arzhel ordered and grabbed her arm, his grip tight as he dragged her out of the bedroom. The Sight bloomed over Airess' eyes, overriding her will and revealing Arzhel's *black* aura. It was so dark, the energy stagnant, unmoving and *strong*. His energy repelled her more than anyone else's ever had. She physically flinched at the sight of it.

She blinked back to her normal vision and hurried her steps to catch up with him, not wanting to appear weak in front of anyone who walked by. Anger bristled within her as she side-eyed the prince who looked like a ghostly vision. He was more physical than usual today.

"Let me go," she demanded, her voice low. Arzhel ignored her, increasing his pace. Airess fumbled after him, his grip still prominent on her arm, dragging her around like she was a piece of property. She snapped—the anger and anxiety mixing together into an ugly, uncontrollable feeling inside. Airess yanked her arm away, her face flushing. "I said *let go!*"

She stumbled backwards as she broke free from his grasp. Arzhel stopped and turned to her slowly, looking her up and down as if he just now noticed her for the first time. "*I* can touch you whenever and however I'd like. You're to be *my* wife, so you are *my* property."

He stepped forward, letting out a bitter laugh. "You should consider yourself lucky, marrying into the royal family despite your halfling *defects*. As much as I disdain this union, I understand my role in producing an heir, unlike you. But don't worry," he continued, lowering his tone as servants passed by. "I'll be sure to give you my heir as soon as possible, and we will both have fulfilled our duties."

Disgust rolled through her like slick oil. The inevitable she had been dreading for so long would be upon her tomorrow night— that is, if her escape plan fails. Arzhel's words only solidified that she would die trying. Airess supposed she should be grateful for such a long engagement. It was a miracle in itself that their union had been pushed off for so long.

Footsteps echoed down the hallway. They both turned to see The queen walking towards them. For once, Airess was relieved to see her.

Airess had known the prince since she was ten years old. Even as a boy, Arzhel had been unnecessarily cruel. He saved that part of himself especially for her—his prejudices against anyone that were not pureblood Elven the reasoning for his wicked behavior. He felt that Airess was beneath him, and treated her as such.

"You both look wonderful!" Melanth exclaimed as she gave both of them a once over. Melanth paused at the locket Airess wore at her neck, her smile melting away. "Where did you get that?"

"The seamstress, my queen. She gave it to me as a wedding gift."

"Is that so?" Melanth asked, more to herself than to Airess.

As quick as her displeasure came, it went. She shook her head and grabbed Airess and Arzhel's arms. "Well, no matter. Come along. It's time for our entrance. Remember, chin up. Smile. Oh, and dance with our guests please. Especially you, Airess. A good queen always dances with her guests."

Airess heard the crowd before they stopped in front of the ballroom doors. Arzhel grabbed her hand—the action looking tender, but the feeling anything but. She felt the discontentment radiating off of him as their hands touched, and she tried her best not to cringe.

Airess stared at her shoes in silent prayer to any Gods that might hear her. *If you have any love for me, if you even exist at all, please, help me escape.*

The doors burst open, the light from the chandeliers overwhelming Airess as they walked forward. Their arrival was announced as they walked, the ballroom lively with chatter and music.

The room, floor to ceiling, was made entirely from white marble. The light from the chandeliers glittered beautifully against the sleek tiles the ballgoers stood upon. Floral arrangements were placed on every surface they could fit—a mix of creams and blues to represent the Lucien House.

The sweet scent of the florals wafted up to her nose, a stark contrast to the bitterness she felt inside. Airess' heart began to thrum, cheeks heating at how exposed she felt with all eyes on her. After all this time, she was finally making her debut into society and all she wanted to do was turn around and hide. A group of musicians played in the corner, grounding her into reality, the music projecting loud into the large space. Airess focused on the sound of the violin as she walked towards the dais, her palms beginning to sweat.

How surreal it was to finally come to this moment, to confront an event that her entire existence in the castle was based upon. Airess went through the motions, her subtle greetings and curtsies to various Luciena aristocrats blurring together. Dissociation set in as she put on a performance, feeling astray from her body. It was as if she were watching herself from the outside.

At last, the formalities ceased and she was relinquished from her social obligations. Airess sat at a table on the dais, away from all the ball attendees and accepted a glass of wine a servant offered to her. She sipped, savoring the bittersweet liquid flowing down her throat.

"I'll have one, as well," said a feminine voice to the servant. The princess walked up to the table and sat across from Airess with a glass of wine in hand.

Morana's eyes dipped to Airess' wrist, the red mark from Arzhel's grip lingering. Airess waited to see if Morana would have a reaction—anything to show Airess her friend was still there somewhere inside. The empty look remained, and Airess felt like a fool for hoping her friend would ever be the same again.

"Cheer up," Morana said bitterly, raising her glass in the air. "You get to be queen one day in exchange for a few hits from time to time. I'd say that's a fair enough tradeoff."

Airess' brows creased together in disbelief. The emotionless words stung more than she expected. Though, she didn't know why she was *still* surprised at Morana's lack of empathy. They weren't the girls they once were. And they hadn't been friends in a long time.

These past few years, Morana had warped into an entirely different person. Airess knew part of it was being shipped off to the northern mountainlands where she resided with her husband. Although they never spoke of the matter, Airess knew Morana had a deep dissatisfaction with her life, being married off at the ripe age of fourteen. Airess remembered Morana begging her mother to change her mind, to not send her away. The queen didn't listen, instead insisting that a member of the royal family must produce heirs.

Since then, Morana's coldness had grown over the years, the princess distancing herself from Airess. At first, Airess thought Morana's sudden change in behavior was due to the fact that it had taken years for her to conceive. But her demeanor never softened, even after giving birth to her now one year old baby. It only grew colder.

Airess drank the rest of her glass and leveled a stare at Morana. "I know you don't mean that."

Morana rolled her eyes, brushing Airess off, and looked beyond her to the crowd. Her dark eyes grew distant. Withdrawn. For a moment, Airess caught a glimpse of sadness in her, like her behavior all along was a facade. An armor.

"All of this, all these people," Morana gestured her hand to the crowd, "will be yours someday. And I've never understood *why* that is."

Airess didn't know. She had wondered about that herself for many years. Surely it wasn't because of her weak powers. There had to be other Magick Wielders much stronger than Airess, yet what the queen wanted, she got.

"I don't know, Morana." Airess inhaled a breath of patience and changed the subject. "Where is Lord Calder?" Airess asked, referencing Morana's husband. "Where's baby Allia?"

To Airess' surprise, Morana smiled slightly as she took another sip of wine. "The baby is upstairs asleep. *Lord Calder* will be running late this evening."

Airess opened her mouth to reply, but Morana stood abruptly, mentioning she needed to check on the baby. Airess watched her walk away, suddenly missing her cold and distant company. She busied herself, picking at her nails to pass the time—

At once, Airess felt an invisible force hit her in the back. An intense, painless energy sent her lurching forward into the table. Her breath quickened at the buzzing sensation within, her body recognizing an aura she couldn't comprehend. Airess gripped the table to steady herself, sensing a foreign energy so strong that it had struck her from across the room.

She whipped her head toward the crowd, blinking to uncover The Sight. Airess scanned the room for the source, struggling to differentiate all the colors of auras in the room, each bundle of energy blending into the next in such close quarters.

Until she saw it.

Or *him*, rather.

It was the most beautiful energy she had ever seen in all her twenty years. Silver and multicolored tendrils of energy flowed around him in a dance, the aura moving with ease. Airess stood up, walked to the dais banister, and stared.

Glowing, silver eyes stared back at her.

He had to have been her age, perhaps a few years older. The male had bronzed skin, suggesting he must have hailed from the southern continent. His brown, curly hair fell over his brow effortlessly. His tattooed muscled arms were on display, as his tunic had been rolled to the elbows. His tall height was evident, even from afar.

The male smirked and brought a flask to his lips. He took a swig, still not breaking eye contact with her, staring through thick lashes. Airess didn't know why he was looking at her so boldly in front of everyone, especially with that *look* in his eyes. Her breath hitched, entranced in his gaze, before she remembered herself and turned away, fighting the heat creeping up to her cheeks.

Before she could think about the male any further, the sound of heels approached. The music began to change to an upbeat melody, cueing the first waltz of the night. "Airess, dear, do go out there and dance with our guests," Melanth instructed with a curt smile, lowering her voice to a whisper. Airess' blood ran cold. This was it. The waltz was about to begin…

"The prince seems to be missing at the moment. You'll have to charm them on your own."

"Of course," Airess replied, her body reacting automatically, just as it always did when her mind was far from the present moment. Airess tried her best to stifle her curiosity about the handsome male across the room and focus on her escape plan.

The Plan: Dance. Get lost in the crowd. *Run*. She descended down the dais and smiled at anyone who looked her way.

Airess stood in formation with the rest of the dancers, knowing this waltz by muscle memory from a lifetime of ballroom dance lessons. It began slowly, only requiring one dance partner. She took the hand of an older Elven male and was whisked away.

The song felt like it lasted forever, the Elven gentleman talking to Airess mostly about crops.

"I find it so strange that my flower field keeps getting raided. Of course, I know my plants are the most desirable in the city, but it's becoming quite problematic. Perhaps this is something you could mention to the queen?"

Airess unintentionally tuned him out, looking around for the mysterious male in the mass of attendees. Curiosity got the better of her. Who was he, and why was he so different from the others? Surely, it was her eyes playing tricks on her—

"It would be very kind of you to pass on a message to the queen, my Lady. My Lady?" The Elven male repeated, yanking Airess' attention back to the present as the first waltz came to an end.

She nodded politely. "Of course, my Lord. I will expedite such matters to the highest of ranks."

The male seemed satisfied with her response and gave his thanks as he departed.

The orchestra wasted no time as another song began to play, the beat much faster than before. Airess knew this waltz well and rejoined the line of dancers, placing her hand in another guest's and moving her feet to the beat of the music.

One. Two. Three. Four.

A dim spark within her lit brighter, a dormant part of her finally coming alive. It was a foreign feeling. Was this freedom? Was this happiness? Whatever it was, she relished in it. Who knew how much time she had left to just be *herself*. Her love for music drove her forward, giving her the strength to live on.

One. Two. Three. Four.

Time to switch partners, Airess swirled in the other direction, coming alive as she met the next dancer. She smiled—a real smile—the feeling foreign as she lost herself in the music. Her feet moved in rhythm with the melody, and before she knew it, it was time to move on to the next person. Leave it to the music to always draw her out of her mind and away from her fears.

She spun, perhaps a little too much, as she tripped into her next dance partner.

Firm hands steadied her arms, preventing her from stumbling. She righted her footing and arched her neck to look up.

Airess gaped, taking in the silver eyes, the color even more intense up close. *Wow.* He was beautiful. A thin scar slashed downwards from his temple and down the side of his cheek, the scarred flesh contrasting against his dark tan skin. Was he a fighter, a soldier? He certainly had the height and build for one, his tall frame towering over her. Lean muscle bristled against his tight suit as he moved.

Her gaze fell to the dangling earring on his right ear. A collection of studs and rings went up the cartilage on his—wait, were those *Fae* ears? She looked down to his full lips that now twisted into a smirk.

"Will you dance with me?" the Fae male asked, his deep vibrato cutting through her entrancement. That smirk was still present on his lips, and she wanted to ask him what was so amusing. Airess noted the slight Runean accent gracing his smooth voice and ignored the tingling sensation she felt at hearing him speak. Airess remembered to nod, forgetting she had stopped dancing in the first place.

He placed a hand on her waist and grabbed her hand with his own, the contact sending a jolt of electricity down her arm. The fabric of her gown felt thin beneath his hand, heat seeping through as if he could brand her by touch alone.

He arched a dark, angled brow at her as they rejoined the dance.

Airess shook her head, remembering to speak. "Apologies for my poor footing, sir—I mean, *Lord*—"

She cut herself off, kicking herself internally for acting like such a fool. Airess let out a breath. "Forgive me. I don't believe I've ever seen you here before. Are you a lord of new standing?"

Airess realized he was the only Fae in the room. Certainly he had some Elven blood to have been let in here, knowing most, if not all, Noborne Fae people were left to live in the outer ring. Taking a quick glance around her, she noticed some people began to stare at them—at *him*. This wasn't good. She needed the people's attention elsewhere. Would this male sully her escape plan?

The male shook his head and laughed. "I am no Lord."

Right, okay.

They moved along with the other dancers. Her dance partner moved with ease, yet she could immediately tell he hadn't memorized the steps as the other dancers had, only making him more intriguing. Airess uncovered her Sight and took in his aura once more, enthralled to see the vibrant colors up close. His aura encased her body like a blanket, the energy behaving in a way she had never seen before.

"I don't believe I asked for your name, sire," Airess said as they rotated, her dress shifting with the motion. He placed his hands firmly on her waist as she dipped backwards, and for a moment she thought she saw intrigue flash behind his eyes. The emotion was gone as quick as it came.

She tried her best to concentrate on normal pleasantries, and to understand how this Fae male had leveled up so high in the hierarchy that he was invited to a noble ball.

It was unheard of for Fae to be a part of high society. Not that Airess cared about such a distinction. She didn't share the prejudices against the Fae and Humans like the Elven people did. Airess had experienced the hatred firsthand due to her halfling status. The disdain had seemed to lessen as the wedding drew nearer, nobles realizing she would eventually be their queen.

Before she's made the decision to leave, Airess had always vowed that when she was queen, she would remake the world—one where everyone lived equally. No outer rings. No discrimination based on lack of Magick or difference in beings.

He caressed a hand along her arm as she came up from the dip, causing tingles to flood her entire body. Airess tensed, and an unknown feeling bubbled in her stomach, that made her question if she was feeling attraction or anxiety. Perhaps both.

They rejoined hands once more as the male opened his mouth to speak.

"My name is—" he began, but was cut off by a loud *BOOM!*

Airess flew backwards as an explosion burst in the room, flashes of lilac light streaking by. She landed on her back, her head cracking against the floor. Pain seared through her skull at the contact. Screams erupted as chunks of marble fell from the ceiling. Dust billowed, blocking Airess' ability to see around her. She groaned as she lay there in shock and brought fingers up to the back of her head. They came back wet with blood.

Airess propped herself up on a jagged pillar now in ruins beside her. Her ears rang. Slowly, she came to stand, suddenly resenting the large, heavy skirts she was dressed in. Her legs wobbled as her blurred vision began to clear. Airess' stomach clenched at what she saw.

The screams became audible as her hearing returned. Some people ran in different directions, others lay unmoving on the floor.

"Oh my Gods," she said, remembering to run. She turned, rearing back as she collided with someone. *Oh*, it was just Esper. She grabbed Airess' shoulders to steady her, the seamstress's eyes hardened with determination.

"Esper, are you all right?" Airess managed to blurt out. The seamstress looked clean, not one hair out of place.

"You must come with me!" Esper yelled urgently.

"What's going on? Where's the queen—"

"Come!"

Airess lurched forward to follow Esper, her body acting on its own accord. Adrenaline blocked out the pain and panic from the fall. She focused on Esper's tight, gray bun as she led her from the ballroom. They rushed down the empty corridor.

"Where are the guards? What's happening?"

Esper ignored her as she turned down another hall, the two now entering the servants' stairwell passageway. Their footfalls echoed against the ceiling of the stairwell as they made their descent, Airess' heavy breathing audible.

Finally, they reached the bottom of the stairwell. They cut through the kitchens usually bustling with servants, but now completely empty.

Esper and Airess barreled through the door and exited onto the castle grounds outside, the fresh night air caressing Airess' skin. It was eerily quiet outside, save for the chirping crickets.

A carriage awaited their arrival. Airess stopped for the first time since the explosion, doubt finally overcoming her. It seemed as if her common sense had returned.

"Esper, what is this?"

"Get in the carriage," Esper snapped. "I'll explain everything inside."

Airess walked forward immediately, stepping up into the wooden carriage. Esper followed and shut the door behind them. Her body jolted backwards as the carriage began to ride away at great speed. Airess' face contorted in confusion as she looked at her legs. What had she done, leaving the castle like this?

"What—what is this?" Airess began, sitting up slightly. Her head throbbed. She felt the blood begin to harden and cake onto her scalp.

Esper's expression was unreadable as she pulled out a folded dress and placed it on Airess' lap.

"What I'm about to tell you will change the trajectory of your entire life, so listen carefully. We don't have much time," Esper said as she placed a pair of brown leather boots at Airess' side.

"My name is Renesper Crawn, High Priestess of House Moros. I belong to an organization whose sole purpose is to preserve the state of the world. That organization is called The Obadiah, and it is one that your mother once belonged to, on the other half of the world."

Airess sat up, her body stilling at the mention of her mother on her seamstress's lips. House Moros? That didn't add up. From what she recalled from her studies, House Moros served *Inntin*, the Mind God, and had been extinct for hundreds of years. The family didn't—*shouldn't* exist anymore.

"Our cause, the entire purpose of The Obadiah, is to preserve the natural state of the world and the lives of the Prophesied Ones. Your mother served her life to our cause, fled her homeland, and relocated to Luciena. She believed it was the best course of action to take in preserving your life. At the time, I agreed it was the wisest move." A wave of grief shadowed Esper's face.

"But we cannot always foresee what lies ahead, and terrible mistakes have been made. I broke away from The Obadiah to search for you."

Airess couldn't believe her words. It sounded like heretic talk, the way she was speaking. Airess shook her head. "Even if this was true, what do you mean *the other half of the world*? This earth consists of only two continents. All land has been discovered. And my mother was *no* Priestess."

Esper shook her head. "Did your mother ever speak to you about The

Tevye Legends?"

Airess recognized the words instantly. Hearing them again opened a floodgate of buried memories from her childhood. She remembered her mother telling her nightly bedtime stories, a collection of fairy tales about a faraway land that was locked in time.

"Yes. My mother used them to tell me bedtime stories as a child."

"They are no stories, child. Have you ever wondered why she told you to keep your abilities a secret, why you are the only Elve that has The Sight?"

Airess shook her head, speechless. She wanted to deny the words Esper was saying, she didn't want to believe that any of this could be true. But when she blinked her Sight forward, and saw Esper's aura shine bright in truth, she could only come to two conclusions—either Esper was crazy enough to think she was right, or everything she said was the truth.

A knock rapped from the horseman outside the carriage. "About five more minutes until we arrive!"

Distracted by Esper's explanation, Airess realized they were no longer near the castle as she peered outside the window, the carriage riding steadily through the woods. Her heart thrummed in her chest as panic set in.

"Arrive—arrive where? Oh, Gods, the Luciens are going to be furious."

Esper placed a hand on her own, kindness and understanding laced in her eyes. "Don't worry about the Luciens. We have orchestrated this escape perfectly. You'll be long gone and far too difficult to trail by the time they realize your absence."

Airess' heart pounded in her chest at the word *escape*. She shook her head furiously. Although she had every intention of leaving during the ball, she had never planned to survive the attempt. She never planned on dealing with the repercussions.

"No. I can't leave. Arzhel will kill me for this."

"You can, and you will. You don't *belong* here."

A silence passed, Airess staring down at the cotton dress in her lap. For once, she felt relief. Airess hadn't ever pictured her life beyond being the queen she was always groomed to be. She looked up at the stars through the carriage window.

Had the Gods really answered her prayers?

"Where will I go?" Airess whispered as she gazed out the carriage window, finally beginning to accept what was happening to her.

"To Rune," Esper smiled. "It's time you meet your people and unite with The Obadiah. You will be free there. We can train you, sharpen your powers to be the weapon you were always meant to be. Every minute detail has been planned for this escape. You'll stay with a friend of mine at her Inn for the night. In the morning, you will be transported south.

"The Innkeeper will have everything ready for your departure. You'll have to lay low and stay out of the public during the day. Here. I'll help you out of this horrid dress," Esper explained as she handed her a dark maroon cloak.

Airess turned around so Esper could unlace the corset. She hurriedly changed out of her dress and into her new one—a much different article of clothing than she had ever worn. It was made of a soft cotton material, plain, the color of cream. The dress was simple, something she had seen commoners wear.

The bell sleeves stopped at the middle of her forearm, the skirt flowing straight down. She was given another article of clothing, a long corset that layered on top of the dress, the dark red color rich. Esper laced the top layer, the fabric cinching her waist. She quickly shoved her feet in the boots and swung the cloak over her shoulders.

"You'll want to take off your jewelry, dear," Esper pointed out. Airess removed them, starting with her earrings and bracelet. She began to unfasten the heart-shaped locket at her neck when Esper stopped her, telling her that it was hers to keep on the journey.

Esper handed her a bag full of supplies and a change of clothes. Airess frowned. "Are you not coming with me?"

"No. My work here is far from over."

"But I have so many questions for you! I don't even know where to start."

Esper smiled sadly as the carriage came to a stop. "If all goes as planned, I will meet you in Rune with the rest of The Obadiah. Then, you can ask me all the questions your heart desires."

Airess pressed her lips together to keep herself from crying, fear and anticipation overwhelming her. She said her farewells to the High Priestess of House Moros. Esper embraced Airess before she opened the carriage door and stepped onto the streets of Holtzclaw.

"You will find your way. This is only the beginning."

Airess watched the carriage ride away until she no longer saw it in the distance. As she turned towards the Inn, she couldn't help but notice the finality in Esper's tone.

She had a feeling she wouldn't be seeing Esper again.

Chapter 4

'Tevye was once part of the physical world, but Evyen Deyanira ascended it to a higher dimension.'

– The book of Tevye

Taryn

He couldn't get her scent out of his head.

In a way, he was grateful for it, the prominence of her sweet scent the only reason he was able to track her after that disaster of a ball. He focused on the task at hand, trying his best to block out the blast that brought too many painful memories back to the surface. He trailed the faintest hint of honey and magnolias, the smell of Lady Airess lingering in the woods he now traveled through on horseback.

The explosion was a problem, an annoying deterrence. An unknown third player had entered the mix, much to Taryn's dismay. He had a flawless plan: dance with the Lady Airess and slowly draw her out of the ballroom using the Compulsion Ring Eryx had lent him. Taryn had compelled the castle guards and any ballgoer around him to act natural, as if he belonged there. He was surprised Eryx let him use the ring, but there would have been absolutely no way he would have been able to get into the castle without it.

Taryn rode twenty minutes south until he reached the small town of Holtzclaw. The clatter of hooves on stone faded as he dismounted his horse and scanned the perimeter. Stone buildings leaned slightly with age, and the town was null of any life bustling amongst the street in the dead of night.

Taryn inhaled the brisk air. The Lady Airess' scent was strong. He tied his horse to a tree nearby, pulled the cloak over his head, and followed her trail.

He stopped before a familiar building, an inn Taryn had seen in passing during his travels across Luciena. The Lady Airess' scent trail ended here. He debated breaking in, but that would lead to witnesses and a commotion he'd rather avoid. Ultimately, he decided on watching out for her behind the outhouses.

Surely, she would eventually come outside.

A brief feeling of shame washed over him as he thought about what he was doing. If circumstances were different, if Eryx hadn't made him swear the Oathmark, Taryn would never be doing something like this. Hell, he wouldn't have done half the things Eryx commanded him to do.

Taking that Oathmark had turned out to be the biggest mistake of Taryn's entire twenty-four years of existence.

After several hours, a soft, feminine humming sound drew him out of his thoughts. He sat upright against the tree, completely out of eyeshot from the outhouses so he wouldn't be seen. The melody graced his ears.

He didn't need to see to know it was her who hummed. For a moment, he closed his eyes and relished in her song. When the door of the outhouse closed, Taryn slowly crept up to the side of the building. He inched around the side near the door.

And when the door opened, he lunged.

Chapter 5

'Us Luciens have always had to connive and claw our way to power, for the other Godlings have pitted against us.'

— *Written entry from Zaro Lucien's personal journal (Pre-Division)*

Airess

She wasn't thinking clearly.

Airess told herself that all the events leading up to this moment had clouded her mind, her judgment, because she could have *sworn* she felt that same familiar energy radiating off the Fae male from the ball at the current moment. She must be feeling things, because when she took in her surroundings before walking into the outbuilding, she saw nothing but a black forest beyond her.

Pulling her cloak over her shoulders, she shoved the outhouse door open. Never had she ever used a building like this, but Airess knew she would quickly have to adapt—

A hand gripped her forearm and yanked her backwards. Her scream was stifled by another hand covering her mouth as she was pushed against the wall. Her gold eyes widened in surprise as she met silver ones underneath the hood of a cloak.

The male towered over her, pressing his forearm against her collarbone to pin her against the wall. Surprisingly, he was gentle, the pressure firm but not enough to cause pain.

"I'm not going to hurt you. Please, **don't yell**," a male voice said with a Runean accent present. He removed his hand from her lips and angled his head down to look at her. She instinctively opened her mouth to yell, to scream.

No sound came out.

Her brows creased at her lack of control. Panic set in, her heart beginning to beat rapidly.

He spoke, his tone low, "**Follow me.**"

He released her and stepped back, lowering his hood, having the decency to give her a chance to look at him. Airess gazed over his disheveled curly hair and straight nose. Those steel-colored eyes glowed faintly, like moonlight casting over a still pond. He wore the same collection of earrings on one ear as before, yet he had changed into different clothes. Her eyes narrowed into slits.

"*You.*" Her tone was pure venom.

The male grimaced, as if her voice had physically lashed him. Without saying another word, he stiffly turned away from her and walked in the opposite direction into the woods.

She inhaled a sharp breath as her legs began to move of their own accord, her body following him, each step betraying her freewill. She pressed her hand on the tops of her thighs, trying to stop them, but her efforts were in vain. She walked right up to the male, walking by his side, her shoulder *touching* his arm.

"What's happening?" she whispered, her breath quickening, her body breaking out in a sweat.

"I've only compelled you to follow me because I do not wish to harm you, and I know you wouldn't follow me willingly," the Fae male confessed, his explanation defensive, as if he too saw the immorality in what he was doing.

"You *compelled* me?" She repeated, realizing how subtle the compulsion felt in her mind. She squeezed her eyes shut, focusing every atom of her body to resist.

Stubbornly, she planted her feet in the ground, refusing to move them. She hissed as she fought the compulsion Magick, feeling a stabbing pain within her mind. Airess fought it, her breath labored as she strained her own muscles to comply. Slowly, one foot moved to take another step, her freewill beginning to shatter. Her leg muscles trembled as she tried to resist.

"Fighting it will only cause you pain. You'll only make it worse."

Her strength faltered. She resumed walking forward, releasing a deep breath. She looked back to the Inn, watching it disappear from view as they walked into the woods, Esper's plan crumbling by the second.

"What do you want?" Airess asked sharply. The male chose not to respond, his gaze forward as if she hadn't spoken at all. His jaw clenched and he refused to meet her gaze. Airess's fear transformed into anger, her face twisting into an ugly sneer.

"Where are you taking me? *Why* are you doing this?"

No response.

The silence scraped her nerves, and although her legs moved against her will, she could still control her arms. Airess had never struck someone before, but desperation had taken over. She succumbed to the basic instinct of survival.

She raised a fist and swung wildly, aiming straight for his face.

He pivoted out of the way with ease, seizing both of her wrists. Airess jolted forward, crashing into his body. She almost tripped, but his firm grip held her upright. She glared up at him, too angry to feel fear in this moment.

"Let me go," she said through gritted teeth, her face taut.

He raked his eyes down her face, and to her surprise, the corners of his lips turned up with amusement.

"**You will not strike me again**." He commanded, and then gently let go of her. He walked forward as if nothing happened.

"You—you—*Who are you*?" Airess asked, her voice shaking with rage. Rage at the fact that he seemingly found their situation *funny*. Airess thought he was going to ignore her again, a beat of silence lasting too long. Finally, he sighed and gave in. "I'm taking you to my Guildmaster."

Airess' eyes almost bulged out of her head. There was only one Guild she had heard of before that used witchcraft, a compulsion Magick powerful enough to compel others against their freewill.

"The Mrkynian Guild?"

More silence. His subtle denial to answer infuriated her. She balled her fists as they trekked forward, footsteps rustling against the leaves in the woods.

Why would they want her? It's not like she had any power to offer them. Unless, they were under a different impression. Perhaps they too were fooled into thinking she was something special, a Magickal prodigy, like the Luciens had.

Oh, were they sorely mistaken.

"I have nothing to offer your Guild," she ground out. "I'm virtually powerless."

"Oh, *really*?" the male retorted sarcastically, "Is that why you were marrying into the royal family, for your lack of power?"

Airess seethed, hating that she was walking so closely beside him. "Yes, *really*. You and your lawless friends will be quite disappointed."

"We shall see," he replied coolly.

Airess scoffed. She was, at last, speechless. He wasn't who she expected him to be, a member of the most notorious Guild in the country. She expected him to look like a scary, ugly male. Much to her dismay, he was the exact opposite of ugly. She studied his side profile, his perfect nose and lips outlined by the moonlight above. That damn earring caught her attention again, and she realized it was a tiny lightning bolt made of copper.

Finally, a chestnut horse came into view, tied to a tree, patiently waiting for its rider as they approached. She scowled as she realized there was only one horse. Did he intend for them to ride together?

"Let. Me. Go. *Now*."

The male shook his head, eyes boring into hers. "I can't."

"Why are you doing this? Do you really have such a lack of morality to see taking a female against her will is wrong?"

The male began to untie the horse's rope, his broad back facing her. She tried to take the opportunity to bolt the other direction while he wasn't looking, but her legs denied her.

He turned around to face her, his jaw tense, "I have little choice in the matter."

What did that even mean?

Airess scoffed in reply, her tone incredulous. "What are you going to do with me?"

"*I* am going to do nothing with you. I am merely a steward of your transportation."

Interesting.

The male looked from Airess to the horse, opening his mouth to speak. She shook her head and crossed her arms. "No, absolutely not. I am not getting on that horse."

He sighed. "Please, make this easier for all of us and get on."

"*Hell*, no!"

The male's jaw ticked. He opened his mouth and closed it, no doubt stifling a witty response he had on the tip of his tongue.

"Contrary to what you may believe, I don't have any desire to compel you again. Just get on the horse," the male said with his chin up, arms folded, daring her to refuse. "Or I will *make* you."

Airess held his stare, contemplating refusing, but she didn't want to lose control over her body again. She hated how it felt, not being in control.

Airess lifted her chin as she strode over to the horse. It was large, much larger than she remembered. It had been ten years since she had ridden. Airess grabbed what she could on the saddle and shoved a foot into the stirrup.

After a few seconds of struggling, the male stepped towards her, his arms out to help her on, "I can help—"

"Don't *touch* me," she snapped, her tone lethal.

Fueled by rage, Airess pulled herself up. Her dress and cloak hiked up her legs as she swung her leg over. She pulled the fabric down, noticing the male had turned away. Was he giving her privacy? The act confused her, his behavior a sharp contrast to his words. Airess kept quiet as he got on the horse, his body behind her entirely too close for comfort.

Warmth seeped off of him, his muscled abdomen molding against her back. She was so close to him, she could hear his breathing. Airess inhaled his scent, the smell of the ocean wafting up to her nose. She loathed that he smelled good, even with the hint of cigar smoke.

Airess was glad she wasn't facing him, her cheeks beginning to warm to a soft pink. Airess tried her best to lean forward, to put as much distance as she could away from him. She was thankful for the silence as the horse began to ride forward, needing a brief moment to take in everything that had happened to her.

Her mind whirled.

First the explosion, Esper's revelation, and now this?

Airess looked down to her hands, disappointed at her lack of golden translucence that was her dreamform. She wished this was some horrible dream she could wake up from. Though she didn't know what nightmare would be worse—being taken by this male, or marrying Arzhel Lucien.

Definitely marrying Arzhel.

Despite herself, she smiled at the realization she had truly eluded him, as she thought about Arzhel for the first time since the carriage.

Gods, she had done it! She had actually escaped!

A laugh escaped her lips. She was unable to contain her joy. She forgot about her current circumstances, her fears about the future, even the male sitting behind her. It was pure ecstasy, she thought, as she realized she had finally got away from her abuser. She could imagine Arzhel's rage as he realized she had left the castle, his pompous ego shattering as his precious child-bearer had escaped. She smiled.

"What could you possibly be laughing about?" The male's deep vibrato rumbled from behind her, his voice vibrating against her back, sending shivers down her spine.

Her smile faded, her burst of happiness short lived as his voice yanked her to the present. Airess didn't reply. Let him think she was crazy. She wouldn't be divulging into her past with Arzhel, especially with the handsome criminal behind her.

Airess thought back to the ball, how she saw the Fae male standing out in the crowd like a sore thumb. He had worn nice clothing then, but looking down at the arms on either side of her holding the reins, he had since changed.

His entire ensemble was black, from the long-sleeved tunic, pants and leather boots. He had various weapons strapped onto his waist and thighs, but it was the double broadswords strapped to his back that caught her attention the most.

"Were you at the ball acting on orders to take *me*?"

"Yes, *my Lady*."

"Why?"

The male sighed behind her. "They want you for your power, that's all I was told."

But how could they have known that?

Airess decided to choose her words carefully, strategizing her next move. She blinked The Sight over her eyes, opening herself to the male's energy. Immediately, she felt uneasiness radiating off of him like fyrelight, mixed with a hint of regret—almost as if he felt *resentful* of his task to transport her. There was also a softer energy, a kindness that spoke to her for him: He would not bring harm upon her.

This surprised her. She didn't know what she was expecting, but certainly not the complicated feelings he was experiencing. Airess looked down at his hands. They were calloused. He had a few white scar lines on the tops of his hands, now healed skin.

Silver energy swirled around him with unrest, as if he was upset with himself. It was his finger that caught her attention. Black, murky energy radiated around a silver ring on his pointer finger. Airess frowned at it and blinked away her Sight.

It was a blessing and a curse, to understand and feel others so deeply, the ability always a teetering balance of self preservation, and open-minded empathy.

She forced herself out of her mind.

"What is your name?" she asked.

His grip tightened on the reins. "Taryn."

Familiarity and unknowingness hit her at the sound of his name. *Taryn.* She had never heard that name before, but she liked it. It sounded like an answer to a question she hadn't even asked yet, a melody she had yet to learn.

"How did you find me?"

The male had the audacity to scoff. "I'm Fae."

Airess' nostrils flared. "That doesn't answer my question."

"I scented you from miles away. Are you not aware that Fae people have much stronger senses than you Elves? Oh, wait, don't answer that question." He laughed bitterly, "Of course you wouldn't know. What would a female of nobility like you be doing near Fae?"

She whipped around, the movement sharp enough to send her hair flying, and shot him a glare. "How dare you speak to me that way? You know *nothing* about me."

His gaze flicked over her briefly. "I don't need to. Your frilly dress and pristine ball told me enough about you."

Her face reddened, a flush of frustration mixed with anger. "I never wanted that. I never wanted *any* of it —" She bit her lip, stopping herself from spiraling off on a tangent. "You're quick to judge, assuming I partake in prejudices I most *certainly* do not. You would be eating your words if you knew the things I have gone through."

That shut him up. Taryn didn't even deign to respond. She didn't need a response. Airess was glad he finally stopped talking.

They rode in silence for the next hour. Dawn fell upon them, the sky tinged a shade of dark pink as the sun began to rise. She fought to keep her eyes open, having now been awake for twenty four hours.

Her mouth and throat felt dry. Airess pressed her chapped lips together, realizing she hadn't drunk water in quite some time. It had to have been hours before the ball that she drank water last. The last thing she consumed was a hearty glass of wine.

"Do you have any water?"

"I'm out," he said curtly.

"Well, where can we get some?"

Taryn laughed. He actually *laughed.* She heard his clothes shifting as he shook his head. "You'll have to try harder than that."

He was insufferable. Did he always think the worst?

"If you're going to take me against my will, compel my body to comply, the least you could do is provide some water. Even *prison guards* understand that principle."

Silence. Then, Taryn guided the reins to the side.

"Fine," he snapped. "Put your hood up and don't make any sudden movements. If you think I can't catch you if you try to escape, you're wrong."

"Whatever you say," Airess retorted, her words dripping with sarcasm. Taryn scoffed in reply.

She gladly put her hood up and began to devise an escape plan. Airess had no desire to be recognized any less than he did. She would have to think quickly, use her wits against him. Surely, other folk would be around if they found a public well.

They came onto the main road. Eventually, a small town came into view—little homes scattered across flat grassland with a strip of buildings at its center. She kept her head low, making sure to hide her features as she saw locals bustling around, preparing for the day. The sun was nearly risen.

They approached the well behind a string of small buildings. To her dismay, it was void of any patrons but themselves. She would have to get away from him and draw attention to herself. Airess counted the steps it would take to walk through the alley and into the main road just beyond the well.

Airess let Taryn dismount first, and when he turned his back, she dismounted as well. He whipped around towards her, dark brows drawn together.

"What are you doing?"

She looked at him innocently. "What? Am I not allowed to stretch my legs?"

Taryn grumbled a response under his breath and began to retrieve a bucket for the water. She looked around—everyday simpletons going about their lives in this small, quaint town. She smiled softly at the different lives she beheld. A boy in the distance leading a horse out from a stable, a mother just a few feet away from him pinning clothing to a line. It was the little things that were often taken for granted.

Did they realize how beautiful their life was to be their own?

Airess looked back to Taryn, busy with fetching the water. She inched forward slowly, each step light as she neared the corner of the building. Just a few more steps, and she could turn the corner and bolt down the street. Before doing so, she peered out, and her heart sank at what she saw.

A group of Lucien guards clad in golden armor stood ten feet away, in conversation with a few of the townspeople, their backs facing hers. The guard held up a poster, the back of the paper facing her so she could not see its contents. She contemplated on what would be worse, being brought to the Mrkynian Guild or being taken back to the Luciena capitol. She shuddered at the thought.

Just as a guard turned around, a hand seized her wrist and pulled her backwards. Taryn grabbed her other wrist and pulled her to him, their fronts touching, her face inches from his. Taryn glowered at her, his tall frame hunching over her, tilting his head to look down at her with a look of scorn. "*Do not* make a sound."

She stilled, realizing how much her curiosity could cost them. Airess heard the heavy footfalls of the soldier walking by, coming so close, all the soldier had to do was look around the corner and he would see them.

Airess took in Taryn's features in the morning light to distract herself. His one earring dangled with the movement of his head. Airess almost didn't see it, his wind blown tendrils curling around the sides of his face and ears.

Taryn's mouth twisted into a smirk, his sultry eyes gazing down on her. Her stomach tightened. Airess dropped her eyes, heat crawling up her neck as she realized she had been staring. Her gaze landed on his hands softly gripping her wrists to hold her in place.

Airess noted red ink peaking out, a hint of a tattoo circling his wrist from under his cloak sleeve. The ring he wore on his pointer finger glinted in the sunlight, as if the universe was trying to tell her something, whispering a solution through the wind that blew her hair.

Finally, the soldier's steps faded as they walked by. Taryn released her, dropping his hands and brushing past her.

"***Get on the horse***. We are leaving," he snapped, nostrils flared.

She turned and followed immediately. Her curiosity shattered as anger set in at his compulsion. She shoved her foot in the stirrup and struggled to pull herself up. Taryn lifted her up by the hips, the touch lasting a millisecond before his hands fell away. He got on hastily, nudging the horse forward as they rode towards the forest.

"You said you didn't want to compel me again," she said stiffly, her back straight as her chance to escape dwindled away into nothing.

"If you didn't try to walk out into a street of Lucien soldiers, I wouldn't have *had* to," Taryn retorted from behind her. His grip on the reins tightened, his frustration clear.

Airess stared down at his ring, blinking her Sight forward. Black energy surrounded the ring, the small piece of jewelry emanating its own dark aura, a harsh contrast to the beautiful colors of Taryn's energy. She began to put the pieces together, an inkling of how exactly Taryn was compelling her.

The corner of her lips drew up in a smirk as she understood what she needed to do.

Chapter 6

The Godlings should have never existed on this plane. They were created out of spite and greed. Destruction is in their nature.

– The Book of Tevye

Taryn

Taryn sat stiff-backed, keeping his eyes straight forward. He gripped the reins tightly, trying his best to ignore the curve of her ass pressed against his groin and her intoxicating scent.

If he was being honest with himself, her scent was making him feral. *She* was making him feral, and Taryn couldn't understand why she was having such a strong effect on him. Although he was to remain professional, he was only male. A Fae male, at that. But after ten years on the Lucien continent, he had learned to keep his animalistic qualities at bay.

Still, being so close to her was torture. The proximity only heightened his awareness of her—the way her body shifted against his, her breathing, the way her heart pounded. He knew his thoughts were wrong, for so many reasons, but he couldn't help but think them. He breathed her in again, smelling the uneasiness and anxiety seeping off of her.

"What am I to expect when we arrive? *When* are we going to arrive?"

The Lady Airess was mouthier than he expected. He had never met a daughter of an aristocrat before, but he presumed she would have been docile, easily pliable. Her stubbornness was certainly evident. He couldn't *believe* how strong her own will had resisted the compulsion ring when she's tried to stop walking earlier. That alone was proof of a strong mind.

"Soon enough, *my Lady*," he retorted, his tone sarcastic.

"Good," Airess fired back. "I can't wait to be rid of you."

"Likewise. I've had enough of your sharp mouth."

"And *I've* had enough of your silent brooding. Truly, it makes for such a boring ride. You were much more enjoyable at the ball, and even *that* was a sham," she said, examining her nails, the words sliding off her tongue like knives.

The Gods were truly testing his patience.

Perhaps he deserved this. He knew what he was doing was wrong, so he didn't bother replying. Let her have the last word, that's the least he could offer her as he took her to Eryx.

And what would Eryx do with her? He didn't know why, but his throat tightened at the thought. He couldn't understand why he felt so conflicted about his actions. Taryn had done so much worse than *this* simple task.

He knew he was more than likely leading her into a fate similar to his. Eryx would offer her a place at the Guild, a bound life sentence to him, disguised as a promise of power.

Taryn looked at the back of her cloak hood. If she truly was powerful like Eryx claimed, why hasn't she used it against him yet? Was it possible she told the truth earlier when she claimed to be powerless?

And if that were true, could he really justify his actions now?

Taryn heard wings flapping above them, followed by a flash of white. He looked up, noticing an strikingly beautiful owl covered in ivory feathers, perched on a branch above them. He made eye contact with it, and Taryn swore he saw a look of displeasure in the animal's milky gray eyes.

As if that was even possible—

A sharp pain tore into his palm and wrist. Airess dug her nails in hard, seizing his wrist so quickly he barely registered her slipping the compulsion ring off his finger. She threw it several feet away from them.

"Fuck!" Taryn exclaimed as he yanked his arm away. Her elbow made contact with his cheekbone, knocking his face to the side. The horse reared back, sensing the energy of its riders, sending them flying onto the forest floor.

Taryn landed on his back, stunned, watching her sprint away as soon as they fell off the horse.

A smile curved his lips. Oh, she was *clever*.

He jumped to his feet and ran after her. Finally, a challenge—someone who possessed enough wit of their own that could rival his.

She was fast, but not as fast as him. Taryn's strong legs propelled him forward. He reached a hand out to grab her ivory hair that flew behind her. She veered left, his fingers barely skimming her locks. Taryn growled in frustration, then held his hand out, wind swirling around his arm like an aura. He reached forward, sending the wind to coil around her ankle and up her leg, and pulled downward.

She fell face-first with a thud. He grabbed her ankle, dragging her towards him and flipped her over, not really sure what he even planned to do. He had vowed before this assignment that he wouldn't bring harm to her. As he flipped her over, pinning her arms and straddling her waist, he realized he was betraying his own morality for his bastard of a Guildmaster.

As he gazed upon the fear in her eyes, her gilded irises glowed brighter. The air around them crackled with static, as if it were charging with energy. A light emanated from her chest so brightly, it showed through her clothing.

"*No!*" she screamed, squeezing her eyes shut.

The light erupted from her chest, growing until it burst into an explosion that blasted Taryn off of her. He went barrelling through the air.

Streaks of sparkling light crowded his vision as his back slammed into a tree, his head cracking against the hard wood.

He didn't even have time to feel shock as he faded into dark oblivion.

Chapter 7

'Never trust a Deyanira.'

– Written entry from Tinyrah Kazimyr's personal journal (Post-Division)

Taryn

Taryn woke up to a burning sensation on the skin of his wrists. He knew that feeling all too well, a familiar side effect of coming into contact with dostenyte poison.

He opened his eyes, taking in the dark cellar he woke up in, and the chair he was tied to. It was dimly lit by two wall sconces on the stone walls. The stone around him was partially damp. Taryn knew they must be underground. Perhaps near a body of water.

How did he end up here?

For reasons he couldn't decipher, his breath hitched at the thought of her. Where was Airess?

The metal door entrapping him slid open, incoming two Luciena guards with a promise of violence on their faces. Airess' scent hit him like a cloud of smoke as the door opened, assuring him she was close by. What did they do with her? Did they... hurt her?

Taryn stifled the constricting feeling in his throat at that thought and wondered why the hell he cared so much. He swallowed tightly and tried his best to focus on the present moment, and how to get out of here.

Taryn caught a glimpse of a hallway beyond them, metal bars on each side of the hall.

Underground. Near water.

His eyebrows rose as it dawned on him where he possibly was. If his suspicions were correct, he was close to the Guild's headquarters.

"Imagine our *surprise* when we find the famous Taryn Seas, notorious assassin of the Mrkynian Guild, lying unconscious in the woods," said one of the Elven guards. "Even more surprised to find you with the prince's betrothed. I'll give it to you, you had us all fooled. Thought we killed you during the raid. Yet, here you are, *alive*. Tell me, what were you doing with her?"

Taryn kept silent, schooling his features into neutrality despite his beating heart. He was grateful they weren't Fae and couldn't hear the sound of it. This wasn't his first interrogation. He had been in these situations several times, but not to this severity. Most times he had been arrested and interrogated took place during his teenage years—before he had reached mastery in his training with the Guild.

If these guards didn't have the upper hand right now, Taryn would have smirked at the words thrown at him. *Notorious assassin.*

It was a title placed upon him after he had taken out five government officials at once during a public event. Taryn had used his lightning, striking all five officials at once in the open courtyard of the Luciena castle. Eryx had ordered the kills and Taryn had delivered, but shortly after his display of power, the monarchy had found the Guild's original location and raided it.

Taryn would have died in the raid that took place in the dead of night if it weren't for Raiden and Eryx. Half the Guild perished, but they continued to work towards Eryx's cause when they moved their base to Lonskeep. Ever since that night, he lay low and was sure not to wield lightning anywhere near the city. Taryn was an asset to the Guild, especially with the Luciens thinking he was dead. Eryx made sure the monarchy was unaware of him still living… that is until he battled the Elve in the alleyway.

The Elven guard before him chuckled and shook his head, cracking his knuckles before sending a fist into Taryn's face. His head snapped to the side, pain blooming over his cheek. Taryn clenched his bound fists as he tried to fight through the pain. He gritted his teeth, steadied his breath and stayed quiet.

He counted down from twenty to calm himself down, something Raiden had taught him to do. Taryn wasn't one to break easily, and he sure as hell wasn't going to give them the satisfaction of hearing him cry out in pain.

"Silence doesn't bode well for you," the male said, eerily calm, bending down to eye level. "We know exactly who you are, *Fae*. I'll give you one last chance. What were you doing with her? Did she conspire with you?"

Shit. Taryn didn't know what to do. He couldn't give away the Guild. He couldn't break, especially with Airess somewhere nearby. He had to get out of here and continue his task. He was *so* close to completing his mission. He just needed to get through this.

Taryn inhaled a deep breath and grounded himself.

Calm. Collected. Controlled.

He could do this. Taryn gathered all the courage he could muster, blocked out the fear blaring within his mind, and spat on the ground in response.

The elven male stood up, clicking his tongue as he cracked his knuckles.

And swung.

Chapter 8

*"I will do everything that is wrong,
so I can achieve what I know is right."*

— Written entry from Evyen Deyanira's personal journal (Pre-Division)

Airess

Airess realized she was knocked into the dreamworld when she materialized before a small, circular hut she had never seen before.

She looked down at her dream form, dressed in the same crimson dress she always appeared in. Her translucent body glowed a golden hue in contrast to the dark night. The hut was made of oak and straw. Through the tiny windows she made out the faint flickering of a fyre. Smoke puffed out of the chimney.

Airess felt a pulling sensation urging her towards the door. She wanted to resist. She needed to wake up. But deep in her soul, she knew she was being called here, whatever this place was. She obliged, accepting the will of the dreamworld.

Airess walked through the door.

To her right were two cots made up with knitted quilts. To her left was a tiny kitchenette consisting of an iron stove, pots and pans hanging upon the walls. In front of her was a fyreplace and a woman sitting in the chair, watching her. She was a plump, dark skinned Human woman, presumably in her later years. The woman's body also glowed in a translucent sheen, similar to Airess, but reflected the color of violets. Wrinkles creased around the woman's brown eyes as she smiled and looked directly at Airess.

Airess stopped in her tracks, her breath hitching. Airess never made contact with others in the dreamworld. She always dreamwalked alone, as if she were a ghost, floating around unnoticed. Unseen.

"My, you're even more beautiful than I ever imagined."

Airess gaped. Usually, if she did see another dimensional being, they ignored her. Like they couldn't see or hear her.

But not this woman. Her eyes shone with a kindness that felt familiar.

Airess remembered to speak, her voice wavering, "Thank you."

The woman before her smiled softly, giving Airess enough time to take in what she was seeing.

"Who are you?" Airess asked.

"A dreamwalker, like you," she said. "You can call me Ima. Please, sit." Ima motioned a hand toward the armchair across from her. Wearily, Airess walked forward and sat down. Ima was knitting, tendrils of emerald and crimson-colored yarn intertwining together as she worked the needles with familiar ease.

"I can only sense so much from here. But I can see you now," Ima said as she knitted. "Which means you must have gotten out." The woman said the words more to herself, eyebrows creased, her gaze falling to her yarn.

Airess sat up straight. "What do you mean? How do you know that?"

"Luciena is a place of many secrets, many betrayals," Ima said. "The Shadow blocks out the Magick of truth, energy of souls, and the river of consciousness."

Airess shook her head. "I don't understand."

The edges of the dreamscape began to blur. Airess' heart rate was increasing in the waking world, her body beginning to wake up naturally. The floor beneath her began to feel unstable, her surroundings blurred, flickering in and out of focus.

This was an aspect of dreamwalking she still hadn't grasped yet. When her body wanted to wake up, she could do very little to force it to stay asleep.

Ima looked around, as if she also realized Airess was on the brink of physical consciousness. "You're waking up."

"I don't know how to stay here," Airess said.

"Listen to me, Airess, this may be the last time I have the opportunity to meet with you. Stay with the male, no matter what, and travel to Rune. The Obadiah awaits the both of you."

"How do you know my name?" Airess asked, opening her mouth to say more, but she might as well have yelled an echo into the void. The dreamscape melted away, Ima's face disappearing like smoke drifting into the sky.

She fell into the darkness at the speed of light.

Airess opened her eyes, gasping for air at the sudden switch from the dreamworld to reality.

The first thing she noticed was a cold, hard surface against her cheek as she woke up lying down.

Then she noticed the prison cell she was in.

Darkness encompassed her, save for the faint glint from the fyrelit wall sconce she spotted through the steel bars. The walls caging her were made of rock. A floor of dirt lay beneath her, smelling of musk.

Panic set in as Airess shot up abruptly, only to be yanked back by metal shackles bound to her wrists and ankles, the chains connected to the floor. She grimaced at the jerking motion. The shackles were dripping in a luminous green substance that faintly burned her skin.

Her heart sank. Had Taryn taken her here? Had he—

Memories of the explosion, her *Magick*, came flooding back to her. Taryn had run after her as she escaped him. She felt pure fear the moment he dragged her down to the forest floor, and for the first time, her power had come to her aid. Airess didn't know how she did it, but she had used her Magick to blast him away.

Had she really done that?

Fear and excitement coursed through her. She held out her palms in front of her and concentrated, trying her best to call to that power that had finally saved instead of damning her.

Nothing came.

Airess sighed in frustration and tilted her head back to rest against the wall, letting out a bitter laugh. Perhaps she would never be powerful, or learn about her Magick. Perhaps she would not live long enough to do so.

She began to hum slowly at that last thought, feeling the music vibrate in her throat. It was the only thing she could do to comfort herself.

A multitude of footsteps thundered down the hallway, cutting her melody short. She made out two male voices conversing with one another, the words becoming clearer as they neared. Airess sat up and stilled in fear. Was the Guild finally coming to retrieve her?

They came into view. Airess immediately recognized the gilded armor of the Luciena guard, sending a wave of nausea through her. The guards held Taryn up by the arms, bloody and battered, his wrists and ankles bound in chains. Displeasure coursed through her at the sight of him in pain. Although he was technically her captor, Taryn had treated her fairly. Seeing him in this state brought up a confusing feeling she couldn't quite place.

Airess brought her legs in close, hugging them with her shackled wrists, trying to remain small enough that they could not see her.

"He's a stubborn one, alright," one guard muttered to the other, opening the door of her cell. The guards shoved Taryn into the cell, the Fae male landing on the ground with a hard *thud*. She backed up as far as the chains let her.

"Luciena will pay a heavy price for the rebellion's most wanted assassin," the guard sneered, "What we've done to you will be nothing compared to what the crown has in store."

Slowly, Taryn propped himself up to a seated position. His face finally became visible as he lifted his head, a mop of curls dampened by blood on his forehead. It seemed he was trying to smirk, but the expression came out grim due to his blackened eye, busted lip, and bloodied face. Taryn spit on the guards' boots in response, and lifted his middle finger in the air.

The guard slammed his boot into Taryn's stomach, the momentum sending him barreling backward. Airess expected to hear Taryn scream in response, but he held it in, as if he were too stubborn to give them the satisfaction of hearing his cry.

The guard turned his gaze to Airess for the first time since they arrived, her hopes of seeming invisible vanishing as he perceived her. "And what a pretty penny you will be, the prince's bride escapee. Don't worry." The guard gestured between Taryn and Airess. "You two will be in the capitol by nightfall, and I will have my reward."

The Elven male grinned greedily as he closed the cell door shut. The sound of the deadbolt locking rang in her head as she watched the guards disappear down the hallway. Airess turned towards Taryn, her eyes sliding down his body.

"Godsdamn," he said as he gathered himself, groaning as he came to a seat. His back rested on the wall of bars behind him. Taryn tilted his head up, looking her right in the eyes, his silver stare piercing into her very soul.

The two stared each other down, gold and silver meeting once again.

Airess cringed at his face. Blood dripped from his lips and nose, a nasty bruise already visible on his cheekbone. She knew she should relish in the fact that karma had already come for him after he had compelled her, but looking at him now, she felt quite the opposite.

"Fancy seeing you here," he joked, a smile on his face, as if what he just went through was a long stroll in the woods. Bringing both bound hands inside the front of his pants, shackles clashing, he fished around in his pocket and brought out a small flask. With a flick, the cap was off and tossed across the cell.

"You're *drinking*?"

Taryn tipped his head back against the cell bars and closed his eyes. "Helps with the pain," he said simply, and drank.

Airess gaped at him. She couldn't believe that he managed to sneak a flask into the cell and that he was speaking to her so casually after being almost beaten to death. This male was *inconceivable*, and has quite literally become the cause of all her problems. If it weren't for him, she would have been on the way to Rune by now, hidden away from the Luciens. Airess tried her best to ignore the simmering anger in her gut.

Taryn set his flask down, leveling a cold stare at her. "Do you want to explain what happened in the woods?"

"I don't know what happened."

Taryn raised a brow. "You aren't a very good liar."

"I'm telling the truth. I've never done that before. I didn't even know that was possible. I just remember panicking and... well, it just sort of *happened*."

Taryn made a sound resembling a *Hmm*. Airess looked down to her shackled wrists, panic rising in her chest, in her throat, constricting and squeezing her. She blinked rapidly, fighting away the tears that threatened to come to the surface. It was a flaw she hated about herself—crying whenever she felt angry or panicked. Airess swallowed the feeling down. She wouldn't cry, especially not in front of him.

"I can't go back," she whispered.

"*Why*? Why did you leave in the first place?" Taryn asked the question like it was on the brink of his mind, the question eager to be asked.

"It wasn't planned," Airess confessed. She wasn't sure why, but she vaguely explained the events directly after the engagement ball explosion. Perhaps it was because she needed someone, even if it were him in this lonely, twisted world. Airess made sure to leave out the details about The Obadiah. She hadn't had time yet to even *think* about that, or what Ima had said in the dreamworld.

"And your *seamstress* orchestrated all of that?" Taryn asked in disbelief, taking another swig of his flask.

"Yes. She knew—" Airess stopped herself before she divulged too deeply into her past with Arzhel. "She knew what I went through there. That is why I can't go back. He'll kill me."

"*Who* will kill you?" Taryn pressed, his tone laced with a hint of urgency Airess didn't understand.

"The prince," Airess chuckled bitterly. "Perhaps the queen, too."

Not wanting to speak of the matter anymore, she changed the subject as she stared at the green substance dripping off of the chains. "What is this? It burns."

"Donstenyte," Taryn supplied. "It's a poison. It can mute out Magick entirely, and given the quantity of it, there's not a chance in hell we would be able to use Magick to escape."

Great. As if things couldn't get much worse.

A beat of silence passed before Taryn spoke, "I'm sorry."

"What?"

"I'm sorry for compelling you, for taking you against your will. I should have never done that. I should have told Eryx *no*."

Airess folded her arms, remembering who she was talking to. "So then why did you do it?"

He looked away. "It wasn't voluntary."

"Who is Eryx?"

Taryn's jaw flexed, as if the question triggered something within him. He huffed out a breath. "The leader of the Mrkynian Guild. The man who sent me to find you."

Airess weighed the name in her mind. *Eryx*. She had never heard of that name before. Why would he want her? How did he know about her power that apparently everyone but her was convinced she possessed?

Airess finally understood what she sensed when she opened her Sight to Taryn's energy. The way Taryn felt repulsed by his own actions confused her at the time, but now, she realized it was because they *weren't* truly his actions. Perhaps he too was compelled. Taryn said taking her wasn't voluntary. Was he a prisoner to someone else, like her?

Stay with the male, Ima had said. Had the dreamwalker meant for her to travel to Rune with *him*? While Airess still had every intention of finding her way there and claiming her freedom, she wasn't so sure about Ima's advice.

"Your accent," Airess pointed out. "You're from Rune?"

Taryn locked eyes with her, lifting his brow. "Yes. Why—"

Footsteps echoed down the hallway, cutting his reply short. Airess sat up, eyes wide in fear. Taryn craned his neck to look down the hall before turning back to her.

"If there is any way you can conjure your power like before," Taryn whispered, "Now would be the time."

Chapter 9

*'It is day one hundred and eleven after The Division.
The mating bonds have ceased to exist.'*
*— Written entry from Tinyrah Kazimyr's personal journal
(Post-Division)*

Taryn

Usually, when Taryn managed to get himself arrested, his power wasn't muted by donstenyte poisoning. He had always gotten himself out of these situations. The last time he *was* chained with donstenyte, Eryx had come to his rescue, much to Taryn's displeasure.

Getting out of this situation was going to be a real bitch.

The guards rounded the corner and approached the prison cell. Taryn counted six guards, more than before. Their armor bore the sigil of a coiling serpent branded onto their breastplates. From Taryn's intel, these were the best-trained guards the Luciens had to offer.

He frowned. Never before had he been in such a dire situation. Bound and powerless from the poison, it would take an act of the Gods to escape now.

Taryn was so fucked.

"Get up," a guard demanded as he pulled out his key out and unlocked the door. Two guards grabbed Airess, hoisting her up to her feet. A growl rumbled in his throat, possessiveness coursing through him as he watched them manhandle her. Why the hell did he do that? The Lady Airess was an Elven female, there was absolutely no reason he should be feeling this type of way, *especially* about her. He clenched his jaw, wishing he could will his natural animalistic instincts into neutrality.

Again, he felt himself wobbling on his mental tightrope, struggling for balance. *Struggling* to do the right thing. If he got away from these guards, what would he even do? Would he return to the Guild with this female, or would he desert them all?

Jaw clenched, he withdrew from his thoughts. That would be a problem for later. Taryn was hoisted to his feet, and a guard grabbed him by the tunic. He and Airess were dragged out of the cell and down a hall, passing prison cells on either side of them. Taryn focused on Airess' silver hair in front of him, her messy locks tainted with dirt. He needed to think of a way to escape, and quickly.

Taryn looked around for anything he could use as a weapon, but there was nothing but dirt and stone. The chains, however…

Who are you without your Magick? Taryn recalled Eryx's words in a training session from the past. *You must learn to use yourself as a weapon, without your power and blades.*

They veered down a hallway and burst through a door, walking into a forest blanketed by the night sky. Taryn looked to the stars, a ray of moonlight touching his face as they walked under the trees. Not a single light was visible beyond the fyrelit caravan, riders saddled atop the plethora of horses attached to it.

"Load 'em up!" an older guard called out as he opened the door to the back of the caravan, a solid wooden box with two barred windows on either side. A prison wagon made for dangerous criminals. They shoved Airess in first, two guards following behind her. Taryn took a deep breath in. This was his last chance to try and escape.

His grandmother's words from the distant past echoed in his mind. *No matter what, you always go down swingin'!*

Taryn slammed his head back, his skull colliding with the guard behind him, resulting in bone crunching and a cry of agony. Taryn spun around, a wicked grin on his bloodied face. He lunged for the Eleven male, wrapped his chain around the guard's neck, and squeezed.

They struggled, the guard flailing beneath Taryn's grasp. The guard beat his hand on Taryn's forearm, gasping for breath. Taryn tightened his grip and snapped the male's neck.

Crack!

The guard fell limp.

Taryn backed away, narrowly missing a swipe of a blade from another guard. It was hard to maneuver with his limbs bound, but he pivoted in time to only feel the metal graze his abdomen. He grunted, gritting his teeth together to stifle his cry.

Taryn scrambled to his feet, moving quickly to move onto his next victim—

Firm hands gripped Taryn's shoulders, slamming him flat against the forest floor in a matter of seconds. Taryn gritted his teeth, baring his canines as he was pressed hard against the dirt. He laughed sardonically as they restrained him.

"Cowards!" Taryn managed to grit out, his lungs crushed under the weight of the guards that held him down. "Unchain me and put up a real fight!"

"Aye! Quit messing around and get him inside the caravan!" someone commanded. They lifted him back up, and a meaty fist struck Taryn's face.

"*Fae trash!*"

Stars clouded his vision. He felt his body being dragged inside the van. They shoved his shoulders down as they forced Taryn to sit on a bench adjacent to Airess. Her eyes were wide in fear as they shackled her ankle to Taryn's, a six-foot chain connecting the two.

Well, shit.

Taryn peered across from him, his left eye already beginning to swell. Two guards sat on either side of Airess, and two more on either side of him. To have them escorted with such heavy security raised Taryn's suspicions. Yes, Taryn was a notorious spy and assassin for the Mrkynian Guild, but the amount of soldiers they sent for his *and* Airess' retrieval was odd, to say the least.

What about us were they so afraid of?

The questions repeated in his mind. The caravan began to move forward, his weight shifting with the movement, only the sound of hooves beating the ground occupying his mind.

Finally, a guard broke the silence, directing his words towards Airess, "You've stirred up quite the commotion with your stunt back in the capitol. From future queen to traitorous noble, your social status has plummeted beyond reconciliation. You best prepare yourself for the trial of your *life*."

Airess' face tightened at the words, her eyes hardening as she looked at the guard. She lifted her chin. "What happened at the ball was *not* my doing. I am innocent."

The guard laughed. "A traitor and a liar, too. Tell me, girl, how did you end up working with the Mrkynian Guild?"

Taryn's chest constricted at the implication. He realized if they didn't find a way to escape, they both were heading straight towards their deaths. Perhaps they would both be beheaded at the guillotine together, the monarchy's favorite method of public execution. He heard her heart beating rapidly in her chest, no doubt due to her rising fear.

"I am not working with anyone," she said tersely, lowering her gaze to her hands.

"How dare you lie to an official guard?" the male sneered. "You don't exactly have the social standing to deflect my questions, *mutt*."

Taryn watched the words hit her like a physical blow, Airess flinching at the words. For the first time, he considered what it must have been like for her to live as a halfling in a noble society. Shame passed through him as he remembered accusing her of sharing those same beliefs.

He shook his head, admonishing himself internally. *I am such an idiot.*

Slowly, the corners of Airess' mouth upturned in a subtle, sly grin. "Did Arzhel say that?" she asked hopefully. "Did he say I have lost my social standing?"

"He is *the prince* to you, not one of your socialite friends!" the guard yelled.

Airess flashed her eyes to Taryn momentarily before turning to the guard, her facial expression now smug. "*Fuck* The prince."

Shocked, Taryn couldn't help but laugh. He couldn't believe what he was hearing. Has this female lost her mind?

The guard drew his arm back and struck Airess' cheek, marking her face with an angry slash of red. Her head whipped to the side, her chained hand touching her bruised cheek.

This time, an audible growl escaped Taryn's lips, his face contorting with disgust with an emotion he couldn't explain, not even to himself. Taryn didn't think twice as he sank low in his seat. He wrapped his feet around the guard's ankles, and twisted, dragging the guard down to the caravan floor. The Elven male hit his head hard, and fell on the ground unconscious. Taryn smirked as he was pinned against the caravan wall by his shirt, his head smacking against the wood.

"This *Fae* isn't worth the trouble!" a guard sneered.

"Take him out," another guard ordered, nodding in agreement.

The guard next to him drew a dagger, swinging it straight toward Taryn's throat. Before he could register what was happening, the air charged with electricity, growing stagnant like a calm before a great storm, as if time itself slowed by a millisecond.

A golden hand grabbed the wrist of the guard, stopping his arm mid-swing. The caravan was illuminated with light, its source coming from none other than Airess. Taryn turned his attention towards her, mouth parting in shock as he beheld her.

Her white hair transformed into an iridescent gold, from the root to the tips of her hair, her stray locks beginning to float in the air as if she were underwater. She looked at Taryn, holding his stare, the whole of her eyes glowing *gold*. Even her brows were gilded, along with her skin. She looked ethereal, her skin glowing a warm hue, encasing her like an aura. Her hair resembled rays of sunlight floating around her.

Airess's face contorted into an ancient rage, the space between her brows creasing as she took her gaze off Taryn. She slowly cocked her head to the male she had gripped by the arm. She squeezed and his gilded armor *melted* from her touch. The Elven male screamed as molten metal dripped onto the floor.

The moment she looked away from him, it felt as if a thousand weights lifted from Taryn's chest.

The guard dropped the knife and fell to the ground, grabbing his melted arm in agony.

"What is she doing!" a guard yelled, the two on either side of her grabbing the chains connected to her arms, pulling her arms apart.

Airess let out a low laugh, her voice layered with others: young, old, voices of other beings he had never heard before. They all blended into one and came out of her mouth. Shock and fear coursed through him as he watched her.

She looked predatory now, her movements fast and calculated. "*You dare restrain me.*" The voices poured out of her as she yanked her forearm up, the chains on her arms immediately cracking open. She slammed herself back, sitting all the way up despite the guards actively trying to hold her down.

She lifted her head towards the sky, light bursting from her chest. A gust of wind blew Taryn's curls as the roof of the wagon blew off completely. She was up in a matter of seconds, grabbing a guard's armored shoulder before throwing him against the back of the wagon, bars denting from impact. A handprint glowed where she touched him, his armor completely melted through.

Yelling had erupted from in and outside the caravan. She—and all the voices coming out of her—*laughed*. Taryn had no other choice but to watch in horror as another burst of light emanated from her body. The caravan exploded into a thousand wooden splinters.

Taryn was temporarily blinded as he flew through the air and hit the ground. He blinked, regaining his sight, and realized all his chains had been blasted off... besides the one connecting his ankle to the female. *Of course.*

Airess stood six feet away with her back towards him. Four guards already lay dead on the ground around them, their faces and bodies burnt beyond recognition. She gripped the male who struck her by the neck with her fist and slammed him down. The male began to scream, but his cries were in vain. Airess' Magick was so hot, his neck disintegrated into nothing, leaving the male decapitated and lifeless.

Taryn watched her, a wild grin on his face. Perhaps he should be afraid, but he couldn't help feeling enthralled with her power.

He sensed an attack from behind. He grabbed a blade lying on the ground and met his opponent, a guard younger and obviously not as skilled meeting his blade. Their blades clashed, but even Taryn knew he outskilled this young Elven male. A flash of guilt thrummed through Taryn as he thrust his blade into the neck of his opponent.

Taryn ripped the sword out. Blood splattered as he turned, ready for another opponent, but the screams had faded into an eerie silence. He looked around, every guard killed, their bodies mutilated.

He dared to face Airess, turning slowly, his eyes meeting hers. She looked like a vision of murder, crimson blood staining her face, neck, and clothes. She heaved for breath as she took a step towards him. Taryn backed away, eyes wide at what she might do to him, but her eyes softened, all that ancient rage slipping away.

She reached an arm out to him, as if she was reaching for him, *pleading* to him. Her hair faded back to white, her eyes back to normal.

That golden aura dissipated.

She fell to her knees as her eyes rolled back into her head. Taryn was already moving, catching her fall so her head wouldn't slam onto the ground. Her face was void of any light. Any emotion. His heart beat rapidly as he looked around for more guards, but he found none living.

Around them lay shards of blasted wood, the metal bars from the caravan lay half melted against the forest floor, the metal still so hot it was glowing orange. The smell of burnt flesh infiltrated his nostrils.

He looked down at her face as he held her, that raging power now void, leaving only her Elven humanity behind. He could see it even as she was unconscious. Despite whatever power she wielded, she was scared and alone. He blinked.

What the *hell* just happened?

And *what* was he going to do now?

He stared down at her beautiful face. He could take her to the Guild right now, turn her in as requested and be *done* with this. But could he do it, after witnessing and hearing everything they both just went through?

A decision was to be made, and he didn't know what he was going to do.

All he knew was that he held a mysterious female in his arms. Everyone around them was dead, and if he didn't move soon, more of them would be on the way.

Gods save me, he thought as he put one arm under the back of her legs and lifted her up, carrying her bridal-style. Her body was limp, arms splayed out, head hanging back. The chains connecting their ankles clanked in response to the movement.

Taryn cradled her head towards his shoulder as he began to sprint as fast as his body would allow away from the massacre. For the first time, he had no plan. No resources beyond his elemental abilities.

Yet, here he was, fleeing with the power of the Gods within his arms, only the sheer determination to live guiding his way.

Chapter 10

And when the God of Gods reigned down after The Division, the entire universe shuddered.

— *The book of Tevye*

The Vulture

The Vulture knelt down next to the scattered debris. Splintered wood and half melted steel bars lay all around them. What the hell had happened? The smell of burnt flesh was pungent. Fresh. Whatever had occurred, it had only been a few hours ago.

The Vulture stalked over to one of the bodies lying on the ground. The head was severed from the body. *Interesting.* The Vulture picked up the head by the hair, inspecting the neck.

"Allow me—" one of The Vulture's sworn attendants started, walking forward to retrieve the head. The Vulture raised their free hand, stopping him. The attendant stopped mid-step and gulped. The Vulture could feel the fear radiating off the attendant in waves, but they sure as hell didn't need anyone to coddle them. The Vulture would be a ruthless leader, any fear of gore and death absent. They would show their subjects true strength.

"This head was severed by heat, not a blade," The Vulture muttered to themself. Could the girl really be that powerful, even now? Even under Luciena's barrier?

"Bring me a satchel," The Vulture ordered. "We have to pay my little *accomplice* a visit. Something isn't adding up here."

Chapter 11

When the world is ready, the Godlings will be born again.
Unity will be restored.

— *The book of Tevye*

Taryn

"A Soul of Mind," Airess muttered, eyes closed. Taryn looked down at her, holding her tight in his arms as he sprinted through the woods.

"What?" he asked, his breath labored. His heart finally ceased thumping in his chest after she massacred those guards.

"Brings forth the Storm."

Taryn frowned, his dark brows drawn together as he realized she was talking in her sleep. He trekked on for another hour before laying her down gently near a stream, determining he had put enough distance between them and the scene. He sat down with his elbows on his knees, his head hanging low. Exhaustion finally overtook him.

"Mark my words...Arzhel," Airess muttered, her tone weak, as if she had given up. "I will haunt you... for the rest..."

Taryn's head shot up. He stared at her. She didn't make any sense, yet her tone conveyed another story.

He'll kill me, she had said in the prison. *Perhaps the queen, too.*

Taryn got to his feet and paced, as much as the chain connecting him to her would allow. He was running out of time. Surely Eryx would be calling him back to the Guild soon enough. He looked back to Airess.

Did she really deserve a fate like his?

He shook his head. *No*, she didn't. How could he lead her to the Guild, knowing how badly it has wrecked his own life? After everything he had seen and heard today, he could no longer deny the simple truth he had come to realize.

He was going to let her go when she woke up, no matter what the consequences were.

He crouched down near the stream and started washing the blood away. He ripped some fabric from his sleeve and dipped it into the water, cleaning off Airess' forehead and neck. He caressed the back of his hand over her cheek, her skin hot against his. Gods, she was burning up.

He pursed his lips as he pressed the damp cloth on her forehead. Never had he known someone else to possess a power so grand as she did. When the whole of her eyes turned a luminescent gold, it was almost as if she disappeared, some other entity taking her over entirely. It was a Magick that could never, *should* never exist on this continent.

Could she be...?

Taryn shook his head, physically shaking away the thoughts. Perhaps his mind raced to impossible conclusions after not sleeping for a day straight. He let go of the damp cloth, exhausted, and finally lay down to rest.

Why am I doing this? Why am I helping her?

He didn't have the answers to his own questions. All he knew was that he was falling. Somewhere along the way, a certain silver-headed beauty had pushed him over the edge of the tightrope. He landed in a sea of golden light as sleep overtook him.

Taryn ran after a head full of red locks, dark purple robes flowing behind her as the woman sprinted through open field of salaroses, the onyx flowers decorating the ground. It was dawn, the sky an ombre of oranges and purples. A wall of turquoise energy stood tall in the distance, but Taryn was unable to see where it began and ended. The woman ran to the edge of a cliff beyond him and stood, her back facing him as she stared at the energy wall ahead.

But something wasn't right.

Taryn stopped running, an awareness taking over him. He observed his surroundings and focused for the first time since he arrived... here, wherever this place was. He tried his best to remember how he came to be here in this field, chasing the woman with hair the color of fyre, but the origins of his travels were unbeknownst to him.

Taryn squinted, noticing the edges of the petals, even the treelines, were a faint blur, as if the image before him was a projection onto a plane he had tapped into. He looked at his hands and gasped, but there was no feeling of air filling his lungs as he gaped at his silver-lined hands. His entire body was translucent, a shimmering ghost of silver.

Taryn wore clothing he didn't recognize, an emerald formal tunic with sleeves reaching his wrists. He was barefoot with dark pants rolled up above his ankles—a material he didn't need to feel to know it was something he had never worn. Deep inside his mind he felt an ancient door open, an overwhelming pool of energy settling itself inside him like it had finally found where it belonged. It hit him then, acute awareness coursing through him like ice in his veins.

For the first time in his life, Taryn became lucid in a dream.

The woman stood still as she gazed at the view beyond them. Taryn began to run towards her. He felt drawn to her, and for some inexplicable reason, he knew he could trust her.

"Excuse me!" he exclaimed as he practically flew towards her. "What is this place?"

Taryn was four feet away when a crack of lightning thundered in the sky above. His head snapped up to the source, a storm hovering above the translucent wall of energy. Odd, he thought, the storm hadn't been there just a few seconds ago.

The wall beyond looked like a collection of auroras in the sky, made of blues and greens that expanded for miles. Even from the cliffside overlooking the oceans, he could hear the buzz of power emanating from the barrier.

When he looked back to the woman, she was nowhere to be found. The woman had completely disappeared. Had she jumped off the cliff? Taryn approached the edge and peered over, but saw nothing but the endless ocean.

Thunder cracked again, and a bolt of lightning struck the massive aurora wall. The wall cracked like an eggshell, the impact from the lightning fracturing it in all directions, splitting in pieces. Fragments of the turquoise wall tumbled from the sky, landing in the water like massive boulders—

Suddenly, the view began to dissipate. The sky above him fell apart *like sandstone. Images flashed before him as he fell through space: Streaks of starlight passing by him, a golden feather made of flames, emerald scales glittering in silver light.*

The images faded, washing away like a river. Taryn screamed, reaching his arms out as he fell into the dark, starry abyss.

Chapter 12

*'I created this land for my lineage. For my House.
We are built from strength and cunning.'*

— *Testimony from Evyen Deyanira's coronation (Post-Division)*

Airess

The sound of rustling leaves whispered all around her like a comforting blanket, nature's melody gracing her ears as trees swayed in the wind. Warm sunlight touched her face, soft blades of grass tickling her palms as she lay flat against the hard ground.

The sounds of chirping birds and rushing waters became more prominent as she gained consciousness, finally awakening from her dreamless slumber.

Wait!

Her eyes shot open, looking onto the canopy of trees, taking in the sunlight trickling through the leaves above.

Where am I?

Airess inhaled slowly and turned her head to her right, her muscles aching at the movement. A body lay next to her. Her gaze trailed up a pair of long legs, a muscled, shirtless torso and finally— Taryn's face, annoyingly more handsome asleep with his features at rest. She stifled a frustrated groan at the sight of him. His black lashes framed his closed lids, disheveled brown hair curling perfectly around his face. His earring dangled as the morning breeze caressed over him. She allowed her eyes to trail lower, curiosity taking over.

From his wrist, up his arm and over his shoulder was a sleeve of tattoos inked in red. Some were symbols she had never seen before intertwining together, creating a beautiful tapestry of art on his warmed skin. It was the particular tattoo on his bicep that stood out: the red ink depicting art of a dragon. Airess ripped her gaze away, willing herself back to reality.

Did they escape the guards? Is he still taking her to the Guild?

Her eyes darted towards his ankle. The chain connecting them still very much intact, though that green poison coating the chains in the prison was now gone. Looking back at Taryn's face, she noticed a golden dagger resting beside his head, ready to use at a moment's notice. There was no doubt it had belonged to a Lucien soldier. Did he steal it to break them free?

Airess frowned. She supposed she should count herself lucky she wasn't back at the capitol by now, however they wound up here, alone together in the woods. But this was another problem entirely. Getting away from this Fae male would be difficult with his enhanced senses. Airess wasn't exactly equipped with a weapon and by *no* means was she trained in physical combat. She stared at the dagger in contemplation.

Would she have to inflict violence to get away?

Could she be capable of such a thing?

The question brought up unwanted feelings. She had never killed before. Hells, she didn't think she would ever have to *hurt*—much less *kill*—anyone. But life had surely taken an unexpected turn. Airess would be smart to adapt to her new reality as it changed.

Here goes nothing.

She sprang up quickly, grabbing the hilt of the blade and rushing on top of him, straddling his hips, the dagger now poised at his neck. Taryn's eyes flew open in surprise, his glowing silver irises striking her. She hated that she found it beautiful.

"Unchain me," Airess said, her voice low. "And I might think twice about shedding your blood."

His gaze slid down her body, leaving heat in its wake, until it landed at the flush of their hips pressed against each other. Taryn's lips curved, maddeningly slow. "Are you flirting with me? I must say, it's working. I quite like when a female threatens to shed my blood."

Airess flushed, his reaction not what she was expecting or intending. Then, he actually had the audacity to laugh. His arm moved beneath her, and a burst of water shot through the air. The water, shaped narrow, rushed into her hand.

The force of the water didn't hurt, but she felt the water *grip* the dagger from her. The water dragged it away, slinging the dagger several feet away from them.

Did he just wield water?

He thrust his hips upward, knocking her off balance. Strong hands gripped her sides as he flipped her onto her back, knocking the wind from her lungs. He pinned his knee between her legs, locking her into place. Taryn gripped her wrists on either side of her head and clicked his tongue.

"Now, *that's* not a very nice way to say thank you." His lips hovered over her, his deep vibrato raspy. "Considering I saved your ass."

"What are you talking about? How did we get out here?" she ground out, fury in her chest at how easy it was for him to disarm her and flip their positions. And with *water Magick?* Last she recalled, the male had used air Magick during their scuffle in the woods. She thought he was a Windborne Fae. Was he… Waterborne too?

His dark brows arched in confusion. "You don't remember?"

"I…" She thought back to everything leading up to this point. They were in the jail, then escorted into the caravan. She remembered Taryn putting up a fight—how she admired his blatant defiance. Airess had mirrored it, finally speaking her mind, but the action cost her when the guard struck her in the face.

Then, it all happened so fast. As irrational and confusing as it was, panic had *drowned* her as she saw the blade heading straight towards Taryn's neck…

And then… nothing.

"I remember they struck me and then—" Airess drawled a blank, "I must have passed out. Next thing I know, I'm here, still chained to *you*." She glared at him.

There was a brief pause. His expression shifted from amused to calculating. He cocked his head to the side.

"Fascinating."

What?

"I'll let you go if you promise not to try and kill me again," he joked with a half smile. "Besides, we are stuck together." He cut his eyes to the shackles connecting them.

Airess uncovered her Sight, revealing his aura. To her surprise, it burned brighter. He was telling the truth. Even in this position—a totally *undesirable* position, his body pressed onto hers, his lips inches from—

Get it together, Air.

"Fine," Airess gritted out.

Taryn let go of her wrists and backed off of her. Airess inhaled a shaky breath, finally released from his weight.

He sat a few feet away, as much as the chain would allow, elbows propped up on his knees. She slowly sat up and placed a hand to her forehead, a slight pounding present.

"What are you?" Taryn asked boldly.

She bit back a scoff at his directness. "A halfling. Half Elven, half Human, if you couldn't surmise. And before you say it, spare me from the *diluted blood* comments." It wouldn't be the first time she was called names because of her parentage. Cross breeding between Fae, Elven and Humans was strictly forbidden, and those who had what was considered to be diluted blood always remained in the lower class, for life.

Airess had been the only exception.

He shook his head. "I don't care about that. I'm talking about your powers. It's Light Magick, isn't it?"

"Is that what your *Guildmaster* told you?" she retorted, remembering that he was here on orders to take her captive. She held onto that fact, not wanting to let her thoughts wonder about him again.

"Yes, but no one has ever actually seen a Light Wielder in hundreds, if not *thousands* of years. What you did back in the caravan is unlike anything I've ever seen. You seriously don't remember what you did?"

Airess frowned at the hole in her memory. Has something… happened?

"I don't remember anything at all." She looked up to him. "Tell me."

So he did. Taryn recounted the events in the caravan, how her pale locks and eyes turned a glowing gold. How she spoke with a thousand voices and laughed at her enemies.

"Your strength was heightened. You threw a two-hundred-pound male across the caravan and dented the metal bars. Your power *melted* anything in its path, as if it's hotter than fyre. I don't know how you did it in the donstenyte chains, but we escaped because of you."

Her stomach twisted. He sounded grateful, but Airess felt horrified. "*I did that?*" she whispered, suddenly feeling small. No way that could be true. She had never been able to produce more than an apple-sized orb of Magick from her palm. Well, besides yesterday evening when she blasted Taryn across the woods.

Airess couldn't describe it with words, but she felt something churning within her, aching to be unleashed, yearning for transformation.

"And did I...kill those people?" She finally had the courage to ask, but knew deep in her heart the answer he was to give.

Taryn's intrigued expression fell. He sat up straight and looked her dead in the eyes, "Yes. All of them."

All of them.

The weight of those words sank into her chest. Airess looked away. There had to have been at least a dozen guards total escorting them to the capitol. Her throat tightened and her stomach plummeted. Airess fought the tears beginning to well in her eyes.

She had never taken a life, and now she was being told she had multiple?

It simply didn't feel real, as if all of this was some sick joke the Gods were playing on her. Perhaps she deserved whatever punishment Taryn's Guild had in store for her. She no longer felt deserving of her freedom or her autonomy. She was a danger to herself and others. She *killed*.

Airess had *killed*.

It was too overwhelming to accept, too jarring to wrap her head around. Her vision blurred as tears threatened to spill, but she forced them back, fists clenched at her sides.

"And now you will finally take me to your Guildmaster?" she said, her voice cracking from emotion, expecting and welcoming her captivity. Confinement is all she's ever known.

A beat of silence caused her to look at him. When he finally answered, his voice was low. "No."

"What?"

Taryn shook his head in emphasis, "I can't do it."

"Why? I thought you were compelled to capture me."

Taryn scoffed, beginning to fiddle with a leaf beneath his fingers, "I am compelled in another manner of speaking, yes. But I… I'm starting to *change*." Taryn sounded confused, his face grimacing, as if he were uncomfortable with himself. He said the words personally, as if they weren't meant for her.

Airess sat up straight at his confession. When his eyes finally met hers again, his determination was fierce. "I'm letting you go. After everything that happened, everything I've seen in the last twenty-four hours…" He trailed off, his face now graced with a subtle smile. "Besides, I don't stand a chance against your power. Your combat skills, however, are quite questionable."

Gratitude welled within her, a warm feeling roaming over the surface of her heart and spreading out to her entire body. She didn't need her Sight to know his sincerity, it was written all over his face.

"But... what will you tell your Guildmaster?"

Airess couldn't voice what she really thought: *Where will I go now?*

Taryn looked at her quizzically, eyebrows arched, as if he wasn't sure why he was sharing this with her. He took a deep breath in, gaze looking out to the rushing stream beside them.

"I'm not returning. I'm going home."

"Home?"

"Yes. I'm going home to Rune."

Airess' breath hitched. She almost toppled over as she recalled what the dreamwalker said in the dreamworld. *Stay with the male, no matter what, and travel to Rune. The Obadiah awaits the both of you.* Airess didn't believe in coincidences, and this synchronicity was far too uncanny to cast aside.

"We can sever the chain and part ways. You can go about your plans to escape the Luciens. We can both forget this ever happened." Taryn stood up, offering a hand out to her. She took it, knees wobbling slightly as she stood, her mind numb from everything she had learned in the past five minutes.

"How long was I out?"

"A day."

Three days since the engagement ball. If that explosion never happened, she would be *married* right now.

Taryn lifted a hand, fluidly guiding a stream of water into the air from the river nearby. The water coiled around the chains. Airess watched, speechless, as he squeezed his hand into a fist, turning the water into ice.

Wow. He really must be Waterborne.

He grabbed two rocks, breaking her entrancement. "The chains will break easier if frozen. Here."

Taryn's hand grazed hers as she took the rock, sending a jolt of electricity down her arm. Airess nodded, unable to conjure the energy to reply. She shook the feeling off, not wanting to get lost in what his touch made her feel. They worked together and pounded the chains with the rocks until they finally shattered.

When that was done, she glanced down at her own clothing. Horror coursed through her as she took in the splatters of blood inked into the fabric of her dress.

"I hope you don't mind," Taryn said sheepishly as he scratched the back of his neck, his cheeks reddened. "I sort of cleaned all the blood off of your face. It was the least I could do after… compelling you."

Airess examined a tendril of her hair, the white strands now crimson as if they were dipped in paint. She tried her best to calm her beating heart as she looked up at him. "Thank you. I—I appreciate it."

A silence fell between them. Taryn shifted on his feet, disappointment flashing in his eyes as he spoke. "I suppose this is where we part ways—"

"Let me come with you," Airess blurted, surprising herself. Desperation boosted her confidence, the realization that she was about to truly be alone in this world fueling her words. If what Ima said was the truth, and The Obadiah was waiting for the both of them, could there be more to Taryn than meets the eye?

"I'm sorry?"

"Let me come with you," she repeated. Airess shifted on her feet, as if she were going to lose her boldness if she didn't say more.

"You're leaving the country and—well, so am I. We both have the same goals. It would be an awfully long trek to the south alone."

Taryn raised a brow in question. "*You're* traveling to Rune?" he asked incredulously.

"Do you have any other ideas where to flee?" she asked rhetorically. Taryn folded his arms and frowned at her. Her smile fell.

"Please, let me travel with you. If—*when*—we make it, we can go our separate ways, pretend like we never even met and leave this country behind us."

His heavy gaze penetrated into her, searching her face. Airess bit the inside of her cheek, on edge while waiting for his response.

"You do realize it's a month or so long journey to the south, don't you? And then an *entire* ocean to cross. It's not necessarily a suitable journey for a Lady."

"If you haven't noticed," Airess said, gesturing to her soiled dress. "I am no longer a *Lady*. Please, Taryn. I have nowhere else to go."

She no longer had the energy to appear strong and determined. Airess tried to ignore the feeling of dried blood caked onto her face, nails, and skin. Her garments were soiled. She was fighting to remain calm, to refrain from shaking.

She was a mess, physically and mentally.

Taryn took a deep breath in. His eyes roamed down her figure, not sexually, but as if seeing her clearly for the first time. He nodded slightly before his face drew into a smug grin. "Alright, Haeleth. You want to travel with *me*? Stay close, don't get caught, and when the time comes, run like hell."

"Run like hell?"

Mischief glinted in his eyes. "You'll see."

Chapter 13

It is said when Death became bored, she created a Godling, borrowing a body from another realm. She Touched him, and the rest was history.

— *The Book of Tevye*

Airess

Airess sat on the forest floor, her back against a tree as she waited for Taryn to return. She hummed to herself as she picked her nails until the hooting of an owl from above caught her attention.

Airess looked up. Above her, perched on a branch, was the same ivory owl from the castle. Airess sat up straight, eyebrows raised, as she met its milky-colored eyes. It cocked its head to the side, watching her. Airess stood up slowly, careful to not make any sudden movements. She didn't know what she was going to do, but she reached her hands out toward it—

The crunching of boots approaching scared the bird off. The sound of its wings flapping snapped whatever trance Airess had been in. She snapped her head to the side and watched Taryn come near.

"Where did you get that?" Airess asked, as Taryn returned with two cloaks. He handed one to her, and swung the other around his shoulders, fastening the clip. She did the same, gladly covering her stained dress, folding her hood over her blood-dyed hair. She tried her best to focus on anything but her gruesome appearance as they trekked through the woods for the entire day, careful to avoid the main road.

"In town," he said simply. "Let's go."

She eyed him warily, wondering if he had bought or stolen the clothing.

They walked over the bridge into Riverstone, a bustling town nestled along the river. Similar to the structures in the capitol, these buildings were also made of stone. The streets were adorned with various shops and cart owners selling their goods in the busy town.

As the golden light from the sunset fell over them, Airess couldn't help but look at the town in awe. Besides her short visit at the Inn in Holtzclaw, this was Airess' first real outing since she was ten years old. They approached the busy street filled with patrons, the scent of cooked meat and herbs wafting up to her nose, making her stomach rumble. Children ran past them, parents telling them to slow down. Airess smiled, her grin concealed behind her cloak hood.

Taryn looked down at her in amusement, before grabbing her arm, and dragging her to the side. The sound of clanking metal and hooves passed by her so quickly, she barely had time to register that the wagon was riding through. "Careful," he said, steadying her.

She swallowed, remembering to be more aware in a place like this. Taryn looped his arm around hers, as if they had been friends for a thousand years. Airess looked down at their interlinked arms. Her eyebrows shot up. "What are you doing?"

"We're going shopping, Haeleth." Taryn's breath tickled down her neck as he spoke to her quietly, "We're going to need more than just the clothes off our backs for our travels. We need food, clothing, weapons."

When he noticed her hesitation, his expression softened. "Follow my lead. We can't afford to get caught. Finding two criminals on the run would be the golden jackpot for a Lucien soldier."

Her throat tightened at the title.

Criminal.

Airess had fallen so far in such a short amount of time, she could hardly keep up. She straightened her spine, falling in step with Taryn. She made sure to be aware of her surroundings and blend in with the crowd, wanting to appear as if she was walking with her companion.

Immediately, they were hounded by every cart seller they passed. Shouts were thrown at them to try their baked goods or smoked sausages. Taryn politely declined each one with ease, a stark contrast to how she was feeling right now. He nudged her lightly as they approached a fruit stand filled with strawberries, blueberries, apricots, and other fruits she didn't recognize. Taryn picked up an apple and inspected it, handing it to Airess as he picked up another to look at.

"Might I suggest the strawberries, sir? They are freshly picked," said the chirpy fruit vendor.

A gust of wind picked up, causing Airess and Taryn's clothing to flow behind them. She grabbed her hood with her free hand. A few baskets on one end of the booth toppled over, the vendor cursing and scrambling to pick up the fruit.

"That damn wind!" the vendor muttered as his back turned from Taryn.

Taryn grabbed several more fruits and handed them to Airess quickly.

Her eyes widened as she realized they were stealing. She opened her mouth to protest–

"Put it in your pockets," Taryn whispered as he handed her two more apples before guiding her away from the stand, his hand hovering behind her back as they turned away. She stuffed the fruit in her pockets reluctantly. Airess' heart pounded as they walked away.

"You just stole!" Airess hissed under her breath.

Taryn laughed as they turned onto another street, this one adorned in fashion booths and weaponry. "And so did you. Do you have a better idea? We don't exactly have enough time to work and save up for all this stuff. Just follow my lead."

He had a point.

They approached a weaponry stand filled with daggers, knives, swords, and other weapons Airess didn't know the name of. Airess observed quietly while Taryn conversed with the weapon maker.

"We just got this yesterday. Do you shoot?" the weapon maker said proudly, placing a bow and a set of arrows on the table. Taryn's expression turned hard, staring at the weapon as if it did something wrong. His brows creased as he answered curtly, "Not anymore. Do you have something suitable for the Lady?"

The weapon maker brought out a dagger from his stack and handed it to Airess. She took it, grabbing its brown leather hilt. The blade was small, the weapon itself light.

Just as she began to inspect it, Taryn picked up a set of broadswords in a strap-back encasement displayed in the middle of the table.

"Ah, yes. Those are a rare find. A little on the older side, but works all the same – *Oh*, for the love of the Gods!" The weapon maker exclaimed at the sudden movement of the water barrel toppling over, knocking down his stand and soaking the weapons.

Metal clattered onto the ground, and Taryn quickly swung the broadsword over his shoulder as the man turned away.

Taryn grabbed her elbow and whispered into her ear, "Get ready to grab some clothing and run."

What?

The pair hit up the next stand frantically, Taryn grabbing articles of clothing from different piles so fast, it was as if he'd done this before. Airess hesitated before eyeing a dress, stockings, and trousers. She grabbed them all with haste. Surely they couldn't keep this facade up that much longer.

"Each item is – Aye! You need to pay for that!" said the booth owner as Taryn guided Airess out of the vicinity of the booth.

"Follow me and run!" Taryn exclaimed as the yelling of the booth owner's shouts caught the attention of everyone around them. Taryn and Airess ran down the alley, her heart on fyre.

"*Hey!*" someone shouted from behind, "*Get back here!*"

The words hit her like a familiar friend, like she had heard them before, but there was no time for further thought. They rounded the corner, leaving the booth owners behind. Airess followed Taryn as he navigated through the streets. Their footsteps skittered against the pebblestones, making an abrupt stop in front of a collection of stables.

He turned to her. "Give me your clothes. Can you ride?"

Taryn hastily took her bundle of clothes and opened the nearest stall. *Barely*, she thought, *the last time I rode was when I was ten.*

But instead, she said, "I can ride well enough."

Taryn brought out a dark-colored horse by the lead and petted its mane, then stuffed the clothing into the satchel attached to the horse's saddle. He scanned the stalls and brought out another horse, white as snow. He tightened the straps on its saddle before holding out a hand, motioning her towards the horse and hoisting her up.

He gripped her hips to help her up. She swore the heat from them burned through her clothing. Airess took in a breath. *He was just helping*, that was all. Taryn mounted his own horse and grabbed the reins.

"Follow me and bolt for the woods," he said casually as he turned his horse out of the stable. She looked down at her own horse and grabbed the leather reins, the feeling familiar yet foreign. Amidst all the rush and chaos, a smile lit up her face.

She nudged the horse to follow Taryn. "What if we are followed –"

"Halt! Don't make another move!" bellowed a voice. The town's guardsmen stood in a group across from them, weapons in their hands. They were more of a rinky-dink version of the Luciena guard, wearing shoddy metal breastplates and swords strapped to their hips.

"Go ahead," Taryn said, inclining his head to the woods. "I'll handle this."

Taryn dismounted, drawing out the broadswords strapped to his back and approached the guards with ease. Her heart thrummed, not sure how he was going to take on five guards at once. Two of the males charged forward recklessly, swinging their swords. Taryn deflected each hit like clockwork, as if each step were a melody in a song he had memorized long ago.

Taryn refrained from spilling blood, striking the guards with the pommel of his blade against the side of the head, knocking two of them unconscious.

Airess would have stayed to witness the rest of the fight if one of the males hadn't turned his attention to her, a greedy smile on his face as he quickly advanced towards her. She tapped the side of her horse with her boot, urging the horse to move. They accelerated into a gallop and headed straight into the woods. The commotion behind her faded as Taryn knocked the last guard to the ground.

This confused her. If he was able to wield air and water, why had he bothered to fight them hand to hand?

Before long, Taryn was bolting on his horse, now only a few feet behind her. With him in range, she faced forward as they rode into the forest. Airess' cloak hood fell back, her unbound hair whipping free behind her. The rushing breeze blasted every inch of her skin.

By this time, she was grinning from ear to ear, drunk on adrenaline. Taryn caught up to her, riding alongside her as the town disappeared in the distance. Airess glanced at him and saw that he too was grinning, his sharp canines prominently on display. She'd better get used to that now that she was to accompany him.

Taryn glanced towards her with mischief in his eyes before facing forward again. She let him ride ahead of her as recognition hit her like a brick–realizing why the words of the booth owner yelling at them felt so familiar, like she had experienced it before.

"Hey! Get back here!"

Her jaw fell open as she rode forward, finally making the connection. It was because, in a way, she *had* seen this before. She had seen it… in the dreamworld.

"Follow me and run!"

She heard those same words the night before the engagement ball when she dreamwalked into that foreign town nestled by the sea, watching those juveniles steal from that old male.

Airess realized in that moment that not only did she dreamwalk into another continent, but she had dreamwalked into someone's *memory*.

Taryn's memory.

Chapter 14

After The Division, time forever stood still.

— *The book of Tevye*

Airess

"You certainly knew what you were doing back there." Airess side-eyed Taryn as their horses walked side by side in the woods. They had ridden for several hours, partaking in some small talk that led to a silence as they avoided large groups loitering amongst the trail. Eventually, they veered off path and traveled directly into the tree line.

"You stole like it was muscle memory. Dare I say, Taryn, you must be the thieving criminal the Luciens have painted you and the Guild out to be."

Taryn looked forward, silver eyes alert as he scanned through the trees as they rode. Airess had learned that his Fae senses were a huge boon– Taryn was able to see, hear, or smell other folk before she could. It was why they had avoided unwanted company thus far.

"I never claimed I *wasn't* a criminal, just that the idealizations programmed into you are false. The Luciens painted the Guild out to the public how they wanted us–*them* to be seen."

His jaw tensed. She reasoned he must be getting used to his new reality, a fugitive on the run and all. Hell, she was too. Airess had seen more today than she had in the past ten years. Her lips pursed as she processed his words.

She pulled the reins and signaled her horse to stop. "Alright, if we are going to travel together, I'm going to need some answers to my questions. And not those faulty almost-answers you've been giving me," she lifted her chin. "A question for a question."

Taryn halted his horse and angled himself to face her. The earring on his sharp-tipped ear swayed as he came to a stop. "Alright. Ladies first."

"So far I've seen you wield wind and water. That suggests you're Windborne *and* Waterborne. Admittedly, I do not know much about the Fae's elemental abilities. Is it common for you to wield more than one element?"

Elemental wielders weren't allowed in Luciena, only a small number of Noborne Fae resided in the capitol as lowborn commoners in the poverty ring, misplaced from the ongoing war on Rune. Any Fae that were capable of Magick were executed, as elemental Magick was illegal.

Fae people were a rare species to come by, even more so if they had Magick flowing in their veins. The fact that Taryn still walked this continent at all proved his resilience.

He shrugged, inhaling a breath before answering. "I wouldn't categorize it as *common*, but rather a rare capability to be blessed with multiple." Airess couldn't help but notice the tension rising within him at the question, but decided to let it go. For now.

He motioned a hand for them to continue forward as they spoke, subtly dismissing any conversation further about his powers.

"And what about your abilities? You said you were powerless, but that display in the caravan obviously contradicts your claim."

Airess expected this question, having been asked this her entire life. Except now, she was truly confused, her body producing Magick stronger than it ever had after she had left the castle.

"Before I was taken to the capitol to marry Arzhel, my mother had advised me my entire life to keep my Magick a secret. Even as a child, I hadn't been able to produce much of my power. It had always been so faint.

"I chalked it up to the Gods gifting me with weak abilities, or perhaps the slowly dying existence of Magick as a whole. What I did to you, to those guards... I have never done it before in my *life*. I thought I knew my own capabilities, but I'm quickly learning I may know nothing at all. Blasting you was the first time I ever triggered so much Magick at once."

"Well, I'm *certainly* honored." Taryn said sarcastically with a hand over his heart.

A bitter laugh escaped her lips. Thoughts of her mother and Arzhel surged forward, traumatic memories begging to rise to the surface of the sea of her mind. Airess drowned the memories deep down, as she always had, and focused on her next question.

What *did* she know about Taryn? The answer was very little. Airess knew he was ordered to capture her, yet he defied those orders. Taryn saved her while unconscious. He even defended her when she was struck in the caravan, showing some semblance of a moral compass, as skewed as it may be with his thieving habit.

To put it simply, he was a complicated person. She felt it, as if his energy was blocked within him. He was kind, funny even, yet showed traits of immorality. He was a walking contradiction. It was confusing and illogical.

"How did you end up joining the Mrkynian Guild?"

He chuckled, the sound lodged in his throat. Taryn smiled bitterly, silver eyes distant as he no doubt recalled the past. "I sometimes ask myself that same question. I was young. The Guildmaster found me in a time of… need. I bargained my way into the Guild. I would have done anything at the time to find somewhere to belong."

The words were raw as they left his mouth. Airess let them linger in the air, weighing them in her mind.

He turned to face her then, his gaze lingering on her ivory hair. "Where are you from?"

Airess understood his curiosity. The Elven people were predominantly dark haired, sharing traits of pale skin the color of porcelain. Airess was an oddity amongst them, her white locks, golden eyes and tanned skin making her stick out in a crowd.

"Judla, a small province in south Luciena near the ocean. My father was the Governing Lord before I was moved to the capitol."

He eyed her wearily but didn't press her further on the matter.

Airess wanted to say, *before the Luciena Guard raided my home and slaughtered my mother and father*, but decided to keep it short. She didn't know him well enough to unpack all her trauma.

"Why didn't you use your Magick on those guards? You had every opportunity, yet you resorted to wielding a blade."

"It wouldn't have been a fair fight," was all he replied, his tone clipped.

"So you *do* have morals."

Taryn gave her a cutting look. Something flared behind his eyes, but she couldn't decipher what the emotion meant. The emotion disappeared, hidden by a mask of a smirk. "I suppose as skewed as it is, yes."

For a moment, Airess caught herself staring. Staring at a male whose deviousness she found endearing. She swallowed and looked forward, but the motion seemed to pique Taryn's curiosity.

"For someone who has lived so lavishly, you certainly don't seem that uncomfortable to be traveling outdoors like this. I find that interesting."

Airess nodded, fighting the blush that threatened to rise. It was a miniscule comment, but one she had never heard directed at her before. No one had ever found her interesting.

"What else can I do but be okay with change? It's not as if I can do anything about it but move forward. I don't need to hold onto the past, there's nothing for me there."

Taryn gave her a calculating look, as if that was not the answer he expected. He nodded approvingly. "That's something not everyone can accept so easily."

Airess shrugged. "Maybe they aren't meant to, at least in this lifetime."

Silence fell between them before Airess realized she never asked for Taryn's full name. "What's your last name? I don't think I ever asked."

For a moment she thought he wasn't going to answer, but slowly, he answered, "Seas. Taryn Seas."

He said the words like he hadn't spoken them aloud for quite some time. She thought it was a nice name. Airess knew names held power, more than most. But his energy suddenly fell stagnant, and when she blinked her Sight forward, she saw his aura dim. Airess couldn't necessarily describe what she felt, but somehow she just knew there was a certain pain that came with his name.

She changed the subject. "And how old are you, *Taryn Seas*?"

Taryn lifted a brow and chuckled. "Someone's curious. I'm twenty-four, if you must know. Four years older than you."

"And how do you know my age?"

Taryn snorted. "You were my target. I was debriefed on everything we knew about you. Granted, the information was very little. You've kept yourself well hidden."

Airess swallowed. If only he knew it wasn't by her design. If only he knew the truth.

They conversed lightly the rest of the way. Airess didn't pry any further into his background, and he returned the sentiment. For once, she just wanted to pretend she was a regular person. She didn't know how much longer that illusion would last.

You've kept yourself well hidden.

Airess' brow hardened as they trekked through the forest, dense with tangled roots and the scent of soil. The reins bit into her palms as her grip tightened. Taryn's words rang in her mind over and over. She tasted the bitterness on the tip of her tongue, she could *feel* the stolen time that slipped from her grasp. She vowed if she ever made it out of this Gods' forsaken country, she would be sure the world knew who she was.

Airess would make sure she was unforgettable.

Chapter 15

What existed first, Death, or the Mind?

– Written entry from Zaro Lucien's personal journal

Airess

That night, Airess sat across from Taryn, a hearty fyre crackling between them as they ate the fruits they had stolen. She tried her best to relax, but still jumped at any sudden sound, no matter how faint. She gripped the hilt of her dagger they looted as she sat stiffly, gazing out into the dark wood beyond them.

"There's nothing there," Taryn said with his back against a tree, legs crossed out long before him. He took a drag of… was it a cigar? She didn't recognize the distinct smell of that smoke. Taryn pointed to his ears as he exhaled, smoke billowing into the night. "I would hear it before you did."

Right. She let out a breath, still not used to his enhanced qualities. She turned to face him, a brow arched, silently questioning the odd smell of the cigar he held between his fingers.

"You want to try it? I should warn you, it's a bit stronger than tobacco."

"No, thank you," Airess said as she shifted into a more comfortable position. "I didn't see you swipe that back in town. Is speed another one of your enhanced qualities?"

Taryn cackled, smoke spurting out of his nose. "Unfortunately, no. We may be the animalistic cousin to your species, but we are not able to move at the speed of light. Speaking of–what qualities do you have? Being half Elven and half Human, I assume." His eyes drifted to her ears, not as elongated as the Elvens.

"In contrast to the Fae's physical Magick and senses, Elven senses are quite the opposite. We are born with a sixth sense, in a way, and are able to sense energies. Emotions. Intentions, even, depending on how strong one's senses are. Although Elven Magick is rare these days, there are some who can still wield energy."

His head tilted to the side, "And you have this quality, even being half Human?"

Airess smiled slightly, suddenly proud of her abilities. She had been so focused on *his* that she forgot her own and how much it had helped her in her life. "Yes," she admitted. "But my power goes beyond just sensing energies. I can *see* energy. It's a rare trait, and as far as I know, I'm the only one with The Sight. It's how I knew you weren't lying, that you wouldn't hurt me. That you were finding your way, just like I am."

"You've seen my energy?" Taryn asked, eyebrows raised.

"Well, yes," Airess admitted. "It's the first thing I noticed about you. Back at the engagement ball, I spotted you in the crowd like the pale moon against the black night. It was actually… beautiful."

"*Beautiful?*" Taryn repeated with a smirk as he snuffed out his cigar.

"Out of all the things females have called me, that has to be the most complimentary."

Airess rolled her eyes. *Arrogant Fae males and their notorious pride.*

"Your aura is the color of your irises, combined with swirls of multicolored energy. It's the first aura I have ever seen that was so vibrant."

Taryn pursed his lips in thought. Airess began to nervously fiddle with her dagger, starting to over think she had said too much. Did she freak him out, saying all that stuff about what his energy looked like? Maybe she was being too open, too–

No. She shook her head. She would not allow her mind to drift like this anymore– wouldn't let her anxiety get the better of her, make her think the worst of everything, everyone. Airess had lived and thought that way for far too long. She wanted to live boldly, unapologetically. She wanted to embody faith and positivity, and that would start with her thoughts.

"Do you know your way around a blade?" Taryn asked, pulling her out of her mind. She met his piercing gaze and shook her head.

"Highborn females aren't allowed to even *touch* a blade, let alone wield it."

Taryn shook his head, clearly not in agreement with the customs that came along with living in court. She examined the dagger that felt foreign in her hand. If they were to be attacked right now, she would have no idea how to use it. That just wouldn't do.

"Would *you* teach me how to use this?"

His brows shot up. Airess studied the way his lips twitched up to fight back a smile, and the stubble that had begun to appear after days on end without shaving. She couldn't help but find him attractive. Airess blinked and withdrew from her thoughts

"I would be happy to. I believe everyone should know how to defend themselves," Taryn said, pausing to glance at her and the blade. "We'll start your formal training after we've covered some distance."

"*Formal* training?"

A wicked grin displayed his canines. "Yes, Haeleth. You're going to need to learn how to use that blade *and* self-defense when the time comes. Because it will. There are creatures and folk out there that will give us trouble. This journey isn't for the weak, and I get the feeling you *aren't* weak. You just need some guidance."

She weighed his words. Taryn didn't think she was weak. That surprised her. No male had ever spoken to her with so much confidence. It was refreshing.

Determination overtook her, "Very well. I'll take whatever you can give me."

They conversed for a little while longer before laying down, each of their cloaks acting as their pallet in the spring night. They spoke of finding a body of water to bathe in, and she looked forward to bathing more than she anticipated.

Airess lay down on her back, the starlight peeking at her through the treetops. She exhaled all the negative energy out of her body and into the open air. With each breath, she melted further into the ground beneath her. The earth comforted her, providing a stability that propelled Airess forward. At last, she had a real plan, a way to get away from here.

She had one goal, and one alone: Freedom.

She exhaled, closed her eyes…

And slept.

"Do you feel that? I think I've reached her–them – it's hard to tell the difference from here," said a young, feminine voice as Airess materialized in front of–what is this?

She stood before a circular portal opening made of swirling, purple flames.

Aside from the portal, she was surrounded by infinite space. It was as if she were standing on an invisible platform, yet nothing was holding her upright.

Looking into the portal opening, her vision cleared as her spirit seeped into the dreamworld. What kind of dreamscape was this? Beyond the flames, she saw two figures, presumably a male and female.

Airess couldn't make out any distinct features beyond a blur of red hair. The other individual, seemingly male from a tall physique and broad shoulders, had a blur of black hair.

"I definitely feel one of them," said the female voice to her counterpart.

"Hello?" Airess asked, her voice echoing into the vast expanse, startling herself.

"Do you hear that ringing in your ear? They must be trying to make contact," said the male voice.

"I hear it," the female agreed. "But it's faint. They must still be within the ward."

Making contact? Within the ward?

"Who are you?" Airess asked.

Suddenly, a black hole materialized to her right, the size of a shield. It started sucking in the black space around her. Her astral body started to stretch towards it. Airess' heart stuttered as she felt her dreamform being sucked in.

"I'm losing them," said the female. It looked like she stepped closer to the other side of the portal, right in front of the flames. "If you can hear me in there, get to Rune! Get to R–"

The female's words warped as Airess was sucked into the black hole. Airess screamed out into the void, disoriented. Was she falling, was she floating? Time didn't exist here. Images, scenes of battle and storms flashed before her eyes.

Then, stars and light as she fell down that familiar black hole. The starry space shifted into a dreamscape revealing a vast ocean before her.

Looking down, she realized she stood at the edge of a cliff, the waves crashing violently against the rocks below. Across from her was a–was that a...wall?

A massive translucent wall made of turquoise aurora jutted out as far as she could see on either side.

Airess couldn't see through it, the barrier was so thick with energy. A storm gathered overhead, the sky darkening quickly. A crack of lightning flashed.

"For Gods' sake, not this again," a familiar male voice complained.

If Airess could feel in the dreamworld, she would feel her eyes bulging out of their sockets. She turned around and saw Taryn standing, his head tilted up to view the sky, completely unaware of Airess' presence.

She couldn't believe her eyes.

His dark tan skin in the waking world was replaced with translucent, silver light in the dreamworld. His curly brown hair wasn't brown here, but a metallic silver, the locks flowing in the air as if he was underwater. He was dressed formally with a fitted emerald tunic that reached his wrists and formal black pants rolled up to his calves.

Airess' jaw dropped. "Taryn?"

His head snapped in her direction, his mouth parting open in surprise before he shook his head in denial.

"Just a dream," he muttered. Taryn stared at her in astonishment, no doubt in shock to see her in her golden, glittering dreamform.

"Incredible," he said, more to himself, as if he didn't believe she was real. Did he not think she was actually here?

Thunder rumbled above them, the wind picking up and swaying the grass at their feet. Behind him was a vast field of dark-colored flowers she didn't know the name of. Strange, she thought. This night's dreamscape had changed and shifted into more unfamiliar settings than usual.

"How are you here?" she asked him in disbelief. Airess was utterly dumbfounded. Before her encounter with Ima, she had never made any contact with other astral beings. She mostly appeared as a ghost, only observing memories or other people in the waking world.

His silvery eyes met hers. "I don't know."

As if his curiosity got the better of him, Taryn stepped forward and reached out a hand to touch hers. His hand went through her own, but for the first time in her life, she felt *something in the dream world. It was faint, but as he made contact with her, a tingling traveled up her arm.*

Taryn took a step back and yanked his hand away, as if he felt it too. He stared down at his hand, fingers splayed out for inspection. "Crazy fucking dream," he muttered again.

She furrowed her brows. "You're a dreamwalker?"

How is that possible?

"A what?*" he said, an incredulous expression on his face, then he*

shifted his gaze beyond her. A crack splitting in the air had her whirling to see what he was looking at. Beyond the cliff and the ocean, lightning had struck the wall of aurora. It cracked like an egg and began to split into pieces. The ground beneath them began to shake. The shaking intensified so much that her vision blurred. It was then when she realized– she was about to wake up.

Funny, how time worked in the dreamworld. A night's worth of sleep equated to about five minutes in a dream. She knew she was about to wake up to the morning sun.

As expected, the view before them melted away like quicksand. Except this time, she wasn't alone as she fell through space. Taryn fell right beside her, his yelling out echoed into the void –

Airess sat up immediately upon waking, sweat at her brow as she heaved for air and glanced at Taryn. He was in the same state as her as he looked around in confusion until he found Airess' face. He shook his head, as if he was denying a simple truth that Airess, deep in her soul, knew to be true.

Taryn was a dreamwalker.

Chapter 16

*'The Gods are punishing us for what you have done.
Now, the world will never be the same.'*

— Unsent correspondence from Tinyrah Kazimyr (Post-Division)

Taryn

It was overwhelmingly obvious that Airess knew something Taryn didn't, by the way she was looking at him, her mouth hung open and speechless. Noticing the alarmed expression Airess wore, Taryn immediately looked around the woods, doused in the morning sun, alert to find the source of her reaction, but found nothing amiss.

Her shock contorted to accusation, her brow furrowing as she pointed a finger at him. "*You* can dreamwalk?"

The recollection of the recurring dream he had awoken from slammed into his mind, recalling the words she had said to him in his dream. But it was just that, *a dream*.

He gave her a skeptical look. "I can do what?"

Airess rushed to her feet and began pacing. "It's not possible. Not once have I ever met another dream walker–well, save for that one recent time – but my own *mother* told me I would probably never meet one. And then you show up in my life with some Magickal aura and a plethora of power, and through all of that, you can dreamwalk, too?"

Taryn stood with his arms folded, amused at how easily worked up she was getting. Even in the early hours of the morning, Airess looked effortlessly beautiful. Her ivory hair fell down her back in loose waves, tousled by their travels. The maroon dress she had stolen from the market fit her body like a glove. The fabric corset accentuated her curves, invoking a need deep inside Taryn that he tried his best to stifle.

"Calm down, Haeleth. I can barely understand you, and we need to get moving. We can't stay in one place for too long."

She nodded reluctantly as they cleaned up their campsite and mounted their horses. They galloped away, their horses' hooves thrumming against the ground as they sped forward.

At last, a lake came into view, nestled in the valley of Mount Yannish. Taryn swung a leg over and dismounted his horse, walking over to Airess and offering a hand to help her down, like the gentleman he was. Her hand was warm, slender, and light as a feather, slipping perfectly into his. The warmth of her touch seeped into his palm. She possessed the grace of a queen.

He gazed out to the lake, "We should bathe here. It could be a while until we get the chance again." Once Airess dismounted, she shrugged off her cloak and turned to him.

"Don't change the subject."

"What subject?"

Airess crossed her arms, looking at him with curiosity.

"Are you avoiding it because you don't want me to know, or do you truly have no idea what you are?"

Taryn's jaw tensed at the words being repeated to him a second time in the past four days, making him instantly skeptical of her. Could he trust her?

Did she even know what *she* truly was?

"I don't know what you're talking about."

He turned away from her, grabbing his waterskin attached to the saddle, and headed to the lakeshore.

"My Gods, you have no idea," Airess whispered in shock from behind, trailing close behind him.

He whipped around, peering down at her. "What are you talking about?" His tone came out more biting than he intended.

She strode to him slowly, letting him digest her words. "We were both there in that field of flowers, you know, with that wall beyond that cliff? *I was there.*"

Taryn furrowed his brows and took a step back. How was that possible? Did she get in his head? Was she a witch? The gentle lapping of water from the river filled the silence between them.

"How did you know that?"

"Because I'm a dreamwalker, Taryn—and so are you."

"What the hell does that mean?"

Airess passed him and sat on the rocky shore, motioning for him to sit. "You're going to want to sit down for this," she said wearily. He hesitated for a moment before sitting down next to her, both of them facing the watery expanse.

"If my mother never told me about my abilities, I wouldn't have known either."

Airess's voice cracked at the end of her sentence, clutching her necklace she wore close to her heart. This was the first time she had ever mentioned anything personal, and Taryn knew to stay quiet.

She squeezed her eyes shut. "I never knew what I was capable of. Not in the beginning, at least. My dreams were like anyone else's. You dream of something and wake up and remember it, as if you were recalling a distant memory. But as I got older, things became different. My dreams began to *change*. It started with flashes of images and voices at first.

"But things started to change around my tenth birthday. Every night when I fell asleep, I would fall into this–this *black hole*. I would end up in different landscapes, places I had never seen before. Sometimes I would be alone, wandering into my dreams aimlessly. Other times I would appear in towns, homes, cities I can't even begin to describe, crowded with people and beings all around me. But I couldn't speak to them, they couldn't see me, almost as if I were–"

"A ghost," Taryn finished for her and thought about how he had observed his own body in his recent dreams, appearing so translucent that he swore he could have been a ghost himself. His stomach twisted as he felt a certain truth in her words.

Airess nodded in agreement. "Exactly. I became aware that my body was… different. It looked like me, but it wasn't me. I wore clothing that didn't belong to me in those dreams. I had no skin, but a ghostly projection of myself. One night I woke up so scared. I thought I had *died*." Airess chuckled, fiddling with her fingers.

"I ran to my mother and told her what happened. She told me what it was that I was doing. She called it dreamwalking. It's a form of astral travel. Our souls leave our bodies at night and travel the universe. From what my mother told me it's a rare trait. Not just *anyone* can do this. You are actually the first person I have ever met who has this ability."

Taryn stared at his boots, taking it all in. He had no reason to doubt her words now, everything she had said was entirely too identical to his own experiences. He didn't know what it meant for him, though.

"And you've been *dreamwalking* your whole life?" he asked her, still getting used to the terminology she used.

Airess turned to face him now, her gilded irises boring into him as she spoke softly. "Ever since I was ten, yes."

"Maybe there's been some mistake, then. This only started–"

Shit, when did it start? He *has* had some pretty weird dreams recently. Airess mentioned voices, seeing flashes of images. Taryn realized when it began for him. "It started the night I saved you after the caravan explosion. I found myself in this dreamworld you speak of…"

Taryn trailed off, not wanting to sound absolutely ludicrous.

"You can speak plainly to me. I'm not one to judge," Airess lightly encouraged, nudging his side lightly with her elbow. Her voice was laced with a soft tone of acceptance. Taryn felt the icy fortress encasing his heart soften ever so slightly.

Has anyone besides his grandmother ever spoken to him with such a welcoming energy? Being a Fae in Elven lands, it was a rarity. Taryn averted his gaze to the watery expanse.

"I was on the cliffside. The same dream you appeared in, only it wasn't you standing there, but another female – or woman – I couldn't see her ears to tell what she was. One moment she was there, another moment she had disappeared."

"What did she look like?"

"It was hard to tell. I only saw her back, but she had red hair and wore purple robes."

"*Red* hair," Airess repeated, the words sounding more like a question. With the sun peaking overhead, Taryn remembered himself, and how they were both on a time crunch to make it out of this country.

"You can bathe first," Taryn said as he stood and turned to leave, giving her privacy. "I have a lot of questions to ask you about this *dreamwalking* you speak of, but if we want to travel in a timely manner, we need to leave soon."

Airess nodded as he turned and stalked into the woods. He walked far enough to be out of sight, but close enough that he was in earshot in case anything came near. He reached his hand out to the saddle –

Taryn stifled a groan as he fell to his knees. The Oathmark flared, searing the skin on his arm. The Oathmark's Magick began to infiltrate his body and mind. He ripped his tunic by the collar to view the mark, its black glow intensifying with the pain. Darkness closed in, Taryn no longer able to hear and see his surroundings as he collapsed entirely.

BOOM!

He heard men screaming around him as he fell to the ground. Taryn's heart pounded in his chest as he watched a Runean soldier get cut down by a Lucien soldier, his head decapitated. The gore splattered onto Taryn as he lay in the mud after being blasted backwards by Shadow Magick. The soldier ripped his sword out of the body, a sound Taryn might not ever forget.

His eyes widened as the Lucien soldier transfixed his gaze on Taryn next, stalking towards him with his blade. He remembered to move, to act. Taryn gripped his bow, trembling fingers fumbling to grasp onto the arrow now that his fingers were soaked in blood.

"No!" Taryn screamed as the Lucien's soldier brought the sword down –

Taryn was suddenly thrust back into reality, the pain from the Oathmark receding. The glow faded, leaving the tattooed ink back to its original red. Panic set in, rooting deep in his stomach and creeping up until his throat tightened. He loathed that Eryx could bring him directly back into his most traumatic memories, even from afar.

Taryn didn't realize he had fallen flat on the ground, but he heaved as he regained his focus, pulling his tunic upright on his shoulders. He wiped the sweat that beaded on his brow as he stood up. *Shit.* Eryx had called on his Oathmark sooner than expected. Of course, he knew it would happen eventually.

He prayed to the Gods he wouldn't have an episode in front of Airess. How could he explain such a thing? It's not like he could tell her what he saw–Eryx forcing Taryn into his deepest traumatic memories when he intended to inflict pain. Eryx knew Taryn could handle the physical pain, so he often resorted to mental torture as well.

Taryn didn't have a plan to rid himself of the mark beyond meeting with the infamous healers in Rune. For now, he would have to conceal his pain. He didn't want Airess to know he was bound by the Oathmark. What would she think of him if she knew?

Why did he care?

Taryn brushed that thought aside as he gathered himself, turning as soft footsteps padded towards him, Airess's scent prominent before he saw her. His breath hitched as he took her in. The blood and dirt she was caked in had been washed away, leaving her glowing beneath the morning light. Her ivory hair had been braided into a crown, save for a few tendrils that framed her freckled face. She wore a dark maroon cotton dress with white stitching. She held the top half of her dress up, her cheeks warmed a soft shade of pink.

"I can't reach to fix the back of this dress. Do you mind lacing up this corset? Unless you don't know how, of course –

"I know how to lace a corset, Haeleth," Taryn cut in, his voice low as he moved toward her. Need bloomed within him at the sight of her–a completely inappropriate feeling he tried his best to block out. He barely knew her, Taryn couldn't be thinking thoughts like *this*. He swallowed at the sight of her bare back on display. He grabbed the strings and began to lace them gracefully, his fingers brushing against her delicate skin felt like electricity shooting up his arms.

Get a hold of yourself, Tar.

Taryn laced slower than he needed to, fighting every urge crawling up his spine, He tied the knot gently at the small of her back. "Is this too tight?" he asked, his voice hoarse with desire that he tried his best to mask. What was wrong with him, losing control like this? Never had a female made him so *weak*. He was holding onto any strength he could muster to not lose control, to hide the desire in his eyes. He couldn't do this, not with her. Taryn didn't even know if he could *trust* her. They were just… unlikely allies working together towards a similar goal. That was all. He reminded himself of these facts and neutralized his expression.

She took a deep breath in to test how much room she had in the bodice. "No, it's perfect."

She turned to face him. The air was thick with a certain tension as she tilted her head up to him, her golden gaze heated. Now that her dress was intact, her breasts were on full display from the tightened corset. Taryn clenched his jaw, a flicker of heat surging beneath his skin. He forced himself to look away with what little control he had left.

"Thank you," she said lightly, as if she too felt the thick energy coursing in the air around them.

"Of course," he said as he turned away abruptly, careful to ignore the sweet scent of her arousal as he descended to take a bath of his own.

Chapter 17

'If you reach hard enough, we can enter the Minds of others, though the cost is great'

— *Unsent correspondence from Paulyr Moros*

Airess

Taryn and Airess sat in front of the fyre pit after a long evening of Airess' training, which turned out to be the complete opposite of what she had expected. She thought she would be learning hand-to-hand combat on the first night, but was quickly humbled when her evening consisted of Taryn verbally teaching her the basic offensive and defensive positions, explaining everything in detail.

He talked expressively with his hands, his voice dipping and rising during his lesson with her. Airess decided she liked that about him, the Fae male eager to teach, and she eager to learn. Although Airess had a fine education in Luciena, there was so much she didn't know about the real world, about society, and she intended to learn everything she could.

She was also glad he was finally coming out of his shell. She enjoyed learning what Taryn had to offer, and he was a fine teacher. In more ways than one.

Taryn strode over to the horses, taking out the remaining apples and feeding each of them. She could see his muscled back through the dark fabric of his tunic, his strong forearm flexing as he stroked the horses manes.

He had cleaned up well since they bathed in the pond earlier that day. He'd shaved, his stubble now replaced with smooth skin.

Airess uncovered her Sight as she watched Taryn, entranced by the never-ending blend of silvery color that flowed around him gracefully. Seeing him now changed her perspective. Although he never went into detail about how he ended up in the Mrkynian Guild, she could sense that there was more to the story than he let on. Airess had an inkling that Taryn didn't have a peaceful past. She would never have guessed Taryn was a spy, or an assassin… or whatever he was to the Guild. His mannerisms were too genuine, too gentle, for her to have ever known otherwise.

Perhaps he was as equally as lost as she was in life.

Taryn sat down across from her and tossed an apple. She nearly fumbled the fruit as he announced, "The last of the fruit. We will have to get more soon. The horses need more food, too." He took out his flask and drank.

"Are we going to hunt?"

Taryn's eyes slid to hers, his mouth quirked up as he took a bite from the apple. "In due time, Haeleth. I was going to suggest we go into town tomorrow and find some tavern food. We will have plenty of opportunities to hunt after we cross through the main road."

She rested a hand over her stomach. "After eating fruit for two days straight, tavern food sounds amazing."

A comfortable silence fell between them as they ate and Airess began to get lost in her own thoughts. She thought of the dreamwalker, Ima, who had instructed her to travel with Taryn to Rune. Nothing about that made sense.

Airess sighed heavily. Ever since she quite literally tumbled into Taryn's life, her entire world had been flipped upside down. What was her connection to the dreamwalker and Taryn? Could she even trust Taryn enough to tell him about Ima, or would he think she was crazy? He barely took in that he *himself* was a dreamwalker. Perhaps she wouldn't need to tell him at all. She would just make it to Rune and be on her merry way.

She thought of the strange dreamscape she had appeared in, standing in space before the portal of lilac flames, two beings on the other side. They were *aware* of her. It was another piece to the puzzle she hadn't quite sorted out yet. She hoped The Obadiah in Rune would have the answers she was looking for.

Airess threw the apple core into the fyre at the thought, frustrated she had more questions than answers.

Taryn raised a brow. "A violent thing you are today."

Her cheeks warmed. "It just – I just –" For some reason, she found herself wordless. Her shoulders slumped as she sat forward, gathering her thoughts.

"I'm frustrated. Everything has changed so quickly in such a little time. Somehow, *you* have ended up being my only ally, and quite frankly, the only person I know. I went from future queen to rogue fugitive, wanted by the most powerful people in the country." Airess laughed bitterly. "And yet, through all this strife, I would do it all over again if it meant getting away from the Luciens."

Saying the words out loud felt like a weight had been lifted from her shoulders. She looked to Taryn, afraid he wouldn't want to hear anymore of her outburst. His brows creased as he took a sip of his flask.

"What could make a daughter of a Lord despise royal society so much?"

Airess contemplated his words, and reached over to grab the flask, taking a swig, not expecting the harsh burning sensation of what tasted like whiskey to go down her throat. As she handed it back to him, she said, "I had been taught since I was ten years old that I belonged to Arzhel, that I would be his wife. That I would... bear his children."

Taryn's face flickered with rage. His eyes darkened, but he stayed quiet and listened.

"The Luciens made sure I was educated the way a queen should be educated. But there were two major problems. My power never grew as they hoped. They were wary of marrying me off to him, so they postponed the wedding."

"What was the second problem?"

Airess tucked hair behind her faintly pointed ear. "I'm half Human. They weren't willing to marry off a powerless *mutt* to their precious prince. They kept my presence discreet, never letting me out of the castle unless it was void of visitors. Guards followed me everywhere I went. As the years went on, the Luciens became impatient with my lack of Magick. They hired countless professors to teach me. But who can teach a dead art? None of the lessons ever worked. Arzhel became the most impatient of them all. He grew... angry. Cruel. He resents me for causing weakness to his position."

Taryn was silent for a beat before he quietly asked, "You didn't have your mother and your father there with you? No friends?"

Airess didn't answer right away. She stared into the fyre, the orange light flickering across her face. The crackling of wood filled the silence before she shook her head, nails digging into her skin. "I had a friend, for a time. Bitterness changed her into someone unrecognizable. We grew apart." She made sure to avoid the questioning about her parents. She wasn't ready to divulge all of her past to him quite yet.

"If they postponed the wedding because your powers hadn't manifested in the way they hoped, why didn't Arzhel marry someone else? Why you?"

"You're asking me," she muttered. "I overheard the queen once. She was talking about how she *knows* I am special and that it is only a matter of time. They pushed it off because Arzhel requested it. He never cared about marrying me."

There was once a time she convinced herself to love Arzhel, or tried too, anyway. That was when they were young, and his cruelty hadn't reached its peak. Airess had hopes of living a happy life, a happy marriage. Those days were lost in time, a remnant of a different girl who looked at the world innocently. She knew better now.

"You didn't deserve any of it," Taryn said as his silver gaze pierced through her. "You belong to *no one*, Airess."

You belong to no one.

The words echoed in her mind. The concept was utterly foreign, but deep in her heart, it felt right. Airess loosened a breath.

"Thank you," she said quietly. Suddenly wanting to change the subject, she angled herself towards Taryn. "Are you mentally prepared to dreamwalk tonight?"

"I'm not sure how one *prepares* to dream."

"Dreamwalk," Airess corrected. "As preparation goes, I find it most helpful to meditate before going to sleep. Entering the dreamworld can be disorienting. Sometimes, it can be so frightening it causes you to wake up and leaves you with a bad night's sleep. It's hard to control that part but you can at least still your mind to ease into it."

She laid her cloak flat on the ground and lay on her back. "We'll start this way."

His eyes widened. "You want me to meditate? Right now?"

Airess laughed. "Yes, Taryn. You teach me to defend myself and I'll do my best to teach you how to navigate the dreamworld."

Taryn gaped at her and retrieved his cloak, laying it flat on the ground before settling onto his back. She looked up to the night sky, filled with twinkling stars, and a sensation of peace came over her. Airess closed her eyes and took a deep breath in.

"When I first started out, I could never still my mind enough to relax. I would breathe in four seconds, hold it for four seconds, then breathe out for four. Over and over again until I was emptied of all thoughts." She turned her head to look at the side of his face, his body laying a few feet away from hers, and smirked at him. "Consider this *my* lesson for the night. In this case, we are getting your mind familiar."

The sound of deep breathing followed as she closed her eyes. Airess couldn't believe she was here, with him, teaching him how to meditate. Just a week ago she was in a lesson with one of the Magick professors getting lectured on how she's not trying hard enough to produce Magick.

Maybe, she thought, things in life came easier to those who accepted things as they are, who were led by their heart rather than greed.

"This is impossible," Taryn's voice cut through the silence, "If this is what you used to do when you started meditating, what do you do now?"

"I breathe. I've been doing this for a very long time, so I'm able to switch over after a few minutes."

Taryn shifted his head to look at her, his expression in disbelief. "You can cross into the dreamworld at will?"

"At will," Airess confirmed. "And eventually you can too if you just focus on… well, *not* focusing."

Taryn shifted and tried it again. "This is quite nice. I think I'll fall asleep soon."

Airess chuckled. "Me too. Goodnight, Taryn."

Taryn looked at her with a softness, his mouth curved into a subtle smile.

"Goodnight, Haeleth."

She saw Taryn falling through space alongside her, his silver dream form a beacon in the vast expanse. Airess shut her eyes as they shifted into the Dreamworld, the uncomfortable feeling passing as she suddenly found herself standing inside a grand corridor–and one that she knew well. They stood there together, grabbing their bearings and taking in their surroundings.

"That was unpleasant," Taryn remarked from her side. She couldn't help but stare at him, his brown curls now silver tendrils, as if touched by moonlight. He raised his arm and inspected the ghostly version of himself.

"It usually is," she said numbly, taking in the familiar hallways of the castle in Luciena. Marble tiling lined the floors, the walls a stark white with intricate crown molding. There were many paintings along the walls, including a portrait of the royal family. It was an older painting, depicting the family when the king consort was still alive before he died of a terminal illness. Arzhel and Morana were younger, mere children, yet she could still depict the cruelty in Arzhel's eyes through the image.

"Are we in the castle?" Taryn asked, sidestepping so that a servant could walk by.

"Yes," Airess chuckled, and stepped in front of another servant. The servant passed through her dreamform, her translucent body flickering at the motion. Taryn's brows rose in surprise, mouth parted open in shock. "You're practically a ghost here. Don't worry about them walking through you. Now, come on, let's go."

She turned and walked down the halls, a place she had never dreamwalked before even though she had lived here for a decade. How strange it was to be back here unnoticed. Her heart filled with dread at what they may see – what *Taryn* might see.

"Where are we going?" he asked her as he fell in stride next to her. Even here, he towered over her by an entire foot. He was so tall, and his dream form was beautiful. Why was he so beautiful? She shook her head, dispelling the thought. She had to stop thinking about how attractive he was.

"Following the pull. Do you feel it–the tug urging us to move forward? The dreamworld is trying to show us something. It is wise to follow it." Airess was familiar with the invisible pull that originated from her chest, that tugged her forward, almost as if it was a subtle push. She hadn't stopped to consider that Taryn might not know what that meant– or what it was.

Taryn stopped walking, causing her to pause. He looked forward to the stairwell, his lips pursing in thought. "I do feel it, like it wants us to go upstairs."

Airess grinned, and elbowed him even though he couldn't feel it, "You're catching on."

"How is that possible? Is the dreamworld sentient?"

"From what I know, yes. It's not so much a person, but more of an entity."

He shook his head in surprise, his stare on her penetrating. She tried her best not to squirm under it and wondered if he knew how powerful he looked. *"That's just... that's absolutely fascinating. I wish I had a pen right now."*

She laughed, *"A pen?"*

"You know, to write things down. This would make for some wonderful research."

They began their ascent up the stairs. *"Research? What for?"*

"Why not?" He countered. *"Being as I've never heard the concept of dreamwalking means there has to be little record of it. Perhaps the world could benefit from such information."*

This surprised her. She had never expected him to care about research, of all things.

"What are you, some kind of academic?"

He glanced at her, a shadow overcoming his expression. *"At best, I am a well-read male. We didn't exactly have time for learning at the Guild."*

She felt the rawness in his words, the yearning in his tone. It was as if he wanted something he couldn't have, and for some odd reason, it made her sad for him.

"You like to research?" She asked honestly, intrigue driving her question.

"Absolutely," He answered confidently. *"The world can only benefit from evolution, and that comes from learning. Researching. Recording. There is still so much we do not know, from the ocean below to the heavens*

above. Knowledge is power. It's everything."

Her brows rose in surprise at his passionate words. She understood, feeling the same about her music. She smiled and glanced up at him, "You're quite the interesting male."

He smirked, eyes cutting to her. "You think I'm interesting?"

"I just –" Gods, he was making her fumble her words. "I just have never met a male who talks the way you do. The males I've had in my life are quite the opposite."

They reached the top of the stairs and walked onto the next floor, feeling the draw to continue forward. She realized they were headed towards the council chambers. Airess' stomach bubbled, dreading what they might walk into.

"And have you had many males in your life?" Taryn asked, cutting through her thoughts. His urgent tone was not one she understood, an emotion flashing in his eyes she couldn't decipher.

"No," She laughed bitterly, and left it at that. Airess didn't feel like talking about her past and lack of experience. Why did he care?

Taryn changed the subject. "Where are we going?"

They stopped before a door and Airess stared, feeling the pull of the dreamworld lurch through her. She knew he felt it too as he took a hesitant step forward, his brows creased in confusion.

"It wants us to go in there." She supplied, wrapping herself with her arms and took a step forward. "Follow me. We can walk right through."

She took another step forward and passed through the wooden door, her dreamform flashing. After a moment, Taryn followed behind her, his silver light in her peripheral. They entered the large chamber. In the center was a table grand enough to seat twelve. The room was draped with royal blue, from the velvet curtains to the ornately patterned rug. A few chairs sat to the side in front of a fireplace. Through the windows beyond, Airess could tell it was light outside. Whatever time period they were appearing in, it was daytime.

The door burst open behind them so suddenly, Airess startled. In came Arzhel, his brows creased in a cruel expression. He held Airess by the arm, his grip tight. Taryn and Airess' dreamforms flashed as a younger version of Arzhel and Airess entered the room and passed through them. Yes, she knew this memory well. It had happened only a year ago, and she hated that she was about to relive it. Hated that Taryn would see.

"Leave us," Arzhel commanded his guards that stood in the doorway. The guard nodded and closed the door, sending a visceral shock through Airess' dreamform. Her golden glow dimmed, her heart rate increasing at what was to come.

Arzhel thrust Airess away from him, sending her stumbling into the conference table. Her physical form caught herself from falling, bracing her hands on the table. She turned around and faced Arzhel, holding his stare.

Even in her dreamform, Airess felt the taut energy radiating off Arzhel. In the corner of her eye, Taryn watched silently next to her, lips in a grim line, jaw clenched.

Leave it to the Gods-damned dreamworld to put some of her worst memories on display for a male she had only just met.

"You've lived here for a very long time," Arzhel said, looking at Airess with beady eyes and folded arms. "And yet you've always managed to keep to yourself. Always so shy. Granted, I never attempted to know you. I never cared to. You showed little promise of power, and I half expected my mother to cast you out on the streets—admittedly, where you truly belong.

"But for some odd reason, she has kept you here. Locked you in your rooms, making sure you are treated like the proper Lady of a nobleman. A shame it was all for nothing. Your power turned out to be mere parlor tricks. Imagine my surprise when I am still expected to take the hand of a weldless invalid. You turned out to be a failure, just like the rest of the Haeleth's."

Airess watched her physical body tense in the memory. This was the conversation that led to her breaking point. Her ruination of her facade.

"Unlike my mother, I am onto your little games," Arzhel stepped closer to Airess, causing her physical body to flinch. "I think you do have power beyond conjuring a little golden orb. I think you're a liar. I think you're doing everything you can to avoid this marriage, and that makes me angry. Do you want me to be angry?" Arzhel asked with a scoff. "You are my property. If you don't show it soon, I will force it out of you."

Airess knew what was coming, remembering the simmering rage at the comment on her family name.

"Do not speak on my family's name," she snapped, standing tall in front of him.

Arzhel's eyes flashed with rage, nostrils flared. He took a calm step forward, grabbing her by the arm once again.

"You dare to speak to your prince this way?" Arzhel spat, then let out an evil laugh, "Ungrateful bitch. Any woman in this court would do anything to be in your shoes."

"Then let them," Airess seethed through clenched teeth. "I have no interest in marrying you. You're a weak, small male and I –

The sound of Arzhel's hand connecting against her cheek cut off her words. It was a hard slap, leaving behind an angry red mark and a split cheekbone.

A deep growl rumbled in Taryn's chest, and Airess forced herself to keep watching. She felt like stone, her dreamform unmoving. She couldn't meet Taryn's eyes, not now. Not after this.

"The next time you speak out of turn, I will be sure you suffer the consequences." Arzhel commanded. "Do you understand?"

The door opened behind them, incoming Princess Morana. She peeked her head in, eyes narrowing on Arzhel. This was right after Morana had given birth to Allia, yet she had intervened that day anyway.

"Airess, the queen requests your presence in your chambers." Morana said, her tone even. *Airess' physical form let out a shaky breath, nodding in acknowledgement before striding out of the room as quickly as she could. Airess remembered how the queen never did come to her room that day. Looking back on this memory in retrospect, did Morana lie to save her?*

The princess entered the room, chin up as she said, "What the hell is wrong with you? She is to be your queen."

Surprise coursed through Airess. She hadn't realized Morana had stayed behind and defended her, despite their falling out.

Arhzel scoffed at his sister. "And I will be her King. I can do with her as I'd like. Now, get out of my way, Mor." *Arzhel barreled past Morana, through Taryn and Airess' dreamforms, and exited the room.*

A blanket of shame fell over her as she met Taryn's gaze for the first time after entering the room. He wore a pained expression as silence fell between them. Airess wished she could leave, wished she could run away.

Why? Why show him this memory? Why make her relive it?

As Taryn opened his mouth to speak, a gaping hole beneath Airess opened up. It sucked her in and her surroundings faded away. She fell through the stars, relieved she was leaving Taryn behind. She didn't want to talk about what he had just seen.

Finally, Airess materialized in an unfamiliar hallway, the walls adorned with intricate crown molding and painted portraits. The floor beneath her was made of dark emerald tiling, expanding as far as she could tell in either direction of the hall.

It was when a servant walked by that she realized she was in a castle, one she had never visited before in the dreamworld. Thunder rumbled beyond the walls. The building groaned as if it was withstanding a great wind.

"So then what would you have me do?!" a frantic feminine voice bellowed beyond a door in the distance. Airess felt that familiar pulling sensation and let it guide her down the hallway to a grand arched doorway.

She walked through the doors.

Airess walked into what seemed to be an office, a room intricately decorated with dark ornate rugs and armchairs. Bookshelves made for walls on either side of her and a large oak desk dominated the space before it.

A massive window expanding from the floor to ceiling gave Airess the view of the nasty storm clouds brewing around them. That is when she realized all she saw were endless clouds, as if the castle was perched in the sky.

Pacing before the window was a young Fae woman with long, wild curls the color of caramel that cascaded to her waist.

She wore sheer fabric that wrapped around her body–and her pregnant belly. An odd fashion, Airess thought, yet beautifully unique. The woman's eyes were a striking green as she turned to face the Fae male leaning against the wall with his face in his hands.

Finally, the male looked up, his black lashes matching his cropped hair. Worry wrinkled between his brows as he looked at the female. "There's only one other option, Rinya."

"No," Rinya said firmly and set a hand on her swollen belly. "Leaving is not an option. The babe will need their father."

The male shook his head. "And if the babe truly is a boy? What then? You know he will be killed the moment he leaves your womb."

Rinya looked away and retreated to the windowsill. "Tevye is vast. We can hide as long as we need to—"

"No, Rinya! Do you hear yourself? Your **brother** *just declared any male baby born this season to be slain! He will have guards waiting the moment you give birth. You have to cross."*

"I will grow old, Tann."

"When the babe is grown, you can come back," Tann said as he took Rinya's hand in his. "There's still a chance for us all."

"No one has ever returned after crossing the wall. We know so little about the Old World. Who knows if our immortality will ever return?"

"It's a price I'm willing to pay if it meant you both lived."

Airess inched closer to the couple as Rinya squeezed Tann's hand, only a foot away as she watched them. Airess looked out the window, the gears in her brain finally flowing at the mention of the word Tevye. The same lands that belonged to the bedtime stories her mother read to her in Airess' childhood.

Airess watched the angry storm clouds, realization dawning on her that somehow, someway, she had dreamwalked into the very fairy tales her mother had told her about.

As Rinya opened her mouth to reply, a gaping hole began to manifest in the floor, warping the furniture around it and sucking Airess in.

"No!" she shouted into the void as she fell into the blackness, desperately wishing she could have stayed.

When Airess woke up in the dead of night, she couldn't help the nagging feeling that the universe was trying to tell her something. Who were those people? What were her dreams trying to tell her?

And if her mother knew Tevye was real, why did she lie about it?

Chapter 18

After Death created her Godling, the other four Gods had to follow in suit. It was the only way to create balance within the world.

—- *The book of Tevye*

Airess

"I'll be right back," Taryn said as he dismounted his horse, gripping the waterskin he intended to fill at the well. Airess nodded, peering at him from under her cloak hood. It was the first time they both had ventured out anywhere public since the incident inside the caravan, and she was especially nervous being around other citizens in the daylight.

Upon their waking this morning, Airess made it clear to Taryn she didn't want to talk about what he had seen in the dreamworld. It was intrusive. It was *intimate*. He had seen more of her than anyone else in such a short time. Of course, he didn't press the matter further, which she was thankful for.

Airess dismounted, stretching her legs before another traveling sprint.

She rested her hand on her horse's mane and stroked it for comfort. She had begun to grow fond of the horse that had carried her nonstop for three days now. Airess blinked her Sight forward, entranced in the warm oranges and yellows that made up the horse's aura. The energy of an animal was always light, always pure compared to other people's —

A cluster of hooves sounded from behind her, ripping her out of her thoughts. She turned, heart dropping as she took in the group of Luciena guards, their golden armor glistening in the daylight. Airess' heart almost stopped beating entirely when she saw her and Taryn's wanted posters gripped in their hands as they neared.

Oh, Gods.

She turned back around and faced her horse, keeping her hands busy with the contents inside her bag, hoping to appear casual enough for them to ignore her as they approached the well Taryn was retrieving water at. Taryn returned as they neared, approaching his horse calmly and stuffing the waterskin in his bag.

"It's okay," he said, his voice a low whisper. "Don't make any sudden movements." They both mounted their horses in unison.

She grabbed the reins hard to keep her hands from trembling, seeing one guard on horseback approach them in her peripheral vision.

"You two, drop the hoods, then you can be on your way. We're searching for a couple of fugitives that could be in the area."

Words lodged themselves in Airess' throat.

"We don't want any trouble," Taryn replied innocently, but the smirk Airess glimpsed on his face under his hood said otherwise.

She swallowed. She had seen Taryn's attitude towards the guards when they were locked up, his persona full of spite and stubbornness. She hoped he wouldn't say anything irrational.

"There won't be any trouble if you aren't who we're looking for. We're interrogating everyone in this town. *Drop the hoods*," the guard commanded, his hand resting on the hilt of his sword.

"Go fuck yourself," said Taryn.

Oh, Taryn.

The Guard drew his blade and charged.

Gods, why did he have to say that? Airess was starting to realize Taryn had a reckless tendency, his stubborn, arrogant behavior always landing him in an even worse position.

The smirk on Taryn's mouth deepened, and Airess tried her best to ignore the physical reaction she had to seeing it, her body heating at his wicked mouth. With a flick of his wrist, Taryn sent a gust of wind barreling towards the guard. The guard fell off of his horse with a *thud*. Taryn titled his head back and laughed–a stark contrast to Airess' growing anxiety.

"*Windborne Fae!*" the guard cried out as he landed on his bum.

Taryn looked to Airess with a satisfied grin. "Time to go." They nudged their horses forward into a sprint. The other guards quickly caught onto the commotion and chased after them. As the horse surged forward, a gust of wind tore her cloak hood back. With her white hair exposed, her cover was blown.

Airess let out a strangled cry as they sprinted through the woods. She heard the guards behind them yell out, "It's her! Airess Haeleth!"

A streak of blackness shot towards Taryn, followed by a hissing of whispering voices. He banked left and missed it narrowly, the blackness landing on the ground and *seeped* into the soil like a dry cloth soaking up a puddle of liquid.

Confusion and fear settled in her chest. Were they Shadow Wielders? She didn't have enough time to think further as terror gripped her by the throat, the possibility of them getting caught scaring her more than anything, and growing more real by the second. The fear grew, fueling her usually muted-power, traveling down her arms and sizzling underneath her palms.

Gold power began to glow at her fingertips, dripping off her fingers like she had just dipped them in a bucket of glowing starlight. She stared at her hand gripping the reins before whipping it backwards towards the guards in a moment of instinct, hoping that she could make use out of her Magick.

She looked back for a split second, catching a glimpse of a guard falling off his horse–a glowing hole burned through the chestplate of his armor. She turned to face Taryn's back as he rode. He pointed forward and shouted, "To the forest!"

Beyond them was a forest of hundreds of skinny, gray trees cloaked in a sea of darkness, the thick treetops blocking out the sunlight entirely. She kicked her horse to go faster as another bolt of darkness swam toward her. Airess veered left but the shot narrowly missed its mark, grazing the top of her shoulder.

She expected to feel hot pain, but instead she felt an icy sting that crept into her veins, spreading through her body like a sickness. The voices of whispering spirits filled her ears before fading away, just as her body began to slow. She tried moving her arm, the motion feeling heavy. Her vision blurred with patchy blackness, like someone had dipped her eyes in ink.

"Taryn!" she called out in fear.

"Almost there!" he said as they neared the forest. She looked behind her one last time, and to her utter surprise, the guards on horseback had reared their horses to a stop, watching them ride into the black darkness that was the forest, fear evident in their round eyes and parted mouths.

Daylight vanished as they crossed into the forest. She reached out to Taryn on her horse as her vision began to blur completely to black.

"Something is *wrong*," she said. Her grip on the reins slackened, her body sliding from the horse as everything went dark.

Airess woke to an eerie silence.

That, and a damp cloth resting atop her forehead. She stirred, her hand instinctively reaching for the cloth, when she heard a shuffling. When she opened her eyes, Taryn was hovering over her with a finger pressed to his lips. He mouthed a *Shh* and removed the cloth from her head.

Her eyes shifted beyond him. It was night–pitch black, even. She had expected to hear the soft hum of crickets and the crackling of a fyre, but to her surprise, it was complete and utter silence. There was no glowing light from the usual fyre they lit every night. There was a chill in the air, much colder than it should be for this time in Luciena.

"What happened?" she croaked. Taryn reached for her elbow, his hand resting softly on her lower back as he helped her sit up.

"You got hit with Shadow Magick. You fell unconscious when we passed through the threshold into The Twins. That was hours ago." Taryn spoke in a hushed whisper, eyes darting around to look for something in the forest beyond. "You'll want to keep your voice low here. We don't know what's lurking."

As consciousness settled within her body, she finally took in her surroundings–horror settling in the pit of her stomach as she focused on the *trees*.

The trees around them weren't just gray from light-colored bark, they were covered in *pale skin*. Purple veins traveled underneath the thin membrane, the veins pulsing as if it were alive. The leaves were a dark red, almost black, as if they were filled with thick, clotted blood.

She could only see the trees closest to her. The rest of the forest was pitch black, besides a glimpse of light that reached through the leaves towards her. They currently sat near the patch of light, the only source lighting up Taryn's worried features.

Not a single soul existed here. Airess' blood turned cold. Every instinct in her body screamed that she did not belong here.

"What is this place?" she whispered, noting the horses bedded down closer than they normally would.

Taryn's silvery gaze slid to hers. "The Twins."

"The what now?"

"The Twins," Taryn repeated. "The only forbidden forest in Luciena."

Airess shook her head. "What do you mean *forbidden forest*? That sounds like something from a bedtime story."

Taryn snorted. "I wish. This forest is ancient, supposedly filled with dark spirits conjured by Bas, the Death God. No one ventures in, not even the guards."

"*Dark* spirits?" Airess asked, horrified.

Taryn waved a hand. "Only according to folklore. I personally don't believe in ghosts, and doubt we will find anything of the sort."

"Such a skeptic," Airess said, rolling her eyes. "I wouldn't go doubting a notorious spirit, you might provoke it."

"*Ha!* I'd like to see it try."

Taryn stood up, brushing off his trousers before extending a hand to Airess. As he helped her stand, she realized he was quite the gentleman. He barely knew her, yet had never failed to help her mount her horse or light their fyres. She glanced at the wet cloth that he had placed on her forehead during her unconsciousness, and wondered what type of person raised such a gentleman–well, that is, besides his crassness.

"What about the guards?" Airess asked, remembering they could very well be waiting for them beyond the treeline.

"We will deal with that when we get there. Let's just… get out of here."

Airess cackled, folding her arms as she looked up at him. "Are you sure you don't believe in ghosts? I would think such a *strong* Fae male wouldn't be deterred by such *folklore*."

Taryn's head snapped towards her, a sly grin gracing his pretty mouth. "You think I'm strong? That's quite the compliment, Haeleth."

"Just get on your horse."

They mounted, riding back in the direction they'd come from. Their horses walked slowly, careful not to make any sudden movements. Spirits or no, there could always be a wild animal lurking nearby.

The darkness of the forest reminded Airess of the Magick the Luciena guards had wielded against them. She knew the Elven people could wield energy–hence how she is able to wield light, but she had thought Shadow Magick was a rarity these days.

"Those guards were wielders," Airess said, the sentence coming out more like a question.

"Shadow Wielders," Taryn confirmed.

"I thought they were extinct."

"I thought so too, until I got hit by one."

Airess' head snapped towards him. "You have? Did you pass out as well?"

Taryn shook his head. "No, but I was severely lethargic. I could barely control my body, but I didn't lose consciousness. Each person reacts differently. Shadow Magick, in a way, is more lethal than a stab wound. It incapacitates you, renders you unconscious or weak, making the opponent's fight much easier for them."

She thought back to her vision, blurred by black splotches when she got hit by the Shadow. Her body felt uncontrollable, her reactions slowed. If she had gotten hit by it on foot, without Taryn, her situation could have been much worse right now.

Yes, Shadow Magick was definitely more lethal than a blade. One hit could bring an armed soldier down. Multiply that by twenty and they could take down entire *armies*. The fact that some Shadow Wielders still existed in the present day made her stomach drop.

The real world was not only full of excitement, but horrors. Like this forest, though unnerving, possessed a certain beauty of its own. Bad things could be beautiful too.

Airess had begun to realize the duality of life, the good and bad coexisting together in an endless cycle of rebirth.

Life and death. Sun and Moon. Sorrow and joy.

"I had always learned about Shadow Wielders growing up, but never thought I'd live the day to experience one."

"There won't be any of that in Rune," Taryn assured. "Darkness doesn't dwell there. Only Elements."

After ten minutes of trekking forward, Airess began to doubt they knew where they were going. "Shouldn't we have reached the edge by now? Surely we didn't stop that far away from the treeline."

Taryn pursed his lips. "It can't be much further."

They kept riding until Taryn came to a stop, scratching the back of his neck.

"We should have been well out of the forest by now."

Airess bit her lip. "Let's try another direction."

Surely it couldn't be that challenging to find their way out of the forest. But as time passed, doubt crept in. They rode through the forest, silent and alert. They saw nothing, but endless trees scattered amongst the darkness.

Airess couldn't help but feel as if she were being watched. As if something were keeping them there. Lurking. *Waiting*.

They never found their way out of the forest that night.

Chapter 19

'I will become the ultimate Godling. I will kill them all. Will Tinyrah still love me? Perhaps not, but I will have the Allpower. I will do it for her.'

— Written entry from Evyen Deyanira's personal diary (Pre-Division)

The Vulture

The Vulture slammed the satchel on the desk. The severed head rolled out like a toy ball, landing perfectly in front of the man. His lilac eyes narrowed as he sat back in his chair, fingers clasped together.

"What is this?"

"The real question, Eryx, is what are you keeping from me? We had a deal." The Vulture stabbed the crystal dagger into the desk, wedging it within the wood. Hot anger brimmed within their chest as they looked into Eryx's eyes.

"You told me to have my spy ready for the Fae male the night before the ball. I did as requested, yet you conveniently left out the strength of his abilities. That plan failed. You say to try again at Arzhel Lucien's engagement ball. *That* plan failed as well," The Vulture sat back in the velvet chair, gaze intent on the man. Eryx sat back in his chair patiently, and The Vulture was surprised to feel the intrigue coming off the man.

"You know, I find your eyes quite odd," The Vulture pointed out. "Intriguing, yet odd. Tell me, why are your eyes the same color of the Magick that blasted apart the Lucien's ballroom?"

Eryx rumbled a deep, rich chuckle. "I can assure you, the attack was not of my doing. That matter is being taken care of."

The Vulture clenched their jaw, their restraint diminishing. "We had a deal. You help me overthrow the government, and I in turn kill your precious targets. Only now I can see they aren't just regular people, are they? This male's head was severed by heat. Her power was so hot, it *disintegrated* his flesh. The girl was not supposed to be able to access her power here. What else aren't you telling me? What else do you know?"

The Vulture could feel in their bones the man was holding back information. Of course, they didn't trust Eryx. Not fully. But their interests had aligned, and The Vulture took the deal. They were desperate for help, but the man couldn't know that. He couldn't know that The Vulture's future–their entire *family's* future depended on this alliance going forth as planned. Failing would be the end. Failing *wasn't an option.*

Eryx huffed out a breath before leaning forward and inspecting the head. He frowned, tracing a finger over the burnt flesh. "This was unexpected. If she can conjure a power this great within the barrier, who knows what she could do once she leaves the continent."

At least he hadn't knowingly sent them and their spies to their deaths. The Vulture needed Eryx to remain loyal, intent on their alliance. Without him, who else could they use as a scapegoat?

The Vulture straightened their spine, remembering themself. They simply couldn't afford to lose this alliance.

Play nice. Keep your attitude in check.

"So what is our next move? What about the male?"

Eryx waived a hand, dismissing the last question. "He will be contained as long as his emotions are in check. His power is buried under a lifetime of pain and suffering, that much blockage stifles Magick. We need to focus on containing the girl, then the male."

"Do you have a plan or not?"

"I do," Eryx said calmly as he thrummed his fingers across the desk, and told The Vulture what they needed to do next.

Chapter 20

And in a moment of rage, Tinyrah Kazimyr created the Everstorm. It was a defense mechanism, to keep out the one person she knew she couldn't deny. Evyen.

— *The book of Tevye*

Taryn

"You just had to provoke a dark spirit, *didn't you?*" Airess asked sarcastically, laying down her cloak as a makeshift pallet to rest after several hours of riding aimlessly through the woods. They were all tired, horses included.

"You can't possibly think that has anything to do with us being lost," Taryn reasoned as he straightened out his own pallet, turning to face her, the darkness cloaking her features. He had learned Airess was quite superstitious, her belief in the supernatural balancing his severe lack of it.

It amused him, truly, that one could have such faith in the unknown. He couldn't relate, only believing what he could see and feel, only accepting anything that had been scientifically proven. Dreamwalking had been the first time he had ever opened his mind to those possibilities, and even that he was still skeptical about.

Airess sighed, ignoring his doubt. "At least we got away from those guards," she shuffled until she came to a seated position, "I'll keep watch first."

Taryn nodded through the darkness. "Keep your dagger on you just in case. I haven't heard anything, but it's just a precaution."

The entire time they ventured into The Twins, Taryn hadn't picked up on any sounds that indicated a living soul lived here. Not even an insect. This had contradicted everything he had heard about the forest, but decided it would be a boon to their travels.

"Dream well," Airess crooned as Taryn lay down.

He hadn't dreamwalked since the night he saw into Airess' memories, and he hoped he never would do it again. What he saw that prince do to her in the dreamworld made him livid. *Furious.* The prince had struck her. How many times had he done that? What else did she endure while prisoner to the Luciens? Airess didn't want to discuss it, and he didn't blame her.

For some odd reason, Taryn just wanted her to feel safe. He wanted – no, *needed* to protect her. As he fell asleep, he vowed he would never let anyone harm her again.

He felt himself being ripped from his body.

It felt forced, like his spirit was peeling away from his physical form. Suddenly, Taryn was floating over his physical body. He had a perfect view of himself sleeping, Airess keeping watch beside him. He wavered slightly to straighten himself as if he was floating in water.

It was when he looked a few feet in front of Airess when he saw it.

A tall, thin creature stood beside a tree, its body resembling a mangled Human being. It was black, as if it were made of Shadow. Its face was covered by long, tangled hair that fell to the ground in thick sheets. It watched him, its head cocking to the side abnormally fast. The creature lifted a knobby finger and pointed at Taryn.

Taryn opened his mouth to scream, to shout at Airess to look up, but nothing came out of his mouth, the words caught in his throat as if his own voice had been silenced. A sinister grin spread beneath the blanket of hair, exposing teeth carved into sharp, jagged shards. It made a clicking sound, something so terrifying Taryn didn't know a sound like that could exist.

Airess didn't react, as if she couldn't see or hear what he was seeing. It was in this sickening moment he realized this spirit, or demon, was dreamwalking.

The demon lifted a finger and pointed backwards, beckoning Taryn to follow. Unwillingly, his body followed, both of them transcending time and Fate as they moved through planes, Taryn's surroundings flashing by him.

All too fast they came to a halt. Taryn was finally standing upright in the dream world, his feet planted on the ground. He looked around and found himself still in The Twins, that same familiar forest all around him. There was a pond of black, murky liquid beyond. Two identical trees, larger than the rest, were nestled next to each other at the pond's edge.

The skin on the identical trees began to stretch, bulging out until a body came out of each, breaking the thin membrane. Two mangled beings crawled towards him on all fours at an alarming speed, both of them looking identical to the demon that ripped him out of his body.

Taryn's scream tore out of him as he turned to run. How did traveling work here? He wished he knew more about dreamwalking, how to defend himself and control where he could go. He tried envisioning somewhere else to go, to free himself from this place, but his efforts were in vain.

Nothing worked.

His body came to a stop, an invisible force halting his steps and forcing him to turn around. The beings slowly stood up, growing to a height taller than he was, that same blanket of hair covering their faces, their appearance identical. Taryn stared at them, something clicking in his mind. His jaw dropped at the realization.

The Twins.

They walked closer to him. He tried to scream, but his voice had been muted entirely, his body stuck still as if he were in paralysis, forced to look at the demons as they both reached for his face with mangled hands.

When their knobby fingers touched his face, the whole world flipped upside down.

Taryn tumbled through the void, no longer in the forbidden forest but suspended in the stars. His raspy yell was all he could hear as he flipped upside down over and over. Then, his surroundings were suddenly solid, the starry space gone as quickly as it came.

Taryn stood in front of two beings running through a field of onyx salaroses, hand in hand, sprinting as if they were crunched on time. One was a male Elve, his white hair cropped, a golden crown upon his brow with a ruby gemstone ingrained in the middle of it. He wore a long, heavy robe the color of crimson, cream rope acting as the belt. His clothes were outdated, as if they were ancient fashions.

Taryn was struck by familiarity when he took in the other female, a pureborn Fae. She shared his bronzed skin, her brown hair falling down her back in a thick braid, silver threads woven into her hair. The Fae wore a similar robe the color of emeralds, the fabric flowing behind her as they ran.

Taryn mindlessly followed the two, as if in a trance, feeling so drawn to them he didn't think twice as one foot moved after the other in effort to keep up.

Finally, they stopped running. They panted for air and gathered themselves, stopping at the edge of the cliffside.

Taryn's eyes widened at the familiarity. He could no longer deny the significance of whatever this place was. It was that same field of wild salaroses nestled by the cliff, only this time, he could see land in the distance where the aurora wall had blocked the view in his previous dream.

The Fae female straightened her spine and spoke with a kind smile. "I think we are far enough, Evyen. Why did you want to leave so urgently?"

The white-haired male mirrored her smile, but it didn't quite reach his eyes as he loosened his grip on the Fae's hand. Evyen's gilded eyes softened. "Tinyrah, I figured it out."

"Figured out what?" Tinyrah, the Fae female, asked cautiously. Tinyrah's kindness melted away from her face, replaced with worry as Evyen slowly pulled out something from his robe pocket. Out came a cloth splattered with blood, concealing something beneath it. When Evyen opened the cloth, he revealed a crystal dagger engraved with an unfamiliar language, also smeared in crimson.

Tinyrah took a step back.

"As you know, I've been searching for the Allpower–"

"Evyen," Tinyrah shook her head in denial. "What did you do?"

"I've found a way for us to be together, to create a world undivided. Nyrah, I did it. I unlocked the Allpower," Evyen lifted the dagger up harmlessly in emphasis. "It's imbued in this dagger. We can–"

"What. Did. You. Do." Tinyrah said harshly, her voice laced with pain as she took another step back.

"You know what I had to do."

"I–I don't believe this! You told me weeks ago you gave up on accessing the Allpower. And now you –" Tinyrah's eyebrows creased, tears welling up in her eyes. She spoke again, her voice softer, barely a whisper, "I can't even imagine what you must have done to get this kind of power. You lied to me."

This time, Evyen's gaze hardened as he lifted his chin in pride. "I know you don't understand, but you will in time. Today, this dawn will mark a new age. We can create a world we both want to live in. Think about the future, Nyrah. Our legacy will carry on through generations. This is so much bigger than just you and me."

Evyen wiped the blade clean of the blood that hadn't yet dried. Tinyrah protested, marching towards Evyen and gripping his wrist.

"Stop this. If what you say is true, you already have enough power to be feared for a lifetime. This idea of… creating another world is meant to be the work of a God. Not you."

Evyen's head turned slowly towards Tinyrah, a wildness in his eyes Taryn hadn't quite noticed before until now, "Is that not what we are Tinyrah?"

"A Godling is not the same, and you know it."

Evyen pushed his arm out forcefully. A blast of light came out of his palm, sending Tinyrah crashing towards the ground. Evyen moved his arms in a circular motion, drawing Magick out of thin air and creating a shield of light around him. As Evyen knelt down, Tinyrah banged on the light shield.

"Evyen, stop!" Tinyrah pleaded, but her voice was drowned out as

Evyen plunged his dagger into the earth, dragging it along the soil. Light cracked through the slit in the earth, shining so brightly it nearly blocked Taryn's view. Evyen began to chant in a foreign language, ignoring Tinyrah's pleas to stop –

The whole world went silent, the light dimming from the slit in the earth.

After a moment of silence, the ground exploded, a massive light surge blinding Taryn's view. The energy began to hum intensely with a power so grand, even Taryn couldn't fathom exactly what it was that Evyen had done.

Taryn blinked, the golden light now replaced with a thick energetic barrier glowing the color of turquoise.

The clicking sound of the demon drew him out of his entrancement of the dreamworld. He whipped around, seeing the Twin demons standing behind him in the salarose field. They drew out their own daggers– blades of decayed bone and rotting flesh, carved into knives–and began stabbing the ground, mimicking what Evyen had done.

Fear rose in Taryn's chest as the demons came closer, hissing and clicking, drawing their knives from the ground and charging towards him–

"Wake up, Taryn!" Airess screamed, shaking his shoulders violently

"Tell yourself to wake up!" she repeated, the urgency in her voice so piercing his eyes shot open. Taryn's head spun, vision blurred as he regained consciousness in the waking world. He didn't know where he was at first, what direction he was lying in, until those familiar trees came into eyeshot.

He looked into Airess' gilded eyes brimmed with worry, and croaked out with a tired, humorous smile. "Remind me not to provoke a spirit next time–

A screech roared in the distance, both of their heads snapping to the source of the sound. Taryn shot to his feet, unsheathing his broadswords as Airess gripped her knife. He pivoted his body in front of hers, angling himself so that he could confront whatever was charging at them head-on. Heavy thuds vibrated at their feet.

Then, eerie silence.

The only sound was the panting of his and Airess' breath. He looked at her wide eyes and gripped her arm, bringing her closer towards him. "Turn around," he whispered, so that they were standing back to back. The thud of her heartbeat increased, her scent reeking of fear. He hated that. He hated knowing she was frightened, and regretted ever bringing her in here in the first place.

Taryn racked his brain on any information he had on The Twins. He had always heard rumors of a predator that lurked here, but assumed it was just folklore. Could it be the demons he saw in the Dreamworld? Could they manifest here too?

The trees rustled above them in warning, followed after a flash of white that landed in front of them. It was no regular animal, but a beast that had to be nine feet tall. Its body was white, the skin the same pale flesh as the trees. It was almost humanoid, with a bald head and distorted face. The beast reeked of death and dirt, the putrid smell flooding his nostrils. The fingers on its hands were clawed and knobby, bending at odd angles. Its eyes were completely black. Void. Decayed.

He had to think quickly. The broadswords would have to be his last resort, and the little water they had left remained in the waterskin. Taryn stepped forward instinctually as it swiped its claw. Taryn pushed his arms outward and blasted it with a burst of wind. Thank the Gods he could at least wield one element that could be accessed anywhere.

The beast toppled over, hissing in rage as it got to its feet.

"The waterskin! I need it!" Taryn called out as he ducked a swipe from the beast. He heard Airess' pounding footsteps retreat to go find the horses that no doubt had fled by now. Its head snapped towards her direction, roaring once more. Taryn sent another blast of wind, smacking the beast in the face.

That made it angry. The beast advanced, this time lunging for Taryn. Taryn jumped backwards, narrowly missing the clawed swipe. He slashed his broadsword downward and drew black blood on its abdomen. It growled, showing its long sharp teeth and pounced again. A zip sounded through the air, Airess' dagger plunging into the beast's back. It whipped backwards, moving faster than Taryn could.

Airess threw the waterskin at him as she ran in the opposite direction, the beast close behind her heels. Taryn uncapped the waterskin and guided the water outwards, shaping it into a small shard–sharp enough to do the same damage as a dagger. He clenched his fist, and the water hardened into ice.

He bolted forward, panic rising in his chest as the beast smacked Airess onto the ground. Fear fueled his steps. He jumped, raising the ice dagger high over his head and slamming the blade down onto the back of the beast's head.

Airess screamed in terror as it writhed. It fell alongside Taryn, snapping its teeth one last time before the light died in its eyes. Taryn grabbed Airess and yanked her from underneath the beast, the pair stumbling back as the ground vibrated from the thud.

Silence returned–only their ragged breaths and pounding hearts filled the air. Taryn looked at Airess, his eyes wide with concern as he gripped her shoulders, steadying her.

"Are you okay? Are you hurt?"

She shook her head violently. "No. No. Are you?"

Taryn shook his head. "No."

He let out a shaky breath, still processing what just happened. Never in his life had he seen a creature of this sort. Was there more? Were they coming?

"Let's get the *fuck* out of here," he said and grabbed her hand without second thought. They rushed to their horses, mounted and rode forward blindly. Surely they would find their way out of here.

Within minutes, they spotted the edge of the forest and sped to it, eager to get out. They passed the clearing, fresh daylight gracing their eyes and rode on as far as the horses could give. Eventually, the pair found a spot in the forest to rest.

Exhausted, Taryn sat slumped against a tree across from Airess later that night. He took out one of those cigars he had stolen and lit the butt with the fyre he had made.

Airess leaned against her own tree as she looked at him, a sly smile on her face. "Still don't believe in dark spirits now?"

"Yeah, yeah," Taryn said, eyes rolling as he exhaled a plume of smoke into the night. "Very funny, Haeleth."

Chapter 21

'I heard the Lucien twins attempted to recreate their own version of Tevye after what you did, but the spell went wrong. The Gods turned them into demons as retribution.'

— *Written correspondence from Pierce Moros to Evyen Deyanira*

Airess

It was entirely too ironic that they had no trouble finding their way out of The Twins after Taryn's horrible dream and the fight with the beast. It was as if they were being held there by a force, waiting to show him the vision he saw while dreamwalking, only letting them out once he had awoken.

She had seen the fear in Taryn's eyes upon his waking, knowing something had truly terrified him.

"It was – it was *insane*," Taryn said as he relayed the contents of his dream with a shaky breath. "It was a memory, but it wasn't mine. And the twin demons–they touched my fucking *face* and I couldn't do a thing about it. I was completely paralyzed in my dreamform."

"What did you see? Who's memory?" Airess pressed, her voice low as their horses trekked through the jagged switchbacks of the unfamiliar mountainland. The air was thick with the scent of damp moss, and fresh rainfall dripped off the canopy of leaves overhead. Never once had she ever been paralyzed in her dreamform. It sounded terrifying.

"I don't know who they were, but they were dressed in ancient robes. There were two people. One was an Elven male–Evyen was his name, I believe. The other was a Fae female. He called her Tinyrah. It seemed as if… they were lovers, and Evyen betrayed her. He pulled out this freshly bloodied crystal blade, stabbed it into the ground, and the world exploded. I don't know how else to describe it."

Airess had never heard of those names before, but she wasn't surprised the dreamworld had shown him something like this. It wasn't uncommon to observe random memories while dreamwalking.

"What do you mean the world exploded?"

Taryn shook his head. "Evyen had done something dark. Something powerful, and Tinyrah didn't want it to happen. He had done it anyway. He said–" Taryn looked up to the sky and bit his lip, as if recalling the memory. "He said *we can create a world we both want to live in.*"

"Do you think they were The Twin demons?" Airess asked, trying her best to piece together his dream.

"No," Taryn answered assuredly. "I don't think they were. At the end of my dream, those demons were trying to emulate what Evyen had done. It was as if they were trying to recreate whatever dark Magick he had attained."

Airess' intuition told her that this memory was important, something she needed to pay attention to. If The Twins were able to dreamwalk, what were they trying to tell Taryn?

"What do you think it means?"

"I don't know," Taryn said. "But it felt like a warning."

Over the following week, Airess and Taryn had traveled from dusk until dawn to put as much distance as they could from The Guild and the Lucien soldiers who were no doubt also on their trail.

In her spare time, she tried wielding her Magick when she could, but it felt impossible. This left her more frustrated, how was she able to wield so much power when they were bound in chains, or when she felt extreme fear?

At this point, Airess would do more damage with a dagger than her own power, and that wasn't saying much, considering Taryn was still only verbally teaching her *the basics*.

During their travels she had learned more about Taryn. Slowly, he began to open up to her. She still didn't know much about his past or how he came to live in Luciena, but she did learn his affinity for science and the heavens above.

At night before they fell asleep, they would lay on their backs so they could face the moon and stars. Every night Taryn would share stories he knew about the constellations. Some nights, he would retell facts he had learned previously from the library books he'd read in the past. Other nights he would stare at the moon and question their vast existence. Whatever it was he had to say, Airess found herself looking forward to his little lessons.

Tonight he pointed to the stars. "You see that one? Just a little to the left."

"I see it. The stars that look like a half circle?"

"Yes." Taryn nodded in Airess' peripheral, his deep voice rich. "But look closer. It's not just a half circle, there are points on the top that resemble a crown. *Yuleon's Crown*, my grandmother called it. Legend says it's the crown of the five main Gods written in the stars, hence all five points of the crown. Yuleon, the God of Gods, froze the Originals within time and space as a result of the five God's catastrophic rule here on earth."

"I've never heard of that story or the *God of Gods*. Is that another part of unspoken lore within Luciena?"

Taryn turned his head to look at her, his silver eyes glowing in the night. "It's unspoken in Luciena *and* Rune. My grandmother told me it is a long-forgotten history."

Airess turned on her side, propping her head up with her hand. "You don't mention your grandmother often."

Taryn looked away. "She taught me everything I know about the constellations and the Gods, it's where my fascination with them began," he paused, lowering the tone of his voice. "She passed when I was thirteen."

Airess swallowed, choosing her words carefully for her response. It was the first personal bit of information Taryn had shared with her and she wanted to respond respectfully. There was still so much about him she didn't know, *needed* to know, about him. Taryn was still very much a mystery, but had become... dare she think a *friend* over the past few weeks of traveling.

"I'm sure she would be proud that you've kept your passion after all these years." Airess finally replied.

Taryn frowned, his dark brows creasing in denial. "Not after what I've become."

"Is this – is this a *fair*?" Airess asked with surprise in her tone. Taryn looked down at her, his face laced with amusement at the excitement brewing in her wide eyes. She grinned.

Her hair had been entirely pulled back and concealed in a scarf, only two strands left free to frame her face. It was necessary to conceal her most distinct feature with wanted posters of her–of both of them–plastered around the town. Taryn opted to wear the hood on his cloak to cover his Fae ears, though it wasn't uncommon for Noborne Fae to walk amongst Zartown, a lower-income area.

Airess noticed the dark blue banners, a silver moon and golden stars stitched on the fabric. The street was bustling with countless vendors, smells of cooked meats and sweet pastries wafting through the air. A musician played nearby, a crowd of people around, singing along. They stomped to the melody, and a certain intensity thrummed through Airess' body at the sight of it.

"What are they celebrating?" Airess asked. They began to walk down the street. Taryn's protective hand hovering behind her back didn't go unnoticed. She glanced at his arm, and when their eyes met, his arm dropped, as if he didn't realize he was doing it. She ignored the disappointment at the loss of his touch.

"The sun and the moon Gods, Ghrian and Gealach. It's the year of the Salamoon. Each year they hold a different fair for each God."

"I wasn't aware people still worshiped the original Gods, much less have an entire celebration for them," Airess replied.

"The capital may only worship Bas, but the rest of the country still worships all five of the original Gods."

"That's right," Airess said. "The year of the Salamoon marks the year of Sun and Moon, only to recur every four years. Isn't it a bit early though for a celebration? The Salamoon is only a month or so away."

"I suppose it is. Though it is never too early to celebrate the upcoming new year," Taryn contemplated.

Airess chuckled quietly to herself, causing Taryn to raise a brow. "What's so funny?"

"Nothing. The Salamoon happens to be my birthday."

Taryn stopped walking, gently gripping her elbow to stop her. "The *Salamoon* falls on your birthday this year?"

"Well, yes," she said playfully, but her features melted as she noticed his doubtful look. "Why?"

Taryn shook his head. "That also happens to be… *my* birthday."

"What?" she said with a surprised look. "You were born on the same day four years before me?"

"I… suppose I was," Taryn said, scratching a nonexistent itch on the back of his neck. His gaze fell to the ground, a look Airess began to learn was deep contemplation.

"What are the odds?" Taryn asked her jokingly as they walked onward. Airess' eyes slid to his as the sunset glow painted his features. She couldn't deny it, he was a handsome Fae male –

"*You there*!" an old voice beckoned. Airess turned to the source. An elderly Human woman, draped in a vibrantly colored shawl, intensely stared at Airess. The woman's long gray hair was in a braid that fell down her back, but it was her stark blue eyes that stood out to Airess the most.

The woman sat in front of a small stand amongst the vendors, her booth enclosed with a tent that encircled her. Intricately illustrated cards, glittering crystals and lit candles were scattered amongst the table. The title of her sign read:

Mara's Fortunes and Prophecies!

"Can I interest you in a free reading, my dear?" Mara asked, a glint of mystery flashing within her gaze. Airess couldn't place it, but there was something about the woman drawing her in–as if the universe was trying to push her in the right direction, urging her to listen.

Out of the corner of her eye, she saw Taryn roll his eyes. Airess smirked, grabbed his hand, and dragged him toward Mara.

"Hello," Airess greeted awkwardly, sitting in front of Mara. The strong fragrance of perfume and the burning herbs on the table blasted Airess' nose. Airess stifled a cough and blinked her Sight forward, delighted to see such clean, pure energy the color of the sky enveloping the old woman.

"Ah, two threads weave together. One crimson. One emerald. What an interesting pair," Mara muttered, eyes darting between the two before she brought out a deck of cards. Airess' brows creased at the cryptic words, and she began to question what exactly she was walking into. Mara's thick stack of bracelets and rings clinked together as she began to shuffle the cards with ease, diverting her attention to Airess.

"Alright. You can choose the cards or fortune, but you can't have both! *That* would cost extra."

Airess glanced at Taryn, who currently leaned against the wooden post, a hand over his mouth to cover his laughter. She bit back her own grin, his playfulness awakening something deeper within her, a heat that spread from her heart, down to her toes.

When Airess realized she was staring at Taryn, she faced Mara and cleared her throat with a timid smile. "I'll go with the fortune, please."

Mara nodded. "Very well. We'll start with the palm reading first. Your hand, miss."

The old lady grabbed her hand, her grip surprisingly strong for her age. She flipped Airess' hand over to examine her palm, running a sharp fingernail down the center.

"Ah, this is certainly interesting," Mara noted. "In the beginning, I see a golden chain–a *cage*. There's struggle and resentment. Not so happy in this area of your life, I see."

Airess stilled, not particularly enjoying this being verbalized in front of Taryn.

"As we move down–oh! *This* line represents change, a new era of your life. This is where your growth begins and you find out your true self. But then…" Mara trailed off, frowning. A slight breeze picked up, bringing in a cold chill and rustling the tent fabric around them.

Airess sat up, her heart beginning to thrum. "What is it?"

"I see struggle and pain. I see anger–and *power*!" Mara chuckled, enthralled, before her smile faded away slowly.

Mara's eyes darkened. "Then… nothing. I cannot read beyond this point."

Silence fell between them. Airess shivered. What did she mean, *nothing*? That certainly was… disheartening. Not at all what she expected to hear.

The woman decorated her face with a smile once more and waved her hand, dismissing the words. "Oh well! Our Fate changes with each choice we make. Who knows what that could mean! Now, time for the fortune. Give me your other hand."

Airess obeyed, lifting her other hand from her lap and placing it in Mara's steel grip. Mara closed her eyes and nodded, as if she were listening to something. Softly, she began to whisper beneath her breath, muttering incoherent words. Then–

The fyre from the candles flared, the heat from the flames licking Airess' face. Mara's eyes shot open, head tilting to the sky. The fortune teller's blue irises had turned a milky gray, sending shivers down Airess' spine. Her heartbeat quickened as the fortune teller spoke–as if the words weren't her own.

"A stolen Death

A touch of Fyre

An earth rebirthed

To be made from desire

A soul of Mind

Brings forth the Storm

Is when the dawn of a new age

Shalt be born."

Mara inhaled a sharp breath and fell back in her seat, eyes still closed. Her grip on Airess' hands slackened. She began whispering rapidly again, her tone dipping and rising, speaking in a foreign language Airess had never heard before. At once, her head dropped. Mara brought a wrinkled hand to her forehead and pinched the bridge of her nose.

"What did you just say?" Taryn asked, suddenly interested, his brows raised. Recognition flashed in his eyes as he took a step forward and leaned over the table, mouth hung open.

"Ma'am, are you all right?" Airess asked softly.

When Mara opened her eyes, they were back to their original blue.

"Yes, I–I'm sorry," the fortune teller said, yanking her hand away, looking between Airess and Taryn. "The – the shop is now closed for the day. You both need to *leave*."

"Do you need any help–" Taryn started, before Mara stood abruptly, the chair scraping against the stone beneath them, cutting him off. Taryn backed off as Mara shooed him away. She grabbed her coin jar and looked directly at Airess.

"Be weary. The Vulture preys on the owl."

It was the last thing she said before she scurried off, as if she was scared of them.

Unsure of what just happened, Airess rose to her feet and watched the woman hobble away.

"What the hell was that?" Taryn demanded, talking with his hands. His face was twisted with confusion, mouth parted open before he closed it again. "What does that mean, *The Vulture preys on the owl?*"

Airess bristled at the thought. Mara had said many things, most of which didn't make sense, but Airess knew better than to brush it off. She was surprised, however, how invested Taryn had suddenly become.

"You seem quite interested for someone so skeptical," Airess teased, but when his eyes flashed with an emotion she couldn't name, she pivoted her body towards him.

"What is it?" Airess asked.

He stared after Mara as she melted into the crowd of the bustling street, clearly grappling with something she had said. Airess grabbed Taryn's wrist softly. His head swiveled to hers, their gazes meeting. There was an urgency she wasn't able to decipher in his eyes.

"Taryn, what's wrong?"

He glanced at her hand, and his expression softened. She watched his face closely as it shifted– first soft, then hardening—-until he wore his usual sarcastic grin.

"It was probably just another part of her theatrics. Don't let it bother you." He said matter-of-factly, brushing off her concern.

"I suppose," Airess commented, wanting to say more, but the growl from her stomach pulled her from her thoughts. She brought a hand to her abdomen. Taryn glanced at her hand, not missing the movement.

"Are you hungry?"

She nodded sheepishly, remembering he could hear far better than she could. Hungry was an understatement. She was *starving*.

Taryn smirked. "I know just the place."

He led her down the street towards the food vendors, guiding them forward with his hand in hers. It was a subtle action, but his touch ignited something within her, heating her entire body. She craned her neck to look at the side of his face as they trekked forward, and couldn't shake the feeling that Taryn was hiding something.

And he had lied about it.

Chapter 22

'I've seen it. When the wall breaks, it is only the beginning. The prophecy will unfold. It is only a matter of when.'

— *Written entry from Paulyr Moros' personal journal*

Taryn

"I'll have ale, please," Airess said to the barmaid and took a bite out of the sourdough bread that was left on the table. Taryn ordered the same and popped a piece of bread in his mouth, chewing as he scanned the tavern.

The crackling hearth cast dim, flickering light across the space. The low murmur of conversation hummed beneath the occasional burst of drunken laughter. The tavern seemed harmless enough, but Airess still wore her headscarf and Taryn his cloak. He didn't want to take any chances on risking them getting caught.

So far, so good.

"What did you think about what Mara said?" Airess asked, her gaze pinned on him, brows creased in determination.

Right. The fortune teller.

It was a completely bizarre encounter. Taryn didn't know what to make of it, but he recognized the words instantly.

A stolen Death. A touch of Fyre.

Those were the words the Elve had said while Taryn killed him in the alleyway. And what Mara had said about The Vulture *preying* on the Owl? He couldn't shake the words out of his head. He knew it meant something, but he didn't know how they connected.

Who was The Vulture?

The question was eating at him. Taryn couldn't tell Airess. How could he possibly explain it without her thinking he was crazy? What would she think of him if he told her? Perhaps it wouldn't matter. Perhaps everything Mara said had been a sham. Taryn tried to rationalize it, tried to make sense of it, but he couldn't. He refused to believe it meant anything at all.

But deep inside, he knew he was lying to himself. He didn't *want* to know or make sense of it.

"Do you honestly believe a word she said?" Taryn asked, brushing off Airess' curiosity. He swallowed the guilt that came along with holding something back from her.

Airess blinked once, scanning him up and down. His heartbeat quickened, realizing she was using her Sight on him. *That damn ability.* He had almost forgotten about it.

Finally, she replied. "I don't know, Taryn. The thing she said about being in a cage… it wasn't inaccurate. What she said afterward about not seeing anything in my future and–and what about that *poem*? It was quite unnerving."

Taryn leveled a stare at her, eyes trailing down her face. He drank her in. The glow of her gilded irises. The two tendrils of silver hair framing her beautiful face. Her lips were pursed in thought, as if Mara's words disappointed her. Taryn wished he could kiss the disappointment right off her face–

He stilled. The thought sobered him and he wasn't even drunk. *Gods.*

Taryn cleared his throat. "Don't pay her words any mind. There's nothing to worry about. You'll have a wonderful future in Rune," Taryn said softly. "I promise."

The barmaid returned with two large mugs of dark ale and turkey legs the size of Taryn's arm, accompanied by roasted vegetables. The smell reminded him of his earlier years at the Guild when he and Raiden frequented this bar during training.

"*Ugh*, Gods. I needed this." Airess said as she took a swig from her mug.

"I thought you said you didn't like ale?" Taryn asked, intentionally changing the subject.

He recalled that she told him she was only ever offered a small glass of wine on special occasions while living at the castle. The thought alone made his blood boil, considering the reasoning was to keep her body pure and healthy for childbearing. *For Arzhel.*

The thought alone made his blood run hot with fury. Taryn swore to all five Gods that if he were to ever see the Luciens again, he would rip their hearts out. One by one.

"I'm trying new things," she said with her fingers clasped together and leaned in. "Here I am, alive and free against all the odds stacked against me–against *us*. I believe this night calls for celebration."

Taryn smirked and raised his mug. "Then celebrate we shall."

Airess clanked her glass against his and took a sip. She slammed the mug down and wiped her mouth with her cloak sleeve. "This has been the most fun I've had in my entire life," she blurted out and blinked, as if the words weren't meant to leave her.

Airess looked around and studied the folk around them. Taryn saw the curiosity in her gaze before picking up her turkey leg and taking a huge bite. Taryn smiled, realizing she was trying to emulate the folk around them. He started eating as well, enjoying the greasy food with the tavern musicians playing loudly at the front of the bar.

"And now we will open the floor to any singers who might be in this tavern tonight!" the Human man at the front projected out. The music died down as he looked around for any takers.

Airess' wide eyes met Taryn's.

He had come to learn her musical talent of singing, catching her humming to herself through the night when she thought he was asleep. He didn't mind it, her voice was a melody he hadn't known he needed, lulling him to sleep with a warmth of a thousand fyres.

One night he had come back to their campsite, and Airess was singing out loud, her back to him as she sat atop of a stone. He waited, letting her get the music out of her system and sparing her the embarrassment of getting caught.

Taryn looked at her now, her face full of angst and longing to perform. She cleared her throat. "Should I..." she trailed off, already losing confidence in herself. Taryn looked around them for any potential threats, any Lucien guards that could possibly stop them, and found none.

"Go for it." Taryn nodded in encouragement, his eyes bright. Maybe it was the ale and the atmosphere that dulled his usual alertness, but tonight he felt different. Lighter.

Lighter, with her. He wanted her to feel this moment entirely. He wanted to experience this *with* her. The thought surprised him.

Airess stood abruptly and sifted through the folk loitering the front. "We have a singer! What's your name, dear?" the man asked her.

"Scarlett," Airess answered confidently, the lie rolling off her tongue like butter. Taryn sat back in his chair, a slight grin on his face as he sipped his beer, nodding to Airess in encouragement as they made eye contact through the crowd. She averted her eyes shyly as the man asked her what song she would be singing. She turned and whispered it into his ear with a smile.

The fiddler began to play a familiar tune. Airess closed her eyes and began to sing a melody so sweet that Taryn's heart quelled at the sound, singing a distant Runean song he heard what felt like a lifetime ago in his childhood.

Her eyes locked with him while she sang. Surprise coursed through him at how fluent the words flowed out of her. Her voice was like a melody that hadn't been heard in a millennia, the answer to all his prayers and the center of all his desires. Her voice filled the tavern like sunlight through an old window, gracing the surface of things that hadn't been touched in ages.

A chair scraped the floor beside him and someone filled the space. "Seat's taken–" Taryn began as he pivoted his body to face whoever dared to sit near him before his jaw fell open.

"I didn't think you would mind." Raiden said, a coldness in his brown eyes. Raiden sat back comfortably with his legs crossed, watching Airess intently. Taryn's heart thundered with panic. Where one Guild member went, others followed. Taryn masked his panic with indifference and glanced around the pub.

"Don't worry, I came alone. Though, it won't be too much longer before the rest catch up." Raiden glanced between Airess and Taryn, suspicion in his gaze. "You have some explaining to do, Tar. Eryx is *furious*."

Taryn had to think of something that would prove him loyal to the Guild, something that would make sense. "I sold my ring to fund my travels," Taryn began. "I've been tracking–"

Raiden shook his head and waved his hand in a gesture to tell him to save it. "After everything we've been through, you would still lie straight to my face? It's as if I don't even know you anymore."

Taryn closed his eyes at the words, and shook his head. "I don't expect you to understand –"

"Then *make* me understand. Were you ever planning on returning?" Raiden's coldness faltered just enough for Taryn to see the brother he had grown up with, trained with, since they were teenagers. Taryn finally understood that Raiden had come alone on purpose, without the other Guild members, to spare him from whatever punishment that would eventually transpire.

"No," Taryn admitted shamelessly, and leveled a stare at him.

Raiden scoffed with a bitter smile and folded his arms, his eyes averting to Airess once more. "You get one taste of aristocrat pussy, and decide to ditch the people that saved your life when you were lying half dead in a ditch at fourteen years old? I've got to give it to you, I never thought a female would have you so tightly wound around her finger you'd betray the only people who were there for you."

Fuck. He knows it's Airess up on the stage.

Taryn's jaw tightened as he leaned closer to Raiden, his voice hushed as he gritted out, "Believe whatever you want but that's *not* what this is. I was thrown in jail with her chained in *Donstenyte*, Raiden, and her power was so great that she broke the chains, and set us free. Did you really think you, or I could simply *capture* her? I don't know what fucked up plans Eryx has for her, but I'm done being a pawn in his schemes. His drug deals. His assassinations. I've got more blood on my hands than I ever wanted. *I'm fucking done.*"

"Godsdamned idiot," Raiden scolded. He shook his head and leaned in. "Two weeks, Taryn. I'm giving you two weeks to get yourself out of whatever *this* is and turn the girl in to us. The only reason Eryx hasn't used the Oathmark is because he doesn't think you've betrayed the Guild. *Yet.* As soon as he finds out, he will obliterate you."

"How do you do it?" Taryn asked with his brows furrowed, "How do you blindly serve him? When we were boys I used to think what we were doing was a service to Mrkynia, to the *realm*. Mrkynia has fallen and will never rise again. Eryx is using us and has his own agenda, Raiden. I know it."

"You truly were planning on leaving, weren't you?" Raiden asked sharply. Taryn's jaw tensed, but he knew better to keep his mouth shut. Friends or not, Raiden couldn't know his plans going forward. He was too loyal to Eryx.

"I'm a Human man, " Raiden said. "What choice do I have, other than staying with the people who made me? I don't have Magick like you or her," Raiden gestured a hand toward Airess.

Airess' brow furrowed as she noticed Raiden from across the room, her song slowly fading off.

"Two weeks, Taryn, or I have no choice but to come after you." Raiden stood abruptly. "And do yourself a favor, if you're going to fuck her, at least don't fall in love with her, man."

"*Watch your mouth.* I told you I'm not fucking–"

"Two weeks," Raiden said stiffly before striding away, clipping Airess' shoulder without a second glance as he stormed out of the bar. She whipped around to say something to Raiden, but he was already gone.

Airess strode to Taryn, when an older Elven male grabbed her arm and stopped her mid-walk, "That was some fine singing, girl. Tell me, do you perform any private shows?"

A deep growl rumbled in Taryn's throat as he approached, Taryn's eyes widened in a rage when he smelt the arousal coming from the male. The male smacked his lips, ogling Airess like she was an object he could use. Taryn's vision ran red, an excessive reaction, but he couldn't control it. He couldn't control the anger that budded within.

"I–" Airess began, but Taryn had already grabbed the male's arm and ripped it away, yanking him up in such a disfigured angle, his forearm snapped. The crunch of bone was so audible, the folk around them fell silent as the male screamed.

Taryn shoved the male to the floor as he replied, "I don't believe she does."

Silence fell over the room. The weight of his actions settled within him after the irrational, blind rage began to fade. He remembered himself, that they both needed to get out of here. Taryn put an arm over Airess' shoulder and quickly guided her out of the bar. "We have to go."

The pair walked out swiftly into the night, cool air hitting their faces, the cobblestone crunching beneath their boots. When they were far enough from other patrons lingering the street, Airess sidestepped away from his arm, her cheeks red. "You didn't have to cause a scene and break his arm, he must have been drunk and wasn't thinking–"

"I don't give a *fuck* if he was drunk. He was touching you," he said emotionlessly. Taryn knew his reaction was... excessive, but he couldn't understand why he had felt such intense anger in that moment. It was uncontrollable. Taryn straightened his spine.

Get a grip.

"We need to leave. We've drawn too much attention to ourselves."

Airess' cheeks burned scarlet, a sight he had yet to see from her. "Who was that man you were talking to back there?" She asked accusingly as they rushed to their horses in the stallhouse.

"A friend."

"A *friend?*" She stopped and blinked, her hands on her hips. "And what friend is this, someone from the Guild?"

"Yes, I promise I'll explain, but we have to *go*. I don't know how far out the others are," Taryn said as he looked beyond her, scanning their surroundings, a hint of panic rising in his tone.

Airess narrowed her eyes, assessing him, doubt creeping over her features. Taryn saw the possibilities she must be thinking of within her mind, a flash of fear coming over her face.

Airess fell silent before lunging at him quickly, her hand reaching for the dagger Taryn wore for her at his belt.

She was too slow, Taryn grabbed her forearms and yanked her towards him, her body slamming into his, their faces so close their noses could touch. Her breath hitched as her chest pressed against his. Taryn smirked, towering over her. She didn't trust him, and he didn't blame her for it.

Airess' brows knitted together in frustration as she glanced to his hands gripping her arms and whispered, "Are you going to betray me, Taryn?"

So close. His gaze lingered down her gilded irises, her constellation of freckles and sultry lips. So close to touching her, kissing her, running his fingers through her hair. His eyes widened, the alcohol letting his stream of forbidden thoughts flow freely now. Taryn no longer shook the thoughts that intruded into his head. He gladly welcomed them now, no matter how wrong they were.

He wasn't sure why he was answering this way, his silver eyes boring into hers, "No, Airess. Never."

It was the first time he had used her first name, their relationship–*friendship*–entering a new depth.

Airess loosened a breath before glancing at his hands on her arms. He quickly dropped his grip and took a step back to put distance between them, not realizing his heavy breathing until they've separated.

It took all of Taryn's strength to turn and walk towards the stallhouse. "Are you coming or not?" He said casually over his shoulder and felt agonizing relief when she fell in step beside him.

Chapter 23

'We are the remnants of burning stars.'

— *Excerpt from House Deyanira's personal history book*

Airess

"A *twig*?" Airess asked as she held the six-inch-long stick up to eye level. Taryn stood across from her, his feet planted to the ground in a position that could only be muscle memory with how easy it came to him. He held up his own stick in a defensive position and cocked his head to the side.

"Did you think we would be using real daggers?" He laughed, his head tilting back in genuine amusement. The sight of it brought a grin to her face. Airess tried her best to fight off, but failed. Taryn's canines glinted in the night from the reflection of the fyre a few feet away from them.

"Unless you want to accidentally hurt yourself, you'll find the *twigs* useful for your lessons. Now, assume a stance similar to mine."

She mimicked his stance, planting her feet firmly to the ground. She held the dagger up with amateur skill as she tried to figure out the best way to hold her weapon. He dropped his stance and walked up to her, his fingers gently tilted her elbow upward. The heat of his touch ignited a fyre within her. Taryn's other hand lightly guided her wrist in front of her center. The softness of his touch surprised her.

Has she ever known a male to be so gentle, besides her own father?

Her brows creased at the intrusive thought, and she swallowed it down. No need to pay old memories any mind. *Focus.*

It was certainly hard to focus as they locked eyes. For the first time, she saw something deeper behind those silver eyes—an emotion richer than his usual amusement, his cloak of sarcasm and humor failing him in this moment. His pupils dilated, his eyes trailing down her face, down to her lips.

Taryn coughed and stepped away, breaking the tension. He assumed an offensive position, clearing his throat as if he didn't just look at her like he wanted to taste her. Her entire body heated at the thought.

"I moved your arms so your weapon would guard your heart. Now, let's see what you've got. Go ahead, strike me." He tilted his head in encouragement, a subtle smirk on his pretty mouth.

Confident bastard.

She struck forward recklessly, not really knowing what her legs were doing as she jabbed her twig toward Taryn's heart. Airess barely registered Taryn swiping her twig out of her hand, the wood now fallen onto the forest ground.

He clicked his tongue. "First lesson," Taryn picked up the twig and handed it back to her, "It's better to start from an angle. You want to be able to cover as much area as you can. You're quick, so this move would benefit you if you ever had to engage in combat. Like this." He drew his twig behind his shoulder and slashed directly across in front of him.

Airess emulated his demonstration, making sure to slash her twig across from her right shoulder to left hip.

Taryn nodded in approval and sidestepped away from the tree. "Good. Now practice on this tree. Get a feel for striking something solid."

She gave him a weary look but obliged—only getting a few slashes in before her twig broke in half. Airess thought they would move on to another move, but Taryn replaced her twig with a thicker, sturdier one each time.

"Again." He said, his muscled forearms crossed as he watched her.

So she struck.

Again and again and again.

Hours later, the pair agreed to find an Inn to stay at for the night. They had both grown tired of camping out for over a month on end, and with them being so close to the edge of the continent, Airess thought it would be a wonderful idea to finally sleep in a real bed.

They approached the small, quaint Inn and walked through its worn-down entryway. Half-torn wall paper hung off the walls, and the Inn smelled of cigar smoke and clean linens. The floorboards creaked as they approached the desk where the Innkeeper sat, currently smoking.

"We'd like a room, please." Airess inquired tentatively, trying her best to muster an innocent smile.

"You're in luck! We have one room vacant upstairs, fourth door to the left. Bathing chambers on the first floor." The innkeeper's wrinkled hands handed the key over to Airess with a sweet smile, "A lovely room for a *lovely* couple. Oh, won't you two make beautiful babies!"

Airess' cheeks immediately heated at the assumption, "Actually, we –"

"Thank you, ma'am." Taryn said stiffly, giving the innkeeper a brisk nod. As they ascended up the wooden stairs in silence, Airess heard the old woman snickering.

That old bat knew what she was doing.

Taryn unlocked the door and abruptly came to a halt midway in the door frame.

"What is it?" Airess asked as he sidestepped for her to come in and closed the door behind them.

Oh.

The room was simple and small. The walls and floor were all made from wooden planks. An undersized rug lay in the middle of the floor. A medium sized bed, just big enough to squeeze in two people, sat flushed against the corner. A painting of an owl hung crooked on the wall and an oil lamp on the bedside table.

How odd. The animal always made appearances in her life, but those thoughts were stuffed down as Airess was still reeling from the innkeeper's comment.

Taryn scratched the back of his neck as he said, "I'll sleep on the floor."

"No, it's okay. I can–"

Taryn laughed, his vibrato deep and rich, "Please, Airess, I insist. If my grandmother were still alive she would have my *head* if I let you sleep on the floor." He set his satchel down and lit the wick in the oil lamp.

Airess shuffled on her feet. "I'm going to the bathing chambers." She spun on her heel, the door slamming shut behind her as she made her way to bathe.

Airess didn't know why her heart was pounding so much, why the innkeepers comments about them making *beautiful babies* drew forward thoughts about him–*absolutely wrong* thoughts she was trying her best to rebuke. She didn't need to think about his muscled chest, the way sweat rolled down the sides of his face, slicking past his scar that she couldn't help find attractive.

She didn't need to think about running her fingers through his loose curls, the dangle of his earring when he laughed, or his piercing silver eyes that seemed to see right through her, or the fact that she had to arch her head all the way up to look at him.

His gentle fingers–

Oh, Air, get a hold of yourself!

Airess walked into the bathing chamber to find a bath already drawn and warmed. She thanked the gods for at least making *this* part of her journey easy. She glanced around the room as she pulled her cloak off and began to undress.

She stepped in the tub and quite literally *sank* into the water, the heat bringing a comfort she had often at the castle. Never again would she take any luxuries for granted. At last, Airess exhaled an audible sigh, releasing a tension that had been building up the entire journey.

One more week. They would make it to her hometown, Judla, and finally cross *Finlan's Passage*. Excitement and dread brewed in her chest. She was ready to meet the priestesses in Rune and learn about her power, ready to make a life worth living for herself. She was more than ready to escape Luciena for good and leave this nightmare behind her.

But along with all of the excitement, came dread.

Airess never expected to feel dread at the end of her travels… but she did. She could no longer deny she had grown fond of Taryn, *more* than fond, that is. Would they go their separate ways for good, or would he leave her behind?

After her much needed bath, Airess finally dried off and reclothed. When she went to grab the heart locket Esper had given her, the locket slipped and fell to the ground.

Click!

Metal clicked against metal. Airess bent down to inspect and realized the necklace had split open. Her heart dropped, thinking the necklace had broken until she brought it closer to her eyes

No, not broken. The locket had opened!

Airess' brows creased as she brought the necklace closer to the oil lamp. Inside the locket was an engraving of text:

Deyanira

It looked like a name, and one that struck her to her very core. *Deyanira*. Why did it sound so familiar?

After a few seconds, Airess closed it, clutching the jewelry in her fist and headed back to the room. Call her superstitious, but she couldn't help but feel like she was on the brink of discovering something life-altering.

Airess finally settled into bed and stared at the ceiling as Taryn rustled to get comfortable on the floor.

"Well, this is certainly better than camping out on the forest floor." Airess said, breaking the silence. "Only one more week."

"One more week." Taryn replied weakly. Airess noted the doubt lacing in his voice and frowned.

"Aren't you excited to finally go home?"

"I am. It's just been so long."

Airess sat up and looked at him. Taryn was lying on his back, shirtless, with his arms folded behind his head. She studied the sleeve of tattoos inked in red on one arm, particularly the dragon depicted on his bicep. She wondered what made him choose the extinct animal.

His gaze snapped to hers, and the thin nightdress she wore. He ripped his eyes back to her face as quickly as he could and swallowed.

"Taryn, what happened all those years ago? How did you end up in Luciena?" Airess whispered, softly asking for an opening into Taryn's mind.

For a moment, she thought that he wasn't going to answer. He swallowed and closed his eyes. "I was fourteen years old when Rune drafted all the young males into the war on Luciena. The war had taken a toll on our population, so we were all that they had left. I was young and eager, and gladly welcomed being shipped off to war after the loss of my grandmother and… becoming homeless.

"But when we arrived on Luciena's beaches, we were severely outnumbered. The Luciens had created these – these *explosives*. A device that wielded power that no war had ever seen before. I fought as long as I could, I really did. But then…"

Taryn loosened a breath. "I barely remember what happened. An explosive landed near me. I woke up ten feet away, in a ditch, bleeding to death. That's when Eryx, the leader of the Mrkynian Guild, found me."

Airess stilled, not realizing she was gripping the fabric of the quilt until Taryn spoke again, "He made me a deal I couldn't refuse, offering me shelter and a place to belong. Hell, I was *fourteen*. I gladly took his offer. It didn't matter how steep the price was."

His gaze slid over to her, and for the first time, she identified the raw emotion in his eyes. Regret. Pain. Loneliness. Airess couldn't bear it.

"Come up here," she said softly.

"Airess, I–"

"We haven't slept in a proper bed in over a month. You shouldn't be sleeping on the floor. Come up here."

A beat of silence passed before Taryn stood up. Airess scooted over to one side of the bed to make room for him as he grabbed his quilt and slowly sank into the mattress. His bulky figure stayed to one side of the bed, careful not to touch her. Airess didn't have Fae hearing, but she was pretty sure his heart was beating just as loud as hers was. The thought at first embarrassed her, knowing he could hear the thumping of *her* heart, but she no longer wanted to deny herself.

Taryn lay on his back, legs out long, and stared at the ceiling. Airess finally got the courage to turn on her side, her hand holding up her head as she spoke to him softly, "Have you thought about the first place you'll go when we make it to Rune?"

Taryn turned to face her, mirroring that same position, looking at her through his dark lashes. Something about this room, this bed, the way they were looking at each other, felt infinitely more intimate than any training lesson or night they had spent together in the woods. They were allowing a deeper part of themselves to be seen, Airess realized.

She didn't know if the thought comforted her or scared her.

"My childhood home. If it's still there, of course." Taryn replied with a soft smile, his canines visible as the moonlight shone directly on him through the window. "Have you thought about what you will do?" he asked hesitantly.

"Well… there's this group I intend to seek out." Airess paused, deciding if she wanted to reveal what Esper had directed her to do. Taryn watched her intently, his facial expression eager to hear her words. Airess had grown to trust Taryn over their travels, and deemed it safe to tell him at last.

"It's called *The Obadiah*, a group of Priestesses who say they can help me learn more about my Magick. One of their members was the one who helped me escape the engagement ball, you know, the one that I told you about."

Taryn sat up, suddenly serious, "Do you mean the temple Priestesses?"

"I'm not sure. When I spoke with Esper, she said there was much I needed to learn. That this was *only the beginning*." Airess looked down. "I'm not so sure what to believe. Hopefully they can teach me more about my power and why it is so rare."

She looked up to him with a grin. She was finally allowing herself to think of the future after so long.

"But I also want more. I want to create a life for myself. I want a flat, a job. I want to *live*."

Taryn's eyes crinkled with kindness. He reached out and tucked a stray hair behind her ear, that caused goosebumps to travel down her body. "I'll support anything you decide."

She looked into his eyes, mesmerized. A palpable energy thrummed between them. Her body ignited, her flesh sizzling with need as his gaze dropped to her lips. Taryn's pupils darkened as he drank her in, and suddenly the energy shifted into something more primal.

Airess reached out her hand to his scarred temple, her fingers running along the side of his face and resting at his jaw, never breaking eye contact. She had never touched a male like this before.

Taryn groaned.

He wasted no time. He cupped her face, fingers running through her hair. Their bodies pressed together, legs intertwined. He angled her head up to look at him and ran his thumb over her lips. Subtly, she nodded.

He ran another hand alongside her face, drawing his touch down her neck and to her collarbones, leaving shocks of electricity in his wake. The heat within her burned hotter. She gripped the back of his neck, needing him closer.

Taryn's nostrils flared, and his eyelids grew heavy. It was a look she had never seen before from him, and the sight of it made the need between her legs *ache*. Airess thought she might burst if he didn't touch her further–

Taryn pulled back, removing his hands from her body. He cupped her face possessively, and forced her head to look up at him. His arms shook, as if he was trying his best to control himself.

"*Say it.*" He growled.

The words sent heat spreading through her body. Airess lost all breath. All words. Her heart pounded incessantly with a mixture of nerves and excitement. She was utterly enthralled by him.

"Yes–" she breathed out, but her permission was lost on his lips crashing into hers. Electricity ignited her entire body at the contact. Even her *Magick* responded, rising to the forefront of her mind. The kiss was urgent, frantic, even. Taryn tasted like the ocean and earth as their lips moved together in perfect sync. She let out a breathless moan.

Airess hadn't realized just how much she wanted–*needed* to kiss him until now.

Taryn shifted, his body hovering over hers in a matter of seconds. His tongue grazed over her lips. Instinctually, she opened for him, their tongues dancing together. Her heart fluttered, never had she ever kissed a male before until now. Her cheeks heated with his hands now weaving into her hair, as if he needed to feel every inch of her.

He broke the kiss, taking a moment to scan her face. His lips were red, hair disheveled. He ran a thumb along her cheekbone.

"Perfect." He ground out, "You are so damned perfect."

And then his lips were on her jaw. Her neck. He sucked and nipped the soft flesh between the crook of her neck. Liquid heat pooled between her thighs as she trailed her hands down his muscled chest–

Taryn abruptly pulled back and hissed in pain. Airess' eyes flew open in shock, immediately drawn to the dragon tattoo on his shoulder now glowing. He rolled to the side, gripping his shoulder with his free hand as he bit down on the quilt to stifle his cries.

Airess sat up quickly, eyes wide as she watched him tremble in pain.

"What's wrong? What's happening?"

In between breaths Taryn breathed out, "It's fine. It'll –" He grimaced again like he was being flayed from the inside out. "It'll pass."

Airess got to her knees and pried Taryn's hand off his tattoo, revealing the black glow that replaced the red ink. "Oh my gods! What is that?"

She pressed her palm onto the tattoo and gritted her teeth as she felt *pain.*

His pain.

She held her hand steady and felt it all–felt Taryn's pain from his childhood, his teenagehood and every terrible moment in between all meshing together to one horrible feeling. In a moment of panic, her hand began to glow, the sparkling light coating her hand like a glove. Without a second thought, Airess pressed her illuminated hand into Taryn's tattoo.

The black light began to fade.

At last, the pain ebbed away unwillingly. Resentfully. Taryn grabbed Airess' wrist lightly and moved it off his arm. "How did you do that?" He whispered coarsely.

"I don't know." Airess admitted, removing the quilt off Taryn and instinctively wiping the bead of sweat off his brow. "Are you okay? What just happened?"

Taryn closed his eyes and sat up slowly in the bed, shifting his body to face her. "There's something you should know."

Airess sat back, her knees touching his in a comfortable vicinity. Her brows drew together in response.

"I did more than swear a simple Oath to the Mrkynian Guild when I was a teenager. I swore my loyalty with the Oathmark." Taryn raised his bicep and ran his fingers along the tattoo.

"I didn't understand what it meant at the time. I thought I was getting a tattoo to prove my loyalty and willingness. Little did I know, I had made the biggest mistake of my life.

"This mark... it controls me. Eryx controls me through it, and everyone else at The Guild. He inflicts pain if we don't comply, physically and emotionally. He can splinter the minds of anyone who swore the Oathmark to him."

Airess' stomach twisted at the words. She recalled Taryn telling her *he didn't have a choice* whenever he had abducted her after the engagement ball. She had thought it was a matter of social coercion, not *this*.

"He uses it to control hundreds of members. Some of them are so loyal to Mrkynia that they *wanted* the Oathmark. Others who started young were unaware such a thing even existed." Taryn's head dipped low.

"I've only made it this far without him killing me because Raiden is steering him the other direction."

Airess' mouth parted. How long had she sat next to him in oblivion of his impending death sentence? How many times had she doubted him, thought he would betray her, when he was literally refusing to capture her despite the Oathmark?

"We can fix this. I don't know how, but my Magick subsided the pain. We can make it to Rune, and I can learn to control my power. I can help you." She reasoned, her voice appearing cool and confident.

Inside, she was trying her best to keep it together.

Taryn gave her a sad smile. "I'm open to anything at this point."

"Just… try to get some rest," Airess said wearily, eyes scanning over his brow beaded with sweat. His shaky breath was alarming. Airess had never seen him so vulnerable before, and it shook her to her very core.

Taryn wore a pained expression, eyes wide and mouth parting as if he was going to say more. He swallowed.

"Okay," he whispered back, his voice faint.

She thought about his Oathmark over and over again until she fell asleep, making a promise to herself that she would save him.

Airess stood at the back of two males clad in onyx cloaks, their boots thumping the puddle-ridden cobblestone street from the rainfall overhead. They swiftly turned around the corner to a street lined with run down wooden apartments and stopped before a door. Airess followed behind as she heard a dagger being unsheathed. The figures turned to face each other.

Her breath hitched at the sight of those familiar steel eyes. "Taryn." She whispered as recognition hit her. It was him–but he had to be in his early teenage years. His curly hair was cropped short, there was no scar running down on the side of his temple and cheek. The plumpness of youth filled his face as his head snapped in Airess' direction, looking directly at her. Her eyes widened—could he really see her?

He looked through her and beyond before turning his attention to his accomplice—who she now recognized to be a younger version of his friend, Raiden, from the tavern in the waking world. Gods, they looked young. Airess never asked Taryn the extent of their friendship, but from the looks of it, they had been friends far longer than Airess had envisioned.

"I can't do this," young Taryn said, his voice slightly lighter than she was used to at this moment. Taryn looked down at the blade in his hand with uncertainty, his hand slightly trembling.

"You have to or Eryx will kill you, remember? To join the Guild you must kill, or be killed. You will be initiated as soon as we return," Raiden stated. "Be quick. I'll be right outside." His friend assured him quietly. Taryn gripped the blade, turned to face the door, and knelt to pick the lock quietly.

The lock clicked. Taryn slipped through the door. Airess walked through it and entered a barren room. There was only a bed in the corner, and a fireplace. A man and woman swayed together in front of the fire, the man holding her hand up with the other on her hip. They startled as soon as Taryn burst into the space.

"Arther Crux," Taryn's voice wavered as he held up the blade. "Eryx Mrkynia, the rightful ruler of this continent, hereby sentences you to death."

Arther grabbed a knife sitting nearby and pushed the woman to the side, "Go!" Arther told her. "Go get help!" The woman ran out of the room without Taryn sparing her a second glance.

"I told Eryx of the shortage, the gate is closed!" Arthur exclaimed.

"I have no choice but to kill you," Taryn said as his voice broke and lunged for the man. The man was quick enough to block Taryn's strike with his knife, using his fully grown height over Taryn's adolescence to sideswipe and cut his abdomen. It wasn't a fatal cut, but enough to make Taryn groan in pain.

Taryn gritted his teeth and struck again, missing, his move falling too short. His mistake cost him as the man swiped his knife on the side of Taryn's face, the skin from his temple splitting all the way down his cheek and jaw. Blood rushed out of the wound like a river as Taryn screamed out. The man lunged for him, the pair tumbling to the ground.

This wasn't the Taryn she knew, the male who had refined his skills so perfectly he had the reflexes of lightning. No, this was an untrained boy who had barely begun growing up, and had fallen into the wrong path in life. Pain unexpectedly welled in her chest. For him. For the boy who was forced to be a male too quickly.

Arther plunged his knife down in self-defense, one hand pinning Taryn's shoulder. Taryn blocked his blade with his dagger, the point of the knife so close to Taryn's eye.

"You're weak," Arthur said. "Not cut out for this kind of work."

Airess' heart pounded wildly at the violent display. Taryn bared his teeth, exposing his Fae canines, and bit down on the arm that pinned his shoulder down. The canines sank in deep. The man cried out, retracting his arm on instinct and losing focus of the hand holding the knife momentarily, giving Taryn a split moment to flip their positions.

Blood ran down Taryn's face and mouth, his teeth stained in the red substance. A tear had begun to roll down Taryn's cheek as he didn't waste another moment to plunge his knife into the man's heart, the fight coming to an abrupt, and brutal end.

Arthur had ceased fighting, his arms falling to his sides. Metal clanged against the floor as Arther dropped his knife and looked Taryn in the eyes.

"Look at me," Arthur said. Taryn stared, mortification overcoming his features as he dropped his dagger.

"You'll regret that Oath," Arthur sputtered, wheezing for breath. "As I h-have." Arthur looked to the ceiling, becoming void, his chest no longer rising with his breath.

Taryn let out a strangled sob before stifling it, reaching out a shaking hand and closed the man's eyelids. He grabbed his dagger and took a step back, his eyes wide in horror as he took in the image of the dead man on the floor. Then, Taryn bolted out of the door. Airess followed.

Taryn ran out and fell to his knees as he vomited onto the street. Raiden knelt down next to him and placed a hand on his shoulder.

"I did it." Taryn managed to get out between sobs, his body heaving. Airess walked up slowly and placed her translucent hand on his back. Even though he couldn't feel or see her, she felt it was the right thing to do.

Airess sat straight up as she jolted awake from her dream. Tears streamed down her face. She had woken up before Taryn, just before dawn, with the sun just beginning to rise. She had seen an intimate, painful part of his past. A side of him he hadn't revealed to her. Airess tried her best to grapple with what she had seen. He was only fourteen years old, and he had become a killer. He murdered that man in cold blood.

At once, guilt welled within her. Airess' chest tightened at the confusing feelings. Not because she viewed him any differently, but because, despite scratching the surface of what Taryn has done in his life... she couldn't find it within herself to care. To hate him. His darkness entranced her, pulled her in. And that was the scariest part of it all.

She glanced at him, his face peaceful as he slept, his head tilted at an angle that gave her the perfect view of the scar on his temple.

Chapter 24

'My brother is an imposter. He is not the man he claims to be. Do not trust him.'

— *Unsent written correspondence from Paulyr Moros*

The Vulture

"I don't understand," The Vulture whispered in the dark alleyway. "Why do you need me to stay in the capitol? Your targets could very well be on their way off of the continent by now."

Even under Eryx's hooded cloak, The Vulture could see his lilac eyes peering down at them from underneath it. His eyes were eerie. Untrustworthy. The Vulture was starting to lose hope that this could work.

"I still feel him through the Oathmark. They haven't left yet. I can't afford to lose track of the Luciens, and neither can you. Someone needs to stay behind. Do you still have the dagger?"

The Vulture nodded, subduing their irritation. Time was running out. The Luciens had gone on complete lockdown, enhancing their security after the ball. More guards had been stationed in and around the castle than ever before. They had even drafted Nobornes from the poverty ring so they could send their best guards to go after the fugitives.

The Vulture glanced around wearily, eyeing the scorch marks in the gravel–remnants of the lightning that had struck down their spy.

"The dagger should remain on your person at all times. Keep an eye on the royals while I am away. If things go sideways, I'll have further instructions delivered to you by my Guild. You will inherit it and all its assets."

"I have no interest in your Guild," The Vulture snapped, annoyed. They removed the satchel of salaroses from their shoulder and handed the massive bag of florals over to Eryx. There had to have been at least one hundred flowers in the bag. The Vulture had spent *days* using their resources to gather that much herb. Whatever Eryx needed them for, it better be a good reason.

"Good. This will speed things along." Eryx muttered as he fished through the bag, ensuring all the flowers were there.

"Why do you need those?"

Eryx plucked an onyx flower out and twirled it within his fingers. Truly, the roses were mesmerizing. Never had The Vulture seen a plant so naturally black. The petals were as soft as velvet, their fragrance sweet. They were rare. It had certainly taken some time to find enough for the Guildmaster.

"These roses weren't crafted by the Gods. They were crafted by Witches. Each petal contains Black Magick, and can be used for casting spells, or portals."

"Portals?" The Vulture asked in disbelief. Magick that could draw portals had died hundreds of years ago. Could it really be true?

"Yes. I need a lot to conjure a portal far enough to where I believe Taryn is. It's not exactly easy casting spells in a land where Magick is near extinct."

"I don't understand. If he swore an Oathmark to you, can't you command him to do your bidding?"

Eryx dropped the flower back in the bag and slung it over his shoulder with a smug expression. "Not exactly. It's a direct tie to a soul. I can inflict pain remotely, physically and mentally, but I cannot compel him with it. That is what the compulsion ring is for."

The Vulture rolled their eyes. "You idiot. You should have just compelled him. Remind me how you got your place at the Guild again?"

Eryx scoffed. "It takes one hit, one crack for a wall to come crumbling down, unleashing all the suppressed power behind it. Compelling him would have been his last straw. Then, we would be up against two powerful beings. Would you want that?"

The Vultured sighed, "No."

Eryx nodded in approval. "Good. You are learning, Vulture. You cannot fight fyre with fyre."

Chapter 25

'Our home is shrouded by stormclouds and rage.'

– Excerpt from House Kazimyr's history book

Taryn

They had traveled day and night to make it to Judla, only stopping at night to rest and always leaving well before dawn. Taryn taught Airess how to use her dagger in self-defense nightly, and though she was nowhere near ready for real combat, he saw a ferocity in her eyes that held true to her strength. Besides, he surmised, that when her Magick got advanced enough, she wouldn't need a dagger at all.

Airess had been practicing her Magick every day since he told her about the Oathmark. She could conjure multiple orbs now and throw them. Anything in their path disintegrated instantaneously. It seemed that her power only amplified to something more during moments of fear, but this led to Taryn's theory that what power she did conjure was only the surface of her true power.

Taryn and Airess had been speaking in Runean to each other during their travels. Airess most definitely had a Mrkynian accent, but she was able to understand Runean and form sentences and converse with him. Taryn couldn't exactly understand why, but he felt pride well up in his chest hearing her speak his native language.

Throughout all their conversations, they had grown closer. Taryn tried his best to ignore the emotion he felt whirring between them when they shared a bed at the Inn. He could kick himself right now thinking about it, and how they had not spoken of the kiss they shared since.

Taryn thought this may be for the best. He was not good enough for Airess. She viewed the world differently than he did, always finding beauty from even the most mundane moments. Taryn had seen it, the compassion in her eyes when she watched the townspeople during their travels. She was an artist, a singer, one who found meaning through words and melodies. Airess was just becoming the person she was meant to be.

She didn't deserve to be tainted by him. She deserved a life in high society, preferably with a prince to give her the life she deserved. Airess didn't need to be with some back-alley assassin like Taryn. He didn't want his own darkness to destroy her.

Besides, if Raiden was only giving him two weeks to either die or betray Airess, he wouldn't be here on this earth much longer, anyway.

Taryn looked over to her then. Her hair had been left unbound, falling in waves down to her waist, dress hiked up to her knees as she rode on horseback. His stomach twisted at the new energy that fell between them.

When they woke up the next morning after their shared kiss, Airess had acted completely normal. Like nothing had happened. He could have sworn he saw emotion brimming behind her eyes, but it was gone before Taryn could name what it was.

When Taryn had tried to bring the kiss up, she had dismissed him.

It hurt him more than he cared to admit, but if she didn't want to acknowledge the stirring feelings between them, who was he to put that on her?

"Are you ready to see your home?" Taryn asked her, diverting his thoughts. They had decided to visit her old manor before leaving. Airess wanted closure, and he wanted anything that she did.

"I'm ready." She said confidently as they came out into a clearing, a meadow of grass so tall it reached their horses bodies. A grand manor made of stone, half in ruins, lay before them. It was completely abandoned, with decade old vines growing up and into the house. Airess paused before nudging her horse forward, Taryn following in suit.

They silently dismounted in front of the building. Airess stepped forward with a hardness in her brow, in her eyes, as she stared down the building. Taryn gave her the space she needed as she took in the place she was taken from ten years ago.

"Destroying the building was a personal touch. I watched it happen as I rode in the back of the carriage. They didn't have to destroy it, but they did. Because they wanted to," Airess let out a bitter laugh. "They had already killed my parents, but apparently, that wasn't enough."

Her boots scuffed against the stone as she stepped forward into a large, jagged hole in the wall. Taryn followed, careful to take one last glance outside to make sure they weren't being followed. No one was. Their surroundings were as desolate and abandoned as the building.

They walked into a grand foyer that had once been beautiful. Rotted wooden beams with intricate gold lacework, now faded, ran along the ceiling overhead. The cracked tile floor had now been littered with rubble. Curtains had been ripped from the walls, leaving the grand arched windows bare, allowing the afternoon sunlight to shine through and grace Airess' now pale face. The manor had been well looted in its deserted years, with nothing left behind but broken furniture.

Airess hesitated, stopping abruptly in front of him as she scanned the space. She sucked in a breath and closed her eyes, her fists clenched. Taryn ached for her, for what she must be reliving. She nodded, the movement miniscule, as she opened her eyes once more.

Taryn imagined Airess as a small child, running through the halls, a smile on her face. He imagined she was happy here, untouched by the cruelty of this world. He hated that it had been taken from her.

Airess lifted her chin up to the bannister, her eyes distant. "I was walking up those stairs when it happened. The royal guard didn't bother to knock, they just busted down the door."

"That can't be legal."

"It's not. They did whatever they wanted. Said they had a warrant out for my mother and father's arrest, that they were traitors to the realm and had plotted an assassination on the Crown." Airess ran her hand along the walls, holding onto a remnant of the past that had no longer held its natural form.

"Do you really believe that?" Taryn asked softly.

Airess furrowed her brows in frustration. "There was a time I denied any possibility of it, that they couldn't be capable of something so evil. But… I'm not so sure now." She turned to face him, her dress rustling at the swift motion. "I'll never know if they did it or not, but would they do it if they thought it was best for the country, for me? Perhaps–perhaps it *was* true."

Taryn angled his head. "And if it was?"

Airess pursed her lips in contemplation, "Then I wouldn't blame them for trying. The crown could view them as rebels, but perhaps they were revolutionaries."

Clap!

Clap!

Clap!

The sound of applause startled Airess and Taryn out of their conversation, their heads whipping to the source of the noise.

"My apologies. I'd hate to interrupt whatever… *this* is." Eryx's cool voice beckoned from another room. Taryn's blood turned to ice as he moved next to Airess instinctively.

How the fuck did he get in here? How did Taryn not hear him?

Footsteps grew louder until Eryx came into view.

"Oh, Taryn. You are a hard male to find. I hope you've had a fabulous field trip away from the Guild you swore an *oath* to." Eryx said, a taunt laced in his tone. His eyes slid to Airess, a greedy curiosity in his eyes.

Taryn bared his teeth at the way Eryx looked at her, as if she were a piece of meat. "Don't even *think* about laying a hand on her."

Eryx waved his hand, "I won't have to. No need to get burned alive from *Lightborne* Magick. I couldn't help overhear your conversation about your parents, Lady Haeleth. Or is that your real name?" Eryx laughed.

Airess stepped forward next to Taryn. "What did you just say?"

"Perhaps I should give you the closure you deserve. It seems fitting, after all, considering I'm the one who planned to assassinate the Crown with your mother."

Taryn could practically feel the rage seeping off of Airess in waves.

"It was your father who connected your mother and I, you see. I was astounded by Aesira's ferocity, her grit, and willingness to stoop so low in order to get what she wanted. I simply could not refuse such an ambitious female," Eryx continued with a smirk. "She came to me with a brilliant plan to get rid of the Luciens once and for all, promising me my rightful throne in exchange for protection. Such a shame she got caught, but that's neither here nor there."

Airess' body trembled with a rage Taryn had never seen.

"Fuck you," she spat, voice wavering. Eryx waved a hand, dismissing the comment. He flattened a hand over his garments, standing tall. "I did not come here to sling insults or cause anger. I have come here with a proposition."

Alarm bells rang in Taryn's mind. He knew exactly what Eryx was going to offer. Taryn wouldn't–*couldn't* allow her to go down that path.

"I don't care *what* you have to offer–"

Eryx held a finger up to cut Airess off. "I'll tell you everything I know about you and your mother, only if you join my cause."

Airess didn't hesitate. "Absolutely not. I will never help you."

Eryx shook his head slowly, a deep chuckle rumbling in his chest. "I urge you to reconsider your words. You have no idea what kind of power I possess. This is your last chance to accept my offer."

Airess boldly took a step forward. "I know exactly what kind of man you are. You use witchcraft to compel your Guild members into submission. I won't have any part in that."

Eryx stared Airess down. The Guildmaster's face twitched, ever so slightly, but just enough to let Taryn know she had disappointed him. Did

Eryx truly think he would convince her? Did he know something Taryn didn't?

"Perhaps you won't have any part of it, for now. Alas, you have made your decision, and I have made mine. Let me show you what it means to be my enemy."

With a cold sneer, Eryx called on Taryn's Oathmark. The dragon tattoo ignited into a glow, searing Taryn's skin ever so slightly. Taryn hissed, shuffling on his feet despite the rising pain. Airess looked between him and Eryx. Her face fell, melting into fear. She returned to Taryn's side and gripped his arm, steadying him.

Realization dawned on Eryx, no doubt seeing the extent of Taryn and Airess' relationship. "Oh my, you two have grown quite fond of one another."

Eryx paced slowly, like an animal hunting its next victim. "I'll sweeten the deal of my previous offer. You come with me, girl, and I'll release this male from his Oath. I would hate to cause any bloodshed."

Taryn shook his head. "She will do no such thing."

"Very well," Eryx said. He raised his fist and squeezed. Taryn fell to his knees and clenched his jaw, refusing to cry out as the Oath Mark's seared his flesh.

Airess took a step forward towards Eryx–

"Ah, ah, ah!" Eryx waived his pointer finger in the air. "You move and he dies. You come with me, and I'll release him."

Airess looked to Taryn, her eyes desperate. He hated what he saw in her eyes at that moment, a promise he didn't want her making for him. A promise that she would do it. Taryn shook his head as he gritted his teeth.

"Cease inflicting pain on him and I'll consider." Airess bargained.

Eryx released his Magickal grip on his body and mind. Taryn loosened a breath, his muscles now relaxed. The Guildmaster nodded slowly, a sardonic grin upturning the corners of his mouth.

"Airess, stop." Taryn begged.

Airess charged forward, intending to strike Eryx before an object zipped through the air and met its mark, a small arrow only a few inches long embedded in Airess' arm, completely covered in the green glow of donstenyte poisoning. It wasn't big enough to cause serious damage. No, these arrows were ones Taryn was familiar with. They were designed to inject a substance or poison into their target.

Airess hissed, her hand instinctively covering the flesh wound, the arrow still in her arm.

"Sorry dear, we can't have you losing control when I kill him, or when *he* kills you."

As Taryn began to move, intending to attack the Guildmaster, Eryx gripped Taryn's body and mind with his Magick once again, this time with an iron fist. Airess screamed to stop him, but someone rushed out to restrain her. Taryn looked up, betrayal rooting deep in his chest.

Raiden had come from another room and had Airess in a chest lock, a bow and arrow strapped to his back. He looked to Taryn for a moment before looking to Eryx for further direction, like the docile servant he had turned out to be. Taryn supposed he should have expected Raiden to choose the Guild over him, it was where his loyalties have always been, and always will be. Still, the betrayal had stung nonetheless.

White hot pain overcame his vision, his ability to hear had been taken away, save for Eryx's condescending voice. "You could have had a long life if you hadn't chosen betrayal. Pity. I suppose it would have always come down to this either way."

Eryx stepped closer. He bent down and whispered, "***Kill her.***"

No.

No.

No!

Hands gripping the floor, Taryn tried his best to fight off the compulsion Eryx set upon him. He would not harm Airess, he *couldn't*. And yet, his body trembled, aching to harm her. Taryn gritted his teeth as pain seared hot in the back of his mind.

"Quit fighting it, boy."

Taryn looked up, eyes watering as he looked at Airess in Raiden's grip. Raiden looked away, letting go of Airess and shoving her on the ground hard. She fell a few feet away from him, and the desire to harm her from the compulsion burned stronger.

"Do as you are told. ***Kill her***!" Eryx ordered impatiently.

Taryn cried out in frustration as his freewill over his body broke. He got up, and strode over to Airess. She was struggling to get to her feet when he grabbed her by the hair and yanked her to standing. She shrieked as he spun her to face him, gripping both of her arms and slamming her against a crumbled wall.

"End this," Taryn pleaded to her, eyes watering. "You can make it to Rune. You *have* to."

Her eyes were a mixture of fear and anger. He shuddered at the thought of her fearing him, at the thought that she believed he would ever harm her.

Slowly, she shook her head and whispered, "You can fight this."

Taryn growled and threw her on the ground, part of it being the compulsion, and the other part trying as hard as he could to stall. She fell like a rag doll, crawling to get away, but she wasn't quick enough.

Taryn pounced on her, dragging her back down and straddling her waist with his own, all the while shaking his head as he watched his own body in horror.

"You can kill me," He begged. "Just do it."

He unsheathed a blade strapped to his waste and held it up to her neck, watching his own limb betray him, betray *her*. Airess breathed shallow breaths, the fear growing all too real, as she angled her neck as far away as she could, his blade grazing her neck and drawing blood.

"Fight it," She whispered. "We have plans. I can't do them alone." She gave him a weak half smile.

The blade trembled in Taryn's hand, the compulsion overriding his free will.

We have plans. I can't do them alone.

Taryn didn't want to leave Airess alone in this world, just as he had been. She deserved better–*more* than that. His heart pounded incessantly, and the ringing in his ears grew louder as he strained against the compulsion. Taryn gritted his teeth, and in a split moment of free will, he twisted the blade, and plunged it into his own stomach. Taryn's scream mixed with Airess' as he fell onto her, his body convulsing, blood inking across his tunic.

"*Bastard*!" Eryx exclaimed, claiming his grip on Taryn's mind through the Oathmark, torturing him. Heat flared within every pore of his body. So hot. *Too* hot. His vision ran red. It was as if his body was on fyre. Taryn screamed in Runean. To anyone, everyone, to help him. Perhaps in the distance he heard Airess screaming. Perhaps he felt her utter terror as Taryn's mind began to unravel as he defied Eryx's compulsion.

Eryx approached them, grabbing Taryn's body and yanking him off of Airess. Pain seared, the dagger sliding out of his flesh as he was tossed to the side. Though the world seemed to shift, Taryn caught a glimpse of the dagger that rested in Airess' hand.

In the split-second Eryx's back was turned, Airess sliced the knife through the air, right across Eryx's achilles tendon.

Everything happened in a blur after that. Eryx tumbled to the ground, shouting in pain as Raiden advanced towards Airess, his blade out. Seeing a weapon heading towards Airess' direction was all the fuel Taryn needed to fight on. Fear for Airess' life quickly overpowered his pain from his knife wound, driving him to move.

Taryn forced himself upwards, tackling Raiden to the ground, Raiden's blade inches away from making contact with Airess. Taryn held Raiden in a headlock, snarling, seconds away from snapping his neck.

Eryx rolled over to face Airess. She was one step, one plunge downward from killing the Guildmaster. Eryx simply lifted a hand and commanded, "***Stop!***"

Airess froze as commanded, blade still in hand, as if she were stuck in time. Eryx's lips trembled as he spoke, a hatred shone in his eyes, "You *bitch*! You will pay for what you have done. ***Come here.***"

"You touch her, and he dies." Taryn threatened, his forearm squeezing into Raiden's windpipe. Eryx's gaze slid over to Raiden, weighing the situation. Without acknowledging Taryn's threat, Eryx looked back to Airess with a greedy smile as she lowered to her knees in front of him. Her brows were furrowed in resentment at the compulsion, now on her knees in front of Eryx's fallen position.

Eryx lifted himself up, holding out his hand, "***Hand it over.***"

No.

Taryn screamed out to Eryx, "I'll kill him! I will fucking kill him if you hurt her!"

Raiden squirmed for breath underneath his arm, his face now turning purple. A messy mix of rage and regret budded within Taryn. How has it ever come to this? Could it have ended differently, or would Taryn have always been destined to betray his own best friend?

Airess' hand trembled with rage as she began to lower the blade down into Eryx's palm. She breathed heavy breaths, squinting her eyes closed as she tried to fight the compulsion.

When she opened her eyes, it was as if the gold in her irises burned slightly brighter, a look of newfound determination overcoming her. Suddenly, a smirk grew on her lips as she yanked her knife back and plunged it into the side of Eryx's neck.

Raiden tried to scream out as Eryx met his silent death, blood splattering onto the floors, the walls, and Airess. The side of Airess' face, neck and chest bore splatters of crimson, the remnants of her murder evident.

Eryx looked up to Airess in pure shock at her ability to resist his compulsion, falling to the floor silently.

How–how was it possible? How had she resisted?

Taryn didn't remember letting go of Raiden. He only watched Airess stand over Eryx, cruelty on her perfect face as she bent down, and ripped the blade out of his neck.

Raiden shifted to grab his dagger that had fallen to the ground. Taryn drew his broadswords from behind his back, rushing in front of Airess and pointed the blade at Raiden, stopping him in his tracks.

"I'll let you go just this once. *Leave*," Taryn bellowed, pain laced in his voice,

Raiden stared at the body on the floor in horror, his eyes looking between Taryn and Airess. Taryn watched the last of his brotherly love wash away as Raiden's eyes hardened.

"I don't know you anymore," Raiden spat as he took a step back. "*Fuck you*. You both deserve each other."

Raiden fled out of the crumbled opening in the wall. Taryn heard his footsteps fade off, until the adrenaline started to fade, and the pain from Taryn's stomach wound surfaced. They stood there, panting, as they both gathered their bearings.

She killed him.

She killed him

She killed him.

The silence was overwhelming, the both of them heaving for breath, covered in blood. Taryn's tunic was soaked from the knife wound and he fought to ignore the pain, as he noticed the miniature arrow still stuck in Airess' arm.

He turned to face her. "We need to get that arrow out of your arm."

"Do it," she said weakly, glancing down at the arrow.

Taryn grabbed her free arm and told her to brace herself, tearing some cloth off of his own shirt for her to bite down on. Once she had the cloth in her mouth, he gripped the arrow.

Taryn grimaced. "I'm sorry," he said, before ripping it clean out.

She screamed as her legs buckled. Taryn snaked his arm around her waist and held her up before she could fall to her knees. Once her breaths finally evened, they stood. She eyed his abdomen and commented, "You're next. That needs to be taken care of."

They worked together, quickly wrapping the fabric from Airess' skirt around his waist. Airess tied the knot, making sure the fabric was tight enough to apply pressure to the wound.

"We have to leave. *Now.*" Taryn uttered, his voice wavering slightly.

They scrambled outside, arm in arm, trudging towards their horses despite the pain.

"We just need one horse to make it to the docks. Untie the other one so it can roam free." Taryn said with a grimace, as he untied the horse.

"Taryn, you need to rest. Surely we can find somewhere–"

"No," he snapped. "You just killed the Guildmaster of the Mrkynian Guild. They will be coming for us, and soon. We have to leave this country immediately."

Taryn mounted, hunched over with blood oozing from his knife wound. Airess climbed on behind him, wrapping a firm arm to add pressure to his stomach. They rode to the docks.

"Taryn, we are a vision of murder. We will get arrested on sight. How exactly are you planning to make it out of here alive?" Airess asked as their horse accelerated.

"We will do what we must," Taryn said darkly. "We have to."

Chapter 26

'My brother will look for you when you cross over to the Old World. Be ready.'

— Unsent correspondence from Paulyr Moros

Airess

They dismounted their horses quickly and sprinted to the docks. Airess's legs pumped beneath her, her muscles burning and her shoulder throbbing as she ran by Taryn's side. She knew he wasn't doing so well, his face was losing color by the second as they headed straight towards their new beginning–or demise.

Commoners shouted at them as they rushed by, their heavy footfalls already fading behind them as they scanned for a boat to hijack. It wasn't their best plan, but it was the only one with two guards on their tail. Luckily, this time, the guards weren't Shadow Wielders.

"This one!" Taryn yelled as he pointed to a small sailboat. He began to untie the boat from the dock, motioning for Airess to hop on. An arrow flew by, Taryn narrowly avoiding it as he ducked.

As Airess jumped onto the boat, another shot flew by. The arrow grazed Taryn's unscathed side as he landed on the boat. Thankfully, they missed, but more blood soaked the fabric of his shirt. Taryn waved his arms, guiding a mass of water and flooding the dock, washing away everyone, including the guards, into the sea. Before Airess could protest his methods of escape, the boat jolted forward.

Airess stared at him in awe, not fully realizing the strength of Taryn's Waterborne Magick until now.

Taryn had both arms splayed out behind him. He moved them in a rotative motion, propelling the boat forward with his water Magick. A wake spread behind the boat as they picked up speed, and in that moment, Airess saw a determination within Taryn that she had never seen before. The wind rustled his brown curls and blood-soaked clothes. Despite everything they just went through, he stood tall amongst the sea.

In the corner of her eyes, she saw a blot of white amongst the treeline. Airess squinted, and her eyebrows rose as she recognized the familiar owl perched on a branch. Its cloudy grey eyes blinked as it watched her ride away. Airess stared at it, not able to explain the pit in her stomach at the sight of it.

It flapped away as soon as she made eye contact with it, leaving Airess bewildered.

The boat began to pick up speed as Taryn wielded it forward. Airess sat up, the air around them blowing her hair and clothing so violently she had to hold her dress bunched in her fist. She glanced back at Taryn. He looked like he could pass out at any moment, his face pallid.

"Are you all right?" Airess yelled over the roaring winds.

"Besides the stab wound, I'm doing just fine," Taryn retorted sarcastically.

Airess bit her lip while she watched him. She knew Taryn was too stubborn to announce his pain, but she didn't know how much Eryx had done to his mind with the Oathmark before she had killed him.

She thought about her kill, and how she should feel remorse. But no guilt came. Airess did what had to be done, and she portrayed a strength she hadn't known she was capable of.

In fact, she would do it again to any other enemy that desired to hurt Taryn. Maybe because Taryn was her only ally, and now friend. Or maybe it was something more, something she hadn't admitted to herself, or put into words yet.

Whatever it was, she realized she would do anything for him.

She would break the rules for him.

Kill for him.

She would even die for him.

That last thought sobered her from her adrenaline rushed haze after the manor. Memories flashed behind her eyes, how it felt to drive the blade into Eryx's neck, feeling the warm blood splatter all over her. She thought she would feel regret, feel some sort of shame because of her actions.

But she didn't. This new world, the real world, had begun to shape her. Airess decided she needed this. It was time to obtain a certain ruthlessness within herself. Her utter lack of it throughout her life had driven her to be docile, pliable.

As they sailed out to the horizon, she would never again be weak. Never again would she be quiet. Never again would she shy away from necessary violence. Airess would do whatever it took to survive, from this moment on.

Taryn wielded the water around them in silence for the next hour. Finally, he let up, dropping his arms in exhaustion and falling to his knees.

Airess rushed to him, steadying his body by placing both hands on his biceps, his tunic soaked in blood and sweat. He breathed heavily, and when he tilted his face up to look at her through his dark lashes, she could have sworn she saw death lingering behind his eyes.

Her stomach dropped.

"Taryn, I need to check on your wounds."

He grunted in reply, slumping against a bench in approval. She lifted the hem of his shirt up, nudging him softly to lift his arms. She brought the tunic over his head and discarded it on the floor.

Taryn smirked grimly, "This is not exactly how I imagined you taking my clothes off for the first time."

Her cheeks burned scarlet at his words. Airess smiled softly. Taryn was such a flirt. She kept her eyes low, ripping his shirt into pieces and began to change the wrapping on his stab wound.

"In your dreams," she said playfully, trying her best to keep her cool and not stumble over her words. Airess couldn't help it. Taryn was a beautiful Fae male, and she was just a halfling with no prior experience with romance... or sex, for that matter. She assumed he must have had experience with both. Her blood boiled at the thought–an ugly feeling bubbling deep within her. The stinging feeling of jealousy.

He reached out and tucked a tendril of her silver hair behind her pointed ear. She met his eyes.

"*Yes*, in my dreams," he breathed out. "Because I'm not going to make it much longer. I think something is wrong with my mind."

Airess frowned, shaking her head. "Quit talking like that. We are so close. How long did you say earlier, just a few more hours? Finlan's Passage isn't that large. We can do this."

Taryn nodded, silver eyes drifting to her bloody shoulder. He picked up the remnants of his tunic now lying on the boat deck and tore one last sliver of fabric.

"My turn," he said gruffly, sweeping her thick sheet of hair behind her back. He peeled away her already torn sleeve and frowned at her mangled flesh.

"I should have killed him."

Airess whipped her head up as he began to wrap her arm. "You don't mean that. He is your *best friend*."

Taryn let out a bitter scoff as he tied off the fabric, not deigning to respond. He braced himself, grunting as he came to a stand. Airess rushed to help him up, steadying him. Once he gathered his balance, he continued to propel the boat onward, bringing them closer to the end of their journey.

After another hour of sailing, a sheer wall of energy came into view. It was a translucent gray that swirled around in a dome-like shape, coming up from the sea and extending up to the sky further than they could see. Taryn ceased wielding, the boat idling forward slowly as they approached it.

"What is *that*?" Airess asked, squinting to get a better view. Taryn put a hand over his brow as he looked, his mouth parting slightly. "I've seen that–*we've* seen that dreamwalking, remember? Only it was that turquoise color in the dreamworld."

"My Gods," Airess whispered. The barrier came closer and closer until they were finally feet away. As they approached, Airess braced herself. She didn't know what that was or what it would do to them. She shielded her face instinctively with her forearm as they passed through it.

Time warped as they passed through the translucent wall. For a split second, Airess heard no sound at all. She couldn't see anything besides a gray static, as if she were enveloped in a pool of energy. They passed slowly, until finally their boat was on the other side.

Electricity surged through her, starting at her head and racing down to her toes. The feeling intensified, her body infusing with an energy she had never felt before.

It was exhilarating, every pore on her body awakening to it. One quick glance to her right and she could see Taryn was feeling the same thing– his teeth gritted as he was hunched over, both hands on his knees for stability.

Finally, it was over. Airess toppled over and sat on the boat floor, the sun beating onto her. She shifted in front of Taryn, sweeping a strand of hair out of his eyes, "Are you okay?"

His eyes met hers with an intensity– a *power* she hadn't seen within him before. It was so powerful, she recoiled.

"I feel…I *physically* feel better. My mind's still a little slow," he explained. Taryn stretched out an arm and examined it. Airess knew exactly how he felt–her entire body feeling stronger, more powerful, than it ever had before.

Taryn stood, leaning on the boat railing for support and punched a gust of wind from his fist that sent him stumbling backward. The boat swayed in response as Airess gripped the railing.

"What was that? You could have flipped this entire boat!"

Taryn only examined his hand, his expression shifting as realization dawned on him. "That energy surge… did you feel it? It felt like *Magick*.

My abilities are stronger."

Magick?

She looked down to her palm and contemplated.

Airess tilted her head before lifting her hand to try–

"Airess!" Taryn exclaimed as he limped towards her. He grabbed her wrist, pointing it away from the boat. "The last thing we need is this boat being burnt to a crisp if you try out *your* Magick. It would make for a hell of a journey the rest of the way to Rune."

"Oh," Airess said, "I'm sorry. You're right. *Gods.*"

Taryn laughed, his head tilted back with that pearly grin. Airess noticed each crease that surrounded his eyes and mouth, memorizing them. The sight of it caused her to crack a smile. His laugh was her weakness.

The laughter faded between them until they were both staring at each other–their first real moment of peace since they arrived in Judla. So many questions, so many words that hadn't been said swirled between them. She still hadn't told him about the dreamwalker, Ima, and how she led Airess to Taryn. Could she tell him now after how close they had grown, after all they'd been through?

Her gaze slid down to his lips.

The kiss.

Airess couldn't believe it really happened. She was still drunk on it, forever haunted by the ghost of his touch after his mouth left hers. Taryn had tried to bring it up, but she had brushed him off. She had never been so emotionally involved with anyone in her life. The vulnerability terrified her. She knew it made her a coward.

"Don't look at me like that," he said, eyes darkening.

"Like what?"

"Like you think I'm a good person. Like you want to kiss me. Like I deserve you."

She straightened her back at his words, at the acknowledgement of what happened between them. She willed herself to be bold, to live unapologetically, and took a step forward.

"And what's so wrong with that?" Airess asked. "You seemed to have no problem kissing me at the Inn."

There it was.

Taryn's eyes fluttered closed briefly. His jaw ticked, and when he met her gaze again, there was a longing she hadn't seen before. Her heart twisted with so many emotions, her head began to spin.

"You deserve better than me."

"What?" Airess said breathlessly, not expecting his response.

"Airess, you don't know what I've done in my life," Taryn said, lifting a hand to touch her face before yanking it back, "I'm not the male you think I am."

Airess thought back to when she dreamwalked into one of his older memories. Back when Taryn was fourteen and had freshly joined the Guild, forced to kill another man in his home to become initiated. She knew that could have only been the beginning of his troubled past, and she had no doubt Taryn was ruthless enough to commit other crimes. But she didn't care. She wanted to know what he had done. Airess wanted to accept every dark corner she hadn't explored yet, so she could see him for who he truly was.

In order to do that, she needed to be honest with him. She needed to tell him the truth about Ima.

"There's something I need to tell you—"

Taryn jolted forward, gripping the railing as his knees buckled. He hissed in pain as he fell to the floor.

"Taryn!" Airess exclaimed as she knelt down with him. He cried out in pain, gripping the dragon tattoo that was his Oathmark.

"What's going on? What is hurting you?"

She scanned his face, frantically trying to make sense of what was going on. Airess gripped his shoulders to hold him upright. When Taryn gathered his breath, he turned his head to look at her slowly. "I meant it when I said I wasn't going to make it."

She unraveled the wrapping on his abdomen, delightfully surprised.

"The bleeding has stopped. I don't understand."

"It's not from the wound." Taryn tapped two fingers on the dragon tattooed on his shoulder. "It has something to do with the Oathmark. I feel…tired. Just give me a few minutes and we can keep going."

"No, we *won't* keep going. You need to rest, that's final."

Taryn looked like he was about to argue, but he held his head low in defeat. They both slumped against the boat railing and sat together in silence, the sun blaring down on them as they drifted through the middle of the ocean.

The boat swaying forcefully from side to side woke Airess out of a dreamless slumber she hadn't realized she had sunk into. She sat up quickly, eyes wide. She glanced at Taryn still asleep and shook his shoulders.

He didn't wake up.

Her heart dropped.

Airess shook him harder. "Taryn, wake up," she whispered frantically. *"Wake up!"*

His limp body made no movements. Airess pressed her fingers to the pulse on his neck, utterly relieved to feel life still pulsing beneath his skin. After several attempts to wake him, Airess realized something was very wrong.

The boat jolted again, harder this time. At once, the boat stopped moving entirely, as if they were being stopped mid-float. She scrambled to her feet and gaped at what she saw.

Land!

They had finally reached land! Airess took in the white stucco buildings perched upon the shore. Every structure had orange clay tiling and circular windows. Her eyes trailed upwards to the castle, made in the same materials as the buildings below.

But then she turned. A massive ship stood before their boat, soldiers atop it with their arrows drawn–all pointing right at her. A massive wave surfaced out of the ocean from her right. Three Fae wielders rode the wave until they landed perfectly onto their boat. Airess instinctively moved in front of Taryn's unconscious body to protect him and faced the soldiers, drawing one of the broadswords out of his sheath.

Three Fae stood before her. Two males and a female had their blades drawn cautiously as they took her and Taryn in. They weren't armed with heavy armor like the guards in Luciena.

The soldiers wore metal chest plates to protect their heart, but other than that, the clothes looked quite comfortable for a soldier. They wore flowing pants that cuffed at the ankles with a matching tunic the color of dark orange. Various weapons were strapped onto their bodies, but Airess knew they were all wielders and could kill her without drawing a weapon.

The guard shouted at her to lower her sword. She did, but did not let go of it.

"State your business here," said a guard in Runean.

Airess scrambled to find the words in her head. She was still learning the language, and could understand far better than she could speak it. "We have escaped from Luciena," she said, the words she had rehearsed with Taryn fresh in her mind. "We mean no harm."

"Yet you wield a blade?" one of the females retorted, eyeing her suspiciously.

Slowly, Airess knelt down and placed the blade on the ground. Everyone stilled. Finally, a soldier in the middle spoke up. "Seize them!"

A blast of water hit Airess, knocking her down. She felt water encase her hands, hardening into ice cuffs that bound her hands together. The guards hoisted her up and dragged her away from Taryn.

"We mean no harm!" Airess exclaimed.

She fought back, her limbs thrashing as she struggled against their grip. They forced her down, but she kicked and bucked, trying to break free.

"Please!" she begged, her voice breaking as she screamed. "Listen, we mean no harm! He–" but she forgot the words in Runean in her panicked state. "Healer! Need healer!"

They paid her no heed as she was tackled to the ground, her face pressed into the wood of the deck, the Runean soldiers binding her limbs with rope.

Chapter 27

The original Gods banded together and created the first five Godlings: Death, Sun, Moon, Mind and Elements.

— *The book of Tevye*

Airess

A Fae guard slung Taryn over his shoulder and tossed him on the ground next to Airess. She immediately scrambled over to him, despite her bound limbs and the rocking of the ship. Her shoulders slumped as she shook him. Taryn was still unconscious.

The world began to spin and her thoughts became scrambled. *Frantic.* Airess' stomach folded in on itself, dread stealing her breath away. She was heaving, her bound wrists going to her chest as she fought for breath. What was wrong with him? Why wouldn't he wake up?

Would he live?

Airess squeezed her eyes shut. No, he couldn't die. She wouldn't let him. Airess needed to calm herself, to fight this anxiety attack. He needed her now more than ever. She closed her mouth and began to breathe in for four seconds, then out for four seconds. Airess inhaled the salty air and focused on the seagulls cawing in the distance.

When her breaths finally evened, she took in her surroundings. They had been moved to the military ship that had stopped them, and now both sat bound in rope. The ship groaned as the Fae conversed quietly across from her.

The crowd parted as a woman, who seemed to be in her sixties, came forward.

The woman's brown skin contrasted against the bright orange headwrap that her graying hair was pulled up in. She wore flowing pants and tunic to match. The woman leaned on a cane with a slight wobble and surveyed Airess with one brow lifted.

"State your names," the woman demanded in the Mrkynian tongue with an accent she didn't recognize.

"My name is Airess." She motioned down to Taryn sheepishly. "And this is Taryn."

The woman's eyes widened slightly before she schooled her features into neutrality, pointing to Taryn. "What's wrong with him?"

"I don't know. He fell unconscious as we arrived. Please, help him. He needs a healer as soon as possible."

Airess couldn't read the woman's facial expression. She blinked her Sight forward to read the woman's intentions, but nothing came. She realized she must have still been drugged from the donstenyte arrow.

"You and your friend will be allowed in Rune temporarily due to such... *odd* circumstances. I will take him to be healed, but immediately after you will be presented to the king." the woman stated as she glanced down at Taryn, lips pursed.

"Thank you so much," Airess began. "You have no idea—"

The woman held a hand up to stop her. "Don't thank me yet. You have yet to meet with the king."

Airess blinked, taken aback. She realized the weight of the woman's words, that she was to be presented to the *King* of Rune. Oh, how she was so ill prepared.

"What is your name?" Airess asked, grasping onto any bit of information she could.

"Ismene," the woman said. "High Priestess of Eileamaid, the elemental God, and loyal member of The Obadiah."

"The Obadiah?" Airess asked, perking up. She was so distracted with worry that she had almost lost sight of the fact that she had actually escaped. "Ma'am, I have traveled all this way to meet you. Priestess Esper Crawn helped me escape the Luciens so that I could train with you—with The Obadiah."

Ismene's eyes trailed down Airess' face and landed on the locket sitting at her heart. "If that is true, you'd best explain that to the king," Ismene said, eyes narrowing. "He will decide if you can stay here."

Ismene turned away and left her alone with Taryn. Airess' head whirled, grasping onto everything that had just occurred. She felt some relief, knowing that Ismene agreed to heal Taryn, whatever was wrong with him. She only hoped the king would accept them.

If he didn't, where else could they go? There were only two continents left on this earth, and one of them wanted both of their heads. Airess swallowed. If they were cast out of Rune, it would be a death sentence. A means to their end. She looked up to the sun and prayed they would be accepted, prayed they would make it through.

Airess sat in silence the rest of the boat ride to shore. She propped up

Taryn's body as best as she could so he was leaning on her. It was as if he was asleep, his body normal, but his mind gone.

She grabbed his hand and whispered, "Please, wake up Taryn. We finally made it to your home."

When they docked, Ismene barked orders in Runean to the soldiers on deck. They grabbed Airess by the arm and one Fae male flung Taryn over his shoulders with force. Airess tried her best to find the specific words to convey her worry. "Careful. *Please.*"

The Fae soldiers snickered at her broken Runean as she was escorted off the ship and to the dock–the same dock she had dreamwalked to when she saw Taryn's past memory the night before the engagement ball.

Her eyes darted to the Waterborne Fae upon the docks, using their hands to guide water from the ocean and into the buckets nearby. It was moments like these where she started to wonder just how sentient the Dreamworld was, to show her Rune for the first time right before her escape from Luciena. Airess knew it had to be deeper than that. She didn't believe in coincidences.

They held onto the rope tied to her wrists as they escorted her by foot through the streets of Rune.

Everything was different here.

Shops and restaurants lined the streets, the scent of spices she hadn't ever smelled before filled the air, burning her nostrils. The town was clean, the buildings a light cream. The windows were just a circular opening in the buildings, not a single glass pane in sight. Layers of different colored curtains hung at the entrances of each building acting as a wall or a divider, as if these people did not need doors. The architecture was very open–and so was the fashion.

Men and women wore significantly less clothing than they did in Luciena. The females primarily wore wrapped tops with matching slitted skirts and flowing pants. Everyone wore sandals here, an odd shoe Airess had never seen before but heard of in her schooling years.

The men had similar flowing pants and hardly wore any shirts at all. Some wore loose tunics or sleeveless shirts that showed off their chest and arms muscles. The men wore armbands, the copper metal reflecting the sun. They also wore different colored threads in their hair, and all of them wore similar earrings to the one Taryn wore. The people here had darker skin of varying shades, and there was a certain lightness in the air here she hadn't felt before in a community. It certainly was hot and humid, and Airess quickly gathered the reasoning for the lack of clothing.

She felt their stares as they passed by. Some looked at her with curiosity, others disdain. One Fae male stared at her greedily, his eyes traveling up and down her body, as if he was trying to assert some sort of possessiveness over her.

"Almost there," said Ismene, breaking Airess from her thoughts.

They approached a dome-shaped building, much larger than the other buildings. It was the temple, Airess realized.

The temple was white on the outside, but as they walked through the front doors, she realized just how sacred this building truly was. Airess could *feel* an energy radiating from down the hallway that they currently were walking down. The hallways were painted with Runean text and elemental symbols, going down the corridor as far as Airess could see.

"What happened to him?" Ismene asked as they rushed down a hall of the temple.

"An Oathmark," Airess started. "Taryn has an Oathmark on his right arm. The man he was Marked to used it before he was killed. Taryn's fatigue slowly increased in the hours we escaped to get here."

They rounded a corner, and two individuals opened twin doors for them as they barrelled forward. The energy Airess felt upon entering the temple hit her body in waves, and she was immediately drawn to the largest hearth she had ever seen in the middle of the room. In the center of the hearth were roseate-colored flames, so pink she thought she was looking at the sunset. If Airess wasn't so focused on making sure Taryn was okay, she would have stopped to admire such an oddity.

Rows of benches surrounded the hearth, and a cluttered desk sat in the corner. Airess realized this must be the sanctuary.

The soldiers rested Taryn on the table and left the room. Ismene walked around Taryn and rested her hands on his chest with her eyes closed. "*Hm.*" She stood there for some time, analyzing him, resting her palm on his forehead, his temples, his heart.

"Which tattoo is the Oathmark?"

Airess pointed to the dragon tattoo that started on his bicep. Ismene gripped his arm and hissed, yanking her hand back. She muttered something in Runean before taking a step back. "This is forbidden Magick."

Airess' heart pounded. "Will he live?"

Ismene looked from Taryn to the fyre with a contemplative look. Finally, she said. "His spirit isn't too far gone, but we are running out of time. The Black Magick has seized his spirit and cast him into the void of his own mind. But, if my theory is correct, he will live if we sever him from the Oathmark."

"Sever him from the Oathmark? The person he was Marked to is *dead*."

Ismene shook her head, "It's not that easy to dispel witchcraft. It lives on, as their soul does. Even in death, a spirit can control the Oathmark."

Horror thrummed through her as Ismene walked to the hearth and swept her hands through the pink flames. When she returned to Taryn's side, she held the flames in the palm of her hand with ease. "Can you conjure?" Ismene asked.

"Conjure what? My Light Magick?"

Ismene's brows drew together in confusion at her retort, then realization dawned on her features. "My Gods, you Mrkynians really *are* in the dark. Your power is not called Light Magick, dear. You possess *Starlight*."

"I don't know–"

Ismene held up her free hand to silence Airess. "I will teach you everything you need to know in due time. Right now, this male needs you more than ever. Can you conjure even the smallest amount?"

"I can't wield it right now, I have Donestenyte poisoning in my system."

Ismene looked at her speculatively. "You, of all people, should be able to fight through such a miniscule setback. Your power doesn't compare. Draw on your Starlight."

Airess didn't have time to think about whatever the hell that meant. She swallowed and splayed out her fingers, closed her eyes and breathed. A buzz emanated from her chest and traveled down her arm.

Airess felt a tingling on her palm, and when she opened her eyes, her golden Magick had wrapped around her hand like a glove. For the first time ever, the Magick came to her with ease.

"Excellent! Carefully press your hand to his heart."

"Ismene, I don't mean any disrespect, but this Magick is lethal. My power—it *burns* things. I can't touch him with it!"

"Don't be ridiculous, girl. For this spell to work we need the fyre *and* your Magick. He will be just fine. Do you want to save him or not?"

Airess looked down at Taryn's face and realized an unspoken truth, a truth she wasn't ready to put into words. She met Ismene's eyes and nodded, carefully placing her hand over Taryn's heart.

Her pulse quickened with fear that she would burn a hole straight through his chest, but his skin remained intact. There was no physical reaction at all.

"Good. Just like I thought." Ismene commented, and placed the rose-colored flames onto Taryn's Oathmark.

"Wait! What is that fyre?" Airess asked, panicked.

Ismene looked at her in disbelief, as if Airess should already know.

"The *Soulfyre*," Ismene said. "One of the many fyres of life given to us by the Gods. It has healing properties, enough to restore his soul, if the Gods deem him worthy."

Ismene left no time for Airess to ask any more questions. The priestess began to speak erratically in a language Airess didn't recognize, her voice ebbing and flowing with her words. Her arms and body shook as she performed the spell.

Taryn sucked in a breath whilst still unconscious, his brows creasing in anguish. Ismene ceased her chanting and looked to Airess expectantly. "Now is your part. In order for this spell to work, I need a Magick only you possess to pull him out of his curse. I can only do so much from my end. Use your abilities, reach his mind, and set him free."

Airess' heart pounded as she looked from Taryn to Ismene.

"How do I do that?"

"How do we reach anyone's mind? By connection. Find your connection, and pull him back to the surface."

How was she supposed to *reach his mind*?

This was madness. Airess started to doubt Ismene's methods, but she also knew the severity of the situation.

How can she reach his mind, his spirit, his... dreamform?

Airess did what she felt called to do, listening to a deeper part of herself. She closed her eyes and breathed, slowing her heart and mind. One. Two. Three. Four.

She let go of her earthly tether and envisioned her dreamform –

Suddenly, she was above her own body–above Ismene and Taryn on the table. Her physical form was glowing, Airess' eyes were not her usual gold, but glowed a soft lilac. Airess realized whatever she was doing was more than just dreamwalking. She reached out a ghostly hand towards Taryn's heart.

"Taryn." *She spoke softly, her voice echoing.* "It's me, Airess."

She lowered her body until she was closer to him, setting her dreamform hand over his body.

Upon touching him, she was transported inwards to the depths of his mind, and she was suddenly falling through darkness. Airess felt the terror, the never-ending nightmare he seemed to be trapped in. She heard the screams of war. Saw blood on Taryn's young hands, desperately scrambling to retrieve an arrow in a battlefield. Then, images of Taryn sitting alone, barely aged thirteen–homeless amongst the streets. It was everything he never said about his past.

She had to think. What was she to do next? His soul felt far, yet so close. So close that if she could just reach a little deeper, she could yank him free from whatever kept him captive. She felt him brimming underneath the surface, whatever this in-between state was.

"I'm not letting you go," she said, and slowly sunk her hand into Taryn's body.

His physical body jerked, muttering vague sentences.

I need to reach your mind, *she thought.*

Airess felt cold, dark Magick recoiled at her intrusion into Taryn's psyche. Whatever it was, it didn't want her there. The sentient Magick struck Airess and gripped onto her ankles. It dragged her deeper within the black void, the embodiment of Taryn's trauma. The black Magick crept up Airess' legs, pulling her under. She cried out, not sure what was happening. Not sure if she could survive whatever this was.

Airess closed her eyes. She had a strong mind. She knew she could do this. She knew she had the strength to fight back.

She called upon her Starlight, willing the energy to expand around her like an aura. She screamed, ripping through the dark Magick's hold until it was nothing but a speck of dust within Taryn's mind.

Airess wasted no time being free of its hold. The world spun as she searched for him under the layers of terror, fear and sadness. Under the layers of memories that had engulfed him. She pulsed her Magick–whatever it was–into his astral body. She reached out into the void, ready to find Taryn.

"You can do this," Airess called out. "You can fight it."

She almost lost hope. Almost lost faith–until finally, a hand brushed against hers. Airess smiled at the recognition, at his touch, and grabbed Taryn's astral hand, then yanked.

She pulled him out of the memories. The darkness. His dreamform glittered silver when he emerged.

Taryn sank back into his body peacefully.

And Airess sank back into hers.

Chapter 28

'Today is my last day. I will see you in the Dreamworld, my dear.'

— *Unsent correspondence from Paulyr Moros*

Taryn

Taryn didn't know where he was. He couldn't feel anything, and he couldn't tell if he was dead or not. He didn't know how long he had faded into this timeless oblivion, but it was agony. His worst memories replayed in a loop, torturing him until he was numb to the pain. It was everything he had been avoiding his entire life.

Taryn's silver dreamform was freefalling in darkness, reaching out to grasp onto anything he could. There was no up or down here. There was no concept of time. He didn't know if it had been days, weeks, or months in this darkness.

But something had changed. Someone had come for him. Her presence was warm, a light in his darkness. A beacon of hope.

Airess.

Taryn felt her reach out to him and send a current of electricity into his psyche. He held onto it with all he could, and–

Taryn opened his eyes and met Airess' golden ones looking down at him in worry. Then, the mural on the dome-shaped ceiling above him. To his left was an old Human woman peering at him, her eyes crinkled with a kindness.

"So he lives," the woman said.

Taryn was enveloped into a firm hug. "You're alive!" Airess said, as she squeezed him harder. He soaked in her warmth, her touch, her scent. He never thought he would be able to again, and now that he was actually alive, Taryn knew he wanted to make his intentions with Airess clearer.

"We made it, Taryn," Airess whispered. "We're in Rune."

His shock faded away when reality hit him. He had held on as long as he could during their journey across the ocean, expending the last tinsel of energy he had to get them close enough to Rune. He never expected to live beyond that, he just wanted Airess to have a chance to make it. To live.

Taryn thought he *had* died, somehow trapped in an inescapable hell that could only be created by Eryx. He had been so entrapped by his darkest thoughts, his worst memories, he had forgotten who he was. That he was a person with a body.

Until he felt her.

He melted into her embrace in that moment as he realized, somehow, it was *Airess* who had pulled him out of it. He had heard her voice, a sweet melody amongst the demons, and had followed it.

"Thank you," he croaked into her neck softly, with a smile. Airess gently pulled away and tilted her head to the Human woman standing next to them.

"It wasn't just me who saved you. Taryn, this is Ismene. She welcomed us into Rune. And… freed you of your Oathmark."

Taryn sat up immediately. "What?"

Ismene began to pace in front of a great hearth of blush-colored flames, something he hadn't noticed until now.

"The Oathmark's Magick entrapped your soul. With Airess' Magick and a blessing from the Soulfyre, you were set free. The Gods deemed you worthy of redemption. " Ismene waved a hand toward the large hearth. "It is because of the *Gods* you live."

Taryn's body ached as he slid off the table and came to stand. He faced Ismene and inclined his head forward. "Words can't express my gratitude for what you've done for me."

Ismene smiled slightly and nodded. "You will want to save your words for the king. You both are to be escorted to the palace immediately, for review– to determine if they will accept you in Rune or not." Ismene turned on her heel without looking back. "You don't want to keep them waiting."

As soon as Taryn was healed, he and Airess were escorted by the royal guard to the palace. The humid air blasted his skin as soon as they stepped onto the street, a sensation Taryn thought he would never feel again. A palanquin waited for them outside of the temple. It was similar to a caravan, but there were no seats, wheels, or horses. Just a cushioned floor to sit on enclosed by walled structure.

Ismene and Airess climbed in first, followed by Taryn. Sheer fabric, the color of clay enclosed them. Earthborne servants wielded the rocks beneath the palanquin, lifting them into the air and propelling them forward. It was a surprisingly smooth ride, and Taryn watched Airess as she observed the Earthborn guards in awe.

Did Rune treat all their guests this way?

Finally, they arrived at the palace. It was just as he remembered. A white castle with several towers and terraces above, giving them a perfect view of the ocean beyond. The courtyard entrance was well-manicured, adorned with florals and palm trees.

As soon as they stepped out of the palanquin, they were immediately led into the castle. Even in his time here, he had never been inside. The floors were a mosaic of colored tiles favoring oranges, yellows and reds. Art hung every few feet, all depictions of the elemental Goddess, Eileamaid. Her raven hair covered her breasts, and she was pregnant in most paintings. Her pregnant belly wasn't flesh, but a blue and green depiction of the world. The goddess held her pregnant belly–the *world*–in her hands.

Although Taryn didn't pay the Gods much heed, he found himself nodding to the painting in respect anyway.

He glanced at Airess walking alongside him. Her hair and clothing were damp, just like Taryn's. She looked so tired. He had so many questions for her. How did she enter Rune? Who was this Ismene woman, and how did she save him? But his questions, however, would have to wait.

Two large white doors opened into a grand room.

The space was entirely empty. Polished colored tiles made up the floors. The walls were covered in gargantuan murals of each elemental symbol: Water, Air, Fyre, and Earth. The ceiling was plated in copper, as were the two thrones at the opposite end of the room. One throne was empty. The other throne was occupied, a Fae male sitting in it with his feet propped up.

"At last! My intruders arrive!" exclaimed the Fae male with a genuine smile, sitting up properly at their arrival. The male couldn't have been much older than Taryn, likely in his late twenties.

It was the male's eyes that struck Taryn first–vibrant royal blue irises with a subtle glow. The male had rich brown skin, his biceps adorned with copper arm links that matched the copper rings in his dark, long dreads. The male wore clothing of royal Runean fashion, a silk V-necked sleeveless vest with matching pants, his muscled chest and arms on display.

"King Roznarr Tozya, I present to you Airess Haeleth of the Judla province in Luciena." Ismene gestured a hand to Taryn. "This male goes by Taryn Seas, an orphan of Rune, my king."

Taryn's chest burned at Ismene's reminder of his origins. *This* male was the now-grown prince–*King*–he had heard about during his time here. Taryn recalled seeing Roznarr when he was a young male, always close to his father during any public event. Roznarr was only a teenager at the time. Even back then he was always polite, never failing to interact with the commoners in town. Roznarr was a prodigy among the Fae, well known for his rare ability to wield all four elements.

Looking at Roznarr now, Taryn could see there was a change within the male. Perhaps the weight of ruling crafted him into someone more bold, more power hungry. There was a glint of greed within the king's eyes, Taryn could see it even beneath his supposed friendliness.

Taryn hadn't known Rune's former king had passed, his son now taking his place. Granted, there was a lot he didn't know by being cut off from society in Luciena.

King Roznarr surveyed them both carefully before locking eyes with Taryn, those blue eyes flicking slightly to Taryn's elemental earring. The king clasped his ring-adorned fingers together. "What an interesting pair to show up on Rune's beaches. Tell me, how did you break through the ward? Last I recalled, Luciena had it sealed off a decade ago."

Taryn and Airess glanced at each other, the look between them conveying a silent message that they both had no idea what this King was talking about.

"We simply…passed through, my King." Taryn said first, taking a step forward. There was a stubbornness in Taryn that didn't want to address this male as King, but he stifled it. "We had no knowledge it even existed. We fled the country and encountered it."

Ismene leaned down and whispered something into the king's ear. Taryn only heard a few words with his hearing, catching the words *suspect* and *like you*. King Roznarr's brows creased as she retreated, thrumming his fingers on the chair arm.

"We have not received refugees from your country in a decade. As unexpected as it was, Rune will not turn down those in need today. We will accept you as our humble guests," the king announced, face animating as he stood. "You will be shown to your quarters for the time being. Perhaps we should throw a feast for our guests!"

The king snapped his fingers at one of the attendants. "Arrange it at once for tomorrow morning. We must give these people time to rest after such a long journey. I look forward to hearing of your travels."

And with that, the pair was escorted out of the room.

Confused, Taryn followed closely behind Airess as they walked out of the palace, leaving as quickly as they came. They were led down a path through what seemed to be the palace gardens. The path led to a smaller looking home.

"The king has instructed you both to stay in the palace guest house for the time being," An attendant said, "Right this way."

Guest house was an understatement. It wasn't small by any means. It was large–almost as large as the Guild manor back in Lonskeep. The servant pushed open the rounded wooden doors and guided them inside.

The house was finely decorated with ornate rugs and plush furniture, all favoring the colors orange and yellow. The doorknobs and handles were brass, as were the cups sitting next to a complimentary barcart. They walked right into the living space of the house: two large couches on one side and a grand table that could fit twelve on the other. The large outdoor balcony across from them let in copious amounts of natural light.

"The house is equipped with several bedrooms and bathrooms upstairs. Dinner will be served later tonight, so please get settled. Tomorrow morning we will arrive to get you both prepped and ready for a meal with the king and Queen Dowager."

The Queen Dowager? Taryn hadn't expected to be greeted with such hospitality, especially a private audience with the king and Queen Dowager.

The attendant left, and Taryn and Airess were left standing in the common room alone. When the door closed behind the last attendant, Taryn finally turned to look at her.

"That was entirely too easy."

"Wasn't it?" Airess asked in agreement, beginning to pace as she usually did when she had a lot on her mind. "I never expected to end up sleeping in a *royal* guesthouse tonight. How could they just accept us so easily?"

"I'm not sure. Something feels… off. I can't put my finger on it," Taryn said, scanning the room. "Fortunately for them, I'm too fucking tired to care."

Taryn stalked over to the bar cart and swiped a bottle of whiskey and a cloth. His stab wound still throbbed with pain, but he would live. It wasn't the first time he had a wound of this severity.

"Let me see it," Airess demanded. Taryn sighed and strode up to her, but she softly pushed his chest backwards, forcing him to sit on the couch. She peeled his shirt up, and Taryn grimaced as the fabric was ripped away from his healing flesh. Pain mixed with pleasure at her touch, and flashbacks of their kiss at the inn flooded his mind.

Airess grabbed the whiskey from his hands and poured the liquid into the cloth. She looked at him, silently asking for permission to continue.

Taryn nodded.

The alcohol stung as it made contact, but it was nothing compared to her fingers touching his body. He inhaled sharply, not from the pain, but to compose himself. A single touch from her made him dizzy.

If they were standing upright, he would have fallen to his knees.

His eyes trailed her every move as she cleaned the wound in agonizing silence. When she was done, she poured the whiskey into two glasses and handed one over to him. Airess slumped on the couch next to him, no doubt from exhaustion.

"Well, Taryn. I'll allow you the honors." Airess commented, raising her glass in the air.

Taryn grinned. He raised his glass as well. "To finally making it to Rune, despite all odds."

"To making it to Rune." Airess nodded. "A month and a half ago I was to be the future queen of Luciena. Now I'm halfway across the world, free, and somehow ended up meeting a sarcastic bastard along the way. Who knew?"

"The Gods knew," Taryn said as he took a sip of the whiskey, bringing his lips to the glass rim.

Airess lifted her cup, a subtle smile on her lips. It was a look he committed to memory.

She nodded, eyes twinkling. "The Gods knew."

Chapter 29

'It has been several months after The Twin's failed attempt to recreate Tevye. Although they perished, they did create their wall. The cost? Magick.'

— Written entry from Zaro Lucien's personal journal

Airess

"Ma'am?"

A voice pulled Airess out of a rare, dreamless slumber. She felt a hand lightly press her shoulder, and when her eyes shot open, she realized she was still in the living room of the guest house.

Airess met the eyes of a servant who looked down at her expectantly, and then glanced over to an unconscious Taryn sleeping next to her. Heat crept up her cheeks and neck as she took in the position they were in. Airess had accidentally fallen asleep on the couch with him, her body pressed into Taryn's, his arm around her.

"It's time for you to get ready," the attendant said with a raised brow.

Airess cleared her throat and nodded, gently removing Taryn's arm from her body, careful not to wake him. She knew he needed the rest.

The attendant led her to a room and got to work. Airess fought the urge to pull her hand away as four attendants filed her nails, scrubbed her skin, combed her hair, and painted her face. She had only been awake in her quarters for ten minutes, yet was admiring the astonishing difference in everything of the Runean culture.

All the furniture was low to the ground, even the masterfully wooden-engraved bed sat on the floor surface. The room was decorated in a multitude of deeply rich colors, the color palette favoring reds and golds that was showcased on the rugs, bed quilt, and curtains.

Even the art was different here, paintings showcasing nude Fae people–of all shapes and sizes–seemed to be the norm here. The windows were constantly left open, letting in a warm, moist air she wasn't quite used to. It seemed as if the people of Rune had nothing to hide, from the way they dressed, to the openness of their architecture.

Airess did her best to not breathe too deeply as they painted a rose-colored substance on her lips and lined her eyes with black paint. Even the makeup was different here, Rune leaning towards a more liquid kind of makeup rather than the powder she was used to back home–

Not home.

The thought stung worse than she thought it would. Even here, even now, she still felt homeless. Hopefully in time she would settle here comfortably.

Finally, they were done. "Beautiful. You will present nicely to the king." One of the attendants admired, stroking a lock of hair in awe. Airess stepped in front of the mirror, her mouth parted open at the sight of herself.

Oh, Gods.

She truly did feel beautiful. Different, a little bit bolder than she was used to, but beautiful.

They had lined her eyes with black paint that winged at the edges of her eyes. A translucent golden shimmer had been dusted lightly on her cheekbones, her bare chest, and shoulders. And – *wow*, her body had never been out on display like this!

She wore a strapless wrapped top that covered her breasts, stopping just before her belly button. The fabric was of fine silk, lined with weaving golden threads.

A matching flowing skirt fell low on her hips, two slits on either side of the skirt. They had given her the sandals with strings that laced up all the way up her calves. Her long hair was left down,

She looked like an entirely different person. Airess stared at herself, and noticed that she felt different. She concentrated on the sensation, and realized it was the hum of power that thrummed beneath her skin. Her Magick felt stronger, more accessible, than it ever had before.

A knock on the door cut her time getting ready short. Airess was escorted out and down to the common room. Taryn was already waiting, sitting in a relaxed position as he looked out one of the windows.

Taryn tensed before immediately standing and turning to face her. His eyebrows lifted as he drank her in, lips parting slightly as his gaze trailed down her body. He walked over to her swiftly.

Taryn lifted a hand to scratch the back of his neck, eyes roaming her figure with adoration. "You are so beautiful."

Airess' cheeks heated at the compliment. "You clean up handsomely yourself," she replied quietly, taking in his clothing, his hair. Taryn wore a billowing V-necked tunic with sleeves rolled up to his elbows, the fabric light. His flowing pants were cuffed at the ankles. Half his hair had been pulled up, save for a single braided strand at his brow. His elemental earring remained.

She looked at him, *truly* looked at him, and smiled. He belonged here. "You've finally made it home –"

An attendant cleared her throat, shifting awkwardly beside them. "We must escort you to the palace."

Taryn and Airess shared a glance. She swallowed down her impending anxiety, but she couldn't help but feel out of sorts. King Roznarr was entirely different than she had expected, despite their brief encounter. She thought he would be a cold individual with a commanding demeanor, but so far he carried himself as a casual friend. Airess bit back her worry and gathered her courage.

I am not my anxiety.

The attendant walked out, Taryn and Airess following through the gardens and into the palace entrance. They were led inside, weaving through several corridors until they were led out to a grand terrace.

"Wait here." The attendant said, and left.

The terrace was as magnificent as the rest of the palace. Perched atop the capitol of Rune, they had a full view of the city and ocean beyond. The pillars making up the balcony railing were intricately curved, the material the same white stucco as the rest of the palace. Sheer curtains billowed along the railings, the humid wind beginning to make Airess' hair frizzy.

The table dominating the center of the space was massive and low to the ground, embroidered cushions placed every few feet acting as the chairs they would be sitting on. Colored rugs lined the floors, each one layering on top of the other.

"I've never seen anything like it," Airess commented, stepping towards the railing, placing a hand on the banister as she looked out to the horizon.

Taryn came up next to her and leaned onto the railing, still a little weak, no doubt after all he had endured in the past day. He pivoted to face her, brunette curls flowing around his face in the coastal breeze. He met her eyes, and sometimes Airess forgot how beautiful she found his molten irises. They glowed, stark against his tawny skin. He was so damned perfect.

Taryn flashed a subtle smile, but she knew him well enough to know he was hiding his pain.

"Airess," Taryn said, tentatively placing his hand atop her own. His touch was warm. *Kind.* It was a small but intimate action, and one that surprised her.

"I owe you my life for what you've done for me."

Airess pivoted her body to look up at him. She saw the gratitude within his eyes as he squeezed her hand, and for a moment, she thought he might kiss her again. Perhaps he would have, if the double doors hadn't burst open behind them.

Startled, Taryn and Airess broke apart and turned towards the doors.

In came Ismene, King Roznar, and another Fae female who had to have been the Queen Dowager.

"My lovely guests! You both cleaned up well. Especially you, My Lady," Roznarr said in Mrkynian, taking Airess' palm and kissing the back of her hand.

She fought her blush as she nodded in respect. "Thank you, King Roznarr. I am very grateful for your hospitality."

"Please, call me Roz. No need for all the formalities."

Airess felt the energy shift in the air immediately, the source of the change coming from Taryn. She glanced at him, shooting him a death glare to encourage him to contribute to the pleasantries, but he didn't see her look, he was staring at Roznarr's hand atop her own.

Taryn's jaw clenched as he looked at the king slowly. "Yes, we couldn't thank you enough for taking us in so expeditiously." His tone was biting, unfriendly. Internally, Airess winced. This was not how Taryn should be acting.

Roz dropped her hand and motioned towards his mother. "This is the Queen Dowager, Rumi Tozya."

The Queen Dowager nodded as she looked to Taryn, and then Airess. She turned towards Roz after her inspection and spoke in Runean, "So *these* are the individuals you say might be the prophesied."

Her voice was neutral, but her gaze was unreadable, speculative eyes lingering on Taryn and Airess.

Roz coughed, replying in Mrkynian, "Mother, let us eat our meal before we dive into such a discussion. Please, sit. Enjoy this meal."

Taryn and Airess shared a glance before sitting down on the plush cushions. What the hell was going on?

Airess blinked her Sight forward, her ability coming easy to her now that the donstenyte poison had worn off. The first aura she noticed was Roz's, his energy a striking blue that swirled beautifully around him, matching the same royal azure as his pupils. Ismene's aura was the color of lilac. The same color of Esper Crawn's power. *Interesting.*

The Queen Dowager's aura was relatively normal, but the energy flowed slower than the others, as if it were not able to travel freely within and around her. Airess knew this was a sign of a mental blockage.

Airess blinked her Sight away when she noticed Ismene eyeing her wearily and busied herself with a glass of water.

Their food was brought out to them, the scent of heavy spices wafting up to her nose. Plates of diced potatoes, rice, various meats, and fruits were placed all around the table.

They began to dine quietly, partaking in small talk about Airess' upbringing and eventual move to the capitol. She made sure to give them the short version of her backstory, and spared them the details of her being taken forcefully.

Taryn relayed how he came to live in Luciena, leaving out key details that he was a trained assassin for an illegal Guild. Eventually, the topic steered towards plans for the future.

"We have a wonderful university in the city–" Ismene began, but was interrupted by the queen Dowager clearing her throat. Everyone's attention shifted to Rumi, who took a sip of her wine with a small smile.

Ismene side-eyed the Queen Dowager before speaking again. "But I would like to take you two on personally, to train you in the art of your power."

Airess perked up at the opportunity to finally mention the Obadiah. She squeezed her skirts as she gathered the courage to speak. "If I may, Ismene," Airess began. "When I escaped Luciena's capitol, it was with the help of Priestess Esper Crawn. She was the one who set me on this path–to travel to Rune and find The Obadiah so I can learn more about my power and how to wield it. I would be honored to train with you."

"And *we* would love to train with the both of you." Ismene's eyes darted from Airess to Taryn, and then to the Queen Dowager and Roz. They nodded to Ismene in approval. Airess creased her brows.

"In fact," Ismene added, "We have all been patiently awaiting both of your arrivals for quite some time."

Whatever Airess had expected her to say, it wasn't that.

"What did you mean for *quite some time?*" Taryn interjected, his face laced with doubt. Airess tightened the grip on her skirt at Taryn's boldness.

"Thirty years ago, one of our Obadiah members saw a vision of a young male and female arriving on our shores. Our Seer couldn't see the faces of the individuals, but she was able to gather the names of who would arrive to Rune and fulfill the prophecy. Those names were Deyanira and Kazimyr."

Taryn stiffened as Ismene let the words linger, sinking in. Airess immediately recognized the name from her locket, her hand already going to her heart to touch it.

"I know that name. It's engraved on my mother's locket."

Ismene nodded in confirmation, letting Airess put the pieces together.

"But… that's not my name. My name is Airess *Haeleth*."

Again, Ismene shared a look with King Roz.

Finally, the king spoke up. "Taryn, Airess, have you both ever heard of Tevye?"

"Yes," Airess answered. "I'm aware of the… tales."

She didn't want to mention her dreamwalking abilities and how she may or may not have stumbled into Tevye by accident. Airess noticed Taryn's silence as Roz chuckled, sipping his wine, "They are more than just tales."

The king put down his glass and looked her directly in the eyes. "This world, these continents, are not all there is to this planet. It is not by natural design. The world was made this way, divided in half by our ancestors.

"Before The Division, our world was grand. Large, even. We had several continents, several nations. Then, The Division occurred a thousand years ago, and the world has been altered ever since. We are what has remained in this half. The other half of the world, lost to us, is called Tevye. It exists in a higher dimension."

The distant sound of birds cawing grew muffled, and the humid wind blew tendrils of Airess's hair in her face. She tucked the stray hair back and tried to reply as politely as she could. "If this is true, we would have already learned about this *Division*. It's–it's just a fairytale." But even as she said the words, Airess knew it didn't resonate with her soul. There had been an internal shift within her during her travels to get here, and she knew whatever seemed impossible in the past now seemed… *possible.*

Roz shook his head. "No, Luciena has kept its people in the dark. They don't teach the true histories of the world. Luciena, in a way, has created its own little world within itself. Brainwashing its people to worship only one God, one House, when it took five Gods to make this world. *Five Houses.* Yet, they claim all the glory," Roz scoffed. "They put Bas on a pedestal, as if the other Gods never existed at all."

"The Luciens altered sacred texts, removing information that could empower the people, only leaving in bits and pieces that strengthened Bas' image. They use a witch-cursed herb to poison your food, your water, so that your power is weakened."

Airess' mind whirled. The food and water? Was it possible that it could actually be *poisoned*?

Airess thought back to when her and Taryn had been jailed. She hadn't drunk any water for hours during that time, and shortly after, she had used her power to escape in the caravan. The same thing happened when Taryn had tried to abduct her when they first met–she hadn't drunk or eaten, and she used her power to blast him off of her in the forest…

Airess blinked her Sight forward. When his aura glowed brighter, she realized the truth of Roz's words.

Her stomach plummeted at the realization, yet something was off.

"That doesn't make sense. The Luciens were hellbent on marrying me off to their prince *because* of my Magick. It wouldn't make sense for them to poison the water. They wanted power."

Roz leaned back in his chair, studying Airess. He cocked his head to the side in thought. "You bring up a good point. I will admit, our intel could only go so far. We had assumed it was the Luciens who were poisoning their people. If not, who is? Who else has access to enough salaroses to create the poison?"

Beside her, Taryn choked on his wine.

"Of course, I assure you that is all behind you now. There is no need to worry about the water and food being tampered with here in Rune," Roz said, nodding his head with encouragement.

"Regardless of the poison, why would the Luciens lie about the world's true history?" Airess asked.

"For control," The Queen Dowager chimed in. "They are a powerful ruling House. They can keep themselves on a pedestal if the people are unaware of their own power. The past can be erased by the present after decades, generations have passed."

"What does Tevye and Luciena's lies have to do with us?" Airess asked hastily, finally bringing forth the question that had been brewing within her this entire conversation. She looked to Taryn, who was currently staring at his plate, and found it odd he seemed so… unsurprised.

"We believe you both are a part of the prophecy that will unite the world whole again," Ismene said, as if her statement seemed simple, and understandable.

Taryn scoffed, finally speaking up, "And you gather that from two strangers you've never met?"

For once, Airess was glad for Taryn's attitude. It was true, this all sounded a little far-fetched. A gust of wind blew harder throughout the terrace, stronger than the usual ocean breeze, making the hairs on her arms rise.

Ismene narrowed her eyes at Taryn. "I believe you know the answer to that, Taryn *Seas*. Or should I say Tarynon Kazimyr?"

Silence fell over them. Taryn physically recoiled, his face blanched, as if he had been reminded of something he had tried his best to forget. Airess turned to him, no longer caring that there were others here.

Tarynon.

"What is she talking about?"

Taryn closed his eyes and let out a shaky breath. It was because of his reaction that Airess knew Taryn had been holding something back. She had an inkling of it during their travels, especially after visiting Mara's fortune teller stand. Airess' heart sank, confusion and betrayal constricting her chest. He had lied about his name.

But why?

Before he could respond, Ismene spoke to Airess directly. "And you, my dear, are *not* a Haeleth. You did not get that name from a Human Lord."

Her pulse thundered in her ears.

"Wait –" Taryn said, holding his hand out to stop Ismene, but she kept talking.

"In fact, that Human man was never your father. Your name, your *true* name, is Airess Deyanira. You are a Lightborne princess of House

Deyanira, Daughter of Stars. And *you*," Ismene bit out, shifting her eyes to Taryn, "Are prince Tarynon Kazimyr, Stormborne prince of House Kazimyr, Son of Moon. But you already knew that, didn't you?"

Chapter 30

'How dare you namesake this abomination of a world after us, Evyen? How dare you.'

– Written correspondence from Tinyrah Kazimyr to Evyen Deyanira

Taryn

Airess stared at him in disbelief, her mouth hanging open. Taryn watched the betrayal take root within her, her face hardening after the initial shock. Her entire body stiffened, brows furrowing as she looked at him. It was a look he never wanted to be on the receiving end of. Taryn's breath faltered.

It was never meant to come out like this.

Airess' nostrils flared as she whipped her head to look at Ismene. Her usually polite demeanor was gone and replaced by a brazenness he hadn't seen from her before. He winced, desperately wishing he could explain himself before things spiraled.

"House Deyanira hasn't existed for thousands of years," Airess said.

It was a fact that Taryn had always known wasn't true.

"House Deyanira still exists, along with the other houses: Kazimyr, Moros, Lucien, and Tozya. Each family house and its members are direct descendants of the Gods, and three of those Houses still stand on the other side. *In Tevye*. Where you both hail from."

Taryn's world spun at the reminder of who he truly was. His real name. His origins. He never thought he would hear the word again. *Kazimyr*. It was a truth he had buried, had ignored, since his grandmother died.

"I don't understand," Airess said angrily. "What do you mean where we *hail* from?"

"You and Tarynon are Tevyen. You were brought over to this side of the world when you were babies, for your own safety. The Tevyen society knew the Prophesied Ones would be born, and they were willing to do anything to stop it from coming into fruition, including killing you both as children."

Alarms rang in his head. The Prophesied Ones? Now *this* was news to even Taryn.

"Why would they want us killed?" Airess demanded, her voice rising. Her face reddened, and Taryn felt the energy radiating off her in waves.

"Because it is *you* who will bring forth The Dawn, unite both halves of the worlds, and make it whole again. The Tevyens don't want that to happen. You'd disrupt a power balance there that had been set since Tevye's creation. It was better for you both to be sent to our side of the world–*The Old World*, they call it–and grow up where people believed Tevye was just a legend."

"So Rune knows about Tevye?" Airess asked–a question Taryn had also wanted to know the answer to. His grandmother was the one who made Taryn aware as a small child that he was a Tevyen being, that he was a member of the Kazimyr House. However, she never once mentioned anything about a prophecy, about uniting the world whole again. Taryn clenched his fists, diverting his attention to Roznarr.

"Only the small council here in Rune knows. This is not information to be shared with the public. It would cause too much panic. The people are not ready for this truth," Roz interjected. Taryn outwardly scoffed. The king's head snapped to him, eyes narrowed.

Who was he to decide what the people were ready for?

There was a palpable tension in the air, an energy radiating off of Roznarr, Airess, and Taryn. Ismene stayed silent, eyes darting between the three, lips pressed into a thin line. Taryn could almost *taste* the power on his tongue, feel it thrumming against his skin, but couldn't discern who it was coming from. Ever since they arrived in Rune, Taryn felt his Magick radiating within his body stronger than it ever had.

The Queen Dowager spoke first, breaking the silence. "Perhaps we should give our new guests some time to process this information. They have traveled a long way to get here. Besides, we have a ball to prepare for. The Salamoon is only a few days away."

"Of course," Roz said icily, dropping Taryn's gaze. Taryn smirked, smug in the fact that Roz was the first to break eye contact. King or not, Taryn would assert his dominance–*especially* after scenting the interest wafting off the male when he kissed Airess' hand. It bothered him more than he cared to admit, and he couldn't deny the protectiveness he felt over Airess. Taryn knew Airess had no idea about the unspoken power struggle going on between the two. The Fae's enhanced senses brought up another layer of emotion that an Elve could not comprehend.

Ismene nodded in agreement and stood, flattening her hands against her clothing. "We will... give you some time to process. I will send someone to retrieve you both for our first lesson, once you've settled in, of course."

They all filed out the door, one by one. The Queen Dowager was last, her gaze lingering on Airess briefly before turning to leave.

Slowly, Airess turned to Taryn. Their eyes met, and the color drained from her face. She shook her head slightly, as if denying the possibility that he had lied. Shame coursed through him, a cold feeling that traveled down his entire body. He knew how it looked. How it sounded. Taryn could only hope she would understand after he explained himself.

Of course, Taryn had suspected over the course of their travels what Airess could be. When she exploded the caravan, Taryn had his confirmation. Even though he had only heard about the power through his grandmother's stories, Taryn knew she was Lightborne–a power only a Tevyen could have.

As for himself... he knew all along what his real name was. That he was a Tevyen Fae, Stormborne from another land. It was why he could control all the elements that made up a storm: water, wind, and lightning. It was why he had made sure to keep his abilities a secret when he grew up here, because there was no one else like him in Rune.

"How did you–" Airess began, then stopped herself. She inhaled and sat up straight, regaining her composure. "Is it true? Did you know this about yourself? About me?"

Taryn's throat closed up, the air around him suddenly heavy. "Airess, I need you to know that I would have eventually–"

She let out a bitter scoff and withdrew, leaning away from him. Taryn's heart pounded at the display–at what she must be feeling right now. He was the only one left in Airess' life. He knew she felt the sting of his withheld information on a deeper level, however new their relationship was. Because they were all each other had, and now he had tarnished her trust.

Gods, I'm an idiot.

Taryn swallowed and forced his voice to come out steady.

"I learned about my true name from my grandmother. She told me the stories about Tevye, about the remaining God Houses that exist on the other side. You have to understand, I was taught to always keep my abilities a secret. I was always careful to only wield water when I lived here, to appear as I were only Waterborne to the other Fae. I didn't know about you until the caravan. I assumed you were a Tevyen being after that... encounter, but I had *no idea* that you belonged to a sacred House."

Airess searched his face, as if trying to sense an untruth. She clasped her hands together, and looked away.

"Did you know about this–this prophecy?"

"No," Taryn confirmed. "That is news to me. Though, I'm not sure I believe it."

Airess pushed up from her chair abruptly, the harsh scraping of the chair legs causing Taryn to flinch. "I don't understand," she said, pacing. "I mean, this is almost laughable. Why is it that everyone in my life is okay with *lying* to me?" Her voice cracked, and Taryn shot to his feet immediately and seized her wrist. She spun around, the lines between her brows heavily creased as she looked at his hand.

"Listen to me. I would never lie to you," he said, eyes pleading. "You have to understand."

Slowly, Airess lifted her gaze to his. Her eyes gleamed–not with anger, but hurt. "You knew your name this entire time, knew the truth about my *lineage*, and didn't think to tell me? I showed you my home, *Taryn*. You let me believe–" pain etched itself across her features. She stepped back, Taryn's hand falling limp next to his side.

Tears welled in her eyes as she spoke, "My–my *father*. Ismene said Haeleth isn't my real name. So who's–" Airess shook her head, as if the motion would dispel the truth. "How can it be true? *Who is my father? Who* really was my mother?"

Taryn's heart cracked. He finally realized the weight of what she was going through. It was more than him withholding information. It was the fact that everything about her life was a lie.

"Airess," Taryn whispered. He stepped closer, but this time she didn't back away. He grabbed one of her hands and caressed her jaw with the other, tilting her head so she would look up at him.

"I should have told you the truth. I just didn't know how to tell you. I–I wasn't thinking about your family or what that would mean for you. Please, I'm an idiot. I've made a mistake. I am so sorry."

Airess studied him before closing her eyes and breathing out. She grabbed his wrist, the one caressing her chin, and let her hold linger. He was grateful for her touch, it was the only thing keeping him from trembling with fear. Fear that she would never speak to him again, that she would leave.

Airess pulled away and walked to the railing, turning her back to him. Her shoulders sank as she looked out at the sky. Taryn waited for her to say something. *Anything.*

Finally, she spoke. "If this is all true, then we have families out there somewhere that want us dead. That threatened our *mothers*."

Taryn approached the banister and stood beside her. She kept her eyes forward, refusing to look at him.

"We don't know if what they were saying is true," Taryn reasoned. "There could be more they aren't telling us."

"You *would* say that."

She cut her eyes to him. The anger within them was gone, replaced with an emotion he couldn't name.

"I know they were telling the truth. I saw it with my Sight." Then as if realizing something for the first time, her eyes widened. She pivoted to face him.

"If what they say is true, that makes you a *prince*, Taryn."

Taryn recoiled at the reminder. It didn't seem real. Taryn didn't think he would ever truly accept it unless he saw his supposed *House* and the land of Tevye for himself. In truth, he hadn't thought about those words in years–had buried them so deep in his mind he had almost forgotten.

Almost.

He couldn't help but smile bitterly. It sounded insane. "Sweetheart, I am the furthest thing from royalty."

Airess searched his face. There was still a subtle hurt present, but also a new understanding. As if learning this information finally gave Airess the permission to be who she was. Who she was meant to be. She certainly was taking this much better than he had. Airess almost seemed comfortable–dare he say *optimistic* about this bomb shell of a revelation.

Taryn's fingers grazed her hand, feeling the warm tingle spread throughout his entire body. "It all makes sense now," he whispered, turning his gaze out to the ocean beyond.

"What?"

"That you belong to a sacred house–that you are royalty."

Airess said nothing for a time. In the corner of his eye, he saw her look up at him. "This changes everything," she said, then frowned as she looked at her shoes. "And at the same time, it changes nothing."

"What do you mean?"

"Somewhere out there, we have a claim to power that was stolen from us. And there's nothing that can be done about it. Tevye exists in a dimension inaccessible to us."

Taryn's brows furrowed as he turned to look down at her. He was surprised to see... disappointment in her eyes.

"Airess, this news doesn't change anything," Taryn stepped forward and cupped her face. "We made it to Rune. We accomplished our goal. We don't have to claim that life. We came here to start over."

"Is that what *you* have done? Ignored your claim–ignored who you truly are?"

Taryn flinched at her words, hearing them out loud for the first time. That's when he saw it. He saw something brewing within Airess that he was afraid to accept. To acknowledge. But it was there. The desire to experience more. To *be* more.

A part of him had always known.

Slowly, he replied, "I have never lived thinking I have a claim to anything. I have been abandoned, orphaned, and left behind as a child to live homeless in the streets. I don't care if I have a family out there who doesn't want me. And you shouldn't either. They are dead to me."

Airess' eyes flashed with a hardness, only for a second, before she looked out to the ocean beyond. He studied her features, the way her lips pursed in thought. They way her brows creased, before they softened as she met his gaze.

"You're right," she said stiffly as she shifted on her feet.

The energy surrounding them was still tense, so Taryn inhaled and plastered a sarcastic grin on his face. He cupped a hand behind his ear.

"Wait, what was that? Did you say I'm right?"

Airess' lips twitched, as if trying to resist a smile, before her slight laugh broke through. "Don't get too cocky, Tar."

"I'm going to need those words in writing."

"You're insufferable."

They stared at one another for a moment before Taryn chuckled and slipped an arm around her shoulders.

"Let's get out of here. We need to find Ismene."

Airess looked like she was going to refuse, but then nodded.

As they walked out, he couldn't help but hear Airess' words ringing in his mind.

That makes you a prince, Taryn.

And, for one moment, he allowed himself to imagine what his life would have looked like if he had never been taken from his homeland. Would he have been a king? Did he have other family members? Would he have ended up a good person if he was never brought here?

Taryn frowned. He hoped he would never find out.

Chapter 31

There is no winning in playing fair.

— *Evyen Deyanira*

Taryn

Later that evening, Taryn and Airess were escorted to meet Ismene at the Temple. Their conversation sure as hell wasn't over, and they both needed to get to the bottom of what this prophecy was.

They walked into the temple room where he had almost died just a day ago. It was beautiful, even more so than he remembered, since he was here last in Rune. He had gone to the Temple occasionally when he lived with Ima, but after Ima's death and his troubled adolescent years, he never bothered to go back.

The arched doors to the sanctuary were intricately painted with the colors of the elements: blue, red, green and white. The depiction told the story of the elemental God, how she harnessed control of all four elements and created the world. It was a story he could recite with ease, even after being away from Rune so long.

As they walked through the doors, they were immediately greeted by the rosy flames within the hearth—so pink they looked otherworldly, as if they were crafted from the Gods themselves.

And now he knew they were.

The Soulfyre. The flames that restored his spirit.

Ismene sat in the corner at her cramped desk, smiling as they walked in. The Priestess waved a hand for them to sit in front of the desk, a book open in her lap.

"Back so soon?" Ismene asked.

"What's this prophecy talk the queen spoke of at breakfast?" Taryn asked as they sat down, getting straight to the point.

Ismene flipped page after page in her book as she spoke.

"How does one control a God?" she asked nonchalantly, ignoring his question.

Taryn arched his brows. "I'm sorry?"

"How does one control a God?" she repeated, as she stood up and moved toward the hearth, reaching her hand in and drawing out a bundle of flames.

"There are several ways, I suppose. You can drug them, take away their ability to think clearly and skew their perception of the world." She began to guide the flames lazily in the air, weaving it in slow spirals.

"You can *trick* them, make them believe another holds power over them, so much so that they believe they don't have power over *themselves*." Ismene's gaze was heavy on Taryn before she averted her eyes to Airess.

"You can take away their knowledge, erase their history, so that they don't even know they *exist*. A God can't act on their power if they don't know they have power, can they?" Ismene asked sharply. "*That* is how you control a God. And that, my children, is what the wretched country of Luciena has done to you."

A silence fell over the room before Airess broke through it. "I suppose you may be correct in regard to Luciena numbing our powers with drugs, but we are no *Gods*." Airess laughed casually.

"Perhaps not that strong of a term," Ismene agreed. "But a step below it, to be sure."

Taryn sat back in his chair and crossed his legs. "And what is that supposed to mean?"

"You want to know of the prophecy and what it has to do with you, yes? We are just getting started." Ismene chuckled, guiding the fyre fluidly back into the hearth.

"If you were regular people, Taryn wouldn't be here right now. That Oathmark should have shattered his sanity, and Airess' magick wouldn't have the strength to bring back his soul. But you are both not regular people. You both are *Godlings.*"

Taryn fought the urge to roll his eyes. Of course, he should have expected this from a priestess, taking her religious ideology a little too far.

"Godlings?" Taryn deadpanned.

"She tells the truth," Airess blurted, her golden eyes set on Ismene, no doubt unveiling her Sight on Ismene to judge her. Taryn pressed his lips together in doubt, but listened to her continue on.

Ismene gave Airess a slight nod in approval. "I'm sure speaking the plain truth that you have been deprived of for so long sounds ludicrous after so many years, so I will convey it in a way you can understand. Each family House is a direct descendant of the Gods. Each house began with Godlings, a God-Touched family deemed worthy of Godlike power.

"As a Godling, you are able to access Spirit–a heightened state of power that allows the Gods' power to flow through you. Think of it this way, the Gods gave you a sliver of their soul when they Touched you at birth. You access their soul when you are Spirited."

Spirited. The word hung in the air between them. Airess leaned forward, brows drawn together in concentration.

"*That* is the meaning of God Touched, of being a Godling. King Roznarr is Touched, an elemental Godling of Eileamaid. We suspect that you both are Godlings as well."

Taryn's eyes widened at the detail. If Godlings were as powerful as Ismene claimed, no wonder the energy at breakfast was permeating through the air like lightning. He glanced over to Airess, her expression a mix of curiosity and belief. He exhaled a steady breath and bit his tongue, listening carefully.

"And how does that tie in with us fulfilling a prophecy?" Airess asked, on the edge of her seat.

Ismene walked to her desk, sifting through the piles of books and papers until she found a singular piece of parchment and placed it in front of them.

"When The Obadiah came to Rune, we brought over many manuscripts of information, including this document written by a Seer hundreds of years ago. Read for yourself."

Taryn leaned in and read the words handwritten in ink:

A stolen Death

A touch of Fyre

An earth rebirthed

To be made from desire

A soul of Mind

Brings forth the Storm

Is when the dawn of a new age

Shalt be born.

Taryn stilled at the familiarity of the words, his eyes flickering with recognition. A plethora of questions brewed in his mind– so many he could barely keep up.

"According to legend, only a Godling can fulfill this prophecy. Only a Godling can unite the world. And because we haven't had a single Godling born for centuries, it would seem that you both, along with Roz and the others, have finally been born to fulfill it."

"When Airess and I were traveling, I dreamwalked into a memory when we were traveling in The Twins," Taryn started. "I didn't have much time to think about it then, but I saw something. Two beings, one named Evyen and the other was named Tinyrah. They were fighting, until eventually Evyen used some sort of Magick and *split* the ground with some... crystal blade. It didn't make sense then, but now I'm starting to think I–"

"Witnessed The Division," Ismene finished. "Yes, that was the cataclysmic event that changed the world. They were your ancestors. They named the new world they created after themselves, the two lovers combining their names to title the other half of the world we know today. *Tevye*." Ismene looked between him and Airess before speaking again, "You're a dreamwalker?" Ismene asked him.

"We both are," Airess answered. "What do you know about dreamwalking?"

Ismene sat back in her chair. "It's an ability *some* Tevyens have. A Dreamwalker's spirit can walk freely amongst space and time within their sleep, viewing memories, places or other worlds. It's quite an ability, and a rare occurrence indeed to have two sitting across from me." Ismene's eyes shifted to him. "Even rarer for a Fae."

"How so?" Taryn asked, his interest piqued. Finally, this woman was saying something that sounded semi-logical.

"The Fae only have control over elemental power, physical Magick. It's not in the Fae's genes to control energetic Magick, including the ability to dreamwalk."

"Is it possible Taryn has some type of Elven descendant?" Airess asked.

Ismene laughed. "That would be doubtful. Your ancestors, Evyen and Tinyrah, never married or had any children together. They became… forbidden lovers." Ismene looked between them. "There is *another* theory, but perhaps we should save that for another lesson. We have discussed plenty for today." Ismene stood up hastily, as if she were in a rush to leave.

"We still have so many questions–" Airess started, but Ismene already cut her off.

"And you will have your answers in due time. Now, I have much to attend to. Meet me back here tomorrow and we shall continue our lesson."

With that, Ismene gathered her things and left the Temple.

They walked out onto the stone pathway that led to the city. The sun had completely set, leaving the sky stained a dark purple as the remnants of daylight faded into the horizon.

Airess was especially quiet, and Taryn couldn't blame her. Despite already knowing about his lineage and the existence of Tevye, all this news about prophecies and dreamwalking was starting to take a toll on him. He didn't know what to think or believe.

"What's on your mind?" he asked her, the glow of the moon outlining her features. They trekked through the main street nestled by the ocean bustling with different vendors, the smells of food making his stomach grumble.

"Everything!" she said incredulously, waving her hands in exasperation. "First the truth about our lineage, the prophecy–not to mention our ancestors *created* Tevye. It's all so much, I just can't help but feel alone."

Taryn didn't hesitate as he grabbed her hand. "You are most certainly not alone."

Airess looked up at him and smiled. It was a sight he imprinted in his memories for the rest of time.

If only she knew what she did to him.

"Good. Because you're all I have," she admitted as they walked forward. Her eyes widened, as if she didn't mean for the words to slip out. Taryn chuckled and put an arm over her shoulder.

"You're all I have too, Air."

A comfortable silence fell between them, their friendship entering a new depth. Of course, Taryn wasn't sure if *friend* could capture exactly what Airess was to him. For the first time in a decade, he was starting to feel at peace and think about his future. Besides all this prophecy talk that he still didn't wholly believe, Taryn started to look inward and determine what his next move would be.

All his life his only goal was to survive–to make it to the next day.

When he joined the Guild, Taryn lost himself. He became something unrecognizable, and it wasn't until he met Airess that he started to see the light. She was a glittering star amongst the darkness, a calm wave in a raging sea. Looking down at her now, he started to have a different idea for his future.

They neared one of the Runean bars on the corner street near the docks. Taryn could already hear the music from here, lively with singing, chanting, and dancing.

He grinned. "Do you want to get a drink?"

"Shouldn't we go back to the guesthouse?"

"Is that what you want?" Taryn asked. "I figured you'd want to explore Rune after all this time."

Airess looked around at all the Fae, and a subtle smile grew on her face. He knew she was still adjusting–to a new culture, a new language, and the freedom to go anywhere she wanted after a life of captivity. He would be patient with her, content with whatever she decided.

"No, you're right," Airess said, looking up at him with a smirk. "Let's go," she ordered, speaking those last two words in the Runean tongue. The sound of his language rolling off her lips made his blood heat. He wasted no time, as he grabbed her hand and led her through the crowd.

They walked up to the wooden outdoor bar. Taryn requested two beers and handed Airess the glass mug. They drank, and Airess looked at the mass of sweaty, dancing bodies in shock.

The Fae danced sensually, grinding their bodies against one another, swaying to each beat of the music. Some males danced upon males, and females danced upon females, or a mix of the two. It was true that Rune had a completely different society than Luciena, his people showing more intimate public displays of affection and an openness toward sensuality.

"I've certainly never seen dancing of this kind before," Airess said as she sipped her beer nervously.

Taryn tilted his head back and laughed at her surprise, her exposure to finally seeing a different culture than what she had been used to her whole life. Hell, even Taryn felt the change, being away from home all these years, and relished it.

Home.

He turned to her and smiled, unable to contain his joy. The vibration from the music traveled up his spine, and Taryn couldn't remember the last time he was truly happy. Until now.

He bent down low and whispered in her ear. "I can show you, if you'd like."

The look she gave him in response could have brought him to his knees, her eyelids growing heavy. His grip tightened on the mug as he awaited her response. She tilted her mug back and chugged the rest of its contents. When she was done, she gripped his tunic and brought him down closer to her.

"Show me," she said in a sultry, low voice.

Whatever restraint Taryn had before was lost. He set his drink down and grabbed her hand swiftly, guiding her into the crowd as the beat thrummed through his body. They entered the crowd of bodies, the scent of beer and sweat mixing together.

"Like this," Taryn said, placing her arms over his shoulders, the front of their bodies now flush together. He gripped the sides of her waist and swayed to the beat of the music, his blood heating at her scent of honey and magnolias.

She followed his lead and pressed her chest and hips against him. Taryn's cheeks heated as the most beautiful female he had ever seen, ever known, danced with him. He held her like he would never let go.

She looked up at him, a subtle blush on her cheeks. Airess leaned up on her tippy toes and whispered, "Am I doing it right?"

"Yes," he breathed. His grip on her waist tightened.

The song changed, the beat faster than before. The crowd responded instantly, moving faster. Taryn trailed his hand up her bare arms, until he grabbed her hands in his, taking a step back so he had room to spin her. Airess twirled effortlessly, her hair catching the light. Taryn grabbed her waist and dipped her low at the end of her spin, their breaths heaving as they stared at one another, their noses inches apart.

When he brought her back up, she spun around and pressed her back to his front. She took his hands and placed them on her hips. Airess mimicked the other dancers, grinding her backside into his front.

Taryn *groaned*. "You keep dancing like that and I won't be able to control myself," he whispered, voice husky, the alcohol blurring his cares and worries into oblivion.

"Maybe I want you to lose control."

When the song was over, they separated, their bodies flushed, brows beaded with sweat. Taryn, for once, was speechless. Airess was not the innocent female he had thought her to be. He was just now seeing a boldness inside of her that she had finally set free.

Airess grabbed his hand and giggled. "Let's get another drink."

They left the sea of dancers and headed toward the bar. The line was long, and Taryn could tell she needed a moment to gather her bearings as she gripped the wall behind her and leaned back.

"Wait here, I'll be right back."

Taryn joined the line that quickly moved forward after a few minutes.

He gathered the drinks and went to go find Airess, but when he turned, a snarl escaped his lips.

There they were, two Fae males standing so close to Airess they had her practically cornered against the wall. A possessiveness Taryn couldn't understand, or control coursed through him in waves at the scent of the male's arousal.

"Come on," One of the males said slyly, "We've never seen an Elven female before. Just one dance. I'll make it worth your while."

"No wish to dance," Airess replied nervously in Runean, her lack of vocabulary causing the males to snicker.

"The bitch can hardly understand us. Just take her–"

Taryn pushed past the males, his shoulders clipping theirs as he wedged himself between them and Airess, forming a physical barrier. Taryn bared his teeth and snarled at them, asserting his dominance as they snarled back in response. They bowed up at his intrusion.

"The fuck–"

"She's *mine*," Taryn snarled, looking each of them in the eyes. "You would be wise not to lay a hand on her."

One of the males laughed and stepped forward. "Last I checked this female is *Elven,* not Fae. She is not yours to claim, male. We have every right to her."

Having heard enough, Taryn drew out his broadswords from their sheaths and pointed one at them. "Say something like that again, and I'll have your head."

The sound of metal unsheathing caught the attention of the crowd, the music slowly fading as everyone slowed and gaped at the scene. The two Fae held out their own swords, accepting the challenge. Behind Taryn, he could hear Airess' heart pounding in her chest.

Bystanders scattered to the perimeter of the outdoor bar. The music had stopped, the space around them falling quiet.

"You would really duel over this female?" one Fae asked.

"Yes," Taryn replied, and advanced.

Metal clashed against metal as Taryn easily avoided each of their strikes, their fighting style no match for Taryn's decade long tenure at the Guild. Taryn sliced one Fae's arm, causing the male to fall, screaming in agony. He intended to make them suffer.

The mouthier one, the one who disrespected Airess, lunged forward. The male's blade barely nicked Taryn's cheek as he sidestepped out of the way. Taryn grinned, the violence bringing out a side of him he was familiar with. He toyed with the male, blocking each hit, but not ending the fight just yet. The male screamed out in frustration as Taryn struck forward. He nicked the male's arms, abdomen and face.

Finally, Taryn grew bored and brought his blade down on the male's wrist. He severed the male's hand from his body, the common price to pay for a duel in the Runean culture.

The male's scream pierced through the silence of the crowd.

Taryn knelt down to the handless Fae, blood sputtering out onto the stone at their feet. "Next time," Taryn said in a condescending tone, "it would be wise to listen the first time a female says no."

"*Fuck you*," the Fae male sneered in defeat.

Taryn stood up emotionlessly, and wiped his blade clean before resheathing his broadswords. Now that the duel was over, the music resumed, the people beginning their dances again. Taryn strode back toward Airess, who was looking at him with wide eyes and a parted mouth. His face had hardened into something lethal, fueled by a rage he couldn't control. At least she was finally seeing him for the menace he was.

"Taryn, my Gods! What–"

"Let's get out of here," Taryn interrupted. He placed a hand on her lower back and guided her down the street. He didn't want to draw any more attention to her than he already had, and he knew other Fae would find Airess curious. She stood out in every way, her litheness contrasting against the Fae's broadness, her hair a light in the dark compared to the Runean people's raven locks.

"I can't believe you did that," Airess confessed. "You didn't have to *cut off his hand.* What the hell is wrong with you?"

"Yes, I did. It was the price for challenging me. He knew that."

"The price of a duel is to cut off the loser's *hand?*" Airess asked in disbelief, eyes wide.

"Yes," he chuckled. "You have a lot to learn about Rune. That is one of the many customs. If I hadn't intervened..." Taryn trailed off, the words lodging in his throat. He wouldn't–*couldn't*–imagine what those males would have done to her had he not shown up at that exact moment.

"Come on, I want to show you something."

"Where are we going?" Airess asked.

Taryn looked at her and smiled. "Home."

Chapter 32

*'I've seen what my daughter will become.
I only hope the world is ready.'*

— *Written entry from Aesira Deyanira's personal journal*

Airess

They walked inland, following a worn-down path that the commoners used to travel between the city and the country lands.

Airess glanced over at Taryn as they walked along the dirt path. She studied the way his brunette curls fell effortlessly over his brow, the curve of his full lips, and the straight line of his nose. It was a face she had come to know well. A face she could recognize anywhere.

Everything about him was starting to make sense. She had begun to put the pieces together–the puzzle that made Taryn the male he was. His time at the Guild, she realized, was not what he truly wanted for himself.

There were still a few things about him that were lost to her. Primarily his childhood years. Airess had gathered he had a troubled past as an orphan, but she didn't know much about the grandmother he kept mentioning. He had yet to open up to her about it, and she found herself wanting to know everything about him.

"Are we going to the home you grew up in?" Airess asked.

"Yes, the one I lived in before my grandmother died."

There was a pause, until Taryn spoke up again. "I met my grandmother when I was eight. She isn't my grandmother by blood, you see. She adopted me when I was an orphan. I lived with her in the home I'm about to show you."

Her heart twisted for him and the pain he endured. Of course he was too stubborn to ever admit such a thing.

"I'm sorry, Taryn. I'm sorry for your loss. I'm sure she was an amazing woman."

Taryn chuckled, gazing at the moon as he was no doubt recalling a distant memory, "She was. She made my childhood–however short it was–worth living."

"What was your favorite memory with her?"

"Oh, Gods," Taryn smiled. "While she cooked, I'd sit on the floor and reteach her history and facts I learned in school. She would always listen to the lessons I wanted to teach. She took me shopping with her everywhere. I miss her smile, her boisterous laugh. I…I hope she's doing okay, wherever she is now."

Airess grabbed his hand and squeezed. "I believe the other side is much better than our world here. Whatever it is like, I believe she is happy and safe watching over you."

"I still feel her spirit existing out there," he said. "Energy cannot be destroyed. It just changes forms. I hope one day I will see her again."

"I have every confidence we will meet again with our loved ones."

Taryn stopped walking and turned to face her. "I've never told anyone about my grandmother before. No one has ever really offered their condolences. Even after all this time, it means everything to me. Thank you, truly."

Airess looked up at him and smiled. "You can tell me anything."

He towered over her, eyes boring into her soul. Airess' smile melted into a frown as she noticed a smear of blood on his cheekbone from the duel. Rising to her toes, she wiped the blood away softly with the pad of her thumb. Their eyes met, their gazes upon each other intense, the moon and stars meeting again.

"I wish you'd stop getting hurt to defend me," she whispered.

"What kind of ally would I be if I let you get hurt?" Taryn said lightly, a touch of sarcasm in his tone. "Besides, this cut is barely a scratch."

Airess rolled her eyes. "A *scratch*? Your cheek is sliced and bleeding."

"You underestimate me if you think that is a problem."

"I don't want you to keep getting impaled by a blade for me. Enough blood has already been spilled."

"Oh, Airess," Taryn said, his eyes darkening, "I would gladly bleed out for you."

Her breath hitched at the words, at the claim they implied. She tried to calm herself, slowing down her quickened heartbeat that Taryn no doubt could hear.

Airess swallowed and changed the subject. "What was that Fae male going on about back in town? He said I'm an Elve, so he had a *claim* to me."

"He was being an asshole, trying to use Fae customs that apply to mates so he could take advantage of you."

Airess stilled. This was news to her. "*Mates*?"

"It doesn't always apply to every Fae, but every now and then a Fae will find their Mate. It's a bond between Fae. Usually a romantic bond, but there have been some exceptions in history before. That male back there was saying that since you're not Fae, I can't claim you as off limits. You're half Elven and Human, and therefore that makes you *available* in the Fae's eyes.

"You'll need to get accustomed to how territorial the Fae can be. We are, after all, the animalistic cousin to the Elven species. Society is different here. Fae people will try and make advances on you, something you aren't used to," Taryn explained.

"Fae people can be *mated*?" Airess asked in disbelief. This was certainly something she never learned about in her schooling. It was moments like these that she realized how sheltered and in the dark she was about the outerworld. Living in Luciena made her blind.

"Yes."

"And... do you think you will find your mate now that you're back here?" Airess asked sharply. She wished she could stifle this sinking feeling in her stomach, an emotion cutting true and deep to her very core. If Taryn found his mate here it would change everything. It would be... *devastating*.

Perhaps this was the moment she realized she was starting to fall for him. Hell, maybe she already had. The thought of someone else having him, touching him, *being* with him, made bile rise up her throat. Her body rejected the idea. Her chest tightened as she waited for his response.

"No, I haven't," Taryn confirmed. "And I hope it stays that way."

Despite her relief, his last comment puzzled her. "Why do you hope it stays that way?"

Taryn shot her a look, eyes boring into her before answering, "I have my reasons. And I don't think I would be a deserving male. You can't choose who you are mated to. I don't think anyone would willingly want to be with me after my past."

Her shoulders sagged in relief, but she couldn't help the nagging feeling of the possible what ifs.

What if he does eventually find his mate here in Rune? What if he wants to be with them?

She realized all these thoughts about something that hadn't even happened was anxiety flooding her mind, invading her self-assurance. She breathed in and out, and let it go.

I am not my anxiety.

She mustered a fake smile that didn't reach her eyes. "I'm sure that's not true."

Taryn let out a bitter laugh. "I am a criminal. I am a killer. I've lied, and stolen, and have done so much wrong in this world. I don't deserve a mate. I certainly don't deserve love."

Airess' eyebrows shot up at the raw confession, at him finally admitting out loud his thoughts and fears. Before she could say anything further, his eyes averted to something behind her.

"This is it."

Airess turned and followed his gaze, noticing the circular hut instantly. The pair walked forward, cutting through the knee length overgrown grass. Something about it looked so familiar to her. Her eyebrows creased as they neared.

"It looks empty."

"Let's go inside," Taryn said, and burst down the door with a gust of wind that shot out of his fist.

Dust clouds swirled around in the moonlight that streamed through the door and into the hut. Two cots, coated in dust, were on one side. A tiny kitchenette was on the other, old pots and pans hung upon the wall. In front of them were two wingback chairs facing a small fireplace.

Airess stopped in her tracks, eyes wide. Yes, it certainly was familiar. She had *been* here before.

"I can't believe it's all here. This is crazy," Taryn muttered, dark brows drawn together. He crossed the threshold into the hut. "Another family inherited this house when I was sent to the orphanage, but it looks like they kept all the furniture." He walked up and put a hand on one of the armchairs and turned to face her, "This is where she used to sit. *Wait*–I'm sorry. I don't think I even told you her name. It was –"

"Ima."

Airess scanned her surroundings, wide-eyed, as Taryn's hand dropped from the chair.

"How did you know that?"

Her gaze met his, "I was trying to tell you on the ship, then everything happened so fast. I... met her. In the dreamworld."

His eyebrows rose in disbelief. "You *what*?"

"I didn't know who she was. I just appeared here." Airess motioned to the hut. "It was such a brief conversation. She told me to *travel with the male to Rune*. I didn't believe her at the time. I thought maybe I truly had gone crazy. It was my first time meeting another dreamwalker. It's why I knew I was safe to travel with you."

"And you didn't think to tell me about this sooner?" Taryn asked as he folded his arms, his tone speculative.

"I had just met you. We were in *jail*. How crazy would you have thought me to be if I told you something like that?"

He studied her, making that face she knew he made whenever he was thinking about something deeply. "Fair enough. I suppose we are even on that end, then."

She visibly relaxed. He strode to her and looked at her with an intense expression. "Tell me everything that happened with Ima."

So she did. She told him everything about their encounter– the chairs, the sewing, and their odd conversation. He listened intently, searching her eyes for more information.

"At the end she said, '*The Obadiah awaits the both of you*'."

"Hm," Taryn hummed as he took a step back. "Ima was Tevyen. It's how I know what I know about my lineage and its forgotten history. She never once mentioned The Obadiah, or being able to dreamwalk, for that matter. This is… an interesting development."

"Wouldn't Ismene have mentioned such a thing?" Airess questioned.

"You would think so," Taryn said. "If my grandmother knew Ismene, that would raise a whole new level of questions. Come on. We need to get answers."

After a brisk walk through town, they finally arrived outside the temple. Taryn banged on the door while Airess tapped her foot impatiently.

What was the connection between the Obadiah, Ismene, Ima and Esper Crawn? Should Airess be taking this prophecy and her Tevyen lineage seriously, or were they being deceived? Ismene claimed the young King Roz was also a Godling, so if that was true, Airess planned to have a meeting with the King first thing tomorrow.

The wooden arched door creaked open a crack. A royal guard peeked out, her face annoyed–until she saw who stood on the other side of the door.

"The temple is closed tonight," the guard said curtly.

"The temple is never supposed to be closed," Taryn retorted, folding his arms. "We need to speak with Ismene. It's urgent."

"The Queen Dowager is occupying the temple at the moment. Come back in the morning."

The guard slammed the door in their faces, leaving no room for any more interruptions.

Airess huffed in frustration. "Unbelievable."

Taryn's jaw tensed as he turned to face her. "We will come back at sunrise, then."

They turned and walked away in sync, gravel crunching beneath their sandals.

"Do you want to walk on the beach with me?" Airess asked softly.

Taryn looked down at her, warmth flooding his gaze. "There's nothing I would rather do."

He grabbed her hand and led her past the buildings in town and onto a sandy path that cut through the tall grassy dunes. They left their sandals in the sand. Airess felt the soft sand glide through her toes each step she took towards the ocean. She breathed in the salt air, the warm breeze ruffling her hair. None of those sensations compared to the sound of the beach–each wave crashing after another. A poetic melody of life's push and pull.

They walked onto the flat shoreline, their surroundings surprisingly bright beneath the moonlight. Airess glanced at Taryn, noticing the breeze rustling his loose tunic and pants as they began to walk along the water. The silence was comfortable. It felt like *home*.

"I never thought I'd walk the beach again," Airess confessed. Her heart rate increased, anxiety welling in her chest at the vulnerability. She breathed the anxiety out again, letting it pass and flow away in the breeze.

Taryn grabbed her hand in response and squeezed. Sometimes actions spoke louder than words ever could. Airess understood exactly what he was trying to convey with one simple touch.

I'm here for you. I know. I'm sorry.

"The Salamoon is in just a few days," Taryn said, looking down at her.

Her eyes widened. *A few days?*

"I can't believe how fast time has passed." Airess elbowed Taryn playfully. "It will be our birthday."

"Indeed it will," Taryn agreed, pursing his lips together in thought before speaking again. "You know, Rune throws a huge ball at the castle every Salamoon. There's dancing and food. The whole town comes together to celebrate. It's customary to bring a date, a companion."

Airess met his gaze at the implication and smirked, waiting for him to say it.

"Would you be my date to the Salamoon ball?" Taryn asked with a grin, a playful hand over his heart.

Airess smiled. "Of course I will."

They walked for miles until they took a break and sat on the shore. They were the only ones on the beach, feet in the sand as they talked through the night. Airess told him things she never had told anyone before: the truth about her anxiety, the night she was taken to the Luciena capitol, and how it was living with Arzhel Lucien.

Taryn caressed her hair as he listened, watching her intently as she spoke. He told her he cared. He told her she didn't deserve it. Taryn listened, and promised they would have a better life here.

Airess hoped with everything in her that the promise would come true.

Chapter 33

A Godling will be marked by their eyes. If you see the glow, you will know it is them who walks the earth once more.

— *The book of Tevye*

The Vulture

The Vulture stood in their usual waiting spot, the back alley where they had met previously in the outer-ring. They were growing impatient, tapping their feet against the gravel, back leaning against the wall. Eryx should be here by now. Had he failed? Had he killed Taryn and taken Airess?

The Vulture felt a wave of overwhelming anger and grief drifting from down the alleyway. Footsteps approached–the frame was far too tall and slender to be Eryx himself. The Vulture's heart sank, not out of emotion, but out of disappointment. Their plan had failed again.

"Is he dead?" The Vulture asked the man who approached. He was tall, dressed in black leather from head to toe. His brown eyes bore into them as the man took his hood off, revealing sandy blond hair. His expression was grim, lips pressed together tightly.

"Yes."

Shit.

"How?"

The man bristled at the question, as if not wanting to be reminded of what had occurred. "That silvered-haired bitch killed him. Anyway, Eryx wanted me to give you this. The Guild is yours now." The Vulture didn't miss the man's resentful tone.

The man handed The Vulture two pieces of parchment. One was Eryx's will, entitling the Vulture to the Guild and all its assets. The other was a piece of parchment titled:

Everything I didn't tell you. This is how you achieve the Allpower.

The Vulture snorted and shoved the will in the man's chest. "I have no intention of being anyone's Guildmaster. For all I care, you take it."

His brown eyes widened, mouth parted open slightly in shock.

"What?"

"*You* take it. I have no interest. When my work is done, I'll be ruling over all of you anyway. Who knows, maybe I will recruit you into serving the crown by then." After a pause, The Vulture's eyes narrowed, crossing their arms over their chest. "Do you accept?"

"Y-yes," the man said, folding the paper. The Vulture nodded, giving him a once over.

"What's your name?"

"Raiden."

"Raiden," they said, testing the name on their tongue. "Well, Raiden, today is your lucky day. You are now acting master of the Mrkynian Guild. I only ask one thing of you in return."

"And what is that?" Raiden asked.

"Transportation to Rune."

Chapter 34

'The prophecy is unraveling. Our son bears the eyes of the Gods.'
— Unsent correspondence from Rinya Kazimyr to Tann Azar

Taryn

Taryn woke up to the cawing of a gull right next to his ear.

He grimaced as he stirred awake. The bird cawed incessantly, forcing him into full wakefulness. Taryn blinked and met the milky gray eyes of the bird staring right at him. He sat up abruptly, shooing the bird away from him and Airess.

They had fallen asleep on the beach last night, talking for hours, letting time get away from them both.

The gull flew over and landed on top of Airesss, pecking at her locket. Airess' golden eyes shot open.

"Oh!" she exclaimed, shooing the bird off of her. It cawed one last time before flying off. *Odd.* Taryn watched it fly away, not sure why he felt so strangely about a common bird.

He stood and offered a hand to Airess, helping her up. They both shook the sand off themselves as the morning sun beat down on them.

"I didn't mean to fall asleep," Airess commented as they walked back into town. Taryn muttered his agreement while rubbing the sleep from his eyes. The events of last night came flooding back. They still needed to have a visit with Ismene–and soon.

The pair agreed to stop by the temple before heading back to the guest house, the matter was too urgent to wait. When they arrived at the familiar domed temple, they found the doors unlocked. Taryn and Airess shared a knowing look before walking back to Ismene's study.

There Ismene was, standing in front of the coral-colored flames as though she were waiting for them both. The faint crackle from the hearth was the only sound in the quiet chamber.

"Welcome," Ismene greeted, turning to face them. She wore the same style of clothing as before, only this time in yellow silk instead of orange. Her hoop earrings bobbed as she turned her head. Her eyes were kind, yet laced with a weariness Taryn couldn't read.

"Where have you both been? The king made an effort to visit your guest house last night and found it empty."

Airess' eyes narrowed. "How do you know Ima?" She asked, ignoring Ismene's question. Taryn shifted on his feet at the sound of his grandmother's name. Even hearing it spoken aloud brought a certain life to her that hadn't existed in a very long time.

"My, I haven't heard that name in ages," Ismene said thoughtfully as she walked to her desk. Airess and Taryn followed behind.

"Airess met Ima in the dreamworld when we were in Luciena. Ima instructed her to travel to Rune, to find The Obadiah. Yet, all we have found here is *you*. We want the truth, Ismene. What do you know about The Obadiah, about my grandmother?" Taryn forced a slow breath through his nose, holding onto the last bit of patience he had. It was as if his tensed body knew the answer to the question he craved.

"Please, sit," Ismene instructed, as she sat down in her chair. The pair obliged as Ismene lit the candles on her desk, igniting each wick with the fyre from her fingertips.

Ismene thrummed her fingers on the desk as she spoke. "I was old friends with Ima back in Tevye. We met during our schooling in becoming members of The Obadiah.

"We were chosen to cross over to The Old World. Only a small group was sent: Me, Ima, and Esper Crawn. Our mission was to give up our Tevyen immortality and help assist the Prophesied Ones. When I came, I had the appearance of a thirty-year-old Human woman. Look at me now, *ha*!" Ismene chuckled at her own joke, meanwhile Airess and Taryn's mouth hung open.

"After a decade of waiting for the prophecy to unfold, we grew weary that it never would. Eventually, we all went our separate ways and started our own lives. That is, until King Roz was born. Then, years later, Aesira Deyanira portaled into Rune with her baby–with *you*," Ismene said, looking directly at Airess.

"Aesira wanted to lay low in Luciena, to hide you away from your own family. She confessed that she crafted a dark spell to cross through Luciena's ward. Aesira told us that a young Kazimyr prince went missing as a babe, and that he was suspected to be the Moon Godling. It wasn't until Ima found Taryn in an orphanage years later that we began to connect the dots. Somehow, Taryn was also portaled from Tevye into Rune and had completely eluded us."

Taryn had no words. No thoughts. His pulse thundered in his ears at the revelation of how he came to be here. He shifted lightly, gaze flicking towards Airess, but she wasn't looking at him. Airess leaned forward in her chair, golden eyes intent on Ismene.

"Esper had volunteered to go and find you, Airess, after many years spent working on mimicking the spell Aesira had crafted to pass through Luciena's barrier. We were going to bring the Godlings back together."

"Wait a minute. Do the Luciens know about the prophecy and the Godlings?" Airess asked.

"We presume they are aware of their prince, Arzhel, being born as a Godling. Given how long they have been cut off from the outside world, it is highly doubtful they are aware of the prophecy. But one can never be too sure of what they know. Their barrier has been a mystery to us," Ismene said confidently.

Taryn shook his head. "You said you were *immortal* in Tevye?" Ima only gave him limited information when he was a child, and she most certainly never mentioned immortality.

"Bah! I don't look it now, do I? Yes, all Tevyens are immortal. We give up our immortality to come to the Old World. It is why no one from Tevye has attempted to cross over, they know what they would be giving up."

Silence fell over them. Taryn wasn't sure what to believe. He had always been a male of facts and reason, and certainly wouldn't be taking this woman's word for everything she had said. Could he even believe the story she gave about how Taryn ended up in Rune?

"You say you serve an organization devoted to preserving the natural state of the world and the Godlings, yet you don't know the full scope of what that means?" Taryn asked skeptically.

"I may be two hundred and thirty years old, but even I was born in an era long after the last Godling passed. Who knows what Tevye has learned after our departure? Time works differently there. Technology is far more advanced than here. It is only a matter of time before we get the answers you seek, once the wall is brought down."

"How do you expect us to believe this?" Taryn asked sharply. He stood, having heard enough of this madness.

Airess stood up next to him, grabbing his arm. "Just hear her out. I can't explain it, but I can't shake the feeling that there is a far deeper truth to her words than we are ready for."

Taryn honed in on Airess. "You can't possibly be buying this."

"I'm just keeping an open mind, Taryn. If we have been lied to our entire lives, perhaps there is some truth here."

Taryn's jaw tightened. He didn't want to hear anything further. He didn't want to know, even if it was the truth. Because if it was… well, he wasn't ready to confront it yet. It would mean his entire life had not only been a lie, but one he might have had the power to change.

"This is a waste of time," he told Airess stiffly and strode toward the doorway.

"You don't believe me, boy?" Ismene called out, voice echoing off the walls of the cavernous sanctuary. "What other connection do you have to dreamwalking, other than drawing from your own *mate's* power?"

Taryn froze mid-step. Her words hit him like a punch to the gut, knocking the air from his lungs. He slowly turned back to face her. "What did you just say to me?"

Ismene laughed bitterly. "Pride. Stubborn pride is the heart of all male's suffering. Be sure to remember that, dear," she said, directing the comment more toward Airess than Taryn. Ismene's beady eyes narrowed in on him. "Shared abilities is the first telltale sign of a mating bond, starting from the very moment you two *touch*. Tell me, when did the dreamwalking begin for you?"

Taryn's mind lurched at the words, his eyes widening as he recalled the mating signs he had learned about as a boy. Shared powers. A signature scent. Irrational protectiveness for one's mate. He hadn't thought about those lessons since he was a boy. It wasn't possible–they weren't even the same kind of *being*. Never once had Taryn considered the possibility.

"When did you scent her, a smell so prominent, so addicting, that it stood out from any other? Did you recognize the innate side of you wanting to protect her from anything and anyone? A side of you that perhaps experienced irrational jealousy when other males–"

"Stop," Taryn's voice cracked as he broke her gaze and found Airess's eyes, her expression confused. It was at that moment he felt the undeniable truth of Ismene's words. It shouldn't have been possible, it *wasn't* possible, yet all the signs were there.

"It can't be true," he practically whispered.

Airess Deyanira was his mate.

Taryn had a *mate*.

Ismene tilted her head, something like sympathy flickering across her expression. "If you would have let me finish teaching you of the prophecy–its *history*–you would find that it is. We have been expecting you both to make your appearance in the world for centuries. We always knew the mating bonds between beings would emerge back into the world, just as it once had. We just didn't know when or who it would be.

"You play a role in this prophecy, your bond between each other is the first sign that it has already begun."

Taryn took a step back.

"I'm sorry you had to find out this way, but we don't have much time to prepare you for what's to come. Please, we have much to discuss."

Taryn looked to Airess, her eyes wide in realization at the simple truth. He couldn't breathe.

Perhaps ignorance truly was bliss, for now he beheld a weight on his shoulders that he never knew could exist. Everything between them would change. Would she accept him? Would she finally see how inadequate he was for such a beautiful person like her?

"I can't." Taryn forced out hoarsely, beginning to back all the way out of the room.

Airess took a step towards him. "Taryn –" Airess started.

But it was too late. He had already rushed out of the temple.

Chapter 35

'If the Gods deemed our Bond worthy, who are we to deny it? A bond between Elves and Fae can only bring us more power. I hope one day you will see that. I hope one day you will forgive me.'

— Written correspondence from Evyen Deyanira to Tinyrah Kazimyr

Airess

Airess reached for him as he disappeared out of the hall. Her head spun with confusion.

"He will come around," Ismene said, cutting through the tension. "A mating bond is a serious thing, especially to Fae males. Let him process."

Airess whirled towards Ismene. "I'm half Human and half Elve, a mating bond isn't possible. Elves don't even have mates, much less Humans."

Ismene clicked her tongue. "Incorrect. You *do*–it only goes by a different name. In Elven history, they call it The Bonded. Only Elves and select Mindborne Humans can have these bonds, though they have been muted in Luciena. Tell me, what does his energy look like to you?"

Airess flushed. "I don't know–"

"I know you have The Sight, girl. What does it look like?"

"It looks like his eyes," Airess admitted. "It's beautiful. His energy is silver, as shiny as armor with an array of colors. It's the only aura I had ever seen like this."

"You see this in him because you are Bonded. Only a Mate, or Bonded, can see right through to the soul. I don't understand the full scope of what your Bond to him means, but we know it is entirely unique to you both. You harness the physical connection between Mates, and the energetic tie between The Bonded."

Airess took a deep look inward, her mind now whirring with every little moment she had begun to suspect something was different about her, about him.

Her supposed Starlight and Dreamwalking abilities that her mother had sworn to keep secret from the world, no matter what happened to her. The fact that she looked completely different than the Elves on the Lucien continent, as if she hadn't hailed from there.

The moment she saw Taryn for the first time at the ball, his aura shining to her as if saying *hello,* her irrational affinity for him from the moment they were trapped together in that jail cell.

Airess' visits to his past in the dreamworld–her visits with *Ima* in the dreamworld. How she accidentally triggered the Godspirit to save Taryn in the caravan while poisoned with donstenyte.

Airess clutched her chest.

"What does being Bonded Mates mean?"

"Right now the Bond is in the beginning stages. Once the relationship is consummated, the true effects of the Bond will take place. Your souls will be completely tied together."

Airess' blood heated. She felt as if she were frozen in place. The relationship needed to be *consummated* for the Bond to take effect?

"I…" Her mouth was dry. "I don't know what to say," was all she could say in response. Airess was speechless.

She didn't doubt Ismene's words like Taryn did. Airess felt Ismene's truth, saw it in her own aura.

Ismene's face softened. "Why don't you go get some rest, dear? We can resume our lesson another time."

Airess excused herself and rushed out of the temple doors. Her thoughts clashed against one another, making her head swim. She was too worried about what Taryn was thinking right now to feel excited. Her jaw clenched as she recalled how Taryn had *just* told her he didn't want a mate.

Would his feelings change? Would… hers?

Airess didn't even fully understand the scope of what being mates meant. It wasn't exactly something she was familiar with growing up in Elven culture, especially living in a land where Bonded connections were muted by the wards.

Despite all this worry, Airess couldn't help but find the entire concept of Mates and The Bonded infatuating. Beautiful, even. The fact that there could be someone out there *destined* to be intertwined with one's soul was the epitome of Fate. The epitome of *love*.

Airess stopped walking, realizing the weight of her last thought. The weight of who Taryn was to her, and she to him, crashed into her. She stared at her shoes. A miniscule smile upturned the corner of her lips.

Of course.

It would be Taryn.

Taryn, whose skepticism in the unknown balanced her faith in it. Of course it would be the male who could never bite his tongue, always challenging any authority whilst she had mastered the opposite during her time in the castle. Taryn, whose elemental abilities were a stark contrast against her energetic Magick.

He was her opposite in every way. And yet, they were perfect for each other. They belonged to one another, like the stars holding the moon upright in the sky, Taryn had been her rock.

Airess lifted her chin. She knew what she had to do next.

Find Taryn.

Airess walked down the path in frustration toward the guest house she shared with Taryn. She burst his door open, finding his room empty, the only thing to stir was the curtain flowing from the breeze. The evening sun had just begun to set as she looked out the window in worry, storm clouds beginning to brew overhead. She had barely begun her walk to the heart of the city when she caught sight of King Roz on horseback heading straight towards her.

Once he was upon her, she noticed the sweat under the casual tunic he had on–strikingly different then the silk embroidered fashions she had seen him in at the castle. He traveled without his crown, a statement Airess surely found odd. If Roz truly was a Godling, he sure presented himself as a common male.

He greeted her with a genuine smile as he dismounted, a noticeable difference from the male she had met back in the castle. "Greetings, Airess of Judla!" He announced playfully as his feet touched the ground. Airess didn't quite know how to respond to such a friendly king, so she opted to bow awkwardly in reply. "Good evening, King…Roz." Airess winced at the awkward tone in her voice.

The king threw his head back as he laughed. "Please, no need to bow." Roz gave her an inquisitive look as he noticed her leaving the guest house alone. "Going somewhere?"

"I was leaving for an evening stroll, if that is allowed, of course." She definitely didn't want to get into the fact that she was actually trying to track down Taryn, her supposed *Mate*. Even thinking about it now felt so surreal.

"Of course. You are allowed to come and go as you please, you aren't a prisoner here." Roz's face flickered with seriousness before the corners of his mouth upturned. "Do you mind if I join you?"

Airess never expected the king to want to walk with her, but she obliged with a polite nod and they began to walk. "It certainly is different here. Where I come from, no royal would ever dare to stroll with a commoner, much less ride on horseback."

"I see, the customs in Luciena are dated, in my opinion. However, you'll find I quite enjoy my horse." Roz mused. "Though, I could hardly classify you as a commoner. You were a woman of nobility where you lived, were you not?"

Airess stared at her sandals as they walked on, "My…father was a governor, yes, before they merged my province to join Luciena. I'm not so sure I could claim to be a highborn Lady now." Airess said with a grimace. She paused, because her father wasn't her father, and her name wasn't her name. She could only wonder who her real father was. The only thing Airess knew about him was that he was a Human man that lived in Tevye.

"I wouldn't be so sure about that." Roz commented, clearing his throat as he changed the subject. "Have your lessons been going well with Ismene?"

"Yes, I've mostly learned the forgotten history Luciena buried. And..." Airess cut herself short, not knowing if she were to mention the brief history of the Godlings or the prophecy.

"And what else?" Roz prodded.

Airess stopped walking and looked at him. "She told me that *you* are a Godling."

Roz stopped and turned to her, a surprised look of relief at her words. "Yes." He admitted.

"Why didn't you mention it sooner?"

"If I would have told you upon your arrival, not knowing everything you do now, would you have believed me?"

"Fair enough," Airess conceded. "However I'm not quite sure what we are supposed to do now that we know the truth."

Roz waved a hand carelessly, "Worry not, my friend. There is plenty of time for that in the future. Tell me, are you a fan of balls?"

If Airess wasn't in the presence of a King, she would laugh at the question.

I'm not quite sure, Roz, considering the last one I attended changed my life entirely.

"I don't mind them." Airess said instead, falling into her old ways of responding mechanically, as if she angered this King enough, he would morph into Arzhel himself.

"The Salamoon Ball is tomorrow night. We would love for you and Tarynon to attend."

"We would love to attend." Airess said as she looked forward, not really present in the conversation as she was reminded about Taryn again. Her Mate. Could it really be true?

Would it be wrong of her to lean into this so-called Bond? Did she even have a choice? Arriving in Rune had been unlike anything she had ever expected, the culture vastly different than Luciena. The Fae lived differently here. She loved it.

Airess loved the idea of starting over, of becoming someone new, chasing after a life she was destined for. Whether this prophecy talk was bogus or complete truth, she felt deep in her heart that everything in her life was about to change. Again.

She wished Taryn would come back, so she could tell him that she wanted to try. That she accepted the Bond. That she accepted him–*all* of him, even the parts he was too ashamed to name. She saw the way his aura flickered with hot shame as they realized what they were to each other. She needed to tell him that she didn't care about his past. She didn't care what he had done.

" – are friends, but I was wondering if you wanted to share a dance with me at the ball?"

Airess snapped out of her thoughts at the last half of Roz's sentence. She remembered to respond, "Yes, of course."

Roz paused and gave her a look, stopping in his tracks. She did the same and pivoted to face him.

"Airess, you are free here. You can speak as you'd like. You can *do* as you like. You are not Rune's prisoner, or even *my* prisoner. Please, be as you are with me. I may be a King, but I am a person too."

Airess truly looked at Roz and blinked her Sight forward. His aura shined bright, the azure tendrils shining true with every word he spoke.

Although it was nice to have the reassurance, she still had many questions about her and Taryn's fates.

"If we are truly free, what does that mean for mine or Taryn's fate here in Rune?"

"You can live here as a normal citizen in society. Given your status, I'm sure we can find a place for you and Tarynon at court."

"What about housing, what about our livelihood?" Though they were living in the guest house, Airess knew they needed to figure out what their next move would be. Everything comes with a price, even if it is free lodging.

"Is it money you worry about?" Roz asked inquisitively.

"One of many worries, actually. What if we don't want jobs at court, what if I want to work and pave the way myself?"

Airess knew deep in her heart she didn't belong in Roz's court. She had lived a life as someone else's pet for far too long. Airess wanted to create a life for herself worth living, worth her mother's memory. Only now, she realized she had the power within her to make her dreams come true. Perhaps her life would have looked different if she would have realized sooner the power she possessed. Now that she knew the truth, things would have to be different.

Yes, Airess would make a name for herself indeed.

"As I said, you can do as you wish. You can reside in the guest house free of charge until you find your way, or you can be a part of my court. You aren't bound here, and if you wish to venture out and live on your own, then you are more than able to do so. You will find Rune is a country of many freedoms and possibilities."

Airess sighed, physically relaxing at his words. They continued to walk onward as Airess said, "Well, then I look forward to the future here in Rune."

"As do I."

She looked out to the path beyond, the buildings from the city coming closer with each step. The warm wind rustled her hair, and when she looked at Roz, she noticed he was looking at her with an unreadable expression. Without thought, she blurted the very question that had been in the back of her mind.

"How does this Godling thing work? Are we immortal?"

Roz snorted. "Something like that."

"What does that even mean?"

"Although your powers now are strong, they will only grow every time you access the Godspirit. Each time you become Spirited, your body begins to glow and your voice becomes distorted. Your power will grow until it reaches its full potential. I heard from Ismene you accessed it once before coming here. Impressive, considering your power was extremely muted from the ward."

The Godspirit? Her mind whirled.

"What do you know about the Godspirit? Have you accessed it?"

Roz chuckled, rubbing the stubble on his chin. Airess had to admit, he was handsome. He had a genuine smile that lit up any space he came around, yet the comparison was null when she thought of Taryn. No one appealed to her like Taryn did, and Airess now knew why.

"You could compare the Godspirit to a possession, the only difference being you can learn to control the Spirit in time, and use it to your advantage. The Godspirit is the God themself channeling their power through you. I have only been Spirited once… when my father died," Roz cleared his throat. "Have you even met your God yet?"

"No, I had no idea that was even possible," Airess looked down to her sandals. *Meeting* her God? What else didn't she know?

"There's so much I have yet to learn. I have barely used my own power, but I feel it thrumming beneath my veins. I feel a calling to use it, but every time I do, I leave a path of destruction."

For a moment, Roz was silent. "Sometimes I still feel that way too, but we were born for a reason. If the Gods Touched a child from all five Houses, then it can only mean the world is about to change. We are supposed to create balance, all five of us."

All five of us. Herself. Taryn. Roz. Arzhel and… who could be the fifth?

Airess hadn't realized her heart was pounding so loudly, but when Roz snapped his head to hers, she knew he heard it. His eyes softened, and he looked forward once more.

"Ah, worry not! All is unfolding as it is meant to be, it is only a matter of accepting it. Now, where are you headed? Anything I can help you with?"

Airess looked at him like he grew three heads. Wasn't he a King? Didn't he have more pressing duties than strolling around with her?

She sighed, internally wincing. She wasn't ready to talk about Taryn. About the Bond. Or the fact that she had been aimlessly searching for him since he fled the temple.

"I was just going into the city for a stroll. No need to accompany me, I'm sure you have much better things to do as King."

Roz studied her before nodding, another friendly smile gracing his face. He grabbed her hand and kissed the top of it. She was startled at the contact, but remained polite nonetheless. "Very well. I shall see you tomorrow. I'll send some attendants to help you both get ready for the ball tomorrow."

Airess gave her thanks as he mounted his horse and rode away. The civilians laughed and waved at him as he rode by. The familiarity between the commoners and King was jarring, to say the least. Melanth and Arzhel Lucien wouldn't be caught dead anywhere other than the inner ring of the city.

A drizzle continued to fall steadily overhead, boosting Airess to move faster in her search for Taryn. Where was he? Why did he leave like that? It hurt her, and she hated to admit that to herself.

She checked the docks, scanning the area for any sign of him. She could feel him nearby, but he wasn't here. Airess then tried countless shops, asking the folk if they had seen a Fae male with silver eyes nearby.

"Silver eyes?" an older male voice from behind cut in as she asked the cashier. Airess turned to the civilian. "Yes. Seen him near?" She grimaced, hoping he understood what she was trying to convey despite her lack of vocabulary.

"Yeah, I've seen him. He's lingering in the bar downtown. Looks rough, if you ask me."

"Thank you," she said quickly, and left the shop. Her steps increased as she rounded the corner and headed downtown– to the same bar her and Taryn danced at. The memory heated her blood. The way he touched her. The way he whispered into her ear that night, his breath tickling her neck. He was seductive, and she liked it. She had mirrored it. She could only wonder if she had the same effect on him.

She walked into the crowded bar nestled near the sea. Males and females alike cheered and laughed, alcohol sloshing out of their cups as they moved. Thick smoke plumed from their cigars, flooding the bar with its scent. She weaved through the bodies, eyes scanning for Taryn. Growing impatient, she blinked the Sight over her eyes.

She saw him immediately, his aura standing out like a sore thumb in the crowd. There Taryn was, currently exhaling a puff of smoke as he sat at a table full of Fae. They were playing cards, and he was laughing at one of their jokes.

As if he sensed her emotion, he looked up. He met her eyes. Taryn's jaw tensed, the smile fading from his face. Did he really loathe the idea of them being mates that much?

She walked forward, hands on her hips as she approached. The Fae at the table fell silent, eyeing her with looks of curiosity. She ignored them, lifting her chin up and addressing Taryn, "So, this is where you have been?"

Taryn stood up so quickly she barely registered that he now stood in front of her protectively, shielding her body in possession. The Fae laughed, turning their attention to them.

"Uh oh, someone's in trouble." One of the Fae commented. Airess's eyes narrowed, her fists clenching. Airess felt power welling beneath her skin, rising into her eyes. Whatever look she had given had shut them up.

Taryn gripped her shoulder, snapping her out of her trance, "Airess."

She turned towards him, eyes hardened. "We need to talk."

He looked down at her, a strand of curls falling over his brow.

"Yes, we do." He replied matter-of-factly. Taryn guided her out onto the patio and down the steps to the beach.

They walked out far enough from the buildings that the noise from the bar faded. Their toes touched the wet sand, the waves drowning out any thoughts of reason. His back stood to her, clothes billowing in the ocean breeze, waiting. The drizzle continued, but she didn't care. She let the water soak into her hair and clothes.

So many emotions flooded her mind as she gripped his shoulder and spun him, her strength surprising even him as his eyebrows raised.

"What is wrong with you?" Her voice cracked at the edges, thick with fury. Airess clenched her fists. She had never been so angry with him before. She had never been so angry with *anyone*. She was never allowed to be. Airess wouldn't hold back now.

"What, you come to get drunk after finding out the truth? Am I really that disappointing to you?" She let the words linger as his face distorted, pain and regret lacing his features.

"Of course not. You could never–" He cut himself off, nostrils flaring as he scented her. He took a step closer, invading her personal space.

"Have you been with another male?"

The rain shifted into a downpour, her clothes and hair now beginning to fully soak. Shivers went down her spine at his possessiveness. Despite her anger, the words made her blood heat.

She looked up at the storm and back to him. Was he controlling this?

Airess gave him an incredulous look, "Why do you even care? You obviously loathe the idea of us being mates so much, you had fled."

"It's not – I don't *loathe* the idea of us being mates, Airess." He closed his eyes and breathed out. "Just–who touched you? Was it forced?"

His voice darkened, laced with a venom that made Airess flinch. She hadn't seen this side of Taryn before, his usual sarcastic demeanor drained of life, replaced with hard resolve.

The sight of it had her stammering, "No–No, it was just Roz. He kissed my hand after walking me into town, so I could find *you*. It was nothing."

Taryn scoffed and let out a bitter smile. "Of course he did. He knew what he was doing."

Airess shook her head in frustration, but decided to ignore the comment about Roz. She wanted to get down to the root of the problem. She stepped forward, closing the gap between them and jabbed a finger at his chest.

"Why are you acting like this? Are you mad? Are you disappointed? Why did you run?"

He looked away, eyes closing. She could smell the alcohol on his breath, mixing with his scent. He smelled like the sea. He smelled like the earth. He smelled like a bad influence. Maybe he was, but she wanted him. Finally, he looked her in the eye.

"I don't want to chain you to me. Do you have any idea what a mating bond means? It's not just a relationship–it's not even a *marriage*. It's a bond that runs deeper than that. It's a soul tie, Airess." He explained, a bitter laugh coming out of his mouth.

"Do you know how many fucked up things I have done? I don't deserve you. *At all*. I'm not a good person. How can I expect you to accept a bond you never even asked for or wanted? My soul…it will tarnish yours." Pain cracked in his voice, raw and unguarded, and Airess felt her heart twist painfully in her chest.

The wind rose, whipping Airess' wet locks wildly around her face and neck. By now, their clothes clung to their bodies, completely soaked through. Lightning struck overhead, and she took a step toward Taryn, rain pelting her from the side. She raised her voice enough to be heard over the storm.

"Has it ever occurred to you that I don't care what you've done? What makes you think I'm this good person? Why is the thought of us being together so unfathomable?" she retorted.

Taryn shook his head slowly, water dripping from his soaked hair.

"You are a good person, Airess. You deserve better than me." He cupped her face with one hand. "To think I would have trapped you forever if the Oathmark hadn't interrupted us at the Inn. I was so irresponsible." He ripped his hand away, as if he were afraid to touch her.

Butterflies erupted in her stomach at the implication. Airess recalled Ismene' words. *Once the relationship is consummated, the true effects of the Bond will take place. Your souls will be completely tied together.*

"What are you saying, Taryn?"

His face hardened. "You're not Fae. How can you understand what this means? I'm giving you the space you deserve."

"You don't get to make that decision." Airess shot back, instilling as much strength in her voice to mask the panic rising in her chest.

Taryn raked both hands through his wet hair. "Don't fight me on this, Air. I'm doing this for – for you."

Airess scoffed in disbelief. "Don't shut me out just because everyone in your life has abandoned, betrayed, *and left you behind*."

Taryn's jaw ticked. "This is for your best interest."

Anger simmered hot in her veins, and the words were pouring out of her before she could stop them. "Oh, that's rich, Taryn. Especially coming from the male who murdered, spied and smuggled drugs for a living. What would someone like that know about my *best interest*?"

Regret closed in as soon as the words left her mouth. He took a step back, recoiling at what she threw in his face.

The rain poured harder than it had been. Water dripped off her nose, and her hair clung to her neck. Taryn's curls soaked around his ears and plastered against the sides of his face. His eyes hardened, the background of the storm adding a shadow of darkness to his features.

Suddenly, a bolt of lightning struck down next to them. Airess was knocked off her feet, and for a moment, her ears rang. Adrenaline flushed through her entire body, and her hands suddenly were coated in Starlight, a natural defense mechanism. She blinked, but hands had gripped her sides and yanked her to standing. She met Taryn's wide eyes.

"Oh my Gods. Are you okay?" he asked, frantically scanning her entire body.

Lightning struck again, vibrating through the ground and shaking Airess to her very core. She stumbled backwards at the force of it. At the force of *him*.

He was causing this.

Her breaths became labored. Not in fear of him, but in shock. Airess had never known the depths of Taryn's power, and when Ismene said it may be heightened outside of Luciena's ward, she had never expected *this*.

Taryn held his arms out and reached to help, but yanked himself away with a pained expression. "I'm sorry. *Fuck.*"

Taryn stared down at his hands, as if they were the enemy.

She came to stand, looking from him to the clouds. She held out her arms, trying to diffuse the situation. "Taryn, it's okay. Just–just breathe."

Taryn shook his head and created more distance between them. "You need to leave."

"It's–"

"I don't want you to see me like this," he rambled, and suddenly he seemed lost. Broken. "You can throw my life in my face, and I would still do anything for you. You can't make me hate you. I never will. My feelings for you are too strong. Please, just leave. I don't want to hurt you."

She stood there, frozen. If she left now, her words would sink into his mind. Fester. *Gods,* she was an idiot. Why did she say that?

"I didn't mean what I said. I'm sorry," she whispered, shrinking into herself.

She turned and left, tears pricking her eyes. She couldn't look at his face anymore. She couldn't look at the pain she caused, that they both caused to each other.

The storm raged on far long after she returned home that night.

Chapter 36

"The Sun and Moon Gods, Ghrian and Gaeleach, will always find one another. In this universe, and the next."

— The Book of Tevye

The Vulture

The parchment crinkled underneath The Vulture's fingertips as they leaned against the ship's salt-slicked railing. The salty air invaded their nose as the breeze caressed their face, and carried the distant cries of restless gulls. They swiftly unraveled the document, eager to read the contents Eryx had left for them.

It was the dead of night, and only the moonlight overhead kept The Vulture company. The ship beneath The Vulture's feet groaned as it sailed to Rune. One way or another, they would accomplish their goals. Only now the goal was muddled by desperation and vengeance, their previous plan crumbled into nothing.

It was true, The Vulture was grasping for power. Grasping for anything they could do to take over Luciena. They had even resorted to using the last bit of Magick the crystal blade possessed to get their ship through Luciena's energy ward. It was a gamble, indeed. If their plan failed, there would be no way to travel back.

The Vulture glanced down at the parchment, loosened a breath and unraveled the paper:

If you are reading this, the plan for myself has failed. Well, that's not entirely true. The plan will be carried on by you. You, The Vulture, the person whom I've seen myself in. I recognized myself in you. It's why I agreed to take on your plan to take over the country. However, you never knew the full scope of my plans. Not really.

Don't be angry. I planned on telling you eventually. You never know what the promise of power can do to a person, and I wanted to see if you could carry your end of the bargain first.

The blade I gave you is no ordinary weapon. The crystal that makes the blade is cut from the tomb of the first Godlings, and has magickal properties. These properties are powerful enough to turn you into a Godling yourself. Though, the price is grave. You must ask yourself if you are willing to do what it takes. I have no doubt you will.

The Allpower is the power of all five Godlings combined. It is unfathomable power. Power enough to heighten a physical dimension into a higher state. It was the power that created Tevye.

This is the lost piece of knowledge I am passing onto you: If you kill a Godling, you inherit their power. If you kill all five Godlings, you inherit the Allpower. This blade is the only one in the world that can allow such a transfer of Magick.

Be warned. This is no easy task. Your best chance is killing a Godling in their resting state. If the Godling accesses the Godspirit, they are completely possessed by their God and can destroy you with the lift of a finger.

You know what to do.

Yours truly,

Eryx Mrykinia Moros

The Vulture dropped the parchment onto the ship deck, speechless. They steadied their trembling hands on the boat railing and swallowed. The price for power was so much more than they had anticipated. It would be unforgivable. It would be ruthless.

A kernel of hope beamed deep in The Vulture's cold, black heart. Because despite the price that had to be paid, it was their solution.

They would do what they must.

Chapter 37

'I ask myself if giving into the darkness was worth losing my mate. What is stronger, the yearning for power, or love?'

— Written entry from Evyen Deyanira's personal journal
(Post-Division)

Airess

Runean balls were surprisingly similar to the ones in Luciena.

The only differences were the styles of music, food, and attire. They held the ball in the throne room where she and Taryn had met Roz. Flickering balls of fyrelight floated overhead like captive stars, casting a soft glow across the room. There was a massive table of finger foods, all the guests flocking to it, eager to eat. Attendants passed out a tray of glasses filled with clear, pink and amber-colored liquid.

Airess took a glass and sipped, the sweet burn of the wine gliding down her throat. She tried her best to relax, but couldn't after everything she had been through. It was so strange how life moved on, no matter the traumas and grief endured by the one who lived it.

The Fae laughed and danced, composing themselves with ease in the presence of the king. She watched Roz interact with his subjects casually, as if he were in conversation with old friends. She decided she liked Roz, and wouldn't mind another friend like him in her life. The world needed more kind-hearted people.

She stood there awkwardly, trying her best to feel comfortable in the clothes the attendants had brought to her. They did give her a choice of clothing, all the options far skimpier than she was used to. After delicate thought, she decided on the perfect dress.

Airess' dress was a deep crimson. The bodice was tightly wrapped around her waist, and her breasts were on display due to the low V-neck. The skirt of the dress had double slits, the sheer fabric showing off her legs. She wore a low heel with golden laces going up her calves.

Her long hair had been left down in waves. Airess wore the locket Esper had given her. She touched the metal heart at her throat, her thoughts going back to the Priestess who risked everything to get her out of Luciena.

Was Esper still alive?

She clutched the glass of wine with a scowl, trying her best to ignore Taryn across the ballroom speaking with the other ball goers. He had returned to the guest house a few hours after their fight on the beach, and when the morning came, he was nowhere to be found in the guest house. Airess did everything in her power not to care.

As if feeling her stare, Taryn met her eyes. He looked devastatingly handsome tonight. Taryn was dressed in a silk Runean suit, his white shirt effortlessly loose on his muscled figure. The sleeves were rolled up to his elbows, showcasing his one red inked sleeve. He excused himself from conversation and crossed the room towards her. Airess stood up straight, eager to talk to him. Eager to resolve things.

"May I have this dance?" Roz asked as he stepped into view, cutting Taryn off. Roz asked it in her tongue, always the gentleman.

Airess blinked. "You may," she replied with a smile that didn't quite reach her eyes. She glanced over at Taryn, whose brows hardened at Roz's outstretched arm. Taryn's jaw ticked, but he didn't intervene.

Roz whisked her into the crowd, the pair drawing hesitant stares that quickly looked away. Airess felt Taryn's stare without having to look over at him.

Roz gently placed a hand on Airess' waist. "There's something I wanted to discuss with you." Roz said lightly as they shifted on their feet. He took her hand in his as they began to dance.

"Times are changing, and quickly. Soon the world will change forever. If we act now, we can assure Rune's survival."

Airess' distant gaze snapped to Roz's attention, noticing the eagerness in his blue eyes as he looked at her.

"Act? Rune is at peace."

Roz's mouth tightened in restraint, hesitating for a beat as if he were calculating his words. "*When* the prophecy comes to fruition, we will be dealing with a new world that hasn't been seen in a thousand years. The Dawn is coming. We need to prepare."

Airess gave him a skeptical look. He was beginning to sound like Ismene, always speaking in riddles, in secret hidden messages.

"Where are you going with this?" Airess asked hesitantly.

Roz closed his eyes and took a steady breath. "We need allies if we are to stand against Luciena, if they dare cross us. My mother has... different ideologies of Rune's success. But I disagree with her, there is another way. With two Godlings ruling, we would be unstoppable."

Airess dropped his hand, stopping their dance in the middle of the floor. "What are you say–"

"I'm asking if you would be my queen, my *wife*. Rule over Rune with me and all its lands. Together, our power would raze anyone who dares to harm us." Roz cleared his throat. "It is prophesied, is it not, that two beings will unite to bring forth a new dawn? It was clear to me from the moment I saw you, that we were destined to bring the prophecy to fruition."

Oh.

Oh, Gods.

Airess tensed. She realized Roz believed that *they* were The Prophesied. Of course he had no knowledge that Taryn was her Mate–that Airess and Taryn were the ones who have been Fated.

She blinked in surprise and cleared her throat to respond. "You're asking me to marry *you?*" She couldn't believe his words. He was definitely coming on strong, and all those sidelong looks he had been giving her started to make sense.

"I know it seems a bit sudden, but unions of this kind are common with people in power. It's not about lust, or love, but we can change the world with our power," Roz grabbed the hand she dropped, "*Say yes.* Rule by my side."

It certainly was ironic, as different and kind Rune claimed to be, they craved power into their line all the same.

Taryn's bitter laugh cut through the shock from her right. Airess hadn't even realized he had approached them, from the whirring thoughts in her brain. Taryn's cheeks were slightly flushed, and his lips were wine stained. His hair was disheveled, as if he couldn't stop running his fingers through it. Taryn's stare sliced daggers in Roz's direction as he sipped his glass, a smug expression overtaking his features.

"I'll give you one second to get your hand *off* her before I cut you down." Taryn snapped, looking between her and Roz, his jaw tense.

Taryn stepped closer to Roz, his silver eyes igniting, glowing brighter than usual.

Fuck.

Airess stepped forward and grabbed Taryn's arm, breaking his attention away from Roz. She knew he had a bold side, but did he seriously threaten the king?

Airess looked between him and Roz. She stepped into the middle, to put a physical barrier between them, for *Roz's* sake.

"Taryn, back off." She hissed, angry at his jealous display. Who was he, denying her and then getting jealous at the next turn?

Roz's laugh was rich and deep behind her, his face amused. He was always amused, and now she saw he could be smug, as well. She needed to get Taryn out of here. The two would be a recipe for disaster.

"I have no quarrel with you, Stormborne." Roz retorted smoothly, choosing his words delicately. Airess interjected before Taryn could respond, pushing Taryn's chest with her hand.

"Excuse us. I need to talk with my *friend*." She bit out the words, not caring if her words sliced him. Let them. His reaction to their bond had sliced her heart open more than she cared to admit.

She grabbed his hand and dragged him away from Roz before things could get more heated. They walked through a sea of ballgoers and out onto the balcony, far from the crowd. The humid air blasted against her skin as they walked out.

"Are you going to marry him?" Taryn demanded, following close behind, his eyes laced with hurt.

"Are you serious?" Airess asked as she whipped around to face him. He was blind if he couldn't see just how much she had begun to care for him. She would *never* betray him. She could never be with someone else. What she felt for Taryn outweighed any hollow proposal this king might give her.

He laughed sarcastically, cloaking his pain once more. "I wouldn't fault you for it. You deserve the life he could give you."

Airess shook her head and groaned, frustration boiling over. "Again with this! I don't want that. I don't want to be *given* a life." She crossed her arms. "Why do you care if you don't even want me?"

Taryn paused, eyes fluttering shut momentarily. He raked a hand through his hair and then slid his gaze to hers. He exhaled slowly and stalked up to her, invading her personal space. Taryn lifted her chin gently with his fingers to look at him.

"*Oh*, I want you," he whispered, sending chills down her spine. He ran a hand along her jawline. Airess' entire body warmed at the contact and her stomach fluttered. Gods, the things this male made her feel with a single touch. A single phrase.

"I want you every day, every night, every *waking* fucking hour. I've wanted you since the day I met you in that ballroom. Airess, you have to know I would do anything for you. I would commit *atrocities* for you if it meant having you by my side. I thought about rejecting the bond–I did," he was shaking his head, as if it were impossible. "I thought I was strong enough to do it. But you're too perfect. You are ethereal. A Goddess in physical form sent to destroy me. I don't want to tarnish you by claiming you, but I am learning that I am a selfish, selfish male."

Airess' eyebrows rose at the raw confession, heart pounding. "You wouldn't tarnish me," the words came out as a whisper.

He shook his head. "I will. I will ruin you."

She grabbed his tunic and pulled forward, dragging him to her with force. His pupils dilated. "Stop putting me on this *pedestal*. I am not this gracious being that you think I am. I've killed just as you have. I'm tainted, and I have a feeling this is only the beginning of what lies ahead," Airess bared her teeth at him, anger and love and frustration melting into one.

"I'll say it for the last time, Taryn. I don't *care* what you've done. I don't care that you've killed. If darkness is where you are, then I'll happily meet you there," she tilted her head back and laughed. "Have you ever considered I have darkness as well? Have you ever considered that *I* might ruin *you*?"

She saw the leash he held on himself break, desire and passion welling behind his eyes. He lurched forward, cupping her face with his hands and slamming her into the wall behind them. Her breath hitched as her back hit the wall. Taryn angled his face towards hers, their lips inches apart. His shaky fingers fanned out against her cheeks.

He was holding onto his restraint by a thread, and she intended to break it.

"Love me. Ruin me. Claim me, Tarynon."

A primal growl rumbled in his chest as their lips collided. He claimed her mouth, pressing his body as close as he could to hers. Her hands gripped his face, as if she needed to hold him, to make sure this was real. Their kiss was a song of stars and light, of beginnings and ends, a push and pull that echoed out into the universe.

His lips on hers felt so right, so at home, that she sighed into him. His hands traveled to her hips and he cupped her breast. The touch had her sighing with pleasure. She was on fire, every inch of her skin igniting with his touch. Taryn ran his tongue over her lips and she obliged, letting him in.

They were a mixture of teeth and lips. A mixture of love and anger. Taryn deepened the kiss, kissing her so hard she wondered if she would ever breathe again after this.

She broke away, her mouth red from the kiss, drunk on passion. "I–I accept you."

His eyes shone bright with longing and desire, and she saw his mental walls fall.

"And *I* you."

He kissed her, gently this time. He trailed kisses down her neck, holding her waist tightly as if to not lose control. She moaned at the kind of touch she only read about in books. But this was real. Taryn was real. Their *Bond* was real.

He trailed kisses down her jaw until he met the crux of her neck. "My beginning and end," Taryn said in Runean, before grazing his canines across her skin. The feeling startled her, but invoked a primal feminine urge deep within her.

More.

She needed *more*. Airess didn't want to wait. She slipped a finger under the waistline of his pants, not caring where they were or who could see. Taryn stiffened, inhaled sharply, and pulled back.

"What–"

"I don't care," she breathed. "I want this."

At that, Taryn smirked, and a deep rumble vibrated from his chest. His hands tangled in her hair as he gripped her ass, and yanked her towards him. His breath tickled her ear as he whispered, "Say it again, Love."

Heat flared in her chest. At him calling her Love for the first time. *Gods.* "I want this. I want *you.*"

His mouth was on hers again. Taryn grabbed her thigh and hiked her leg up, then her dress, and pinned her upright against the balcony wall. He grazed his fingers against her inner thigh. Airess shuttered. Every part of her was on fyre.

"You know," he whispered into her ear, fingers slowly creeping up her thigh, "I've thought about this moment since you opened that wicked mouth of yours."

He grazed the sensitive flesh that was her core, and Airess' head fell back. Taryn yanked her undergarment to the side and moaned as he began to stroke the most sensitive part of her. She sighed, breathless. The sensation was almost too much to bear. Never before had she experienced anything sexual, never before had she been so exposed to a male.

Every muscle in her body tightened at his touch, and a foreign pleasure budded within her and spread through her entire body. Her world spun, her body flushing and growing hot. Taryn began to trail kisses down her neck and sucked, claiming her as his. Airess gasped as he continued, taking matters further. She had not realized it could get any better than this.

Airess felt him smile against her neck as she shook, the feeling intensifying. Airess slid a hand under his tunic, her breaths quickening. Taryn moved faster, his touch both possessive and careful. She didn't know how much longer she could last.

Taryn lifted his head and looked at her through his lashes. He tilted her chin up to look at him. The damn bastard was smirking.

"Look at me."

Three words, and Airess was unraveling. She moaned as her pleasure reached its peak, but kept eye contact with him. Taryn drank her in, eyes roaming down her face with a devious half smile upon his lips. When her breaths evened, his grip on her waste loosened, and he withdrew.

Airess gasped for breath and reached for his belt, intending to go further, but Taryn seized her wrist.

"As much as I would love to take you right here on this patio, I prefer to be away from spectators, under the stars, only the Gods as our witness," Taryn tucked a strand of hair behind her ear as he lowered his voice. "And if you tempt me now, I won't be able to uphold that."

The words sent shivers down her spine. Airess loosened a breath and slumped against the wall, wordless. She watched the corners of Taryn's mouth upturn into a slight smile as he took a slight step back.

"What is it?"

Taryn didn't hesitate. "I want you to know I didn't leave the guest house today to avoid resolving our differences," he explained as he fished in his pocket, and pulled out a small, wooden box. "I know I let my power get out of control on the beach, and for that I am so, so sorry. You must know I would *never* endanger you. I am still learning the scope of my power. I wanted to make it up to you, in the way you deserve."

Taryn opened the box, and inside it was a gilded piece of jewelry. Airess' heart pounded as Taryn withdrew it from the box.

"I know your birthday is tomorrow, but I couldn't wait. Happy twenty-first birthday, Love."

It was a bracelet. The gilded chain was delicate, but it was the center of the jewelry that caught her eye. In the center was a small, delicate sun adorned with tiny, red rubies that glittered in the pale moonlight that cascaded down upon them from above. Airess' mouth parted open as she looked back up at him.

"The sun is to represent your familial house. I spent the entire day crafting this with the blacksmith in town, along with this," he said, laughing nervously. Taryn's eyes were warm as he retrieved a second item out of the box. It was one copper earring, similar to the one Taryn wore, only it wasn't a lightning bolt. It was a small, dangling star. Her breath hitched, and her eyes shot to his ear. He had replaced his elemental earring with a crescent moon symbol, the other half to hers.

Airess' eyes brimmed with tears.

"Taryn," Airess started, voice breaking slightly. She was overcome with emotion, at the thoughtfulness of his gift. Gifts *he* had made. The bracelet was breathtaking. The earring was stunning, entirely unique, and she was honored he was sharing a part of his culture with her.

"I've never been gifted anything like it. They are beautiful. Thank you *so much*," she exclaimed and rose on her tiptoes. She cupped Taryn's face with her hands and kissed him softly. Although they hadn't solidified the mating bond, there was not a doubt in her mind that she wanted to, and soon. He wrapped his arm around her before pulling away, gripping her wrist lightly.

"Allow me," he said, and fastened the bracelet onto her wrist. She looked at it in awe, twisting her wrist and watching the rubies glitter in the night. Taryn swept her hair back and fastened the earring onto her ear, the other half to his.

Taryn smiled and backed up a step. He held out his arm, as if he was about to ask her to dance. Then, Airess heard a whirring sound. Something landed and hit Taryn in the back. His eyes widened in surprise and he spun around to face their assailants. Upon turning, she saw a tiny arrow embedded in his shoulder.

Neither of them managed to react in time before another arrow zipped by and hit Airess in the thigh. She hissed as Taryn drew out a dagger she didn't know he was wearing and stood defensively in front of her. Whatever drug the arrows had been injected with had made Airess' body feel so heavy, she could barely keep her eyes open. She took a disorienting step forward to do something, *anything*, but it was no use.

They both faltered, falling to the ground together as the whole world went black.

Chapter 38

A stolen Death. A touch of Fyre.
An earth rebirthed to be made from desire.

— *The book of Tevye*

Taryn

The sun glared down on Taryn's face, momentarily blinding him as he opened his eyes. He stared at the ceiling–a barred skylight window ten feet above him, the source of the light. It was dawn, the golden hue of the morning sun painting the sky in a blend of pink and orange.

His eyes widened as he took in the four stone walls surrounding them, familiarity coursing through him, a Runean prisoner cell he had managed to score himself in during his youth. He sat up, chains encasing his wrists and ankles clanking with the movement. His skin burned, and he didn't have to look down at the green substance to know they were drugged with donstentye. And a *heavy* dose of it.

Airess lay unconscious against the wall opposite him. He sighed in relief that they were together. She looked unharmed, only dirt caking the side of her face and legs from the cell floor. They were both still in the clothing they'd worn at the ball. He leaned over to wake her but was yanked back, the chains linked to the walls separating them with distance. He steeled himself away from panic, trying his best to formulate a plan. He could get his mate out of here–he *had* to.

"Air." Taryn whispered, his voice scraping against the parched feeling in his throat. "*Airess*."

She stirred awake, bringing her hand to her forehead, the chains grazing her body. At once, she shot upwards with panic in her eyes, until she found him.

Taryn smirked, trying to keep the energy light. "Fancy seeing you here. We've truly got to stop making a habit of getting incarcerated together."

Her face contorted into a panic, brushing off his humor as she looked up to the skylight. "They drugged us."

"We've been betrayed." Taryn confirmed. "A bold move for them, considering none of them will be left alive when we escape this place. We need a plan. How did you access the Godspirit back in Rune?"

"I don't know how I did it. I saw you get hurt and became so angry. It *consumed* me–

"It doesn't matter." said a dark feminine voice in Mrkynian, her Runean thick. "You won't survive long enough to set yourselves free."

A figure stepped near the skylight, bending over to peer down on them.

It was the Dowager Queen.

"Happy to see you're both awake, just in time for the *fun*. So sorry it had to be on your birthday, of course."

Taryn's brows drew together as understanding washed over him. Hot anger ran down his body in waves.

"How dare you betray us?" Taryn barked.

"Are you really so surprised?" the Queen Dowager asked as she let out a cruel laugh. "I am a queen and a mother. You are a danger to my son, and you are a danger to Rune. I'm protecting the best interest of both, and that means getting rid of any threats that may pose. You two, for example. You may have pure intentions now, but in time your power will grow," the Queen Dowager smirked. "My sweet, idiot son thought we needed you for the prophecy, but I think we need to get *rid* of you."

"Where is Roz?" Airess called out, her face twisted into a scowl.

"Let's say my son is... indisposed at the moment. By the time he wakes up, you will be *long* gone."

"We would never have ill intentions. We came here in *peace*!" Airess countered, straining against the chains.

"Power breeds destruction, girl. It's only a matter of time until you both realize what you are capable of. Now, you'll never get the chance. You will be negotiated back to who you belonged to. Did you really think by coming here, Luciena wouldn't declare war on its lost bride?"

Airess blanched, the words hitting her like a physical blow. "What are you talking about?"

The heat simmering within him increased to a boil, his sight turning red at the words he was hearing. How she was speaking about Airess, as if she were stolen goods. As if she were an *object*.

"We have changed the course of history for the better. For the first time in a century, we have reached a peace agreement with Luciena.

Prince Arzhel has arrived on our shores, and we will begin our negotiations for peace. Perhaps you can view this as a victory—you being a small price to pay for the peace of the world."

Taryn snarled. He would kill them all if they dared to touch her. He would destroy this fucking continent and everyone in it.

Airess' frantic words cut through his reaction. "You're being manipulated! Arzhel will stop at nothing to expand his empire. Letting him come here to claim me as his bride was a mistake!"

The Queen Dowager chuckled, her voice like velvet. "You think he would take you back after being sullied by this Fae male? After the intellect we've shared during our correspondence, we are negotiating your *life*. An exchange of power for peace." Her words slid over Taryn like cold water. She turned her head toward him with the slightest curl of a smile. "With my plans in place, I am assuring Rune's success and victory." she said bitterly as she stepped out of view.

"Bring the girl."

The rock wall behind Airess shifted into a door opening, two earthborne guards grabbing hold of her chains. Taryn shifted forward as they grabbed her arms, and he barely noticed that the movement tore the skin on his wrists.

"Don't you fucking touch her," Taryn roared, thrashing against his chains with an incessant rage. The guards lifted her up, and the panicked look in her eyes was the last thing he saw before she was dragged away. "Airess!" he called out as he threw all of his weight against his restraints. Pain tore into his limbs as he fought to free himself, but it was no use. "I swear to all five Gods if you touch–

The panicked look in Airess' eyes was the last thing he saw as The wall slammed upwards, leaving Taryn alone.

He released a cry to the skylight, the space now void of anyone who could hear him. Never had he felt so powerless. Never had he felt such despair. His hands trembled, his heart cracking in two.

"You're fucking dead!" He spat. "You're fucking dead! All of you!"

Chapter 39

A soul of Mind brings forth The Storm.
Is when the Dawn of a new age shalt be born.

— *The book of Tevye*

Airess

Airess thrashed as the guards held her up by her arms, her feet dangling just above the ground. They removed her blindfold and threw her on the floor, securing her chains and binding her upright on a wooden stake. They gagged her with a cloth rag.

She breathed heavily as she took in her surroundings. They were outside on a stage in the city courtyard. Fifty or so Lucien guards stationed themselves in front of her, Runean guards stood at her sides. Beyond the guards were hundreds of Runean civilians gathered to watch whatever was about to unfold.

The Queen Dowager leaned over a desk with Arzhel as they signed the treaty that would forfeit Airess' life. She instantly broke into a hot sweat as she stared at Arzhel, a face she thought she would forever be safe from. Airess looked to the sky, the morning sun now visible. She felt so small, so powerless against him.

Gods be with me. It can't end this way.

Finally, the treaty was finished. With one sign of a quill, her life would forever change–a slow descent into darkness. She closed her eyes and tried–*willed* that Godspirit into her body like it had done back in the caravan. Nothing came. Not a single spark. She felt an empty void where her power should have been.

Airess opened her eyes to the sky, her expression contorted in anger at the heavens above. *How dare you choose me and neglect to come to my aid?*

She gritted her teeth against the cloth gag, her breaths shallow.

Why Airess? Was it all for nothing? Did the prophecy *mean* nothing?

Where was the king? Where was Ismene?

Arzhel turned slowly after shaking the Queen Dowager's hand. They walked up to the stage where Airess was staked.

The crowd quieted as the Queen Dowager began to speak. "Today marks a day in history where the world will be ruled by Godlings once again! May we forever have peace in our humble sacrifice. We declare the war between Rune and Luciena *over*!"

The masses cheered at the declaration. For the first time since this nightmare began, Arzhel turned to face Airess. Her heart hammered against her ribs at the sight of him, but her expression remained still, defiant. The familiar hatred in his glowing red eyes struck deep. His mouth twisted into a cold smile as he stepped toward her, their faces close enough so no one could hear.

"Did you really think you could elude me? " He spoke in a low whisper. "I must say it truly is *impressive* you made it all this way. Your little stunt cost me much embarrassment. At first I was so – so *angry* you had left me. You were to be my wife. You were supposed to give me *heirs*." Arzhel softly dragged his fingers along her jaw, taunting her. Bile threatened to rise in her throat at his touch, and she tried her best to angle her body as far away from him as she could.

"But after we came into communication with Rune in recent months," he continued, voice laced with malice, "we learned of something far more valuable than your womb. Your travels were not all in vain, you see. Because of you, I am now about to become the Godling I was always meant to be." Arzhel jerked her face upwards.

"I am going to kill you and take the power that is rightfully mine. This is the end of your miserable, weak existence." he taunted with a smile, trailing his fingers down her neck and back to her mouth, removing the gag. She flinched at his touch.

"Do you have any last words?"

Airess let out a crazed laugh, tears welling in her eyes, sliding down the sides of her grinning cheeks. She laughed and laughed–an unexpected reaction even she couldn't comprehend. Perhaps it was all she could do to take control, to comfort herself in such a fucking crazy moment of her life. It was a laugh of panic.

Of desperation

Sorrow.

Anger.

She looked at Arzhel. It was such a shame that in her last moments, she would be seeing his dreadful face as she took her last breath and not her Mates.

"Mark my words, Arzhel Lucien," She heaved out, her voice clear, "I will haunt you for the rest of your days. Not even Death will save you from me. And when you finally die, I will gladly meet you in hell." Airess spat in his face with a wild grin, unleashing a more sinister part of herself she had always felt stirring deep in her mind. The floodgates of her darkness burst open in her last moments, forever unleashed. She averted her eyes to the sun, what she wanted to be her last image as she left the world.

What a miserably wonderful existence.

Chapter 40

'The Gods deemed us worthy of their power. Are you worthy, Evyen?'
— Written correspondence from Tinyrah Kazimyr to Evyen Deyanira (Post-Division).

Taryn

Taryn tried his best to draw out his power. He strained against the donstenyte poisoning his mind and came up with nothing. No Magick at all. Whatever they had here was infinitely stronger than what was in Luciena.

He had tried to pull and break the chains, but it was impossible. Every second was crucial, his rising panic starting to take over. He sat back against the wall and looked inwards. How could he escape this?

Taryn could only think of one solution. Accessing the Godspirit Ismene said he had within him. He had seen Airess do it. He knew it was possible to draw on that power–a power so strong that it could break the drugged-coated chains bound to him.

"*My power is within the mind, a different kind of Magick.*" Taryn recalled Airess saying once, during a past conversation. Could it be possible to tap into her Magick? If the mind was truly separate from the body, could it still hold some power that could aid him in breaking out of here?

Taryn closed his eyes and meditated. He had been unintentionally drawing from her dreamwalking abilities for months now. Maybe he could draw on something deeper if he purposely tried to access it. Access *anyone* who could help him.

He lay down, trying his best to calm his raging breath.

One. Two. Three. Four–just as Airess taught him.

Calm. Collected. Controlled.

After several minutes, he slipped away.

"Tarynon." A voice spoke. "At last, you've finally reached the higher dimension."

He looked down at the armchair he sat in–one he had sat in many times in his life. In front of him was a small fireplace, and to his right sat his grandmother, Ima, her lips curved in a soft smile. She was knitting as she usually would, crimson and emerald yarn intertwining, as if she had never died at all.

"Ima!" He said, slipping out of his chair and dropping to his knees in front of her. "Is it really you?"

Ima nodded. "It's me," she set her yarn aside and took his hands in hers with a soft smile. "Why have you come, my dear?"

Taryn didn't know it was possible to cry here–wherever this dimension was, but there were tears streaming down his face. It seemed to be a step beyond the dreamworld, his movements more fluid and controlled.

"I am so lost," Taryn confessed. "After you died, everything changed. I have–I have done terrible things." Taryn looked away. "If you knew what I've done, you would never look at me the same. I'm sorry I couldn't make you proud."

Taryn sobbed. There were so many things he had felt but never voiced, never formulated into words from all the sadness and shame he felt. Ima drew him in an embrace. "My dear," she drew back, looking him in the eye.

"I have always been with you, through every hard trial and decision you've made. I know what you've done. I know what you've gone through. You are more than worthy of happiness, of a good life. Your mistakes have been forgiven."

Taryn's mouth parted open, half in shock that he was really talking to her, and the relief that her words had brought him. Feeling a sense of urgency, as if time was about to run out, he blurted. "I found my mate. Oh gods, Ima, she's even more beautiful than I deserve."

Ima smiled. "I know. What a wonderful match Fate has made."

Taryn frowned, suddenly remembering why he was here. Where his body really was. "She needs my help. I'm trying to fight through the poison and access the Godspirit, but it's too strong. I don't know what to do."

"Let go of your shame and let your spirit be free. Only then will you access what you desire."

Ima pressed her thumb in the middle of Taryn's brow, sending a feeling of Magick coursing through him. "Until we meet again."

As soon as the words left her mouth, electricity filtered through him, blinding his eyes. He was falling through space now.

All Taryn knew was that he had to try and let go of his shame, his guilt.

He needed to access the Godspirit. He needed to save Airess.

Words whispered around him as he fell,

"Killer!"

"Liar!"

"Thief!"

Taryn yelled out into the void as each word clashed into him, reminding him of who he once was. Each word was accompanied by a memory that flashed in his mind.

He saw himself homeless at thirteen, stealing from another family, barely making ends meet.

He saw himself at fourteen, killing another man to join the Guild.

He saw himself at sixteen, alone and drunk, wandering the streets as he tried to fill a bottomless void.

A void he now knew was Airess. Airess, his light in the darkness. Airess, a star holding up the moon. It was always her. It would always be her.

He stopped resisting the memories, his goal becoming suddenly clear. It was about more than him now. This was about his Mate's life. He faced the ugliest parts of himself and accepted the shame. Accepted the regret. He could not change the past or who he once was. But he could shape his future. Taryn would become the person his Mate needed.

A Godling.

The memories faded, and in the distance, he saw a figure sitting upon a silver throne, floating in space. The being was massive, the body made of pulsing energy the colors of black and silver. It had a face, but the features were unreadable. Two silver glowing eyes stared at Taryn. In the palm of the being's hand, it held the moon. Taryn sank to his knees.

Gealach, the God of Moon and Storm.

It was an innate fact Taryn knew without thinking, felt in every fiber of his being. His God. The one who Touched him at birth. The God Taryn shared his spirit with.

Gealach's gaze upon Taryn was heavy with an energy so strong, he felt it pulsing through his astral body. Taryn stilled at the sight of the God.

'You are ready.' The God bellowed, its voice a plethora of beings all meshed into one. Taryn heard the voice in his mind, despite not seeing the God's mouth move. Gealach extended a hand, sending tendrils of silver light towards Taryn.

Taryn reached for it and touched the light. His vision turned white, astral body fusing with the Moon God. He screamed out, not in terror, but because the power was overwhelming.

'Go.' Gealach commanded. Taryn was sent barreling forward, flipping through space. His spirit fell back to earth, back to Rune, back to the prison cell his body was in.

Taryn opened his eyes.

Wind whirled around him as his eyes began to glow, his brown hair fading into an iridescent silver from root to tip. His skin turned a glowing metallic, and when he yanked his chain from the wall, the entire prison cell began to crumble.

He pumped air upwards, blasting the skylight bars into the sky.

Chapter 41

*'Soul slaying is forbidden. If you destroy a soul,
you destroy your own as well.'*

— *Excerpt from House Moros' book of Minds*

Airess

Arzhel unsheathed his dagger at her words.

Act.

Act.

Act.

"A threat from the grave," he mused. "I think I'll give you a slow death for that statement, put on a show for our crowd." Arzhel turned to face the audience and raised his dagger in the air, their chants growing as her death neared.

Airess closed her eyes when a thought struck her. She had saved Taryn, hovering over his body as she reached into his heart and pulled him out of his curse.

Could she do it now?

Could she die trying?

Arzhel turned around, bringing the blade to her neck, taunting her. "See you in hell," he said.

Airess' eyes began to glow lilac as she looked up. Before he could press down his blade –

Airess peeled out of her body, the feeling so uncomfortable it felt like taking off wet clothing. She watched above her and Arzhel's body, the movement of him striking his blade happening in slow motion.

"No!" She screamed, and reached her arm through Arzhel's back, dragging his spirit out with her bare hands. It was hard, his spirit was so intact with his physical body, she had to pry it out of him. Ghosts of darkness followed, attached to his body by their tales.

His spirit was dark, so very black. She could barely make out his eyes as he looked around in confusion, looking down at his spiritual body. Airess took advantage of his hesitance, grabbing his neck with her hand, yanking his face close to hers with a snarl of rage.

Despite the blackness of his spirit seeping into her fingers slowly–dying the tips of her golden hands black–she grinned and squeezed her hand around his neck. "What is this?" He said, his voice sounding smaller here, less menacing.

"Look at me." Airess commanded. He did. She saw him recognize her, saw him look below to their physical bodies moving in slow motion. By now, his physical body had seized, frozen in the act of murder, the blade inches from impaling her physical throat.

"Look at my soul as the last thing you see before you die." She said

and thrashed her arms, ripping into his soul, tearing him apart. She raged. She screamed and shredded his soul. She was so lost in her frenzy that she missed Morana walking onto the stage.

Morana withdrew a blade made of crystal, engraved with text she couldn't recognize.

"No!" Airess said, screaming into the void, wanting Arzhel to die by her hand.

It was too late, Morana had already plunged the crystallite dagger straight into Arzhel's back.

His black spirit vanished as quickly as the blade struck into his heart, disappearing from Airess' grip.

The sound of screaming overcame her as she forced herself back in reality. Arzhel's blood splattered on her, and Morana as he fell to his knees. He fell on his back, his eyes wide in shock at his sister's betrayal.

Morana smirked at him, holding him up by his tunic. She was wearing dark, tattered clothing. Her cloak was dirtied, as if she had been traveling for quite some time. A simple gold, gilded broach in the shape of a vulture rested on her chest.

The Vulture.

"You were never deserving enough to be a Godling," Morana spat at her brother. "But *I am.*"

Morana dropped his shirt and climbed over him, pressing her hands to his temples, red tendrils of power drained out of him and traveled up her arms like veins. She was screaming, her brown eyes suddenly fading into an iridescent red. Morana fell back, crying out with a wicked smile on her face. She thrashed, receiving the power of Death in all its glory.

When it was done, her body glowed red. Her ebony hair had turned a dark crimson–red, for the Godspirit of Death. Morana looked down at her hands and shot a fist upwards, a hiss of dark spirits audible as the Shadow Magick shot up in the air. Morana's burgundy glow faded, the color only evident in her eyes as she returned to her normal state.

Airess watched Morana steal Arzhel's power in shock. The world trembled at her newfound power. Airess knew how detrimental it was, and–

Thunder bellowed, bringing Airess' attention overhead. The sky darkened, storm clouds drawing together. The temperature had dropped, carrying the feeling of calm just before a storm. Everyone was screaming now, people running away in all directions. Airess tried to shake her arms out of the chains again.

Morana looked at her, a mix of greed and pity in her expression. "I'm sorry, old friend. I need the Allpower, and unfortunately, that means killing you."

Airess looked at the crystal blade like an old foe. Recognition ran through her being, as if her ancestors were whispering to her through space and time itself. *The Allpower blade.* The weapon that could take a Godling's power for itself.

The weapon her ancestor, Evyen, used to create a new dimension.

As Morana took a step toward her, lightning cracked through the air, a figure emerging from the clouds. The sky bellowed, a sound so loud it verberated through Airess' body. A bolt of lightning struck the space in front of Airess, causing Morana to roll to the side, missing the electricity by inches.

Airess looked up to see the source of the strike.

It was Taryn.

Airess beheld him. His face was his own, but contorted with an ancient rage she had never seen before. His brown hair and brows had turned completely silver, matching his glowing silver eyes and skin. Raging storm clouds whirled around him before he shot down on the stage, breaking the wood he landed on. He pumped a fist and blasted Morana away with silver tendrils of pure energy.

He looked to Airess, his eyes not truly his own. They melted for a split second as he looked at her before a blast of darkness shot towards him. Taryn laughed and pivoted out of the way, several voices coming out of his mouth. *"We meet again, Bas."*

Airess' eyes widened at the mention of Bas, the Death God, Taryn's Godspirit speaking through him

Morana's jaw dropped at the sight of Taryn. She shot out another string of darkness, her amateur skill from being previously powerless was evident. Taryn moved lethally, pushing his palm forward and blasting her with a lightning strike. He met his mark, just barely, and grazed her bicep with electricity. Morana cried out in agonizing pain. Her sleeve singed away, leaving an angry burn in its wake.

Morana moved to her feet quickly, gripping her burned arm. She fled the stage, running into the fearful crowd. Airess watched her disappear into the bodies, leaving as quickly as she had appeared. Morana had gotten away. Despite the fact that Morana had almost killed her, Airess felt relieved her old friend had fled.

Taryn continued to rage. Heavy winds increased and ripped pieces off of the buildings nearby. The clouds thundered above, and she pivoted her bound body to him. He needed to stop destroying this city.

"Taryn!" Airess screamed over the raging winds, her hair and dress whipping around. He looked to her like he would strike *her*, his movements quick and precise. He looked confused, then recognized her and smiled. "*My Ghrian.*"

Airess realized his Godspirit was recognizing her as the Sun God, and was calling her as such. Her heart pounded incessantly as she met the eyes of a God, speechless.

Taryn moved his arm and her chains broke off instantly. She tripped forward, now loose from her chains and fell to her knees. An arrow pierced itself into the wooden board in front of her hands.

Taryn growled, moving in front of her protectively. He reached his hand to the sky and drew lightning from thin air. As he brought his hand to the ground, lightning raged down like a shower, electrocuting everyone around them. The scent of burnt flesh and singed hair filled the air. The ground trembled as bodies dropped like flies at Taryn's power. Airess' breath hitched as she watched him, his facial expression void of any emotion. His eyes, wholly silver, struck her true and deep. It was in that moment that Airess truly knew fear.

By then, even the guards began to flee, the power Taryn holed up inside was even more powerful than Airess could have ever imagined.

"*We must unite the realms as it once was, Ghrian.*" Taryn–and the voices coming out of him–bellowed, "*The world has lost its way.*"

He stood, his back to her as he breathed heavily before raising both hands in the air. Airess saw the temple ceiling blast apart in the distance, outpouring the pink flames–the Soulfyre. The flames traveled through the air like it was sentient, traveling towards them both. When it reached Taryn, the flames collided into him forcefully.

"*A touch of fyre,*" Taryn–and all the voices inside him – recited, "*An earth rebirthed to be made from desire.*"

His other hand was conjuring lightning, shooting it upwards into the sky. The electricity and Soulfyre merged, weaving itself together as it shot up in the air. Airess thought it would dissipate in the sky, but the lightning hit an invisible wall. Upon impact, a green translucent dome across the ocean revealed itself. The dome began to crack, its remnants falling into the ocean.

Taryn turned and gripped Airess by her waist tightly, bringing her in possessively to his chest. *"Let us go home."* The voices spoke to her.

For the first time, Airess truly feared Taryn.

Horror coursed through her veins. He was not the sarcastic, stubborn male she had fallen for. No, he was a vision of the Gods, consumed by the power he was Spirited with. Taryn held her tightly with one arm and shot into the sky, their bodies bolstered by the pressure of storm clouds swirling beneath them.

Her stomach lurched as they ascended upwards, over Rune's capitol. The teal wall had finally broken away, revealing a cliff in the distance. She didn't realize she had screamed as they flew through the air so fast, the world blurred around them. She gripped Taryn's neck and buried her face in his neck as they flew.

"I sense your fear. I will not hurt you, Ghrian." He said as they passed over the ocean. They landed on a cliff that hadn't existed before Taryn's lightning. Airess looked at Taryn's glowing eyes. Gently, she reached up and placed a trembling palm to his cheek. She felt the faintest jolt of electricity beneath his hot skin.

"Taryn," she whispered, searching his face for any trace of him. "come back."

Taryn's face twisted into betrayal, before it slowly faded. His eyes rolled into the back of his head as he fell down into a grassy field of black salaroses all around them.

Chapter 42

'Our son will be the One who brings forth the dawn.'
— *Unsent correspondence from Rinya Kazimyr to Tann Azar*

Taryn

Taryn emerged from a dreamless slumber.

His entire body ached as he came back to reality. The world spun. He groaned. His head was *throbbing*. Taryn propped himself up, bracing his arm on a soft surface. Soft fabric grazed his fingertips.

"He's awake."

It was Airess' voice. His eyes snapped open.

A single candle flickered on the bedside table, its flames the color of violets. He was in a bedroom, and a small one. A single bookshelf dominated the dimlit setting, the shelves cramped with books and trinkets. There were no windows in this room, just dark walls painted black.

The end of the bed sank as she sat down next to him. He felt her before he looked at her. "It's okay." Airess said, and grabbed his hand. He exhaled. Safe. His Mate was safe.

Thank the Gods.

Agonizing relief flooded over him, and suddenly nothing else mattered.

Another pair of footsteps walked up beside Airess. Taryn blinked as his vision cleared. Purple robes came into focus, revealing a familiar woman. Her round face was framed by long, red hair. The woman's lilac eyes crinkled as she spoke with a bright smile.

"Welcome to Tevye, Tarynon."

Epilogue

The Vulture

Morana descended the dark steps of the prison. The air was thick with the scent of must and decay. She held her head up high, still adjusting to wearing the crown that was *rightfully* hers. After an adjustment period, it was time to finally resume her plans and start on her first order of business.

Morana walked by her mother's cell. She heard her mother cry out to her, begging her to be released. "I can make things right!" she said to her, "I can get you the help you need!"

Morana would *never* free her. Her mother was the reason her lover was killed. The one who married her off to that rapist of a Duke at the age of fourteen. When Morana fell pregnant with the child after all those years, she knew she had to act. She would make the world a better place.

She *needed* to create a world where no one would sell off her daughter as a child bride, like her mother did to her.

No, Melanth would *never* be free.

Morana would make her suffer, as she had for four years.

She passed another cell, this one entrapping a beast Morana had only heard stories about. A nasty beast that dwelled within The Twins–all grey flesh, black eyes and claws. It snarled and thrashed in its cage. That is, until it saw *her*. The beast calmed when Morana neared, holding its head low in submission.

"Silence," she commanded. It obeyed.

She turned down the hall to visit her *special* prisoner, holding her lantern up to peer down at the female in rags on the floor. Gods, she really did look just like her. The Elven female was no older than forty, her long pearly hair falling in tangled sheets after almost a decade of not being cut. She was barefoot, her dress ripped and dirty as she sat against the wall. Morana extended her sixth sense, feeling for the female's energy–but found her null of anything. No emotion at all.

The prisoner's eyes were milky white, her eyes void of anyone inhabiting the body, as if nobody were home.

"After all this time, you still live," Morana said, voice echoing out into the cavernous prison. The Elve did not stir, sitting motionless. Morana began to wonder if her mind was truly lost–the woman now just a shell of a person.

Morana set the lantern down and gripped the bars. "I must say, my mother has done a great disservice keeping you locked in this cell. You certainly have far greater potential, if you can mirror anything close to the level of power your *daughter* has achieved."

The prisoner inhaled a deep breath, her body remaining still as those gray, milky eyes shifted to look at Morana.

Morana's red lips curved upwards in a sinister smile.

"Hello, Aesira."

Acknowledgments

Soulfyre is the first book I have ever written. In this process I have learned that I may be the author of this story, but I couldn't have done it without the minds, support and love from the people in my life. It truly takes a village to write a book.

Thank you to my husband. The one who listened to all my story ideas. You have and always will be my best friend. The Taryn to my Airess. The moon to my sun. Your support has gotten me through the hardest parts of writing a book. I love you and Millie Dog so much!

To my editor, Monique, there has been a touch of magick added to this book that could only derive from you. Thank you for taking me on and reading my story. I truly believe the universe connects people for a reason, and I couldn't be more grateful to find such an amazing editor. Soulfyre wouldn't be the story it is today without your expertise. Thank you, thank you, thank you.

Thank you to my writing group and all of my writer friends. From answering my endless questions, to reading my book before any editing had taken place. Soulfyre wouldn't be here without you. *I* wouldn't be the writer I am today without you. Thank you so much.

A big thank you to all of the alpha and beta readers who read this book. Your feedback was essential, and helped me shape the story into the best version of itself. Thank you, truly. It meant the world.

Thank you to my family members for teaching me responsibility and perseverance. For passing down your wisdom and kindness. I have taken traits from each of you that live on in this book.

To my Papa for instilling a creativity and a humor in me that I know only comes from you. To Grandaddy, whose kindness and artistic side have seeped into my bones. I miss you both more than words can express, but I feel your souls out there. I know you can see these words.

To my best friends. There are too many to count, but you know who you are, and I love you all. Thank you for all of your support while I was writing this book. <3

And to you, reader, for reading the very essence of my soul and mind. If I even made one reader feel something while reading this book, my mission is complete. Thank you for taking a chance on my story.

www.ingramcontent.com/pod-product-compliance
Lightning Source LLC
LaVergne TN
LVHW091658070526
838199LV00050B/2192